SILICON VALLEY EAST

SILICON VALLEY EAST

GINA MARIE WILSON

Published by Bayfront Press, an imprint of
System Strategies, Hockessin, Delaware, USA, in 2025.

Library of Congress Control Number: 2024927025
ISBN 978-1-7370829-3-4 (pb)
ISBN 978-1-7370829-4-1 (ebook)

Cover images: Freepik.com and Shutterstock.com

To purchase books in bulk for promotional or educational use, contact the author through her website,

www.ginamwilson.com

*For my mother, Helen DeSantis,
who has always believed in me*

SILICON
VALLEY
EAST

PART I

1973–1983

CHAPTER 1

SHE'D RIDDEN THIS route a thousand times—pedaling down her sloped driveway, then pounding the pedals with all her weight uphill for a block and carving a wide right turn without slowing, before the thirty-second thrill of a three-block downhill plunge. Her long wavy black hair fanned out behind her like a contrail of the Concorde, until she skidded to a halt at the dead end.

Twelve-year-old Christina Como possessed a strength belied by her small stature, developed from days of biking through rolling fields to a nearby estate where she hoisted saddles and bales of hay in exchange for a chance to ride the horses. Other days, she and her hand-me-down ten-speed traveled the newly paved roads of her suburban Delaware neighborhood to Terry Merullo's. The girls had been friends ever since six-year-old Christina followed a moving truck and station wagon full of kids to the Merullo's new house.

Today, as always, Christina closed her eyes as the wind whipped her face, the lay of the land etched in her mind's eye. Only the rattle of her bike chain on the bumps around the manhole in front of the sixth of ten houses she'd pass interrupted the quiet in the brightness behind her closed eyelids. The sun warmed her face with the promise of an early summer. Unconcerned about traffic that wouldn't appear for another ninety minutes, when the clocking dads returned home promptly from their shifts, Christina savored the great freedom her modest bike offered. Something inside her was set free with the flash of acceleration and adventure she enjoyed each time she rode to Terry's.

But today seemed especially quiet.

Christina's eyes jolted open. Where was the steady hum of her rear wheel rubbing against the brake pad, the sound that lulled her into a meditative state on long rides?

From her front porch, Terry watched Christina racing down the hill and rolled her eyes because her friend did this every time. Just before the Merullo's driveway, the bike would skid to a stop, and Christina would hop off, shake her long locks back into place, and claim, "Phew, that was fun!"

This time, Terry saw a wild look on Christina's face as the bike careened past the driveway and skipped up the curb before coming to an abrupt halt against a tree stump. Her friend's body was hurled over the handlebars and landed in a thicket.

Christina woke inside an ambulance as two medics yanked its doors open, clanged the wheels of the rolling stretcher in place, then wheeled her into the emergency room. A kind nurse took Christina's hand, patting it gently. "Your mother is on her way. Your friend said you got thrown from your bike."

Completely awake and startled into a state of hyperalert, Christina watched as a small army in scrubs and white uniforms darted around her bedside. One used scissors to cut away her frayed jeans below the knee. Another swabbed a brownish liquid along her bloodied leg. Someone was shining a flashlight into her pupils, asking her to follow the light as he moved it back and forth.

A physician who looked like he could be a classmate's older brother pushed back the curtain surrounding her bed. "Does your head hurt? Can you touch your fingertip to your nose? Can you wiggle your toes?" He peppered her with questions, and as she began to feel normal again, she decided she liked this game of twenty questions, as long as she didn't have to look at her leg. Once the nurse had covered the gash below her knee with a notebook-sized gauze pad, she became the one asking questions. "What's that for? Why are you looking at my pupils? Is my leg broken?"

They whisked her off to get a CAT scan and X-rays just as her mother arrived.

"No concussion. Saved by the brambles. Though there are quite a few burrs in her hair," the doctor assured Mrs. Como. "And we'll stitch her leg up." Christina, the patient, winced at the shot of lidocaine. Christina, the curious, went on to interrogate each action the nurse and doctor made, no longer feeling pain. The kind doctor peered into the girl's dirt-streaked face with its intelligent almond-shaped dark eyes and smiled. "OK, I'll give you a detailed synopsis."

"You've got a laceration on your calf extending from the gastrocnemius down to the soleus. Fortunately, you missed all the tendons."

Christina stared at her leg like it was the frog on her lab table in science class.

"I will first irrigate the wound with a spray of saline, which is basically a mild salt water, to get any debris out. Then I'll stitch internally and externally. The white bubble-like tissue you see is subcutaneous fat."

She didn't expect the spray to hurt, but her eyes watered. "Take some deep breaths, and it'll be done before you know it," the doctor said. Christina grimaced, then pictured the air going in and out of her lungs as her mother turned to read the various notices posted on the wall of the clinic, still holding her daughter's hand. As she relaxed and the local anesthetic began working, the doctor inserted clear suture thread through a wire shaped like an eyelash.

"This suture material will dissolve in your body. I'll use black thread for the external stitches to close the wound. You'll have to return here to get them removed in ten to fourteen days."

Christina paid more attention than she ever had in science class, hanging on his every word, marveling at what she saw. "This is just so cool, Mom."

Her mother shuddered. "Oh, Christina. It's just awful. I don't know why you insist on racing around on that bike like you do."

As her mother turned into their driveway, Christina saw a posse of neighbors and family gathered there. "Sweetheart, we were all so worried about you!" Her father rushed to help her from the car. Her younger siblings, six-year-old twins, fearfully eyed their sister as she hobbled with one crutch and grinned.

"I have twenty-eight stitches and more inside. No head injury, thanks to Mr. Merullo's bushes that saved me. But I need a good shampoo."

"What were you doing, racing down that hill?"

"Dad, I can ride to Terry's with my eyes closed. I actually do. But this time, I didn't hear my brakes rubbing the wheel."

Her older brother Dominic appeared with her bike, pointing to the wheel. "Your brake line is severed, Christina. That's why you couldn't stop."

"Dom, really? How can that be?" Mr. Como frowned at the bike, then looked up as Christina's oldest brother, Sebastian, turned and walked back to the house.

"Dad, who knows?" she said. "I knew it wasn't my driving. But Dad, I'm going to be a doctor!"

CHAPTER 2

FROM THE DAY OF her bike accident, Christina set out to become a doctor, convinced she was meant to be a surgeon. In high school she worked hard to make the honor roll, and she spent more days at the estate, observing the horses' anatomy. Craning her neck to watch the vet's actions when a horse was in trouble, she analyzed everything she saw with a critical eye. Soon the vets let her help with minor procedures and encouraged her to consider vet school. Her guidance counselor advised, "Christina, you should study engineering because you're good in math. The world needs more female engineers." But the skeptical Christina wanted only to study pre-med. "Doesn't the world need more women doctors?"

Her family scoffed at the idea, never taking it or Christina seriously. "No one really gives a rat's ass what you do in life," her oldest brother, Sebastian, said, flipping back a strand of black hair falling over one eye. "You can peddle makeup at the mall or do heart surgery. It don't really matter when you quit to have your babies." Her hair tossing brother, six years older than Christina, took any opportunity to emphasize her insignificance. He talked over her as if she wasn't there and pushed Christina around, sometimes grabbing her hard enough to leave a bruise. Sebastian made her the subject of his endless cruelty, usually exercised when no one else could witness, pulling her long hair until her scalp went numb or pressing his fist into her stomach until she nearly puked.

Christina's sister, just three years ahead of her in school, had married right out of high school and moved across town. It was an unstated tradition that no one had dared to question until now. Daughters raised a family; sons got jobs. "Why?" Christina asked her mirror and her friend Terry and would ask herself for years, a million times.

Her father was not keen on Christina going to college, dismissing her summarily one night over dinner. "It's not needed when you raise your family," he said before turning his attention to the platter of braciole and meatballs as she blinked at him with set jaw.

Her mother felt otherwise. "You'll never regret a good education, Christina," she said, heaping a few meatballs onto her daughter's plate.

Dominic tried to smooth things over as he passed her the bowl of grated parmesan. "Make enough to pay the bills is all you need to do, Teen. Don't need to put all that pressure on yourself." He was the only one of the siblings who affectionally shortened her name. Dominic, four years older than Christina, tried to take care of her, though he himself couldn't stand up to Sebastian. Christina thought her older sister was lucky to be out of the house.

"We're not a family of doctors," Sebastian shouted over his shoulder as he left the table, unexcused. "So why should you go to medical school?"

By Christina's senior year, the Como mailbox bulged with glossy college pamphlets inviting her to apply. Much as she would miss her family, Christina knew she had to get out of the house and make it on her own before the traditional ways would overtake her and sentence her to a mundane life in the shadow of security and suppressed ambition.

Christina's fascination with medicine had grown ever since that day she was stitched up in the ER. She was convinced she, too, could help patients like those who had helped her. Her teachers encouraged her. She wanted to use her brain for something other than perfecting a casserole or committee work at the PTA. Going to college would be the ticket to her future, the beginning of her life in medicine on her own.

When Boston College offered her an academic scholarship, Christina was determined to study pre-med there. The scholarship covered only tuition, though, and her parents refused to accept the remaining expenses. It wouldn't be fair to the rest of the family, they said. Her brothers had commuted to the local state university for far less than what board cost at BC, though Sebastian flunked out before finishing, and there was the twins' future schooling to consider. Her sister forfeited any money for education by getting married at eighteen. *How in the world can I get them to agree to Boston?*

"Why did you get so excited about my scholarship if you had no intention of letting me go?" Christina asked her mother. "I could've worked to offset the expenses."

Her mother looked away before answering.

"Your hard work will pay off wherever you go and whatever you do. Your father and I hoped the scholarship would cover all your costs. We can't justify the added expenses when you can go here to State for almost nothing. We have your brothers to support and the twins' future to think of too."

"Really? Dominic works hard, but since he joined the union, he's already ticking days off the calendar until retirement. Sebastian still has no aspirations and no steady job. Neither won a scholarship. The twins are six years away from applying to college. It's just not fair."

By May, Christina had applied nowhere else and had no plan. One day when Christina came in from school, her mother handed her a large white envelope obnoxiously labeled with the state university logo, printed in full color with their mascot.

"C-O-N-G-R-A-T-U-L-A-T-I-O-N-S" was printed in huge type across the back.

"What's this, Mom?"

"It looks like an acceptance letter, honey!" Her mother's face brightened as she looked up from where she stood by the stove. She began scooping spheres of meat from a bowl and dropping them in a pan sizzling with olive oil.

"I never applied there!" Christina looked confused as she plopped her books on the kitchen table.

"Well, honey…" Smoothing her apron of invisible wrinkles, her mother stammered, "I-I sent an application *for* you when it didn't work out with Boston College."

"You what? You applied for me?" Christina ripped open the envelope. "Ha, they're offering me, or you, I should say, since you are the one who applied, first year tuition, room, and board, paid. Like that'll make me want to go."

Her mother's smile faded as Christina stormed out the front door and sent the envelope rocketing into the bushes.

Three months later she was moving into a dorm only twenty minutes from her family's home, with no idea how she would realize her dream. On campus, Christina met with her advisor, Dr. Solokoff, a pudgy academic who sometimes taught an introductory biology class to a sea of three hundred faces. She told him of her interests and medical school aspirations as he studied her exemplary high school transcript and SAT scores with indifference.

"We don't offer biomedical engineering, and pre-med isn't a major," Dr. Solokoff deadpanned like a poker player with a lousy hand.

"I know. That's why I'm here. For advice."

"Most pre-meds major in biology," said the biology professor.

"Exactly. I want something different."

He looked at the impudent student in front of him. "Let me remind you, to be eligible for medical school, you'll have to take the required pre-med courses, in addition to whatever your major requires, before taking the medical school admission test."

"Yes, and I want to study something that will offer an alternative job if I don't get in right away. Something challenging that will enhance my application for medical school."

"Nursing."

"No, thank you. I've read that medical schools now value applicants with more diverse areas of study, unrelated to medicine."

"Bio is your best bet and easier because the major requirements overlap."

Welcome to state university, she thought. This is an advisor who's been spitting out canned advice for decades to invisible advisees between hours when he is otherwise holed up in his office like the jarred organs floating in formaldehyde upon his shelves.

"I choose electrical engineering." Christina blackened in the blank ovals on her registration card and handed it to him to sign. It was a stretch. "Electrical engineering might be something I can use to develop medical devices. If I never make it into the operating room, I can still help people lead better lives through prosthetics."

A dubious Dr. Solokoff shook his head after scribbling a signature on the form and shoving it back to her. She left his office, thinking, I guess I'll have to do this college thing myself.

On the first day of classes, the petite, suntanned Christina, wearing her new Calvin Klein jeans and a pink Oxford button-down shirt tied at the waist, sat in a lecture hall filled with more than three hundred students. She scanned the enormous room for an occasional ponytail, flowered halter top, or lipsticked mouth. Where are all the girls?

The dean of engineering droned on and on. "It's an exciting time to be an engineer. Technology is exploding. You and your classmates could change the world."

By only the second week, just three of the original six females remained in Electrical Engineering, in a class of ninety-seven "EEs." Trying hard to convince herself it didn't matter that nearly all her peers were male, Christina entered the world of circuit boards, capacitors, and transistors. She tinkered with sensors and diodes, though she had never in her life, unlike most of her class-mates, disassembled and reconstructed a radio. A quick learner, spending countless hours in the microprocessor lab after classes to compensate for her inexperience, Christina held her own.

"Where on earth did you learn that? And when?" she asked a lab partner one day, as he arranged capacitors and resistors on a circuit board and connected a DC power supply, all before reading the lab assignment.

"I followed my dad around his workshop ever since I could walk, so I picked up whatever he did. I was six years old when I started with circuit boards," he said, measuring output on a voltmeter.

While she had been busy babysitting, riding horses, and bak-ing pizzelles, her male peers had been constructing robots and building potato canons. They'd already deconstructed engines and made flashlights from Altoids cans. Even the marginal student she barely knew from high school was doing well in EE, though he asked Christina for help with calculus. "Can I make a living calculating integrals?" she wondered.

She joined engineering study groups but had trouble connecting to the others who were laser focused on engineering and interested in nothing else. Christina tried to strike up conversations, cracking an occasional joke or asking about their weekend plans. She was puzzled by those who seemed uncomfortable with her questions and couldn't maintain eye contact when she talked about anything other than the problem set they pored over.

Some students spoke like the robots they built, in steady monotones, matter-of-factly spewing formulas and computations with stone-faced authority and palpable condescension. Prospective lab partners seemed disappointed to find that the *C* in "C. Como," as she signed her name, was for Christina, not Charlie. She found herself wearing a baseball cap, stuffing her hair up inside it, and wearing nondescript T-shirts with her Calvin Klein jeans to blend in. Stifling her natural friendliness and curiosity to fit in and stay under the radar, Christina became less chatty and all business, though she had never been considered talkative. There were a few downright hostile classmates, sneering at her when an instructor commended her answers or when she finished a test early.

Not fitting in wasn't new to Christina. She had struggled to overcome self-doubt after years of Sebastian's baseless but relentless ridicule, which her parents dismissed as normal sibling bickering. Christina remained silent during his attacks, holding back tears until she was behind the closed door of her bedroom.

In middle school she struggled with her looks because she stood out among her homogenous, fair-skinned peers. Her olive skin, small stature, and dark features never reflected back from pages in magazines or from beauty-product commercials on TV. "Christina, you'll never be a model or an actress," Sebastian warned. "You're too short and dumb." Christina's appearance stood out, a noticeable anomaly in the school cafeteria. "What *are* you?" some curious, boorish classmate asked every year she went to school.

In one physics class, an EE classmate took notice not only of her thoughtful answers but also of the inquisitive nature of the dark-haired girl who smiled with her eyes. Drew Dawson knew her lab partner and made it a point to be sitting next to their station when

Christina arrived. The lab partner introduced them, and Drew interrupted their lab session several times to ask for a spare resistor, borrow a pendulum, and use her calculator. By the end of lab, Drew asked Christina if they might study together. She cautiously agreed, hoping this friendly guy was different.

Christina dove into her schoolwork, discovering that she learned quickly and understood what others struggled to grasp. She started studying regularly with Drew Dawson, who seemed to master much of the material before she did, though he never let on that he did. He was patient when she got stuck, encouraging her and dismissing any doubts she expressed. "You're bright and inquisitive, Christina. You just don't know how much you know," he told her.

Drew was genuinely kind, a good-natured companion everyone liked. A former high school tennis player, he was solid and lean, and with his winning smile and soulful eyes, he had his choice of dates until he found Christina. He never doubted his choice to study engineering. He was one of those who could repair anything from a carburetor to a stereo speaker.

By the end of freshman year, Christina and Drew began dating. The two shared many interests outside school—live music, swimming in the ocean, hiking. She didn't believe his praises, thinking Drew was just being a sweet boyfriend.

Dozens of jabs from others in her classes chiseled away at her resolve. She had beaten back her insecurities during high school to land at the top of her class and become a respectable track runner. But in college, those anxieties again crept into her psyche, threatening to thwart her success. She didn't share these feelings with Drew and outwardly presented a resilient, determined student, undaunted by the unwelcoming environment.

Her pre-med cohort was not much different from the engineers, consisting of mostly arrogant guys buoyed by their high school valedictorian or Presidential Scholar titles. Christina shared her frustrations with her roommate, a math major, as they walked to their dorm after a long night studying in the library.

"Can't we simply be good students? Why must the few girls in my classes be stellar, acing every exam, justifying why they deserve the rare inclusion in this group?"

"Yeah, there aren't many in math either," her roommate observed, shifting the books in her hand.

"The guys sitting next to me, mediocre students themselves, hardly suppress their condescending smirks when the TA returns my B+ exams, seemingly justifying their views that women don't belong in engineering or medicine," Christina bit her lip.

"It stinks, but you show them. You heard that physics instructor tell us, 'Look at the students on your left and right. Only one of you will be here at the end of the semester.' You stick with it and be that one, Christina." The girls crossed the quad to their building.

"I can't help feeling it's not enough to just be very good."

CHAPTER 3

CHRISTINA WAITED PATIENTLY outside her sister's hospital room. The sisters had been close as children but drifted apart as teenagers. While Christina was buried in books, her sister spent more time with her boyfriend. Once married, the couple planned their family. Any minute now, Christina would be summoned to photograph the birth of her new niece or nephew. Secretly delighted to be asked to witness the delivery, Christina was glad there were no other takers in the family.

Christina knew her stint as an EMT more than qualified her to work the camera without fainting. Sitting on the hard metal chair in a stark Labor and Delivery corridor, Christina thought about the job she'd been lucky to have had since January of freshmen year. As a pre-med at State, she was instantly hired by the local ER as an EMT, and her on-the-job training began.

She quickly mastered taking vital signs and memorized loads of medical terminology. Christina learned the medications commonly used in the ER, reading the voluminous *Physicians' Desk Reference* when things were slow. Patients mattered to her, and she chatted calmly when checking their vitals and taking their medical history. She made a game out of trying to anticipate the physicians' needs based on her own triage for each patient ushered back to a curtained stretcher.

Minor laceration? Suture kit and gloves just the right size for that doctor, supplied before the provider even stepped behind the curtain. Unable to bear weight on that leg? Plaster kit, fabric sleeves to line the cast. *Foreign body in the eye?* Those were the ones she found tough to watch. Christina had passed out upon first putting contact lenses in her own eyes. Nonetheless, she'd have saline and a flush set unpacked, fresh from the centrifuge and lined up, ready to go. It was her ability to anticipate what came next that set Christina apart.

The physician in charge, Dr. Aboud, took her under his wing, teaching her more than he should have.

"Countless aspiring nurses and doctors come through our doors as volunteers and tech staff. Many find it gruesome, dull, or simply not for them."

"Not me," said Christina, "I can't get enough of it, Dr. Aboud."

Christina often took a second shift to work a sixteen-hour day, including the overnight. That's when things got interesting. Fight injuries, gunshot wounds, car accidents, domestic violence, and an occasional homeless "patient" feigning an injury, looking for shelter. Night shifts showed a slice of society that had never before made an appearance in Christina's world, though she was fully aware that not everyone had been so fortunate. Standing before a victim whose relationship left them battered or someone in debilitating pain elicited a profound empathy in Christina, affirming her commitment to use whatever talents she possessed to make things better for the sick and injured. In the ER, Christina temporarily replaced all her anxieties with responsibility and action.

On night shifts, skeletal staff meant that before triaging a patient, she had to first check them in. She asked for their personal and insurance information, typing with one finger on each hand onto a multipart preprinted form that became their first chart document. The typing presented the most challenging part of the job for Christina. She had elected woodshop over typing in high school, determined never to become someone's secretary.

Her mother had warned her not to be judgmental. "Christina, some people have no choice." Considering those wise words, she vowed to become a voice against injustice. Still, Christina was not one to wait on the sidelines, never comfortable just watching. It was her incessant penchant for doing and running in perpetual overdrive that propelled Christina through the world. Terry, her childhood friend once admitted to her, "Sure, Christina, you're smart, but what really makes you different is your spunk."

True to form, while Christina watched the ER doctors like a hawk, she took in all she could and was soon able to administer basic care. The sudden onslaught of patients from a multi-vehicle accident became Christina's cue to take over. Dr. Aboud had been suturing a femur laceration on a Chrysler assembly-line worker, but when he saw the arriving emergencies, he motioned Christina forward.

"Christina, you know what to do. Finish up the last six sutures and bandage him up," Dr. Aboud said before rushing from the procedure room to greet the medics unloading accident victims. She had studied Dr. Aboud's careful dexterity, watching him quickly pierce the skin tissue a millimeter from the clean edge of the wound with the semicircular tip of the suture needle, raising the point to the opposite edge of the wound and drawing the suture thread across the opening to bind it and repeating the action consistently until the wound closed like a zipper. This was not too different from the sewing she had learned for a Girl Scout badge in the fourth grade, except for the suture needles being curved and the fabric being human tissue. How different can it be? She went immediately into action, calling up her acquired skills and quashing any self-doubt.

Dr. Aboud stopped in to check her progress as Christina delicately blotted the closed wound with a gauze pad moistened with Betadine after completing the sutures. "Could there be remaining bacteria on the skin? I wanted to prevent infection," she said as Dr. Aboud nodded. She skillfully wrapped the patient's thigh with gauze and advised him to return in ten days for suture removal. The man had told her he liked her gentle but purposeful style more than Dr. Aboud's tugging at his skin. Performing minor procedures soon became second nature to Christina, and Dr. Aboud appreciated the help.

A code blue during a shift that was short-staffed led her to become the relief "bagger," alternating stints with the RN to push oxygen into the lungs of a patient who went into cardiac arrest upon entering triage. Bagger became her official role during codes. They once spent forty-five minutes doing CPR on a fourteen-year-old boy who had suffered a cardiac arrest. The youth had received a lethal jolt while working a power drill in a wet workshop. "This one is too young to stop trying," Dr. Aboud announced to the team, so they continued tirelessly until the doctor resignedly removed his gloves and pronounced the patient deceased. The experience stuck with Christina long after.

Once a middle-aged woman was carried into the ER vestibule and left at the reception desk by two young men who immediately jumped into their car and sped away. One glance at her and Christina saw the deepening red pool growing on her chest like a blossoming rose in time lapsed photography. "Gunshot left upper chest wall!" she shouted into the air, furiously pressing the call button to summon the physician who was resting between patients. She hopped over to the shortwave radio and called an ambulance. This one would have to be transferred to the medical center for emergency surgery. Christina and the RN deftly packed the wound to stop its bleeding before loading the patient onto a stretcher, and in less than two minutes, the woman lay stable in the ambulance on its way to the hospital, where a surgical suite and trauma team awaited.

One curious case still had Christina chuckling and grimacing, even now as she waited outside her sister's room. A man and woman entered the reception room, exchanging furtive glances and taking care not to brush up against the door or people waiting nearby.

The harried husband said, "My wife had an accident in the kitchen and is in extreme pain."

Christina recognized the woman. She lived two streets from the Comos. The neighbor wore a tablecloth draped over her right arm and hand. Removing the tablecloth revealed a hand disfigured, purple and swollen, fingers entangled in the beaters of a kitchen mixer. Christina bit the insides of her cheek to keep her jaw in place. Note to self—never reach into a mixing bowl while the beaters are still turning! An injection of a muscle relaxer and swift cutting of the metal blades relieved the entanglement and freed the woman's fingers. Dr. Aboud proceeded as if this was an everyday occurrence while Christina shuddered at the thought of baking anything for a while.

Nor did he visibly react when a scantily clad patient, a regular in their ER, entered late one evening complaining of lower abdominal pain. Acting as the female witness required by state law for any pelvic exam, Christina watched, perplexed, when Dr. Aboud requested the forceps. She lurched backward, her hand slapped over the chasm that had been her mouth, as Dr. Aboud extracted a set of false teeth from the woman's vagina. He advised the patient, "I think I've found the source of your pain."

This was an education no classroom could provide. Christina had found something that challenged, intrigued, and fascinated her. She was becoming a valued asset to the small ER, and it became her second home, away from her troubles at home and school. She took as much responsibility as they gave her, and staff relied on her, despite her young age. Though Dr. Aboud had noticed, Christina failed to realize how competent she had become, always trying to do better. He encouraged her, recognizing a compassionate, driven young woman who could make a difference. Christina could stomach the sight of blood and unpleasant treatment situations. When her sister asked her to photograph her delivery, she leaped at the chance to witness a joyful and hopeful demonstration of the marvels of medicine.

An abrupt opening of the hospital room door startled her back to the present.

"It's almost time," her brother-in-law called, waving her inside. Christina donned a protective gown, gloves, and a face mask before sliding behind the curtain. Her sister, only slightly winded and flushed, reclined in the hospital bed, her legs apart in stirrups.

"Got the camera?" Her sister grinned like a vacationer getting off the tour bus at Niagara Falls.

"Sure do! I'll try to be discreet," Christina assured her, adjusting her mask.

Her niece shrieked her way into the world on the last day of Christina's summer break. What a way to start off the school year! I can't wait to tell Dr. Aboud about this.

CHAPTER 4

SOPHOMORE YEAR, Christina settled into a routine of spending weeknights in the microprocessor lab or the library and weekends working in the ER. She and Drew studied together many weeknights during the semester and on weekends treated themselves to off-campus outings and concerts whenever she wasn't working. By the end of the term, they had become nearly inseparable. When the condensed winter term started, Christina wanted a break from her rigid EE schedule and squeezed in two social science classes. Drew went home to work for the few weeks and returned to campus to visit Christina on weekends.

"Drew, I miss you here every day. But I'm so thrilled with these classes! I really can't believe this is the same college."

"Technically, those are in Arts & Science, not in the College of Engineering."

"Well, it's a welcome change I didn't know I needed."

Here were classmates who endlessly pondered world issues and valued witty conversation and reflection. Christina engaged in stimulating exchanges that challenged conventional ways of thinking. She wrote papers analyzing current theories, from child psychology to social justice. When Christina resumed classes in her major for the spring semester, she felt renewed yet slightly unsettled.

Then came the infamous day near the end of her sophomore year. She had been consumed with trying to pass organic chemistry that term. Though she had aced two chemistry classes during her freshman year, organic seemed a different kind of science. It required sheer memorization. Christina's uncanny ability for analytical thinking would not suffice. Hundreds of equations on flash cards and seemingly random compounds simply had to be committed to memory. She couldn't fall back on her usual "let's figure it out" strategy. The class was a wholly foreign breed of *hard*. On the last day to drop courses, Christina called an end to the misery. I'll try again over the summer when I can devote more time to it, she decided. She could no longer delay the meeting with her advisor, Dr. Solokoff. She needed his approval to drop Organic and take it over the summer.

"Hello, Dr. Solokoff." Christina smiled and reminded him as she entered his office, door ajar, "I'm Christina Como." Since that sour first meeting to declare a major, she'd met with him only once, when she needed his approval to allow eighteen credits to fit in Microbiology.

His flippant dismissal at that time—"Microbiology! You're wasting your time since nearly half of entering freshman are pre-med these days. Good luck."—had left her feeling like the fading print on the list of nameless advisees, noted only by their social security numbers, posted outside his office. Now, returning a year later to this gatekeeper of student futures, she felt hopeful he'd agree it would be better to focus on Organic over the summer term.

"Yes, hullo. What can I do for you?" Solokoff mumbled as he sat there, head buried in a journal. He didn't look up.

"I'm here to get approval to drop Organic Chemistry. I want to take it over the summer, instead, when I can focus on all that memorization and get a good grade before the MCATs."

Raising one eyebrow and with a slight turn of his head, Solokoff half asked and half stated, "MCATs." With this he put down his journal and picked up a file folder with her name in bold black stick-on letters affixed to the edge. "I don't see how you'll be taking the MCATs."

"Oh, yes," Christina assured him, "I'm signing up for the December test date, after I've taken Anatomy & Physiology and Organic this the summer."

"I don't think you understand. I've seen your grade report," Solokoff said to the folder.

Aghast, Christina wondered if he had mistaken her for another student. Christina found it strange this professor still hadn't viewed her face. She noticed the patched seams on his sport coat and a coffee stain that encircled the buttons on his wrinkled button-down, perhaps indicating a carelessness that bled through to his work.

"My GPA is solid, and I'm doing well in everything this term so far, and once I drop Organic, I will have more time to focus on the other classes."

Still, the folder held his interest, not her. "I'll sign your drop form, but forget taking it over the summer. No need to. You don't need it for EE, so you'd be wasting your time."

"I'll need it before the MCATs."

"No, your 3.78 GPA is not good enough." Dr. Solokoff continued, shaking his head. "You're better off concentrating on engineering. Forget medicine. Even if you ace this term and summer, you won't be close to a 4.0. As your advisor, I can't endorse you or sign your med school application." Now he was speaking to the bookshelves.

Christina recounted her achievements, hoping he would suddenly realize he had missed important facts about her. "I know it could be better, but you see I've taken a challenging engineering curriculum, upgrading both the math and physics classes far beyond what is required for pre-med. I've done well in those. And I've been working in the ER."

Turning now to the window, Solokoff lectured a bird that had just alighted in a nearby tree. "There are only twenty spots in the medical school class for our students, and there are plenty of students with better grades than yours. Some with a master's degree will also be applying for one of the twenty. Of course they're likely to get those coveted spots."

Christina could only stare at him.

"Did you know," Dr. Solokoff said, "the teaching assistant for your Organic Chemistry class has already applied?" Christina knew the man had also worked as his research assistant, poor soul. "No, I'm afraid your grades are simply not good enough." Dr. Solokoff snapped the folder shut and tossed it onto a pile, as if chucking a garbage bag into the dump.

Christina was shattered, like stemware dropped on a tile floor. Her dreams blown to bits. She wouldn't make it. Her advisor had told her so in plain words. He could have been telling the time. He said he wouldn't sign the med school application when the time came.

Not good enough…not good enough…not good enough. The words kept repeating in her head. She hobbled out of his office, lame from the crippling judgment. The figure that left Solokoff's office was nothing like the self-assured force that had entered just fifteen minutes before.

With the clap of a manila folder, dreams she'd harbored since middle school were vanquished by one myopic biology professor. His sole job as advisor had been to facilitate student success. *My* success. Did he offer me advice or suggest any other way to pursue my goal? Did he offer alternative paths? No, my advisor failed in his duty to advise, instead taking on roles of judge, jury, and executioner. An open and shut case. *No 4.0 GPA?* No med school admission. There was no mention of applying instead to less popular schools or securing a tutor or lightening my semester load to improve my grades by the .22 percentage points he deemed necessary. He gave no consideration to my dean's list recognition, the rigorous engineering and math courses I mostly aced. What mattered to Dr Solokoff was solely the number on a printed transcript of my four semesters and a winter session, and it simply wasn't good enough.

Christina staggered through the quad like those returning to campus after last call at the local bars. Her equilibrium was off, not from intoxication but from debilitation. *I've been so sure I could be a good doctor. I know I have the analytical skills and aptitude and more importantly, the passion and empathy to help patients. I'm fascinated by the human body. I know I can learn and perform well in medicine, given the chance.*

"Grades aren't all there is to being competent and capable," she cried out to no one in particular, garnering suspicious glances from students rushing by on the gravel path. She knew what she could do but wondered why others, like Dr. Solokoff, didn't believe in her.

In her nineteen years, Christina had little experience handling failure, especially in school. She was all too familiar, though, with the pain of criticism, ridicule, and bullying. Growing up with Sebastian had been a never-ending cycle of achievement and humiliation. When Christina got an award at school, her brother would "accidentally" bump it off the table, sending it crashing to the floor in pieces. When Christina received accolades for her piano recital performance, Sebastian dismissed it with, "I've never been so bored in my life." When the little kids in the neighborhood played kickball, Sebastian, weighing nearly twice as much as his sister, appointed himself as pitcher and referee. He'd tackle Christina just before she crossed home plate, leaving her bloody or limping, invariably ending the game. In eighth grade, Christina arrived home from school to find her parents confronting Sebastian, who had just been suspended from college. He'd yelled, "Get her out of here." When they left the house, he barged into her room and pinned her to the floor in a choke hold, his hand over her mouth, yelling, "What I do is none of your goddamned business."

Two years after Christina's bike accident, Dominic was searching the garage for a lacrosse ball when he found Sebastian's letter jacket balled up behind paint cans. Inside the sleeve was a wire cutter, clamped shut with a short length of brake cable and its white rubber casing stuck between the blades.

He showed Christina, and her eyes filled with tears, her hands clasped over the locket she always wore around her neck. "Don't say anything to anyone, Dom. If he knows, next time he'll do something worse."

Dominic, younger and smaller than Sebastian, tried to intervene a few times, but he couldn't physically overcome his brother and became the target if he confronted Sebastian or told their parents. Her older sister escaped harm by never being home and, whether intentionally or not, by never upstaging her brother. Their parents continued to assure each other that Sebastian was merely a bit high strung and that he'd grow up to become the prized elder son they could be proud of. Neither Dominic nor Christina could bring themselves to dispel that hope.

Christina spent less and less time at home. She went to Terry's or to the estate to relate her troubles to the horses and ride the fields in peace. As she got older, Sebastian's attacks were infrequent, but the constant threat left Christina continuously anxious. When Christina received a dean's list announcement from State in the mail, she left it proudly on the kitchen table for her parents. Sebastian took one look at it and ripped it to shreds. *I have to get* out of here! she thought.

Working toward her dreams and immersing herself in the ER had offered Christina a respite. Busy with work and school, she had put the dark days at home completely out of her mind—until she encountered a different kind of bullying. Then it all came back in buckets. The classmates who belittled her exam scores, those who laughed at her inexperience with circuitry, the teaching assistant who humiliated her in front of class by announcing she came in for extra help sessions, and now her advisor, demeaning her attempts to prepare for medical school—all formed a chorus, singing the refrain, "You can't do it."

Finding the put-downs too much to bear, Christina floundered in self-doubt despite knowing her abilities. She wondered if it had all been just wishful thinking, that maybe she really wasn't smart enough or good enough. Maybe I don't deserve the future I've dreamed of. Maybe I shouldn't dare to hope for a future where I can use my brain in meaningful work and help the world in some small way. Maybe I don't really have talent after all. Maybe I'll end up doing nothing with the rest of my life. Maybe I'll have to live at home and battle Sebastian forever. Maybe I'm as pitiful as Sebastian. Maybe I, too, will be unable to make it on my own.

Though her old friend, Terry, described Christina as a go-getter whose fire in the belly pushed her to go on and do what most of her peers would never even contemplate, that fire was all but embers after Dr. Solokoff's rejection. Without her advisor's recommendation and support, Christina lost her way forward. Her family didn't get it. After all, her father questioned why she should even go to college. Her mother brushed it off with, "You'll find another line of work. You're smart," not comprehending the lost dreams' emotional toll.

Weeks passed and the semester dragged by. Christina forced

herself to complete her remaining classes. Although she continued working at the ER over the summer, her white nurses' shoes now shuffled, no longer skipping over the buffed sterile linoleum. Still, she worked overtime, happy to be out of the house.

Taking the summer term off gave her time to scrape together a way forward. Mustering what was left of her initiative, Christina stoked the remaining sparks in her belly. She decided she was done with engineering. *I've gritted my teeth and busted my butt and discovered the truth—EE lights no fire in me. The thought of two more years of circuit boards and their adoring fans sounds more like a stint on a chain gang. EE at State has no medical focus. Who am I to invent a major?*

She recalled the electives she had taken during the winter session, classes in which she could express herself through writing and critical thinking. This prompted her to switch her major to philosophy. The computer science classes, all the engineering classes, the science and math she had taken were superfluous and would now be considered her electives. In the remaining eight semesters, Christina also cobbled together a minor in computer science.

She requested a new advisor. This one was supportive and remarked on her unique combination of studies. Christina knew with this approach she could graduate on time and with a market-able skill. She hoped it would enable her to move out from under her parents' roof. It never occurred to her to extend beyond four years. *Where would I get the money?* Her parents had agreed to pay the $1800 annual in-state tuition after the initial scholarship money ran out. She was sure they would not spring for an extra semester or two, all because she had decided to switch her major.

Sebastian spat out his mouthful of soda when she announced at dinner one night that she was now studying philosophy, then mopped his face with a corner of his T-shirt. He snapped his head to the right to flick his black curly locks away from his right eye. "What are you, Aristotle?" He made no mention of her computer classes.

"At least I'll know how to think, something you'll never learn," Christina shot back.

"I think it's pretty cool, Teen," Dominic said. "I couldn't see you behind a circuit board all day, anyway. You'd die working without people around you."

With her renewed sense of direction, Christina took a campus job in a biopsychology lab, convincing herself it would be a good use of all that science she had taken. The required data collection and analysis might help her get a job after graduation. She reluctantly gave up being an EMT and joined the lab's research team, studying brain manifestations of cats' behaviors in response to various stimuli. Her main job was to record observations and monitor subjects' brain waves on the oscilloscope, identifying patterns, data trends, and anomalies shown on the printed tracings, but other tasks were required.

When the team prepared new animals for the study, Christina assisted during the complex surgical procedure. To sedate them, she inserted a small syringe into a vein in the animal's foreleg for the intravenous anesthesia. She was relieved to defer to the lab director when it came time for the cranial incision used to implant a source of electrical stimulation. Christina monitored anesthesia and tested the electrical stimulation during surgery before closing the incision with sutures.

When animals didn't survive surgery, the team performed autopsies. Christina did the routine task following any autopsy— procuring tissue samples for study. Using what appeared eerily akin to a deli counter's meat slicer, she shaved wafer thin slices of brain tissue and mounted them onto slides for microscopic review. Initially horrified, she came to consider the slides as works of art, beautifully captured cross sections of the cortex. Hours alone in the lab had her examining the slides as one might view a Rorschach image. Once she finished tissue sampling, Christina placed the body inside a thick plastic bag, carried it through a windowless hallway to the adjoining Life Sciences building, and deposited it in the incinerator room. The act seemed a perfect analogy for the turn her life had taken. She wished she could just as easily dispose of her dreams.

CHAPTER 5

GRADUATION WAS BITTERSWEET. Christina had looked forward to the day for four years, but now that it was here, the joy she had anticipated was preempted by a desire to put the past four years behind her and an urge to move on. Her few friends who had found jobs would be scattered across the nation. Others moved home, searching for work. Jobs, after the Carter years, were hard to come by, especially for liberal arts graduates. Christina's friends with degrees in engineering were the lucky few who landed the $30,000 salaries. She could've been one of them, she thought, except that the only thing that interested her in engineering was the computer and its new sidekick, the CRT screen.

Christina had counted on her computer skills being an asset in job hunting, and she was right. Global Life hired her on the spot at a campus recruiting fair in April of her senior year. It wouldn't have mattered if she had studied equine science or ancient Greek. Computer skills were enough to land a job in 1982. Two weeks after graduation, she was waving goodbye to her parents. Her father, wiping a tear from his eye, and her mother, filled with hope, wondered why their middle child chose this path. Christina's other hand unconsciously moved toward her neck to clutch the delicate heart locket containing their photo, keeping them close to her heart. Since vowing to wear it forever when they gave it to her on her thirteenth birthday, she removed it only for showers and swimming.

Now, their big black Sedan DeVille inched away from the curb, dragging an empty U-Haul. Just twenty-one years old, the petite Christina, her long dark hair billowing behind her as soft winds ushered in a refreshing change, smiled broadly. She had been looking forward to living on her own, with no one to answer to but herself.

Fully outfitted with hand-me-down furnishings and kitchen essentials, the first floor of a once-suburban two-story house was now home to Christina and Heidi, both eager to join the ranks of working Americans. Blindly swept into the current of computing, Christina neither knew nor cared where it would take her. She was happy for a steady job.

Christina wanted to believe a job with Global Life carried a certain cachet. The insurance company's headquarters was the tallest building in Newark's tiny commercial district near Penn Station, which consisted of exactly three hubs of "good jobs"—the insurance giant, Bell Telephone, and Blue Cross Blue Shield. Despite Newark's grim reputation for homicides and car thefts, its proximity to New York City dangled a small carrot that enticed young people like Christina to take jobs there.

For the girls, knowing the company had security guards to escort them to their cars offered a semblance of safety in the notoriously dangerous city. And the companies held unwritten policies of workdays ending at 4:30—before dark. Heidi and Christina departed their building promptly, accompanied by escorts, then with their carpool companion sped seven miles upriver to Bloomfield every evening. Heidi had joined the pension department. She hoped to attend law school after getting work experience and saving money. Christina was accepted into the competitive paid programming course the company offered.

She would emerge with a coveted credential—IBM Mainframe Computer Programmer—and a guaranteed job in the insurance industry.

Christina found life at Global Life to be a perpetual hum of paper shuffling, which, in the manner of tectonic plates, slowly inched toward automation through computerization. The company hoped to hasten the process along by introducing a training program to fill its need for programmers. Global Life's inaugural class consisted of a disparate group of twenty. Several middle-aged Global Life lifers were plucked from the manual systems departments because of their industry knowledge and aptitude for logic as demonstrated by a passing grade on the algorithm and flowchart test. A few thirty- and forty-somethings from nearby employers jumped from telecom or transportation into insurance in search of a better salary. A smattering of recent grads from local universities rounded out the group. Two instructors from within Global Life led the motley crew into the world of computer mainframes for the next six months.

Christina befriended two peers in class. Erik Lundstrom, a few years older, was a local from Fort Lee and a recent Rutgers graduate. One girl from south Jersey, land of pig farms and tomatoes, was friendly and fun to chat with during breaks. The carpool team of her roommate, Heidi, and a classmate named Wayne became weekday-only friends. When the work week ended both took to the highways to return home to nowheresville, Pennsylvania. Wayne had a fiancé back home and, at age twenty-two, already had a plan for the rest of his life. Passing the programming course and earning his insurance certifications would guarantee him a steady job for years to come, and what more could he want? Heidi retreated to the safety of small-town living and Mom and Pop. Christina wondered if she was hoping for life to find her in the two-day reprieve between five-day stints of processing pension policies.

Christina liked Heidi and Wayne in the way she might enjoy the company of a friend's mother or father. Conversations during their commute to work were pleasant but dull. Heidi talked about making pies for her neighborhood yard sale. Wayne relayed his trouble fixing a leaky gutter or finding just the right floor mats for his car. Christina only half listened as she looked across the river at the Manhattan skyline. She had so little in common with them. Somehow, their youthful spirit seemed to have already been extinguished. She still held a steadfast drive toward something bigger, yet what that something was had eluded her since she'd abandoned her medical dreams. Christina started, once again, to succumb to self-doubt. There had to be more ahead, but could she get there? She had her sights set on doing something in the world, herself. Independence, despite frugal beginnings, tempted her with its sweet taste of freedom, adventure, and choices.

Evenings went by fast. Sometimes there was work to be done, assignments to complete before the next class day. Christina enjoyed working through the problems, debugging the programs, writing hundreds of lines of code. It's what had attracted her to computers in college. She'd look up and find it was after eleven, marked by Heidi's nightly pilgrimage to the sink to fill her nightstand water pitcher and then to the bathroom for a shower before bed. Christina laughed to herself as she admitted she had never worked this hard and this long at one task in school. The job reinforced her penchant for problem-solving. She found it satisfying, like solving a lengthy geometry proof or completing a thousand-piece puzzle.

"It's gratifying. I have something to show for it. I get to use my brain," she told Dominic over the phone.

"I like climbing telephone poles," Dominic said, referring to his job with the phone company.

"That's why they make chocolate and vanilla," Christina answered. Her brother didn't fully understand that she wanted to make a difference or why she had to make it on her own, but he was the only one in the family she could talk with about it.

When she wasn't working on a class assignment, Christina spent weeknights jogging the winding suburban roads of Bloomfield's middle-class neighborhoods, rarely passing a soul. A nagging fear that she'd collapse in the bushes along the route and not be found for weeks or meet the likes of the Central Park rapist and suffer an untimely death helped to increase her pace. During these runs, she held a tight grip on her locket, though in hindsight, a can of mace might have been a better choice.

Unlike the neighborhood where she grew up, this place epitomized suburban decline, with tattered curtains drawn tightly across windows mounted in off-kilter frames clinging to cracked asbestos siding whose paint had long ago bleached to varying hues of cement gray. There were no teenagers shooting hoops in the driveways. No kids playing hopscotch on the sidewalks or freeze-tag on front lawns—this neighborhood seemed devoid of life. Here, when a car pulled into a driveway, a briefcase-carrying driver would enter the house and disappear until the following morning when he reversed those actions exactly.

The apartment she and Heidi occupied was a step up from the dorms she had called home for the prior four years. It had been converted from the downstairs of a generously sized two-story home. The living room and den became two "railroad" bedrooms. The dining room became their living room, a crystal chandelier dangling from the ceiling.

Their landlord was local police chief Bud Campanelli. This fact allayed Christina's parents' fears about her safety so far from home.

Campanelli stood only a few inches taller than Christina, with a face weathered by grime and smoke, half-occluded by a grizzled beard like the coat of a wirehaired terrier. His mouth posed oddly to one side, permanently misshapen from cradling a cigar in the right corner, and his pot belly obscured his uniform's belt buckle. He wore a badge with a bent corner, no longer shiny. The Comos imagined he would keep a good eye on the place and look after their daughter and Heidi, though they'd never met him. Christina didn't share their optimism about him.

Despite its odd layout and outdated kitchen, the apartment was clean. Light poured in through its generous windows. The $550 monthly rent was steep, though, and after Christina forked over $275 for her half, the rest of her meager paycheck paid for utilities, gas, groceries, and little else. She liked walking to the drugstore on the corner but hated the awkward conversations when she asked the pharmacist to recommend cheaper alternatives to Crest toothpaste or Noxzema skin cream. Sweet-smelling shampoos, nail polish, and magazines never rose to the top of her affordability list. She would have to wait for a future trip home where those items were stocked as a staple in a house with daughters and a mom who understood. Though Christina had worked since age fourteen, her earnings were spent on going out to the movies, buying riding gear, and saving for a used car. Necessities were provided by her parents, and whenever household items ran out, there was what Mom called "pin money" hidden in the vase on the dining room table for anyone in the family to use. Christina had never considered budgeting for toothpaste and dish detergent until now.

Her mother had generously provided Christina with five work outfits to seed her wardrobe. Two suits already occupied her closet from days of campus interviews. The resulting seven outfits became a rotation as predictable as the changing of the guards at

Buckingham Palace. If it's Tuesday, it must be the green flowered skirt and matching blouse that ties around the neck.

Black, navy, and gray mid-heeled pumps, worn only at the office, were spared the daily wear of pounding the pavement for several blocks from the parking lot to her building. Instead, a broken-in, dingy pair of Tretorn tennis shoes, stored in her briefcase upon arriving at her desk, saved both her pocketbook and her feet. New heels cost five dollars—a luxury she couldn't afford. Christina was grateful to her mother for the practical send-off. Though repetitive, her wardrobe was classy and served her well until she grew tired of it months later.

"Purchase tailored, classic clothing, Christina, and your wardrobe will never go out of style," her mother had advised. It was good advice that Christina adopted.

Weekends alternated between out-of-town adventures and trying to establish a life for herself in her new home. She'd joined a gym, hoping to meet other runners, and started doing aerobic dancing. She asked around at work for places to shop and slowly learned her way around towns up and down the Garden State Parkway.

Drew lived and worked in Allentown, Pennsylvania, after graduating with honors and landing a job with Keystone Cellular. Initially, Christina visited Drew on weekends, and they had fun whenever she was willing to drive two hours to Allentown. She loved him and every minute they spent together. She knew he was a good boyfriend, and he loved her, though she casually understated their relationship whenever Heidi or her classmates asked about him.

After a couple of weekends in the old steel town, the fun faded. There was simply nothing to do there for twenty-somethings. The couple saved up to drive to the Jersey Shore twice over the summer, spending days romping in the ocean and walking the dunes.

They'd pass warm evenings on thrill rides at Great Adventure before heading back to their respective grinds. A few times, they met at a mountain resort equidistant between them.

By Labor Day, Christina realized Drew had never made the trip to Bloomfield since her first weekend there. When she visited him, he took her to watch his tennis matches as he and an opponent volleyed back and forth or along to Sears, where he searched for tools for his latest project. They alternated calling each other on weeknights, and as September approached, she asked Drew to come to her place more often.

"Sure, darling," he'd said. "Maybe on weekends when I don't have tennis."

"Couldn't you skip a match? I'm so close to New York, we could have fun exploring the city."

"Maybe later this fall."

Christina knew Drew's family had spent a lot of time in New York when he was growing up in New Jersey. He'd seen shows and museums and knew all the landmarks, but she wanted to experience them with him. Meanwhile, Christina fell back into her routine, including a few more trips to Allentown. Between Drew's tennis and projects, they toured open houses, Drew wondering how they might decorate a house they'd buy next year.

"Darling, do you like cherry cabinets? Take a look at that granite!" Drew would place his hand behind her back and guide her through the homes.

"What style kitchen do you prefer?" the Realtor asked Christina.

"Maybe one in the back of a restaurant?" Christina quipped.

At one open house, the agent asked, "How many children do you plan to have? That will tell me how many bedrooms you'll need."

"Oh, we don't have any children. We're just looking." Christina politely replied, annoyed at the presumption. Why do people think we're planning children? Am I wearing a sign on my back?

"We'll probably need four bedrooms," Drew clarified.

Christina liked viewing model homes, but the lifestyle they suggested was something she envisioned for her *parents*, not herself, at least for the next ten years. Drew was rushing ahead of her to see the finished basement and backyard pool. This is my parents' life. It seems Drew, like Wayne, has his life planned out already, and he is counting me in as well!

The sparkling new houses could have been in any suburban neighborhood across America. The lifestyle was comfortable, secure, and admittedly great for raising children. Hers had been a privileged and happy childhood, aside from her brother's venom, thanks to the lifestyle her parents had adopted when they moved from the city to the burbs. They had joined the country club and played bridge with the neighbors. Every kid waited for school buses on the corner. Drew's family two states away had the exact same life.

Christina began to question their future together. He never asked about the volleyball team she joined at work, about how her class was going, or about her few trips into the Big Apple. Drew has a vision of our future together yet hasn't discussed it with me. It's as if he has skipped past my life after college, ahead to my life in his.

In college, they'd shared lots in common and never run out of things to talk about. They had both worked in labs, liked computers, gone skiing and to concerts, enjoyed frequent escapes to the beach. They had friends in common. Their dorms sat adjacent on the same quad. They'd spent days, nights, and weeks together. Their lives intertwined without effort and with enough overlap that talking about one's interests naturally interested the other. Now, however, away from the contrived, artificial world of a college campus, where real choices could be made, the twine began to unravel.

CHAPTER 6

WEEKDAYS FLEW BY. Christina dedicated herself to learning all she could to become a proficient COBOL programmer, taking special delight in finding and correcting defects in lines of code. Captivated by the idea that a single bug could halt processing of thousands of policies, thereby costing the company hundreds of thousands of dollars in delayed billing and payments, Christina felt herself discovering for the first time the impact of human error. She was determined to write thoughtful, deliberate code that hummed along, bug free. A simple syntax error or a missing punctuation mark was a costly mistake that prevented a program from compiling.

Unwelcome images of Sebastian laughing at her throughout her childhood when she made a mistake in a card game or missed a catch or colored outside the lines or got sick on an amusement ride flooded her mind in the middle of class. She developed careful attention to detail in order to avoid the shame of a compiler error.

After only a few days of class, she quickly dispensed with mundane components of a program—defining its purpose, name, and data types—eager to get to the meat. Christina flexed her logic abilities in COBOL's Procedure Division, the section of a program that offered her a chance to make the system *do* something. A clever programmer could construct it into a work of art, though Christina found code like that to be a rare occurrence.

The old programs more often proved to be a clunky, unwieldy series of steps that sucked up the computer's resources unnecessarily, requiring a concise rewrite by a more skilled programmer. When the instructor presented subroutines—chunks of code written to perform a single function and stored in a library for new programs to use—Christina appreciated the efficient means of sharing commonly needed functions, freeing up programming effort to devise new solutions instead. It made perfect sense to her.

In the early days of mainframe computers, processing time and memory cards were expensive. The ability to expedite processing and reduce memory requirements could separate a brilliant developer from the rest. Those who saved time and money through succinct algorithms and efficient code were in demand. Christina became one of them. She wrote code, letter by letter, on preprinted paper templates, eighty columns wide. Relieved at not having to poke commands onto a punched card as she'd done in college, Christina typed code from her carefully desk-checked template sheets directly into the system. Programs were often tens of thousands of lines long.

Her fastidious work resulted in programs that passed through the compiler without failure. Even so, a clean compilation assured only accurate syntax. Once compiled, programs could still suffer logic flaws and endless loops of circular instructions that had no exit condition. Faulty logic could also result in undesirable and unexpected output. Carelessly misplacing a decimal point could falsely report profits by millions of dollars when thousands of payments are processed daily. Sometimes, programs came to an abrupt halt upon encountering an unexpected input or a condition for which the code didn't stipulate an instruction. These "abends" meant someone on the support team got paged in the wee hours of the night to come in to fix the problem. No programmer wanted to claim authorship of those lines and bear the wrath of whoever was called in overnight.

Christina acquired a knack for understanding data. In insurance processing, numbers and computations were the primary data types, with text representing policy holder demographics. Converting decimal numbers to binary representation as a series of 1s and 0s and hexadecimal numbers using digits 0–9 and letters A–F was necessary because data was stored in these formats. For some, this math was challenging. Christina, having mastered calculus, tutored her classmates on number systems over breaks.

The biggest challenge for Christina was learning about the hardware itself. From her engineering classes, she knew microprocessors, but Global Life used equipment she had never seen. When the instructor led the class through the computer center at Global Life, machines of all shapes and sizes came to life. Disk drives were lined up motionless, while inside, mechanical heads traversed the drums and platters reading volumes of content at the speed of light. She chuckled when she heard the clickety-clack of magnetic tape drives when an end of tape was reached because it sounded like cards in a bicycle wheel. Card punches and readers made a deafening cacophony of sounds.

Christina strolled between dozens of line printers positioned like corn plants in a field. They spewed yardage of lined greenbar paper until the rolls piled up on the floor, pages folding over each other. Some spat out specialized forms, checks, and invoices. Spending hours in the frigid computer room, Christina eventually replaced her trepidation with knowledge.

Still, Christina, who barely knew how to operate a lawn mower, found operating and troubleshooting all these components daunting and was more comfortable designing their software. Descending to the subterranean level of the skyscraper that shook when the PATH train rumbled by, she would flag down Deidre, the operations director, for help.

Diedre, who was always willing to talk about "her babies," had come into her job quite by accident, Christina learned as they bent over to mount a disk in a drive. The lean, single woman with heavy tortoiseshell glasses had been working in the procurement department, where she negotiated deals for much of the equipment Global Life purchased from IBM. She got to know the sales team well and was invited to IBM headquarters in Poughkeepsie, New York, to learn more about the machines.

The new computers piqued her interest, and Deidre enrolled in night classes to learn more. Over time, she became the resident expert on all things computer at Global Life. While Deidre liked working alone among the machines, she welcomed any opportunity to share her world with anyone who asked.

Adopting Christina as her student, Deidre revealed secrets of the machines' internal workings. Christina, clad in a heavy sweater over her suit, spent hours puttering around the computer room. With practice loading tapes, handling platters, unjamming paper feeds, swapping out boards and replacing burnt memory cards, under Deidre's guidance Christina soon became proficient. She savored the sweet taste of satisfaction at having beaten the machines. *If only my former radio-building classmates could see me now.*

For weeks, Christina was intellectually consumed by the intense training. She had found a chance to use her skills. *It may not be as exciting as the ER, but I'm good at this, and I will make enough money to support myself, and live on my own.* She'd be more than ready by December, when class would end, and she'd interview for a real job in the company.

Still, her social life in her new home was dismal. Determined to find her own pastimes and not rely on Drew every weekend,

Christina journeyed out to Allentown less and less frequently. He was too busy with tennis and projects to visit her. Weekends in Bloomfield became solitary gaps she filled with running or going to the gym. Christina endured, entertaining herself by recording cassette tapes from her favorite album tracks. She was determined to plow through and enjoy her newfound independence—anything but going home for the weekend. Missing her parents, Dominic, and the twins, Christina reminded herself that going home would mean seeing Sebastian. She had enjoyed peace these past few months, despite admitting to herself that life in Bloomfield was not *all that*.

At one point during a September lunch break, Christina's loneliness was interrupted by a spark of possibility.

"What do you guys do up here on weekends?" she asked the other young people at her lunch table.

"I surf whenever I'm not here, at Manasquan," said one classmate, who lived at home on the Jersey Shore and commuted seventy minutes to Newark on weekdays. Christina thought that could be fun if it wasn't so far.

The girl from south Jersey admitted she went home like Heidi and Wayne. Christina remained silent, dumbfounded.

Erik Lundstrom, however, chimed in with, "I go to The City."

"New York?" Christina's espresso eyes opened wide.

"Where else?" Erik's blond eyebrows arched.

Christina looked up at Erik, noticing for the first time his handsome chiseled jaw, his delicate and angular nose, the way his summer-blue eyes reflected the afternoon light. His stretched-out limbs and cornsilk hair couldn't deny his Nordic ancestry, in stark contrast to Christina's southern Italian features.

"I go to clubs, museums, festivals…whatever is going on." Erik studied Christina. "Maybe you can come with me sometime."

CHAPTER 7

ERIK KNEW HIS way around New York City, all right. He'd spent his college summers as a chauffeur to a big bank executive who popped in and out of businesses during a typical workday. Erik drove the exec where he had to go, killed time for as long as the banker remained in a building, then returned to pick him up and cart him off to the next meeting. Erik knew just where the underground clubs were, the galleries and speakeasies, the hidden parks, and street food joints where he could leave the car idling while he grabbed a quick lunch. He also knew which areas to avoid—where drug deals went down in broad daylight, where hoodlums harassed passersby on the sidewalk, or where the stench of piled-up trash became putrid in the summer sun.

Not long on words, Erik took it all in with astute observation. His slow and deliberate swagger could turn in an instant to jackrabbit leaps, darting around corners and springing into the Lincoln after inadvertently discovering a thug suspiciously fumbling at the doorway of a brownstone clearly far beyond his financial reach.

Yes, Erik Lundstrom is the right person to escort me around the city, thought Christina. If Drew won't come here with me, I'll go with Erik. His easy confidence yet diffident demeanor offered the allure of a mild suggestion rather than an invitation. He was unflappable and steady, equally adept at gunning the gas pedal or deftly maneuvering around a stopped delivery truck. The city posed no obstacle for him. Erik took delight in sharing all he knew with his inquisitive new friend Christina.

At first, they took afternoon spins around town, stopping to eat steaming hotdogs from a street vendor outside the Port Authority parking garage. Erik pointed out Studio 54, Caché, and other clubs he frequented. "You're going to love these places when we go."

Christina peered at their discreet or flashy entrances as Erik rolled by, some with nondescript doors in back allies and others with glitzy marquis. He told her about the lines that formed after dark. She envisioned edgy youth hoping to get selected by the stoic, broad men wearing dark sunglasses, the gatekeepers to Oz.

"The best time to go is on a weeknight around midnight," advised Erik, "when the crowd is not full of tourists and middle-aged Jersey salesmen looking to recapture their youth." He wove his car into the left lane to get around a stopped taxi.

"You go in at midnight on a weeknight?" Christina turned to stare at Erik.

"Yeah. The line forms about nine thirty, and usually the women get in right away once they open the doors at eleven. I know a lot of the bouncers, so I get in no problem. Some people never make it in—they might be awkward, too old, unattractive, creepy, or whatever. The crowd is highly curated for the right look. These places pride themselves on exclusivity."

Finding the admission practice incredibly unjust, Christina stared out the window to hide her shock. As she watched anonymous New Yorkers hustle across a street before the traffic light changed, she thought about the clubs back home that allowed everyone in and still never filled to capacity.

"Erik, what does it take to be one of the chosen? Should I take up smoking to look cool?" Christina wondered what they wear and mentally traveled through her closet of work clothes. Her gaze brightened as she recalled a pink miniskirt, white booties, and a trendy polka-dotted top that looked like something the Go-Go's might wear in concert. Even if I have the right clothes, I don't have the right face or the right body. Who am I kidding? I've never looked cool, I can't stand cigarette smoke, and I really don't want to conform to someone else's arbitrary standards of cool, even to get into a great club.

"I don't know. They just size everyone up and decide." Erik seemed unfazed. Christina decided to take her chances and go anyway, then wondered when he would ask her to go along.

They walked the Battery and the Bowery. Christina discovered more stores selling lighting fixtures of all styles, prices, and tastes in one block than in her entire home state. They frequented the Italian market, eating cannoli, calzone, and bacalao along Mulberry Street at the weeklong celebration of all things Italian—the San Gennaro Feast. Christina's long dark curls and olive skin blended in with the locals. Erik, slender, soft-spoken, and fair-haired, towered over the boisterous crowd. Christina liked knowing he kept guard when she darted ahead to inspect a vendor's fresh artichokes or get closer to the accordion player fingering "O Sole Mio" with closed eyes. She could easily spot Erik among the throng of people.

They consumed immeasurable quantities of dim sum in poorly lit cave-like establishments under the busy streets of Chinatown, accessible only through a creaky corrugated metal door in an alley she would have avoided if alone. They knelt and prayed at St. Patrick's cathedral, then window-shopped along Fifth Avenue. They chatted with the elevator man at Saks, who Erik knew by name. Christina admired the lovely wooden display cases exhibiting one or two expensive handbags or three glittering necklaces. Though she'd never owned an expensive piece of furniture, she appreciated the craftsmanship in their finely hewn scrollwork. The cases themselves, even emptied of their pricey interior content, were works of art in the 1920s building.

After riding the Empire State Building's elevator up to the eight-sixth floor observatory just before closing, they'd witness the twinkling view of lights coming on in the Big Apple. They went to Canal Jeans, their favorite stop for cheap and trendy wardrobe staples any up-and-comers like themselves needed, where they maneuvered between savvy shoppers to sale racks. Italian-made leather shoes at bargain-basement prices, inexpensive fashions made in the garment district, and handmade jewelry from street vendors in the Village were too good to pass up. *Not the wardrobe from Nordstrom's my mother recommended,* Christina thought.

Any news that reached Christina now came through the lens of *The Village Voice*. From popular music to film reviews, social issues and gay rights, Christina embraced the paper's views, making a point to read the *Voice* cover to cover every week. The Village, as Erik so casually referred to it, became one of Christina's favorite neighborhoods in the city. Walking down Christopher Street, popping into the Stonewall Inn and mingling with people from every social class, Christina remarked about the huge crowds showing up to the bar in the early afternoon, but Erik told her, "The best time to go there is between 1 a.m. and closing."

With Erik, she wandered streets traveled by the literary greats and jazz musicians of days gone by and traced the steps of its more recent inhabitants, the beatniks and bohemians of the '70s. Christina loved its sense of acceptance and its artsy vibe. She felt as if just by breathing the air, she, too, could be one to change the world and champion a social movement.

In Washington Square, NYU students demonstrated in protest. She had never seen that on her suburban college campus.

"Do people actually protest anymore?" she asked Erik.

"Let's go see."

She thought demonstrations ended in the '70s when the Vietnam war was over. But here, in New York today, students shouted their passionate disapproval of nuclear weapons. She read their signs, scanned their pamphlets, and became fearful of a world threatened by world powers wielding weapons of mass destruction. Christina got swept up in the cause, grabbing a sign extended to her by a raggedy co-ed. Marching along, she, too, was indignant that our country might allow this to happen.

The city was a smorgasbord for the senses, and she consumed it, mouth wide open, with the reliability of her trusted friend Erik beside her. Theirs was not a romantic relationship, more artisan and apprentice, scholar and student. She physically and cognitively felt her world expanding. She had seen more in the few months with Erik than she'd seen in her whole life. No stranger to city life, Christina knew downtown Philadelphia, less than an hour's drive from where she grew up. City sights, from bums to bus stations, high-rises to historic buildings, expensive restaurants to street food vendors, were not new to her. But New York, or The City as Erik so affectionately called it, exuded urgency. She was enamored of its diverse, progressive persona. The city beckoned Christina, welcoming her with open arms.

The last week in September, Erik finally suggested she come along with him to the clubs. They were refilling their coffee mugs in the break room before class resumed.

"I'm going on Wednesday about eleven," Erik casually mentioned as he piled two spoons of sugar into his cup.

"Is Thursday a national holiday? Aren't you worried about driving to work the next day?" Christina stopped, the coffee cup half-lifted to her mouth.

"No! You may be a little tired that's all."

Erik really doesn't know me. I need sleep. I can't function on less than eight or nine hours, let alone solve a problem. Going out at eleven is ludicrous. But I'm game.

"OK." Christina agreed as she recovered enough from the idea to take a sip of coffee.

"Meet me at the Meadowlands parking lot at 10:45, and I'll drive us in." Erik turned and walked to his desk, and nothing more was said about it.

Christina's head was spinning. OK, she thought, I'll get home from work at 4:50, grab a quick bite, have a glass of wine, and sleep for four and a half hours. After a quick shower, I'll drive over to meet Erik. I can sleep a few hours when I get home and then get up for work.

"Heidi, do you mind driving carpool Thursday morning?" she blurted after the security escort brought her to her car in the parking lot.

Heidi was already buckled in. "Sure. Are you taking the day off?"

"No. I'm going out Wednesday night and may be too tired to drive." Being tired, Christina would soon learn, was only part of the challenge. There were the sweet cocktails to metabolize before dawn, and the dizzying set of memories and experiences to digest, all before eight the next morning.

"Wednesday?" Heidi grimaced. "Are you out of your mind? Where are you going and how late will you get back?"

"I'm going clubbing with Erik, and we're meeting around eleven. I'm sure we'll be back by one or two."

Heidi's shocked face could have been that of Christina's mother six months ago, when she had announced she had accepted the job in the most crime-ridden city in America. "I hope you'll be quiet when you come in because I will be sound asleep." Heidi rolled down her window as they waited for Wayne.

"I'll be careful not to wake you. Unless, of course, I get locked out or attacked in the city..." Christina's joke went unnoticed.

And so, it began. Clubbing nights became a regular occurrence. Most clubs were in the city, but occasionally they'd venture out to Morristown for a punk club with a more upscale clientele. Erik drove like the expert chauffeur he had been but always from a meeting point that Christina drove to, if only a couple of miles from her apartment. That meant driving home at ungodly hours when he dropped her off at Meadowlands. Along the turnpike. Or along the parkway. High-speed roadways, middle of the night, young girl compromised by lack of sleep, too many drinks. An occasional high posed a new set of concerns. Christina almost couldn't recognize herself. Who are you?

The dancing was hypnotic. Base boomed from refrigerator-sized speakers, lights spun and dappled the floor, beautiful people in all manner of clothing undulated with glee. No judging or pushing. No bullies or ridicule. There was nothing like it. Christina became powerful and anonymous simultaneously. She felt blissfully free, sometimes forgetting where she was. She just danced and danced, feeling alive. What harm could come from a night of simple fun?

At first, she passed when Erik offered a line. After several weeks of clubbing, she noticed he never seemed out of it after snorting. He didn't get obnoxious or act dumb like drunk frat boys did at campus parties. If anything, he became more alive. That appealed to Christina. She didn't want to zone out, like when she smoked pot, or get more gregarious as she might from drinking too much. But energized? Christina found that enticing.

Erik skillfully rolled the twenty-dollar bill to make a straw, then held the small mirror and tapped out a neat white line from the small baggie he drew from his pocket. Using his American Express card, he corralled any stray grains and shaped the line to the straightest, most beautiful etching. This seems sophisticated, genteel, observed Christina. Not like the many low-life habits I've witnessed at college parties. No one sloppy and staggering. No one laughing raucously loud, vomiting, or passing out. Well dressed and well behaved, these aren't the drug users I've witnessed. I can do this. I want to do this. But not yet, not tonight.

Her paychecks started going to clothes bought in the city on a solo Saturday afternoon, forcing her to eat PBJs for dinner some nights. Christina became more comfortable weaving her way into the city after boarding the PATH train to cross the river, then walking or hopping onto a subway to her favorite spots. Short skirts, super-pointy flats, bright colors, glittery fabrics, and stretchy Lycra garments began populating her closet. She carried a distressed leather jacket when traversing city blocks on crisp fall nights.

An easy-going and free club persona took root in Christina, though she maintained an observant regard for human nature. She noticed patrons in the clubs who looked lost, drugged-out, or too old to be doing this sort of thing. Most seemed like her, having fun, working out for themselves the many choices of friends, entertainment, interests, and habits they would adopt on the way to becoming adults. Erik never pushed anything on Christina. She loved that about him. Most of the clubbing nights included just her, Erik, and occasionally another friend of his. Often, they made new friends there.

Heidi once commented that sleeping during the car ride to work on Fridays didn't seem like a great path toward promotion. Heidi had set her sights on becoming a team leader and did her best to appear as mature and levelheaded as she thought necessary to land the job. Christina, though, didn't see herself staying too long at Global Life and was not concerned about promotion there. The training course was going well, but now the instructors were plugging the insurance training that would make any programmer more valuable to the company, especially those who made it to level nine. There would be sessions to prepare for the level exams after work on Wednesdays and Thursdays. Ah, there's the catch. There's not a chance in hell I'm going to do that. On club nights! To learn more about insurance! Instead, Christina became increasingly more focused on finishing the program at the top of her class in order to land the best assignment, despite not pursuing the levels. Besides, I have other plans for those nights.

One of those Wednesdays, they went to the punk club in Morristown. Dancing for hours to music by A Flock of Seagulls, David Bowie, DEVO, and Modern English, Christina couldn't think of a better set list. As smooth beats gave way to punk rock, the dancers morphed into jerky, erratic popcorn kernels popping in a hot pan. Under flashing strobe lights, people gyrated all too close, and an occasional cocktail splashed her clothes as someone sashayed by. It was hypnotizing. But where is Erik?

Christina looked around and spotted him at a table with three guys she hadn't seen before. They were standing in a way that blocked a full view of Erik. Only his long legs were visible, stretched out with his unmistakable shiny pointed shoes crossed leisurely at his ankles. She stopped dancing and went over to the table. The guys tried to wave her away, but Erik motioned, "She's OK," and made room for her beside him in the booth. One glance at the table strewn with empty plastic bags and Christina knew what had gone down. "I want to try it, Erik."

He looked startled at first, but his gaze softened, and he smiled. "You sure about this?"

"One hundred percent. I'm more than ready," Christina announced, moving in closer to Erik as she slid into the booth.

He carefully took out a fresh clean twenty and rolled it into a neat straw, then offered it to her gently. He slid the tiny mirror from his pocket, set it in front of her on the table, and emptied a pea-sized sprinkle of white powder onto it. The guys were now huddled in close, enjoying the exaggerated demonstration. Erik carved the neat line as Christina watched, trying to look nonchalant. "Whenever you're ready. You've seen me do it. Just take your time."

She sniffed a straight line and felt a tingling in her nostril. It was done in an instant. An unexpected rush caused her to clench her teeth as her heart pounded. She felt herself on high alert. Each of her five senses came alive. Erik suggested she blot up the remaining few grains with her finger and then rub her gums. Aware only of her gums and teeth, Christina jetted through a time warp. She witnessed, as if suspended from high above her own body, the blood molecules pulsing through her veins from her heart to the inside of her mouth. She slid her tongue over her gums, feeling each crevice between her teeth. Isn't the human body truly fascinating? The lights became more intense, the music more emotional, the people more glamorous. Ready for anything, Christina threw her arms around Erik and pulled him to the dance floor.

That night seemed endless. With every beat of the music, she rocked and spun and bounced and laughed. She couldn't stop smiling. Erik smiled, too, that wry, half smile of his, enjoying her delight. At last, it was time to leave. She gulped down two glasses of ice water and plopped down on the front seat of Erik's car, still on top of the world. Even the highway looked pretty. Few cars passed by, but bright shiny streetlights steadily punctuated his vehicle's progress back to Meadowlands. As Erik pulled up to her car, Christina started worrying about driving herself the few miles back to her apartment. She had a personal rule to never drive after drinking. She had aways sipped water the last hour of a night out to clear her system. But this was altogether different. That heightened alert state so welcomed a few hours ago now nagged her brain with logistical details she hadn't considered.

"You OK?" Erik looked concerned.

"Yeah, but I'm not sure about driving like this." Christina's thinking brain took over.

"You'll be fine. Just take it easy, and you'll be home before you know it. Just don't get stopped. I'll see you bright and early tomorrow, I mean, in a few hours, at work." Erik rolled up the window and made his way past the stadium, heading north to Bergen County.

Christina smiled weakly and started the car. What if my car breaks down? She prayed it wouldn't be tonight, shuddered when she felt her locket beneath her shirt, and pulled away, as Erik's car faded in the rearview mirror.

Christina deliberately looked for the Hackensack River and made sure to aim away from it, heading west down Route 3. If she lost focus and went too far, she'd run into the Garden State Parkway or Montclair Country Club, where there were likely to be cops along the route. Instead, she took the Passaic Avenue exit and Bloomfield Avenue through neighborhoods, finally turning onto the street where she lived. It was deserted this time of night. Annoyingly conscious of and desperately fighting her desire to stomp on the pedal and scream out the opened windows, her usual levelheaded self took over and steered her slowly and carefully back home, teeth clenched as she held on to her last shred of rational thought. She crept through the front door, which led directly into her room, then crashed on the bed in the dark. What was I thinking?

Christina finally drifted off and slept through the alarm just a few hours later, rising only to Heidi shaking her to get up for work. "Must've been some night, you didn't even change out of your clothes!"

Not wanting to share details with Heidi, Christina clumsily made her way into the bathroom and got ready for work. While Heidi drove in, Christina dozed for most of the ride. "Take it easy on her, Wayne," chided Heidi, shooting a look in the rearview mirror, "she had a hard night."

"Ahh," nodded Wayne, smart enough not to ask.

In class, Christina could hardly look at Erik. *Do I remember everything that happened? Or is it like drinking, where people don't remember doing stupid things?* She worked with her head down, until Erik approached her desk midmorning. "I had a great time last night," he whispered, "and I hope you're good with it."

Christina couldn't deny she'd had a blast! But it scared her. *What if I hadn't been able to drive back? What if my heart stopped suddenly? Who would ever know to look for me near Meadowlands at 4 a.m. on a Thursday? Was it really worth all this worrying? And isn't Erik concerned about those things too?*

She simply replied, "Me too," and returned her gaze to the lines of code on the continuous green-bar paper that spilled over her desk.

There were a few more club nights after that, some with lines, some without. Erik was selective about his supply and never settled for the crap cut with God knows what. Christina, though, made a point of enjoying it early in the night, deluding herself that the drug would be flushed out of her system by the time she had to drive back. At least the teeth clenching and lead foot impulses were gone by then. They continued the club nights once or twice a week through the fall. Nights brought cold winds that slashed through her leather jacket and bit her bare legs. Erik kindly offered his jacket. She readily accepted but wondered if she had seen Erik lean in imperceptibly closer to her cheek before she had abruptly skipped ahead.

We're just good friends, aren't we? Not that I'm not interested. Erik is sweet and looks like the leading man in a Hollywood film. But we work together, and he knows about Drew. Drew! I wish Drew would have visited and gone clubbing with me in the city.

We would have had so much fun dancing and soaking up the city together.

Then one night, Erik pulled up at the Meadowlands with a woman in his car. Sarah, tattooed with snakes and swords on all visible ghostlike skin, sported a severe, side-shaved and blond-tipped spiked haircut. A long cigarette hung lazily from a black slit of a mouth. Christina couldn't picture a woman more unlike herself. Erik introduced Sarah as his friend from home, and Christina as his friend from work. All true, and off-putting for both of them.

"Nice to meet you, Sarah!" Christina smiled self-consciously and cautiously climbed into Erik's back seat, never having sat there before. Instantly regretting her trendy outfit and dramatic makeup, which screamed "Not cool," Christina knew she would be considered edgy by exactly no one. Nor would she be considered intimidating by anyone—unlike this real-life goth.

Sarah's cursory "Hey," muttered as she blew a puff of smoke up into the heavens, in no uncertain terms told Christina they were not going to be friends. Christina knew Sarah didn't like this arrangement—meeting up with her at Meadowlands for a night of clubbing. Sarah, seizing any chance to take Erik's hand, sitting with one leg draped over his knee, whispering into his ear while her lips ever so lightly grazed his neck, then looking into the distance whenever Christina uttered a word, showed Christina she thought of Erik as more than a friend. After a few nights out with them, Christina begged off from the weekly clubbing. She queued up excuses. It was becoming too hard to get up the next day. She had too much going on at work. She wanted to be sharp now that class was finishing up.

Erik initially protested, "Aw, come on, Christina."

I wish Erik hadn't let it go so easily. The glory days are over. I'll find adventure elsewhere. But boy, it was fantastic while it lasted.

CHAPTER 8

AFTER THE NEW YEAR, as the programming class wound down, each student was notified of open positions available for their permanent assignment. Christina accepted an offer for her first-choice role, a spot on a team that wrote and maintained code for the daily policy processing cycle that began at midnight. Their code managed changes, premium billing, and maintenance for over sixteen million policies. Huge volumes of data were processed each night. A halting error could affect company cash flow by millions of dollars and could leave a policyholder unprotected, while their policy remained in suspension during the resolution of a computer system flaw. These high stakes, the need for accuracy, and high impact were what attracted Christina to the team.

Christina's classmates took roles working on payroll, benefits, and other internal systems. Others left the company after class ended. Christina thought that audacious until Erik explained that the company took a significant research-and-development tax exemption for the training program expenses, regardless of attrition.

"Don't feel too bad for the company, Christina, they still get the tax write-off if someone leaves."

"I clearly know little about the business world," admitted Christina. "That's what years of science and math classes will do to you."

"Welcome to the real world," he said. "And what happened to your hand?"

"Two broken fingers. Horsing around with my brother. Don't ask."

Christina had stumbled and fallen while hanging Christmas lights over the holidays with Dominic. Her brother had been teasing her about knowing why once one bulb goes out on a string of lights, the entire string stays dark.

"Only you, Christina, make a lesson out of hanging Christmas decorations," Dominic said.

"You should know that yourself, Mr. Telecom," she chortled, lunging toward him with a length of evergreen garland in her hand. Her leg got tangled up in the greenery, and she came down hard, catching herself with one hand. "Dang it, Dominic!"

The next day, her two purple sausage-like fingers couldn't move. "Teen, that looks bad. I'm sorry. I'll take you to the ER, your old stomping grounds," Dominic said. She returned wearing a cast.

Erik winced when she showed him the colorful bruises peeking out from the plaster. "Ouch. At least you have a couple fingers left to use the keyboard."

Still, Christina felt an obligation to the company for investing in her, and it never occurred to her to leave after getting paid to learn their systems.

Christina approached her new job with gusto. She spent several weeks shadowing her mentor, Doug, as he wrote code and moved it from the development region, where code was written, to the test region, where it could be validated, and finally into production.

Christina soon learned that writing code as part of this team really meant writing merely a few lines of code or correcting syntax errors. Removing an extraneous space or reducing the number of iterations in an algorithm that looped one time too many was hardly the development opportunity she had expected. She had envisioned writing thousands of lines of complex code to solve real-world problems, but that had already been done by others over the last decade. Nowadays, what was left for this team were simple corrections to lines of code never-before-accessed. Due to an obscure set of conditions, some errors went undiscovered until years after the program went into production.

The work didn't require three weeks of shadowing to get the gist. Christina felt silly following behind Doug as he walked over to the code librarian's desk to check out the code he'd work on. Sometimes Christina nodded off when she was watching over Doug's shoulder as he typed in a few characters on the CRT screen. She found herself drumming her fingers on the desk when he sent internal messages to the team about an upcoming change going into production. No, this is not what they trained me to do.

Having sat through two years of engineering classes to master machine language and programming of the microprocessor, then providing care in the ER, then conducting research in the cat lab, Christina knew she could do more than fix careless errors of programmers gone before. To relieve her boredom, Christina resorted to counting the tap-tap-taps of keys fingered by nearby coworkers. She imagined deliberately planting a bug so that the team would immediately mobilize in search of a fix, just to liven things up. She checked her Swatch far too often and longed for the class days when her fingers cramped from writing hundreds of lines of code.

When she corrected one of Doug's mistakes or suggested a fix he hadn't considered, Christina felt marginally satisfied. However, she quickly realized that the possibilities for making any type of important contribution here were limited. Particularly since this team's members had eight to twelve years of experience and still worked in the same roles. Christina could foresee no possible upward mobility.

Little more than a month into the role, she knew she had to make a change. When she was called into a meeting with her former classmates, Christina almost skipped to the conference room in anticipation of what she hoped would be a new project announcement. Instead, management announced more classes for insurance industry certifications. Christina's short-lived excitement plunged into disappointment. She had zero interest in becoming a certified insurance *anything*.

While waiting for programs to compile, her daydreams became more frequent. Sometimes she revisited the ER in her mind, but she tried hard to close that chapter and not look back. But something kept popping into her head about the darn typewriter they used to check people into the ER. Life and death may hinge on a typo a clerk makes when they manually check you into the Emergency Room, yet your life insurance policy renewal is cleanly inked, error-free, on a computer-generated letter sent precisely thirty days before expiration. How can the country's priorities be so screwed up? As Christina thought increasingly about how computers could revolutionize patient care and streamline hospital operations, she started making notes of her ideas to help pass time between Doug's excruciatingly slow corrections. Christina thought more about healthcare problems than insurance while tagging behind Doug like a new puppy.

Wouldn't it be great if all that manual collection of patient information we did in the ER was automated and retained for the next time a patient comes in, so we don't have to collect it all again and manually type it onto a multipart form? What if the computer could prioritize treatment for patients with the highest acuity? Couldn't we collect data and track all the failed surgeries and poor outcomes and then evaluate trends to determine patient risk factors, flag errors in care plans, or catch medications before they prove harmful or fatal? Couldn't patients' medical histories be carried forth to subsequent medical visits, better informing practitioners of patients' risk factors and known disease states? Couldn't the computer anticipate a needed medication like it determines when to send an insurance bill? Her mind raced with solutions.

Then she remembered a company who had come to campus during her college recruitment. Hospital Systems of America, or HSA, as they came to be known, had been in business for less than a decade. Their headquarters occupied a sprawling valley in Philadelphia's western suburbs. They developed, sold, and managed software for hospitals. She had wanted to interview with them before graduation, but their recruiter explained that they were interviewing only computer science majors. Though Christina had inquired, her campus career office couldn't persuade them otherwise.

But now, a year later, things were different. She had skills. She had experience. She had knowledge. And she was motivated. Determined to get in with this company, Christina crafted a letter to Hospital Systems of America, explaining her prior and renewed interest in interviewing, her recent certification in IBM mainframe programming, her short time in a job assignment with little growth potential and even less responsibility, and her desire to combine her passions for health and computers to improve healthcare.

Christina had no reason to stay in north Jersey, though her affinity to the city still tugged at her wild side. Allentown was of no interest, though if she worked at HSA she'd be closer to Drew. They'd spent little time together other than a few days at Christmas, but those few days together reminded her how much she loved Drew. I hope he'll come visit more often if I get a job closer.

Bloomfield had felt a bit unwelcoming anyway, she admitted to herself, for she still had not connected with anyone besides

Erik. Joining the health club left her working out next to dozens of silent weightlifters whose conversation consisted of only an occasional breathless grunt. The hordes of young aerobics enthusiasts and joggers she had expected to meet were figments of her imagination. The dancers departed the gym immediately after Jane Fonda's workout routine ended, without so much as a glance Christina's way. Joggers on treadmills next to hers were oblivious of their neighbors, wearing headphones plugged into a Sony Walkman and staring straight ahead at an imaginary trail.

A call came through late one afternoon in early February as she returned to her apartment and dropped her car keys on the kitchen table.

"Is this Christina Como? I'm Valerie Parks from the Human Resources department of HSA."

"Yes, this is Christina. I've been so eager to hear from you."

"We appreciate you contacting us again this year, and we have a hiring manager interested in speaking with you. Would you be able to come to Lenapy for an interview next Thursday at nine? You would spend the morning interviewing, then take our entrance exam in the afternoon."

Silently cheering and pumping her fists in the air, Christina kept her cool. "Certainly! I can make it then."

The next week dragged by. She would drive home Wednesday evening after work, take off work Thursday and Friday, and make the forty-five-minute drive to Lenapy from home Thursday morning. She had her navy suit dry-cleaned, polished her black pumps, and packed a notepad and a few copies of her résumé into the beautiful cordovan-leather briefcase that screamed, "Don't mess with this girl!" if only to an audience of one—herself in the mirror. She turned up her nose when her gaze fell on the pesky cast on her left hand, knowing it put a cramp in her otherwise confident style.

"How will I hold the briefcase and shake my interviewer's hand?" Christina asked her mirror image. "I'll just have to set the briefcase down to shake hands. Even Michelangelo's David once had a broken arm," she told the girl staring back at her.

Rehearsing in her mind what she might say in the interview, Christina assumed an air of confidence that comes only when one decides to pursue one's dreams undaunted. She stared at the hopeful figure in the mirror.

"Won't HSA want to hire someone who wants responsibility, someone dedicated to their mission, someone willing to learn and work hard?" she demanded, as the girl in the mirror echoed with indignant posture. She couldn't picture herself working for any business that didn't appreciate drive. Clock-punching was not her style. I want my work to be interesting and worthwhile. I will do my best, as I always do. I will not be content to simply coast along for the next twenty years. The embers in Christina's belly were rekindling.

Mrs. Como smiled upon hearing Christina might leave Newark and made a fuss over her daughter coming back home for a long weekend. "Oh, and by the way, do you know they're predicting snow for Thursday?" Mom had a way of changing subjects abruptly.

"What? No. I had no idea. I don't get Philadelphia news stations." Christina held the phone away from her ear just a bit, frowning.

"I'm sure it'll just be a dusting. Lenapy isn't that far. Your car should be fine. I'm glad you're coming home Wednesday." Mom's not-to-worry voice achieved its goal.

Driving down I-95 Wednesday evening, Christina tuned the car radio to WIOQ-Philadelphia. "A storm is coming overnight," the reporter cautioned. Christina knew a couple of inches was enough to wreak havoc on the roads, close schools and businesses, and shut down the state of Delaware. This sounded like it could be a bit more than usual, but Christina dismissed the thought. She smiled at an unexpected image of Erik chauffeuring the banker through New York. I can drive like a pro too. She sang along to the radio "Break down, …give it to me" and sped south along the New Jersey Turnpike.

CHAPTER 9

RISING AT DAWN to a howling wind, Christina thought for a minute that her shades were down. Where her bedroom window should be was a gray rectangle on a pale green wall. Blinking sleep from her eyes, she gasped, realizing she would be driving to her interview in a snowstorm. Springing from bed, she went to work gathering up what might be needed for a dicey drive in the snow—long johns, boots, mittens, hat and scarf, snow pants, snacks, and cans of Tab. Retrieving items from the hallway closet, her sister's old dresser, and the kitchen, she raced past her father as he deposited an empty coffee cup in the dishwasher.

"Good luck, sweetheart! And be careful on the roads," he called, stepping into his galoshes before leaving for work.

Clad in the interview suit and heels, briefcase in tow, Christina piled her supplies on the back seat. She thought if she was prepared with everything she might need in a worst-case blizzard, she would have absolutely no use for them when the snow storm amounted to nothing. Confirming that her army surplus shovel and sandbags were still in the trunk, she set out amid snowflakes the size of quarters just after daybreak. Ever responsible, Christina allowed two hours for what would normally be a fifty-minute drive. Back roads were the last to get salted or plowed, so she stuck to the highways, going seven miles out of her way. After a few skids and slippery stops along Route 1 in Chadds Ford, traffic crept along Route 202 through West Chester, as everyone had the same idea.

"School buses aren't out, thank *God*!" she announced aloud.

Ninety minutes later, she arrived in Lenapy. Pulling into the parking lot, she squinted through a clear slit on her windshield at what looked like brownies sprinkled with confectioners' sugar, only their wheels revealing the cars' true identity. She had time to collect herself and freshen up before announcing herself to HR fifteen minutes early.

"Wow," a pleasant Valerie greeted her. "I can't believe you came in. We've had lots of candidates call us to reschedule," she tittered, exasperated hands waving in the air, leading Christina toward a conference room where her day would start.

Was that even a possibility? Christina had never given a thought to rescheduling. Who would let a little snow keep them from something as important as this? "It wasn't so bad getting in," she assured Valerie, "and I took it slow."

"You'll first meet David Stokes, senior manager of our Aura Installations group, then his team leaders and programmers. We'll give you a voucher for lunch here in the café."

"Thank you," Christina nodded.

"This afternoon you'll have the entrance exam. You did know about this part, right? It's just an assessment we do to ascertain your logic, analytical, and flowcharting skills, a way of measuring aptitude for the programming. Everyone who works here has taken it, except those of us in Human Resources, of course." Valerie sounded relieved.

Christina wasn't worried about the logic test. She had taken Logic as a self-paced pass-fail course to satisfy a philosophy requirement and had completed it well before spring break. Too bad I didn't take it for credit—would have boosted my GPA.

Valerie poured her a hot coffee, while Christina held her own internal pep talk. *Flowcharting?* No problem. I designed a matching algorithm for a dating service, in Pascal, for cryin' out loud. *Analytical skills?* Those three semesters of calculus and differential equations better have prepared me for this. She stirred the black coffee, searching for invisible Boolean expressions, while Valerie left her to wait for Mr. Stokes.

Minutes later, an energetic, smiling Mr. Stokes burst into the room as Christina jumped to her feet. Christina's smile widened upon seeing his youthful face, guessing him to be in his thirties. Mr. Stokes took one look out the window at the blustery day.

"You get the candidate-of-the-year award for showing up today," he joked, extending his hand to Christina. She fumbled nervously to set down the power briefcase so she could shake his hand, and he graciously waited, putting Christina at ease. "I'm Christina Como, with a broken left hand," she apologized.

"Oh, snowstorm applicant with injury—bonus points!" He winked. "Glad to meet you. And call me David."

He began by telling her he was still getting used to the new building and how much he loved working in this site where all the meeting rooms overlook the rolling hills of Chester County. "You see," he squeezed his arms together into a hug, "we started in claustrophobic office space in King of Prussia, the town of office parks and shopping malls, with sometimes four of us packed into a tiny office, until this campus was built. A few times I thought I might have to work out of a closet, but Jack kept reminding me that the Emerald City was our next stop."

Jack Walters, he explained, was the brains behind Aura, the new product being built on in-house minicomputers for registration and clinical data. Before that, their hospital clients used HSA's mainframe-based product for billing, with no clinical systems or systems written in-house. Jack was a Stanford prodigy with a vision—to bring the next generation of computing to *help patients* in the healthcare system, not just bill them efficiently. Christina already liked David within their few minutes' conversation and Jack, whom she hadn't even met.

"My team," he explained, "takes the model product Development puts out and customizes it for each client to their specifications. We build that custom solution, then go out and install it on-site, train them how to use it, and bring it LIVE a couple of months later. I have three teams of Install programmers now, the west, the east, and everywhere else. Each team needs more people. We've installed nine sites so far and have forty-three on the books.

"Our sales team is insane. We can't keep up right now. They're selling vaporware at this point, stuff we only dream of, but that means job security for all of us. Our Aura product now offers patient registration, a patient index, order entry, and reports and requisitions. I'll stop talking for a minute to see if you have any questions."

"What kind of customization is done? Don't the hospitals all have to collect the same information on a patient and order the same kinds of testing based on a patient's symptoms?"

"Good questions! Well, no, we follow the Burger King model, Have it Your Way. The government only last year introduced a uniform billing standard, the UB-82, for data on bill forms. Some hospitals are still not using that, so their demographic data isn't standard. Besides, hospitals collect all kinds of other data, unique to their sites.

"For example, they might want to know who referred you to them, your food preferences, religious affiliations, shoe size. I'm kidding about shoe size. But that's the idea, we can do whatever they want, within reason. The orders vary depending on the type of facility. A women and children's hospital has no need for prostate screening, and an osteopathic hospital might have four variations of hip X-rays. This means we take our base product and hone it to what they need, starting with our model. They buy a license for the model and pay for the customization and ongoing maintenance fees. It's already a huge revenue stream for the company, and we're just starting. There are eight hundred revenue cycle clients on our billing system, and they could all become Aura clients, potentially. You can see why we've tripled our size in the last two years."

Christina was impressed. "So, what do the programmers on your team do, since the model code already exists?"

"They interpret the specs and change or add code to make it work for that client." David's eyes were bright with enthusiasm. "They load client profiles into the database after clearing out model data. Each hospital's profile is unique. We program custom forms, reports, and notifications to look just like the hospital wants. And sometimes, if the hospital has an innovative idea for functionality we don't have, my team creates a whole new solution. Often, that solution gains the attention of other clients, and pretty soon everyone wants it, so we get Development to standardize it and add it to the model. I like to think we are on the leading edge."

Chrstina couldn't disguise her excitement. *This is exactly what I've been looking for.*

"That sounds incredible." She hoped she didn't sound like a giddy schoolgirl. "I like problem-solving and writing new code. In my current job, there's so little novel programming. The code has matured for ten years, and it works well for the most part. We were trained to do new development and program from scratch, but the reality is the job doesn't require those skills. There are teams of programmers whose work overlaps, and so many degrees of corporate review, it takes forever to enact a simple code change. In the short time I've been there, I feel overqualified, underutilized. I want more responsibility, but it seems like a dead end. I also have little interest in insurance, so any problem-solving there may be requires me to feign interest."

"Hmm. What makes you want to work here?" David asked.

Christina summoned confidence. "I'm not sure if you reviewed my résumé, but I worked in an emergency room and did research in a lab in college. I'd been given and have managed a great deal of responsibility in those jobs. One thing I loved about both of those jobs was that I learned a lot. I'm passionate about health. I was a pre-med student until I discovered a love of computers. I wanted to apply to HSA last year during campus recruiting but wasn't eligible to interview because of my major. Now, I have programming experience. I'd like to combine my interest in health with my computer expertise. I want to work here, for you, and I'll work hard, so you don't regret hiring me."

"That's quite a compelling pitch"—David nodded—"and I have a hunch you'll do just that. Let me introduce my team." He led Christina out of the conference room toward the open staircase in a plant-filled two-story atrium to the second-floor offices.

She had never before seen palm trees and gigantic rubber plants, with flowering orchids and lilies perched in limbs overhead, in an interior space other than in Pennsylvania's Longwood Gardens or upscale hotels. I guess this is what corporate America looks like in 1983. And just think, working here, I'd get a chance to bask in sunlight every day walking the halls! The walls of glass on the far side rose several stories high, and even in snowfall, Christina could make out an indentation where the fitness trail traversed the lawn and exercise stations scattered on the hillsides surrounding this building and its adjacent data center. It couldn't be more unlike her current worksite, the sterile office tower of Global Life's headquarters.

HSA was a whole different world. For the last ten months, her daily routine had consisted of commuting down a smog-filled industrial corridor through boarded-up neighborhoods, to an urban tower-cum-cubicle farm. Every floor was an identical grid of half-height gray fabric walls punctuated by a cadence of fluorescent ceiling lights that illuminated the work of near automatons.

I would enjoy coming to this place every day, decided Christina. The atrium, awash with daylight, exploding with foliage, and whose frameless windows invited the outside in, together with the expansive surrounding lawns, beckoned her to stay awhile.

Rhonda, a reticent but smiling team leader, welcomed her and warned her not to take anything David Stokes said too seriously. Gary Wentworth and Robert Coney, two officemates, joked they needed someone on the team who could improve their image, and Bryce, introduced as "not on our team but spends an inordinate amount of time in our offices correcting our logic." It was a friendly, fresh-faced group. She wondered if the oldest employees might have been college recruits when the company started up a decade ago. At Global Life, a generation separated her from most of her colleagues.

Gary and Robert gave her the ten-dollar tour of the imposing, windowless building, the data center. Its exterior blended in with the brick campus, except for its high-domed roofline and telltale air handlers off the back corner. Once inside, Christina's wide-eyed grin gave away to amazement as they paraded down rows of humming machines under soft ambient lighting to the beat of occasional beeps and the whir of spinning tapes. Unlike the sterile and frigid white computer room in the basement of Global Life, this space was warm enough to wear street clothes without a parka and gloves because of its efficient design. Heat radiated up through the cavernous dome, affording a comfortable climate that enabled people to work in the ball-field-sized data center without violating OSHA regulations. Hot air given off by the machines was piped out and used to heat the corporate offices during winter. An entire gym-sized area remained empty, allowing for future growth. This state-of-the-art facility could have been a set from *Star Wars*.

"We like to take our prospective customers here and wow them with jargon and techno-gibberish. We have them stand in front of the blowers so they can't really make out what we're saying," Gary said with devilish glee.

Christina laughed.

"But seriously, this place processes billing data for over eight hundred hospitals across the USA. We run these mainframes in a shared computing environment, so no one client has to foot the bill and invest in a huge computer system of their own. They each get the processing they need on a rotational basis. It's an innovative solution our founder, Elliot, came up with over ten years ago." Elliot McMaster, aptly named, was the mastermind of the shared hospital computing concept.

Robert beamed as he interrupted Gary. "Our product, Aura, however, is not shared among clients. They each get their own machine on-site. The allure of the PDP computer we use to run the registration and clinical systems is its affordability and small size. Soon the new VAX computer will have even more power, memory, and efficiency to replace the PDP."

Gary added, "Those of us on the minicomputer side of the house are partial. We like to think we are trailblazers."

It was the second time that day Christina heard about the innovations going on here. Being at the forefront of modern technology intrigued her. The tour alone, with its entertaining guides, was worth the trek through snow.

Just as Christina returned to David's floor to have her last conversation with Rhonda, David hurried over. "Good news—they're letting everyone go home early today because of the snow."

Christina had forgotten all about the snow. "I thought I would be taking the entrance exam this afternoon. How bad is it out-side?" she peered out the window only to find a blanketed hill. Its frosted evergreens poked through periodically like marks on a percussionist's sheet music.

David warned the accumulation was already a couple of inches, adding that main roads seemed passable. "We have people com-muting from west of here, and the back country roads become a sledding hill. You're welcome to stay for the exam if you want to, but we sure don't want to make you stay and drive home in a blizzard. We could reschedule it for a clear day."

"If it's OK with you, I'd prefer to take it while I'm already here," she asserted, willing to take days to drive home, if need be, just to improve her chance of getting the job.

"Sure, that's great. I'll be here, and I'll let HR know they can scoot out." David was as kind and easygoing as they come. Christina couldn't imagine anyone she'd rather work for. After a quick lunch where Gary and Robert led her through the café line, pointing out what was good and what to avoid, Robert insisted she try a slice of pie—"They're homemade here by Mrs. Kennealy and have zero calories"—she found her way to the conference room for the exam. It sat empty. Christina admired the room's watercolor prints of Chester County farmhouses and grazing horses, stone walls and wispy fields. She wondered if the Andrew Wyeth paint-ing might be an original.

David rushed in moments later, handing her a packet. "HR said here's everything you need. I'll check back with you in a while, but you have ninety minutes."

Christina reached for the packet. "I'm ready."

By the time she finished, seventy-eight minutes later, and thanked David not once, but twice, for the opportunity—did that sound stupid?—her buried car was one of only a handful left in the ivory indentation that yesterday was a sea of asphalt. Concluding that the day had gone better than she'd expected, Christina exchanged her pumps for snow boots and her suit jacket for the parka. She cleared snow off the windshield, hood, and windows until her blue '78 Honda CVCC became recognizable. The barely visible lanes where a snowplow had gone through a few hours ago hinted at the way out of the corporate park. Christina turned onto a salted Route 29, gripping the steering wheel with one gloved hand and one hand stiff with cold, left exposed because a glove didn't fit over her cast. Upon reaching 202, she exhaled knowing she could take this plowed highway all the way into Delaware and pick up another highway to get within a few miles of home. Turning up the radio, the music she sought to keep her nerves in check was interrupted by an obnoxious beeping. An emergency alert announced that Pennsylvania's Chester County, the city of Philadelphia, and the entire state of Delaware had been declared a state of emergency.

What? It's just a few inches! Christina stroked the locket around her neck, and her father's advice came to mind. "Stay calm and pump your breaks."

A salesman for most of his life, Mr. Como drove over sixty thousand miles per year. He had become an expert driver in any conditions. He instilled in her and all her siblings the basics of safe driving in the snow.

"Use low gear in slippery conditions; make no sudden moves or stops," Dad said in an even-keeled tone. He had outfitted her car with a shovel, sandbags, flares, and a blanket for emergencies. She remembered the time he drove the family's station wagon, pulling a pop-up tent trailer, down an icy Mount Washington in New Hampshire's White Mountains in July. His six children and their mother held their breath while he pumped the brakes in a slow, steady rhythm. He sometimes resorted to coasting uphill onto the truck pull-off lanes to interrupt the station wagon's acceleration as he skillfully maneuvered down treacherous switchbacks. At just eight years old, Christina somehow cemented every detail of that ride into her gray matter so she could replay the scene in her mind. It was a lesson Christina was grateful to have had.

This is no Mount Washington, and there's almost no one on the road, so I'll just take it easy, and lay off the brakes. Then it dawned on her, as she crossed the state line, that a state of emergency in Delaware means that only police and rescue vehicles, snowplows, and salt trucks are permitted on the roads. With twenty more miles to go, she hoped for the best and wondered what she would tell a cop if she were stopped.

You see, officer, I stayed to take a test following my interview after the company closed for the day. . . or, I need that job and wanted to be the last candidate standing in a snowstorm, so they'd just have to hire me. She could just see the cop rolling his eyes as he wrote out the citation on his yellow carbon copy.

In Pennsylvania and Delaware, at three-thirty in the afternoon, even in February, the sun should be visible. At least, one should be able to detect that it's still daytime. Not that day. A bleak gray nothingness loomed in front of the car, until an occasional traffic light or taillights of a distant vehicle appeared before her, jolting her out of the hypnotizing lull of the overheated cabin and whish-swish of the wipers. A 7-Eleven arose from the abyss up ahead, and Christina pulled in. Recalling the two cups of coffee she had during the interviews, Christina opted instead for a mug of piping hot chocolate that could provide just enough sugar and heat to get her another twenty miles.

"You an EMT?" The cashier eyed her as she handed over two quarters. "State of emergency out there. No cars allowed."

"Not an EMT, just trying to get home," she waved for him to keep the change and darted out the door.

Sitting in the car while it warmed up, Christina paused to

think about that question. She was an EMT just a few years ago. That job in the ER had taught her not only emergency first aid but also an understanding of the care process, a process that was sometimes as painful as the injury itself. With exceptions for chest pain, gunshot wounds and motor vehicle accidents, everyone waited in a queue while a mundane process delayed them before receiving care. Bleeding, moaning, wincing and suffering did nothing to hasten their wait. Delays were often exacerbated by a person behind the desk, like herself, who was inept at the typewriter, jamming forms in the machine and backspacing with x's to correct typos in slow motion, while blood dripped on the floor and people cried out and sometimes screamed. The care process seemed ripe for automation. If only I get a chance with the company poised to make a difference.

Back on the road, Christina got lucky and followed a snowplow for miles to Wilmington. As the rising moon peered out from behind snow-laden clouds, she turned with trepidation onto the final snow-covered back road that led home. It had been hours since it had been plowed. The few cars around crept soundlessly along. Headlights wasted their energy against walls of white before them. The sky began dumping snow in truckloads and the near whiteout conditions forced her to slow the Honda to five miles an hour. Christina checked her seat belt and skidded around turns without braking. She slid through redlights, offering prayers for forgiveness and protection.

Shoot, I could run faster than this!

Less than two miles from home, the last road mounted a steady incline she had run up hundreds of times before on the hottest of summer days. She passed the graveyard and church where, for six years, she had spent Tuesday nights at Girl Scouts. Headstones she had hidden behind and made rubbings of with giggling friends were now mere bumps in drifted snow. The wind kicked up and drifts arose like Whac-a-Mole figures in the middle of the road. Her impotent wheels spun out just beyond stone piers that marked a long driveway for the Judge Morris Estate and her car slid backward at an angle. With no vehicles in sight, a little slide was not too concerning. It was only when the Honda slid into a drift that buried the back windows that Christina began to swear.

"All this way, and now I get stuck! Judge Morris, would you please offer me a cup of hot tea?" she yelled into the white nothingness.

Using her body weight to push the car door open against the snow mound, Christina retrieved the collapsible army surplus shovel and sandbags from the trunk. She pushed snow away from the rear wheels, then spread sand in front of and behind each wheel. Shifting rhythmically first into drive, then into reverse, and steady on the gas pedal, Christina rocked the car backward and forward as her father had taught her. It was a gallant but futile effort. The semi-bald tires could gain no traction.

Why did I put off buying new tires until they were completely bald? Poor decision number one thousand and two.

After another few tries, she decided to leave the car there, walk the rest of the way home, and return for it tomorrow. Night had already fallen when Christina stomped into the garage, icicles falling from her hat and glove, cheeks red with cold. Grateful that she'd had the good sense to throw a pair of snow pants into the car, she felt warm despite the blizzard happening around her.

Her mother loomed in the doorway, aghast. "We were so worried about you! Come in, honey, I've got a hot cup of tea ready for you." Christina let out an exhausted sigh. Her mother wrapped a cozy blanket around her and held her tight for just a little longer than usual.

Who needs Judge Morris when you have Mom?

Her family spent the weekend digging out from a record

twenty-seven inches of snow. Though her hand prevented her from shoveling, her parents asked Christina to maintain a continuous supply of hot drinks to fuel her siblings. She was glad to keep busy while waiting and wondering about the interview. Valerie Parks had told her she'd hear back early the following week. David had thanked her for coming to interview under the worst weather conditions, saying "Elliot would be impressed." Christina carried a thermos of hot cocoa back and forth from the house to the shovelers, imagining palm trees and giant rubber plants adorning a warm, sun-filled atrium.

CHAPTER 10

MONDAY AFTERNOON, SHE got a call just after getting home from work. It was David Stokes, congratulating her on a high score on the entrance exam.

"My team demanded I hire you. 'We need her!' they implored. And I agree, one hundred percent. Could you start on March 14?" he said before she could utter a word.

Having rehearsed in her mind what she might say and how soon she could start, Christina forgot all of it and blurted, "Yes, March 14 sounds great."

David told her she'd be getting a formal letter from HR, but he didn't want to wait to get her on board. "I hope your drive back wasn't too terrible."

"It was slow, and I ended up walking the last mile or so home because the snow was just too deep for my car to move another inch," she conceded.

"What? Now that's determination. I knew I made the right decision to hire you. I'm glad you made it back safe. We can't wait for you to start."

Imagine that. He sounds as if I'm doing them a favor by taking the job. With a fifteen percent increase in salary for interesting work, Christina couldn't believe her good fortune.

That night she penned her resignation letter to Global Life, thanking them for the training and indicating that she had decided to leave for a job closer to home. It was true, just not the whole truth. She skipped to the mailbox and dropped the letter in, never once looking back.

The call home was filled with excitement on both ends. "You're moving back home in two weeks?" Mom's high-pitched questioning voice revealed her delight.

"Yes, and I start on Monday, the fourteenth! But living at home will be temporary, until I can save up and find a place closer to work. It'll be quite a commute to Lenapy, and after only a seven-mile drive to Global, I'm not looking forward to now driving fifty minutes in traffic each way." Christina wanted to be clear about her plans after being on her own for ten months now.

She would rent a smaller U-Haul van to move out, and not surprisingly, Drew was keen on helping. She'd be closer to Allentown, and he told her he was glad she would not be so far from him. Heidi had considered relocating to a smaller place anyway, farther from the city and closer to her home, and Christina's move gave her a push to do so. Their month-to-month lease could be terminated by either tenant or landlord, so moving out was not going to be problematic.

The roommates spent the next few evenings deep cleaning, and Christina began packing. Heidi took on the kitchen, which could have been taken from a *Leave It to Beaver* set, scrubbing down the pastel appliances and checkerboard linoleum floor. Defrosting the refrigerator was next, and she removed the few food items inside. Their fridge contained more condiments than food anyway. Christina tackled the living room and dining room. Standing atop a ladder to clean the chandelier, Christina heard Heidi scream, "Oh, noooooo!"

It was all Christina could do to keep from falling off the ladder. "What is it, Heidi?"

"I messed up. I put a hole in the freezer."

Christina ran into the kitchen to find Heidi on a step stool, peering into the freezer compartment above the refrigerator door and gripping an ice pick. It looked like a scene from a low-budget horror film. A bluish fluid puddled on the floor. Heidi had punctured the lining of the freezer when trying to remove the several inches of ice that had built up, and now the liquid coolant was spurting out from the freezer.

"I had no idea Old Faithful loomed inside our refrigerator!" Christina exclaimed.

"What kind of freezer has antifreeze in it?" Heidi looked at Christina, her brows furrowed.

Christina scrunched her face and studied the rounded powder-blue mammoth. "This thing is ancient. It's got to be older than us! It's an antique. No one should have to defrost a freezer in this day and age. I hope Campanelli doesn't charge us."

Heidi's eyes grew large. "Could he? I mean, would he really try to charge us to fix this blasted old thing?"

"I hope not, but you know he did collect two months' rent as a security deposit," Christina reminded her, "which seems excessive in hindsight. We could offer to pay a small amount toward repairs instead of him keeping our whole deposit."

Their feared prediction came true. Withholding their security deposit was exactly what Campanelli did. The protective policeman figure her parents imagined had never materialized. The girls explained to him that they took great strides to clean the place and return it shipshape when they left, but the snow and ice coated the freezer so densely, they couldn't remove it without using force. They had thought letting it thaw on its own, unplugged, might result in a flooded kitchen, which of course they wanted to avoid.

"Couldn't you simply deduct fifty dollars from our deposit and get it repaired?" they suggested.

Campanelli wasn't having it. "I'll have to replace the whole refrigerator!" he grumbled, "and that's going to cost me a pretty penny, so no, you will not get your deposit back."

Christina hung up the phone and shook her head, frowning at Heidi. "He is nothing more than a greedy landlord looking for a quick buck."

Christina and Heidi couldn't believe he would keep everything they'd put upfront. They waited for their refund to arrive in the mail. Neither Heidi nor Christina heard from their landlord.

Eleven hundred dollars was a lot to lose. Each of them could use their half to start their next lease or make several months of car payments. The value of that old refrigerator couldn't be much more than fifty dollars, if that. Christina and Heidi consulted the latest Sears catalogue to find out just how much a new refrigerator might cost.

Heidi slammed the catalogue shut. 'Heck, a brand-new state-of-the-art Frigidaire with ice maker costs only about eight hundred dollars.'

Campanelli's audacity in keeping the entire security deposit enraged Christina, and she was determined to call him out.

First, she wrote him a respectful letter again restating their willingness to relinquish fifty dollars security to pay for the fridge repair, reminding him of how clean they'd left the apartment and that they were aware of just how old that appliance was. Calling around to used appliance stores, the pros confirmed the girls' hunch that it had little value. Aside from its rounded edges, chrome trim, and antiquated freezer technology, it was no longer in production. Her own parents' fridge, purchased new sixteen years ago, looked light years more modern than the old dinosaur Campanelli valued at more than a thousand dollars.

In her cogent letter, Christina stated that she had also researched tenant law and found deposits could not be kept in entirety unless any damage exceeded the deposit, which of course didn't apply in their case. Her final point was that as a public servant, his job was to keep people safe, not to take advantage of young women who took responsibility for their mistake and offered a fair compensation. The latter point was admittedly snarky, but Christina didn't like being taken advantage of and wanted him to know she would not back down.

The letter went unanswered. Campanelli didn't return her phone calls. In researching New Jersey's legal system, Christina learned tenant-landlord claims are managed by the small claims court. Believing in a just world, she filed a claim. A police officer is an easy target for serving a subpoena to appear in court. Campanelli spent his days in the police station or riding around town in his patrol car. Christina fully expected him to offer a settlement after receiving the subpoena, but he did not.

Days before Christina moved out, a patrol car passed by their house several times, circling the block slowly as if stalking the girls. She couldn't make out the driver's face beneath the police cap, but felt sure it was Campanelli. A chill crept up her spine and she stiffened. Christina pulled down the shades, expecting a knock on her door, which never came.

Weeks after moving out, Christina and Heidi appeared in Newark's small claims court to contest their landlord's withholding of their entire security deposit due to a damaged freezer, which had spent more time on this earth than each of the two tenants. Christina's mother accompanied her daughter for moral support. Christina acted as her own legal representative, stating their case, the condition of the apartment, and their history of punctual rent payments as documented by canceled checks. She painted a picture of two responsible tenants, showing the canceled checks she and Heidi received after the landlord had deposited their security deposit the same day they signed the lease. They also submitted a snapshot of the refrigerator.

Campanelli sat facing the judge, unswayed and stone-faced, while Christina relayed the facts. Christina wore her best navy interview suit and carried a legal pad with notes and her power briefcase. She stood tall before the judge. Her stomach was in knots, and she had to clench her teeth to hide her quivering lips. Nervous but convinced she could win, she was not about to let someone walk all over her and Heidi. We may be young, but we're not naïve, she thought. She knew she had a case and suspected Campanelli knew it as well.

"Will the defendant please stand?" An impatient judge stared into the courtroom.

Campanelli took his time lumbering to his feet.

"State your full name and occupation."

"Pasquale Campanelli, or Bud. Town of Bloomfield police officer for twenty-three years," he mumbled.

"And landlord?"

"Yeah, I rent properties for extra income. Police work doesn't pay much."

"Do you agree with the facts stated by Christina Como involving the security deposit and refrigerator?"

"Well, Your Honor, they broke the refrigerator by poking an ice pick through the freezer."

"Yes, the plaintiff stated that and that they're willing to give you money toward repairs."

"I'm going to have to replace it, not repair it!" Campanelli barked at the judge.

"Why's that?"

"It's too old. They don't make them anymore!" He caught his breath as if to erase the words he had just uttered.

"Exactly. So just how old is that refrigerator?" asked the judge.

"I don't know. It's been there since I bought the house."

"And when was that?"

"I bought the property in 1971."

"Oh, so twelve years ago. Was it new then?"

"No."

"And when was the last time you had it serviced?"

"It's never broken down, so never."

"So, it's at least twelve years old, and you've never serviced it."

"Yes."

The judge paused and motioned to a court clerk, who handed her the Polaroid photograph of the refrigerator that Christina had submitted.

The judge suppressed a laugh. "OK, I'm looking at the photo of the appliance. Is this your fridge?"

"Yes, that looks like it. I don't know if it's my actual fridge."

The judge paused a minute to consider Campanelli, then began her assessment.

"OK. I'm thirty-nine years old, and we had a fridge like this when I was growing up. Appliances have little resale value, especially if they're more than ten years old. This is at least twenty-five years old. It is not worth eleven hundred dollars. Your right as a landlord allows you to retain funds from security deposits for damages incurred, but there are no rights for taking advantage of tenants and keeping their deposit indiscriminately. The value of this item is less than one hundred dollars. You may not, by law, keep the full eleven hundred dollars the tenants paid as security, in exchange for the damage to a worthless appliance. This is hardly the conduct expected of a police officer or anyone entrusted with protecting the public and our communities. It is also not conduct befitting a respectable landlord."

Bud Campanelli's eyes were fixed on a small insect crossing the toe of his boot. His beard twitched. He stood motionless as the judge continued.

"The court rules you may withhold one hundred dollars from the tenants' security deposit, refunding the remainder to them by check today before leaving court. Case closed," the judge shouted with a hard clap of the gavel.

Christina, Heidi, and Mrs. Como rose to their feet, cheering. "Thank you, Your Honor," they chorused as they exited the courtroom and were escorted by the court clerk to the cashier's office where Campanelli would hand over a check, cleared by the court. "Christina, you were terrific!" Heidi grabbed both her hands, jumping up and down. "I can't believe we won."

"As they say," Christina smiled, "crime doesn't pay." She exhaled a long breath she'd been holding throughout the hearing.

The girls, each clutching their $500 check, followed the scowling Campanelli out of the court building, then said their goodbyes to each other and to the whole unpleasant experience.

CHAPTER 11

IT WAS A BRISK March day when the sun teased of an early spring, but the air still had a biting nip. Christina traveled along a scenic back road into Pennsylvania and through the small town of Kennett Square, known as the mushroom capital of the world, where the musky smell of its steaming piles of manure seeped through the slight opening in her car window. Traffic was light until she met the main highways that wound through the easternmost side of Chester County. She hardly recognized the short stint on Route 29 without snow and wondered if she had taken a wrong turn. Soon Christina spotted the familiar fieldstone wall, ruins from a crumbling colonial barn, adorned with gleaming metal letters that spelled Springton Grove Corporate Park. It became an inviting welcome beacon she looked forward to seeing every morning.

Valerie from HR met Christina in the lobby, as she stood once again admiring the giant terrarium. After filling out employee paperwork and having her photo taken for a badge to swipe into the buildings and into the data center, Christina started to feel she belonged there. Valerie asked if she wanted to purchase company stock at a seventeen percent discount through pretax payroll deductions, which the company matched. Christina knew this sounded good—getting discounted stock with company matching seemed like free money.

With the formalities out of the way, Valerie led her through pale-yellow open corridors lined with art to David's office. Along the way, Valerie mentioned her interview during a blizzard. Christina didn't think it was anything special. *Don't other people who interview want to work here as much as I do? Am I really any different than anyone else?*

While others would describe her as driven, motivated, and hardworking, she saw a girl with nerdy determination, overcompensating to no avail for a long-held insecurity, one that had grown like a festering wound since that day with Dr. Solokoff. Or maybe it had started even earlier than that, when Sebastian constantly belittled her as a child or when her father insisted that she didn't need a college education. Those doubts had a nasty habit of turning up at the most inappropriate times.

David's welcoming smile at once put those thoughts right out of her head.

"Good morning! And welcome. Glad to see the weather cooperated today and there's not a flurry in the sky." He winked. "We thought it would be nice to have you share an office with Gary and Robert, and Gary will be your buddy."

"My buddy?" asked Christina.

"We assign a buddy to each new hire, and it's their job to introduce you around, help you get started on whatever project you're assigned, and generally be your go-to person. They also have the important responsibility of providing donuts, enticing others to stop by your office to meet you."

Christina already liked this place, no matter what the job would be, after being there less than an hour. She looked up at Gary, a full head taller than she was, as he sauntered over from his office down the hall, carrying a tray of donuts.

"In your honor, so of course you get to be the first to choose."

Christina had never been comfortable eating in front of strangers. "Thanks, Gary. Won't you have one?" His willowy frame could use some fattening up.

She selected a plain glazed donut instead of a cream-filled powdered mess that was calling her name.

"In a minute. Come along now, we're going shopping. We'll stock up on any supplies you'll need." Gary left the donuts in his office and led her to the supply room, where he selected the usual inhabitants of an office desk—a stapler, boxes of pens and pencils, tape, scissors, folders, notepads—and hesitated for a couple of seconds before offering her a bright blue notebook. "This suits you, I think."

Christina smiled and took the stack of items from him. "How did you know blue is my favorite color?" No green tablets of eighty-card-column paper here. In this job, she would enter commands directly into the dumb terminal's screen. There would be no fifty-thousand-line COBOL programs either. Here she would use MUMPS, an efficient and succinct fourth generation language. No one would be counting her attempts to compile.

Back in Gary's office, he and Robert had moved furniture around to squeeze her desk between theirs.

"This way, we can sandwich you with information." Robert joked. "I'm one of the first people David got on his team, and Gary came last year, right out of Penn State."

"That's right. Don't mind all the Nittany Lions paraphernalia I have in here. You a football fan?"

"Not exactly," she confessed, "but I do like the Eagles, at least when they're winning."

"Well, we can work on that." Gary moved the tray of donuts to her desk and picked one piled high with toppings for himself. Christina likened his casual and unassuming style to a favorite sweater plucked from the drawer on a crisp autumn day.

Robert's desk had no fan tchotchkes, but in the corner sat a framed photo of a beautiful smiling dark-haired woman. Seeing Christina notice the photo, Robert beamed, 'Oh that's my wife, Faith. She is a saint to put up with me. We met when I wrote code for the bank, and she worked in their Cherry Hill branch. She was the one calling me whenever the system crashed. It got to where I planted bugs just to have an excuse to talk with her.'

"So slick, dude," Gary shook his head and eyed Christina. "And the thing is, Faith is great, but I can't figure what she sees in *that* guy." He flicked his thumb at Robert.

And so, it began. The daily banter in their office was a back-and-forth exchange of jabs and quips with two guys and a new girl who got along famously. For Christina, it felt like having two old pals showing her the ropes. She had never laughed so much in any job. Their jovial manner didn't fool her, though. They were both bright, teaching her whatever they could in the first few months before she entered formal product training in June. By then, Christina was way ahead of her cohorts.

David's group seemed to live by the motto, Work hard, play hard. On her very first day, Gary mentioned matter-of-factly, "A group of us will be going to the St. Patty's Day Happy Hour on Thursday, and you should join us. It's at Flanagan's, a cool place in King of Prussia."

Going out on a Thursday evening wasn't new to Christina, but now she had a long commute to consider. When Thursday came, she wore a stylish jacquard dress and black heels, sporty enough for a happy hour and still professional enough for a workday, and she tucked a bag of makeup into the power briefcase so she could touch up before leaving work. Later she stood shivering in a trench coat, stockinged legs, and heels as they waited outside in a line to get in the door while March fought to keep a hold on winter. The twenty-minute wait went by fast, though, as Gary made sure to introduce her to anyone in the group whom she hadn't already met. Many from the Aura team were there, along with a few "other siders."

"What do you mean, the other siders?" she whispered to Gary.

"Oh, they're not on the Aura team. They work on the IBM products or on interfaces between the two product lines. But we like them anyway," Gary said with a smirk.

The camaraderie was apparent, despite an age range spanning fifteen years among the revelers, and Flanagan's would become one of her favorite nightspots. Christina wasn't used to dancing in work attire but observed how everyone managed to do so. Men in dress shirts loosened or removed their ties. Gary tossed his into the back seat on the car ride over. Women ditched their suit jackets or left them draped over a barstool. These truly were the so-called beautiful people—full of vitality, youth, and unlimited potential, known by their parents' generation as Yuppies—young, urban professionals.

The best happy hours provided all-you-can-eat appetizers, and Flanagan's didn't disappoint. Overflowing platters and baskets occupied every inch of the club's lavish buffet, obscuring any hint of the tablecloth under them. Gary and Christina skipped along the spread, dipping into bowls of shrimp, plucking cubes from cheese towers, assembling a colorful assortment from the char-cuterie boards, sampling green and creamy salads, and choosing among skewers of meat as if playing a game of pick-up sticks. They piled food onto their plates, amassing a full meal to counter the indulgence of half-priced drinks. Gone was her timid nibbling from that first day of work. She forced herself to eat enough to absorb the drinks before her drive home.

Dim lighting became a gentle haze in the wafting cigarette smoke. Spinning disco lights mesmerized and hypnotized inebri-ated dancers as they swung and rocked and shimmied. Few punks with shaved heads appeared in Flanagan's as the corporate crowd took over the club in a mall parking lot in a once-sleepy suburban town. Richly upholstered banquettes provided a luxurious respite from the workout on the dance floor. This was an extravagance Christina hadn't seen in the clubs she frequented with Erik.

The HSAers were not only friendly with one another, many had brought other friends. Christina left that night with more than a dozen new acquaintances. Gary called them the regulars, noting that a Friday night group would be even larger. She looked forward to that.

Her group started departing near the 7 p.m. end of happy hour, as the locals, recognizable by their markedly more casual dress, entered the building and shoved their way directly to the taps dispensing green beer. She had switched to drinking water by six, so she was fine for driving the long way home, and she enjoyed replaying the events of the last four days in her mind as she motored south. New job, new friends, and a new life in what seemed like an instant. Even rising early for the commute back on Friday morning didn't bother Christina. She was excited to get back into work to see what the next day would reveal. Already, Christina felt the change filling her mind and her heart.

CHAPTER 12

IN APRIL, DREW drove to Delaware to visit Christina, who was living in her family's home. During a phone call earlier in the week, he'd said he looked forward to seeing her and being only a few miles from his alma mater. He reminded her of the fun they'd had as college sweethearts and suggested they go to the local Shipwreck tavern on Main Street. "Remember, darling, all those Friday happy hours we spent there, downing one-dollar drafts? And celebrating you becoming legal on your twentieth birthday?"

"How could I forget, Drew? And that night the rocker from Jersey played at the Shipwreck was unforgettable!"

"I got only an occasional glimpse of him that night. I was squeezed in between the bar and the barstool, holding a tight grip on your ankles as you teetered atop the bar for an unobstructed view." Drew teased her over the phone.

The crowd had gone wild that night, exploding with shouts and applause, welcoming the rising star from New Jersey to their local hangout, goading him and his band to play well beyond last call. While that night the Boss came to town lived on in history and in their memory, they marveled at how many new groups got their start at the Shipwreck over the years. Drew and Christina had never missed a show.

"We'll have to go, then, for old times' sake." Christina smiled into the phone.

"You know, Christina, we've shared so many special nights. I can't imagine going to any concert, or any event, for that matter, without you." Drew's tone turned low and serious. Christina got the feeling he was discovering something. She didn't dare to ask what it was.

Days later, Christina was in the garage, helping the twins build a straw basket for an egg drop competition in their upcoming science fair. When she heard the roar of Drew's red Saab 900 Turbo in the driveway, she bolted outside to greet him.

"How was the drive?" Christina asked, as she leaned forward to kiss him through the window of what she called the boot on wheels.

"Definitely better than the drive to Bloomfield," Drew said as he got out of the car, wiping an imperceptible speck off the shiny red door. "It's been too long since I've seen you, darling. I've been looking forward to this weekend." He scooped her up in an embrace.

"Me too."

Christina had missed his warm hugs and how easy it was to talk with Drew. The month since he helped her move from Bloomfield to home had seemed to fly by at work, yet inch by otherwise. She had busied herself helping her mother select new paint colors for the house and spent evenings running along her familiar routes, riding horses, or hanging out with Terry. Christina often sat on the porch after dinner, chatting with Donny Meddleton, a teen-ager who lived across the street. Donny was now graduating high school and earning money doing yard work for her dad.

Christina shared a special bond with Donny, who was five years younger, since she had been his after-school babysitter. His mother, Edith Meddleton, had approached her mother six years ago to ask if Christina could meet Donny at his bus stop and watch him until she got off work at the hair salon. Christina was grateful for the steady job. She came to enjoy her ninety minutes with the then sixth-grade Donny on school days. Mrs. Meddleton, with her bleached-blond bouffant hairdo, ruby red cat's-eye glasses, and orange pursed lips, would return to find Christina and Donny at the kitchen table playing chess, in the backyard tossing a baseball back and forth, or making a batch of Christina's favorite ricotta cheese cookies or biscotti. Mrs. Meddleton would stop in the doorway, holding her arms wide apart waiting for Donny to approach and be gathered up and smothered in her tulle skirt or encircled by her itchy boiled wool maxi coat.

"Thank you, Christina, that'll do for today," Mrs. Meddleton would say each time, as she alternated between kissing Donny's forehead and drawing back to study his face for any new bumps and bruises.

"Goodbye, Donny, until tomorrow," Christina would say to the boy who had extracted himself from his mother's voluminous clothing.

After Donny had a few more years of throwing baseballs around, he had become the high school's star pitcher. To Christina, it seemed he had grown by ten-pound and two-inch increments each time she returned from college, until he was somehow towering over his petite mom who could no longer clasp her hands together when she wrapped her arms around his muscular chest. Coming home from school after graduation, Christina didn't recognize him from across the road.

Seventeen-year-old Donny waved to Christina and Drew as he rolled his lawnmower into his garage. He had already met Drew at the Comos' Christmas party. "How's it going, Donny?" Drew called over to him, lifting his duffel bag out of the trunk. Turning to Christina, Drew kidded her, "I can't believe you babysat for that six-foot-three, two-hundred-pound athlete!"

"I know! I still see him as the scrawny sixth grader learning to play chess. In hindsight, I might have spent that time disassembling our TV instead of being Mary Poppins."

"What does the TV have to do with anything?" Drew asked.

Christina rolled her eyes. Drew wouldn't understand. He was one of those kids who had always tinkered with electronics. He still didn't understand why I left engineering. No one ever made him feel less than. And he thought I willingly changed my mind about medical school too. He's been set on engineering his whole life and never faltered.

"Never mind," Christina said. "Donny's still a big kid at heart, though, and now he helps my dad with the yard because Lord knows my older brothers are too busy or too lazy to do anything remotely helpful. I'm glad my dad pays him well. I have Donny's mother to thank for supporting my album collection when I was his age."

"That reminds me," said Drew, as Christina led him into the house, "are we going to the Shipwreck tonight, you know, for old time's sake?"

"Who's playing?" asked Christina.

"I forgot to check. But does it matter? It'll be fun to walk Main Street again, have a few beers and listen to *live* music. I sure don't get much of that in Allentown. Besides, with my job now, we won't have to count our dollars between us before ordering." Drew's salary easily paid his bills, and he was saving a few hundred dollars each paycheck. He could afford to spend a little on a night out in a college town.

"OK," said Christina, before adding, "and I have money to spend, too, even if I'm saving up for an apartment close to work." She could see Drew leaving an extra five on the table and dismissing a server who said he'd be right back with change. Drew was generous, and his wallet allowed for it.

Paying her parents only a token amount for "rent," Christina was saving for a deposit on a lease. She already had her eye on a neighborhood close to the mall, near Flanagan's, and close enough to Valley Forge park to stop there and run on her way home from work. Her paychecks went right into the bank, forcing her to think before withdrawing money.

Though she wasn't keen on reliving old college memories now that they'd graduated, especially since she had frequented the best clubs in New York, she could tell Drew wanted to go to the Shipwreck. "I could call Terry and see if she's not doing anything. She may want to join us."

Terry still lived at home. Never a serious student, Terry was just finishing up her degree after five years. While the two friends never had classes in common during high school, other than choir and yearbook, and their college paths rarely crossed, Terry and Christina knew each other well. They had listened attentively and commented on each other's dreams and maintained their close friendship for over a decade. They were more like sisters to each other than their own sisters. Terry could always make Christina laugh, if only from the unfiltered innermost thoughts she voiced.

Christina and Terry had gotten together whenever Christina came home from Bloomfield, but their worlds were farther apart than the 130 miles up the Jersey Turnpike. While Christina began her quest for stimulating work and financial independence, Terry actively sought someone to settle down with. By the end of the summer, she had started dating Ryan, a friend of Drew's. Christina had introduced them at her graduation party. At Christmas, Terry and Ryan announced their engagement when Christina had stopped over with a present for Terry. The wedding would be as soon after Terry's graduation as they could manage. Gulping the eggnog Ryan handed her, Christina revived herself enough to utter a sincere "Congratulations!" She gushed accolades on the beautiful ring shimmering on Terry's pale hand and gave her friend a warm hug. "How wonderful!" she had managed to add, before darting out the door.

To Christina, Terry was still the stifled teenager who dreamed of escaping through the back door when her parents went to bed. Theirs was a strict household with early curfews, endless chores, and three teenage siblings with no car. Someone or other was always grounded for a seemingly mild transgression. Terry's ticket out was a college degree or a husband. Terry had always talked about having a large family of her own one day, and Christina dismissed the idea, wondering why Terry would want to escape one confinement for a different one of her own making.

Even now, Terry sat down to dinner with her family every night and lived by some arbitrary house rules despite being old enough to question them. While Ryan was busy establishing himself in the accounting firm and passing his CPA, Terry focused on finishing school. Ryan visited Terry occasionally on weekends, but Terry went to his place far more often. Neither one liked the fact that her parents made him sleep in the basement. "They're not married yet," Terry's mother had reminded Christina when she had seen Ryan carrying his bag downstairs.

While Mrs. Como welcomed Drew and sidelined him with questions, Christina called Terry. This weekend, Ryan was not coming, and Terry was up for going out. She loved the Shipwreck and dancing to live music. It was the one experience the friends could enjoy together, even when their interests, boyfriends, and college selves pulled them apart. Christina hung up the kitchen phone just as Drew and her mother came down from upstairs laughing. They seemed to be up to something.

"It's always so nice to see you, Drew," her mother was saying as Drew swallowed a laugh. Whipping around the kitchen, Mrs. Como started to cook dinner. The smell of garlic and basil and briny clams floated through the air while steam billowed from a large pasta pot on the stove.

"Drew, do you eat clams? It's Friday in Lent, and linguine with clams is our go-to meal."

"Sounds delicious, Mrs. Como. Is there anything I can do? Set the table? Pour drinks?"

Drew had impeccable manners, and Christina liked that about him. He talked with the twins about their egg drop strategy for the science fair, patiently answered the questions about his job and family that both her mother and father asked throughout dinner, and joked with Dominic. Sebastian ate in silence, with his head fixed over the plate. When dinner was over, Christina and Drew made a quick exit to pick up Terry and head for the Shipwreck.

Drew suggested they park a few blocks away and stroll down Main Street to see what may have changed since last year. Terry walked ahead like a tour guide, pointing out Drip and Dribble, the new basketball-themed coffee shop on the corner, and expanded outdoor seating in front of Yukon Jack's. Drew and Christina walked arm in arm, hardly listening. Drew looked at Christina and started to say something a few times, then turned away as if something distracted him. She thought it odd.

Once, he interrupted Terry and asked, "Hey, Terry, what kind of ring is that? Did Ryan pick it out?"

"Ryan asked a million questions before getting the ring, so he knew what I liked. I made sure to be specific because you know how exact Ryan is about details. I told him I wanted high clarity and color, pear-shaped, white gold. You know what? That's just what he got me!"

"Isn't it pretty, Christina?" Drew said.

Christina wasn't looking at Drew or the ring. Her gaze was fixed on a familiar figure walking toward them.

"Dr. Aboud!" she called, waving her hand in the air.

"That's my old mentor, Dr. Aboud!" she told Drew and Terry. "I have to talk with him."

The man approached, and upon getting closer, broke out in a broad smile.

"Christina? It's great to see you. What are you doing here? I thought you graduated a while ago," Dr. Aboud said.

"Hi, Dr. Aboud! These are my friends, Drew and Terry. Yes, I graduated last year, but I recently moved back home, temporarily."

After shaking hands with Drew and Terry, Dr. Aboud turned back to Christina. "What are you doing these days?" he asked.

"I had been working in Newark, New Jersey, for an insurance company, but I took a job with Hospital Systems of America not long ago. Writing hospital software. I just love it." Christina said.

"I'm sure you'll do well there. We really missed you when you left the ER. Maybe you can put that experience to work and write us a program for the ER. Can you believe we still type charts on multipart forms?"

"That's very kind of you," said Christina. "I missed working there, too, when I left. It's hard to believe that so many practices are still not on computers these days."

"I'm sorry to run, but I must start my shift. Why don't you stop in the ER someday when you've got time? I'm always there, and most of our team is still around from when you worked there. I want to hear more about this medical software you're working on."

"I'd like that very much." Christina, excited by the chance meeting with her old friend, smiled, grateful for his efforts to school her in emergency care. Whatever she and Drew had been talking about had slipped completely from her mind.

The bouncers at the Shipwreck checked their IDs just as they did for every college kid and anyone before them in line. The crowd grew quickly as the local band, Sax Appeal, was about to take the stage. Drew guided the girls to a side wall bar where he grabbed the last two barstools for Christina and Terry and waved down the bartender. Sax Appeal had been around since Christina's high school days, and they now did a Delmarva circuit followed by their beachgoing and student fans. They covered popular rock and roll dance tunes, nothing new age or punk and most certainly not anything construed as disco. The lead singer's raspy crooning and the sax player's talented riffs kept fans coming to see them again and again.

Christina, Terry, and Drew had only downed half their beers before succumbing to the call of the beat and jostling their way to the dance floor. Squeezed close to the stage, they bounced in place and mouthed the words to every song. Conversation was impossible, and only after sweat dripped from Drew's forehead did he motion he was going back to the bar for a cold drink. Terry and Christina, undaunted by the overheated throng about them, carried on like they'd done in Christina's bedroom in the seventh grade. They had sung into hairbrush microphones and adopted outrageous moves from *Soul Train* and *American Bandstand* before falling to the floor giggling and exhausted.

That scene repeated itself again and again as they moved through high school. Christina's dad often volunteered to drive her and six other teenage beauties packed into his shiny black 1975 Cadillac Sedan DeVille to the teen disco, Electric Gramophone, which had become the new occupant of an old grocery store in a mostly vacant shopping center across town. The girls spilled out of the behemoth as would celebrities arriving to walk the red carpet, looking coyly around to see who was watching.

This wasn't a neighborhood the girls knew, and Mr. Como spent the first evening he dropped them off there waiting in the parking lot. Any parent could hang back after drop-off and see just what kind of characters went in. The place was off-limits to anyone over age twenty-one, and it didn't serve alcohol, which eliminated a certain element. After the girls entered, groups of two to ten paraded into the venue—a few of Christina's classmates and kids from the football and basketball teams, some kids from their neighborhood, and others Mr. Como wouldn't know. When the stream of patrons slowed, he left his post long enough to get a taco at Jack-in-the-Box drive through before returning to wait out the evening. After a few weekends of this surveillance detail, he dropped them off at seven and returned at ten. They wouldn't leave one minute before closing and couldn't arrive late. He'd always give Christina a few dimes to be sure she could use the pay phone to call home if needed. Christina would roll her eyes when she took them, stuffing the coins into her shoe or coat pocket. There was nowhere in her tight-fitting jeans to stow even one thin dime.

Mr. Como was a silent figure on the drive home as his passengers emoted about so-and-so's new haircut, the dreamy new boy who was too shy to dance, the strange pairing of Michelle and Ernie, and their favorite songs, oblivious to his eager ears. He coughed when they chatted about their elaborate plans to stand in just the right place at about 9:45 so they could catch the eye of their heartthrob just as the DJ started "Stairway to Heaven." Christina saw him bristle when Terry concluded, "Since the slow dance is eleven minutes long, it's important to choose the right partner." When one of her friends mentioned she'd seen Frankie Dubanowski retrieve a flask from his tube sock and pass it around, her father swore, gesturing to an empty highway.

"Can you believe he snuck that in?" said Terry. "It's disgusting."

"It's too bad he needs a flask to have a fun time. Everyone else in there has fun dancing and hanging out with their friends," Christina added.

The other girls had wholeheartedly agreed. Mr. Como visibly exhaled after holding his breath when the flask situation had been revealed and dismissed. That night after dropping her friends off, he had cautioned Christina to stay away from "this Frankie character" and decline any drinks other than those the Gramophone sold. "Dad," she had said, "I'm not stupid. I know what those boys are like and have no interest in them or their alcohol. They probably can't even read the labels."

Her mother had reminded him Christina had a good head on her shoulders. "Don't worry," she said. "We can't exactly keep her locked in the house until she's twenty-one. She's an honor student and has earned our trust. You know, Terry's parents allow their daughter to go to the Gramophone only if Christina is going."

Back on the dance floor at the Shipwreck, Terry found a few of her school friends, and Christina went to the bar to speak with Drew. They tried to talk over the music but couldn't and were content to lean on each other and listen to the band. Staring at the comic lead singer of Sax Appeal, Christina could sense, out of the corner of her eye, that Drew was looking at her. She turned to him and smiled but couldn't help thinking he had something to say. On the short drive home, Terry chattered nonstop from the back seat about the band and her biology lab partner, whom she hadn't seen since sophomore year, and how Ryan should have been there too. Christina and Drew just looked at each other and laughed. Christina knew something was up with Drew but couldn't put her finger on it.

CHAPTER 13

"MY GOD, CAN Terry talk." Drew said, smearing his bagel with a dollop of cream cheese at the Comos' breakfast table.

Mrs. Como poured him an espresso to go with it and said, "Terry comes by that honestly, Drew. You should hear her mother."

"Drew is right. We couldn't get a word in edgewise. Terry did have us laughing." Christina poured herself a cup of espresso. "Mom, I'm taking Drew out to Carousel Park today. Teach him to ride."

"I rode a horse at the state fair once, Christina, so I'm not completely green," Drew said.

"Those horses could walk with a pot of water on their back and not spill a drop. They train them for every possible cowboy-loving tourist that could want to ride them. But I'm going to teach you to ride. If you don't guide the horse, he might try to shake you off," Christina warned.

"Sounds like . . . fun?"

"You'll love it. There's nothing like cantering across an open field on a day like today, when you can smell the sweet spring grass warmed by the sun and see the tree limbs heavy with buds just waiting to pop. Carousel is a beautiful estate that's now a park on land bequeathed to the county by a duPont heir. That's where I've been riding for years."

"I'm game. If the horse doesn't work out, we can go for a nice hike."

They drove two miles to the park's vehicle entrance, where they could see a hook-shaped lake in the valley, just beyond a pine forest that smelled like her mother's cedar chest. One look at the lake and Christina smiled, filled with childhood memories of learning to ice skate. After the frozen lake melted, she would turn her attention to the herd that grazed and loped in white-fenced corrals. She would offer the carrots and apple slices she had stuffed in her pockets to mares who dared to approach. Spotting one of the springtime foals was a special treat, and Christina never tired of watching them hobble around on their spindly new legs, always within view of the watchful mare.

The stables perched atop a hill beyond the pine forest, set back from the main road by more than a thousand feet. While suburbia sprang up all around the estate, the rolling hills of the duPont acreage maintained its bucolic serenity, shut off from the encroaching suburbia by a whitewashed fence that stretched for miles. As a teen, Christina often escaped to the park when she needed a break. She found peace riding alone through its expansive fields.

"Drew, did you know that I spent many afternoons hanging around the barn here?"

"You worked here?"

"No. I'd just bike over and do whatever needed doing—brushing a muddy colt, riding a boarder named Chester whose owner rarely came around, or dumping a scoop of grain into an empty feed bin. I got to know the stable hands. They welcomed my help and let me ride any horse that needed exercising. I liked organizing the tack room. I'd take a deep inhale, pulling the intoxicating smells of leather and horse into my lungs. Sometimes I sat in there reading *Practical Horseman*, imagining I was one of those foxhunters in full dress soaring over jumps and following the hounds."

"I led a boring childhood," Drew shrugged, "spending my afternoons watching *The Brady Bunch* and *Dark Shadows*."

Christina glanced at Drew. "And building radios and clocks, don't forget."

She led Felix, a stately but not young seventeen-hand chestnut gelding out of the last stall for Drew.

"This handsome guy, Felix, will be good for you. You already look the part, and quite dashing, I must say, with that hat and those cowboy boots. Too bad we're riding English today, though."

"Thanks! It was nice of Dominic to lend me his riding gear, though the boots are a bit snug. If I go down, I want to go down looking good." Drew puffed out his chest.

"No worries there. I'm so happy you're willing to try this—something I've always loved."

"What did you mean about riding English? I don't know any other languages."

"English is a style of riding." Christina first laid a blanket, then hoisted the saddle above her shoulders onto Felix's back. "Western is more of a working style. Our saddles are lighter than a Western saddle, and see, they have no horn on top. Cowboys use the Western saddle's horn to carry a lasso, like you see in Clint Eastwood movies. New riders use the horn to hold on to." She adjusted the cinch and stroked Felix's withers.

"That sounds like what I need," said Drew.

"Sorry, you'll have to use those muscular legs of yours instead. Squeeze your thighs together to stay put on the horse."

"Can't I just step hard on the stirrups and hold the reins? I thought we were going for a ride, not a workout." Drew eyed Felix as if sizing up a formidable tennis opponent.

"Lord, no! English reins are connected to a metal bit in the horse's mouth. Moving the reins signals the horse to turn or stop, based on the pressure on the inside of their mouth. We use a soft hand so as not to hurt them. It's a matter of finesse, which I know you have." Christina winked at Drew.

"I see." He raised an eyebrow. "And the stirrups?"

"Stirrups are there mainly to help you mount the horse and maintain your balance and posture."

"What about when I'm galloping?"

"We will not be galloping today unless Felix takes off on you. I'll have you trot and maybe canter."

"Trot sounds good, keep it slow. Remember, I'm a novice."

"A slow trot is the most work and the most uncomfortable for new riders. The horse clops along one foot down at a time, in a 1-2, 1-2 pattern. It requires the rider to post—rise up like they're getting up from a chair and then sit back down, in the rhythm of the horse's movements. It can be a rough ride, especially for men, if you don't rise up when the horse's front feet rise."

"Ouch!" Drew grimaced. "Is there a less painful alternative?"

"When we canter, the horse's feet move in a 1-2-3, 1-2-3, 1-2-3 rhythm. It's smooth and there's no up and down motion, just fast forward." Christina readied her mount, Chigger.

"Perfect! Let's do that!"

"We need to give the horses a chance to warm up, and you a chance to get acclimated in the saddle. First, we'll walk and trot, and if all goes well, we may canter."

"I really don't know why I agreed to this, Christina. Must be because I love you. Let's do it." Drew lifted one foot into his stirrup and swung his other leg over the horse, landing hard in the saddle. Felix pranced ahead a couple of steps, testing the novice on his back. Christina stroked Felix's neck to settle him and laughed when she saw Drew's face.

"It'll be OK, Drew. We'll talk through the basics and walk around in the ring before we set loose on the trail. Relax and trust me."

Two hours later, the lake stretched before them, down a slope and past the pine forests. Drew had weathered the trotting, though he admitted his thighs might regret it tomorrow. "I'm not too sure about going down this hill fast, Christina," he said.

"Now's time for the canter. It'll be easy downhill! Just lean back a little in the saddle. You're a natural," she said, leading the way so Felix would mimic Chigger's pace. "I have a surprise for you when we get down there."

After the exciting dash downhill to the water, Christina guided Chigger and Felix to a shady spot and dismounted. Helping Drew down, she nearly hit the ground as he fell toward her, losing his balance as he swung a leg around.

"I made it." Drew landed on his feet, teeth glinting in the sunlight, arms clutched around Christina's shoulders. "What's the surprise?"

Christina dug into the cantle bag behind her saddle, patting Chigger's flank. "I packed a picnic lunch for us. We can find a quiet spot in the pine forest to set our blanket down and rest."

"A picnic has never sounded so good, darling." Drew took off his cowboy hat and kissed her as Chigger snorted and munched on sweet leaves below.

When they spread the blanket among the evergreens, their secluded enclave could have been in the Colorado Rockies or Sierra Nevada mountains. They were far enough from the road to hear only the sounds of squirrels scrambling up a tree trunk or a plop when a pinecone dropped from above. Christina handed Drew a sandwich of prosciutto with provolone and tomato between slices of crusty Italian bread.

"What did you think of the ride, Drew?" she said, snatching a green grape from a clump she had wrapped in a kitchen towel.

"It was more fun than I thought it would be. And peaceful, riding through the woods and fields. I can see why you like it here. The trot was bone-jarring, though, I have to admit." He stopped to chew the prosciutto, then continued. "Mm mm, this is delicious! Walking was better, until Felix suddenly stopped to grab a bite of something green along the trail. Watching you ahead of me, sitting tall and lithe upon Chigger, I would have followed you anywhere."

"Only then?" Christina stared at the checkered blanket's alternating red and white squares.

Drew looked puzzled. "What do you mean?"

"It's just that you didn't seem too interested in following me or visiting me much, for that matter, in Bloomfield." Christina looked away. Why did I have to bring this up now? Drew is here now. I should enjoy that.

"You know Bloomfield isn't a big draw."

She couldn't let it go. "Yes, but we could have gone into New York and had fun there together. You were happy when I came to your place, and you showed me around town. I would have liked to do that for you, take you around the city. Instead, I went with a friend from work. And Allentown is not much of a draw either." Christina turned to the lake.

"I loved having you come to my place. And you're not in Bloomfield anymore. You're closer, and I know you don't want to stay at home on weekends."

She wanted him to know it felt one-sided to her, even if he didn't see it that way. Yet he didn't acknowledge her concern. "That's true," she conceded. "But I'm not staying in Delaware. I'm saving up to get my own place near work. With a roommate. I hope you'll come to see me there. I've already found good places to go out and made friends I'd like you to meet," Christina said.

"OK, sure. Maybe once you get settled in your job, we can look for a place between Allentown and Lenapy for both of us?" Drew coaxed his tone into a question.

Instead of responding, Christina studied the horses. "We need to water the horses and get them back to the barn. I'll take them while you finish lunch."

There is even less to do in the endless farmland between Allentown and Lenapy than there was in Bloomfield. Moving in with Drew is not part of my plan. What part of living on my own doesn't he get? She started packing up the picnic.

Drew reached for her hand. "Christina, I missed you. Why don't you sit with me a few minutes, and then we'll take the horses together?"

She couldn't resist those knowing eyes that bore right through her, and for a moment, she forgot about the apartment and everything else but Drew.

When they arrived back at the barn, Christina took Chigger to his stall. When she went back for Felix, she found Drew patting the nose of his new friend. Drew had a way with animals. His three Airedale terriers at home were well trained and well cared for, and he was the one who had introduced Christina to the idea of dogs being part of the family. Even Barney, the old father, whose head overlooked the kitchen table, exercised manners. He never once drooled at the food while posing in dignified restraint next to Christina like just another dinner guest. Though new to horses, Drew's connection with four-legged creatures was obvious. She knew he would be just as gentle with children someday. Why am I pushing him away?

After a day on horseback, they spent the evening playing rummy with the twins. The day's fresh air and exertion got the best of them, and they fell asleep stretched out on the sofa, awakened by a ruckus when Sebastian and his friends came into the foyer, carrying on about the bad calls they'd witnessed at the university hockey game. Sebastian cursed as he stumbled over the riding boots she had left near the door. "Damn that idiot sister of mine!" Darting up the back stairs, Christina and Drew narrowly avoided the group.

Next morning, the rest of her family had left the house for nine o'clock mass. Christina and Drew enjoyed a quiet breakfast of a few biscotti with their espresso, alone in the kitchen.

"This is nice," Drew said so softly Christina wasn't sure she heard him.

"You like anise? Mom makes these biscotti from scratch. I can make them, too, but it takes a lot of time. You need to bake them twice to get that crispiness."

"I wasn't talking about the cookies, though they're delicious—"

Drew stopped midsentence as Donny appeared just outside the kitchen window, trimming the boxwoods. The whir from the electric hedge clippers deafened them.

With only a glass pane and less than three feet between them and Donny, Drew and Christina waved and held up their mugs in a mock toast to him. Donny glanced up from his work and flashed them a "gotcha" smile. Massive sound-deadening earmuffs covered his ears, and he wore a Phillies T-shirt cut off just below his chest. The sleeves, too, were cut off so the shirt exposed his washboard abs and bulging pitching arm. The couple exchanged glances, both admiring this picture of all-American youth.

Just then the hedge clippers jumped from Donny's hands, tipped up by a stubborn limb. Now rocketing towards Donny, the machine spewed bits of leaves and bark in an explosive spray. The menacing black cord snaked about. Entangled on an adjacent boxwood, the taut cord jerked the machine backward. Donny reached into the air to steady the clippers, his left-hand landing on oscillating blades.

CHAPTER 14

"AAARGH!" HE CRIED, his bright smile turning to a grotesque distortion of lip, tongue, and teeth. A blackish-red glob hurtled toward the window. Blood splattered everywhere. Christina dropped her mug, spraying espresso across the table, as she shot up from her chair and sprinted to the back door. She crossed the patio with a single leap to find Donny, dazed, in a heap in the grass, holding up his gushing mangled hand. Drew followed, just steps behind her. Christina barked orders.

"Drew, go into the laundry room, top left cabinet. Grab the stack of rags and scissors if you see them. Get a bucket from the utility sink and fill it with water."

Drew dashed into the house and returned with the requested supplies within seconds. Christina knelt on the grass next to Donny, holding his left hand above his head with both of her hands applying pressure to the gash, reassuring Donny. "Don't worry, Donny, we got you covered. You'll be OK. Hands bleed a lot, but it's not as bad as it looks."

"My glove hand . . . ," Donny mouthed as Christina blotted at the hand with a clean old towel. The three-inch slice across his palm filled with blood as quickly as she dabbed blood away.

"Let's have you lie down on the grass so I can work on this." She smoothed his hair back from his face.

Drew appeared at Donny's side and lowered him back onto the grass, rolling a towel to place under Donny's head. "At least it wasn't your pitching hand, Donny."

Christina glared at Drew and put her index finger to her lips. She wadded up more cloths and packed Donny's wound after wiping around its edges with a clean damp cloth and flushing it out with water. "Donny, remember that time you took a baseball on the forehead when I was babysitting? You threw it up in the air so high you lost it in the sun on its way down. You were twelve then. I was so worried your mother would think I whaled you with a baseball bat! And you hardly even cried." She wanted to make Donny laugh.

"Yeah, I remember that. I had a goose egg for a month," Donny said, color returning to his face.

"And a mean black eye too. You looked cool, like a tough guy. All the middle school girls at the bus stop fawned all over you," she said, winking at Donny.

Christina asked Drew to find an old undershirt from the pile of rags he had brought out to the backyard. "Cut it into three-inch continuous strips for as long a length as you can, until I've finished wrapping him up."

Turning to Donny, she said, "Your mother wanted to fire me that day, but I'm glad you owned up to missing the catch, Donny."

"That may have been the last catch I missed," Donny said with a half smile. He glanced at the hand and grimaced. Drew started telling a story of how he once got hurt straddling the net after a tennis game, distracting a fearful Donny with an account of his aching crotch and damaged pride. Christina was busy wrapping the packed wound with the undershirt strips and saw the growing red blotch at the wound site despite heavy bandaging.

"Drew, get the car. We'll need you to drive us right to the ER. On Main Street, where we were on Friday when I saw Dr. Aboud."

While Drew started up the car in the driveway, Christina readied a tourniquet. *Gosh, I hope I remember how to do this right.*

"Donny, brace yourself for this part. I'm going to stop the bleeding with a tourniquet."

She wrapped the cloth tightly around his forearm, helped him to his feet, and supported the weakened athlete as best she could as they made their way to the driveway. Her family pulled up just as Drew got Donny into the car.

"Dad, we're taking Donny to the ER in town. Call them. Tell them we're on our way with an injured teen, about ten minutes out. We'll need sutures for a severe hand wound from a power tool. Ask for Dr. Aboud."

Drew deposited Christina and Donny at the ER entrance. The team was ready with a gurney and ushered them right back to the procedures suite. Donny's bandage was a soggy ochre mass. One nurse said, "Christina Como, I recognize you! Is this your handiwork?" pointing to the bandage. She didn't wait for an answer and muscled the gurney down the hallway.

Dr. Aboud appeared at the bedside and, noting Donny's youth, made some lighthearted comments to reassure him. "Looks like you got the business side of something sharp, young man."

"Electric hedge clippers and a boxwood with a vengeance," Donny managed to croak, as a nurse injected a local anesthetic, saying, "This might be a little pinch." The frigid liquid was already in his vein.

Christina and Drew gave Donny's information to the receptionist and took a seat in the waiting room while Donny was being treated. Minutes later, her father came in. "How's Donny? I went over to his house to tell his mother what was going on. Said I'd call her once we had any information."

"Thanks, Dad. Dr. Aboud is back with him."

"Christina, what happened? When we left for church, Donny was mowing the lawn."

They proceeded to tell Mr. Como what happened, and he looked at Drew. "I'm amazed at your quick thinking."

"I had nothing to do with it, Mr. Como. Your daughter sprang into action. I just fetched what she needed."

"And Drew drove us safely but swiftly to the ER, only running through a few yellow lights. Drew was so good, distracting Donny. It was a gruesome sight. Getting him to look away really helped." Christina smiled gratefully at Drew.

"Heck, I had to distract myself," Drew said. "I felt weak just looking at it, but Christina had the presence of mind to fix him up."

Dr. Aboud came out to the waiting room, his scrubs blood-stained from waist to chest. Christina rushed over to him. "Dr. Aboud, how's Donny?"

"Christina, they told me you brought him in. He's doing fine now. It took thirty-two stitches, but he managed to avoid hitting any tendons or ligaments and barely nicked an artery. That's why there was a lot of blood. The laceration needed a bit of irrigation, which was the worst part for Donny. The wound was expertly bandaged. The tourniquet decision was a good one. I'm guessing that was yours, Christina."

She nodded. "Will his hand recover? He's a star pitcher, and we're in baseball season. I just kept thinking we can't let him lose use of his hand!"

"His hand will recover. Is he left-handed?"

"No, he's right-handed. That's his glove hand." Christina said.

"Shouldn't affect his pitching at all then. Worst case, he may miss a few weeks of the season. He's lucky you were there. He could have gone into shock if you hadn't stopped the bleed. You sure you don't want to come back and work here with us?"

"That's so kind of you, Dr. Aboud. Thank you for taking good care of him."

"That's my job." Dr. Aboud walked back down the corridor, then stopped, calling back to her. "And, Christina, I'm still interested in hearing more about your work these days."

"OK." She smiled. "I'll get back in touch. Thanks again."

A nurse walked Donny out to the waiting room. His left hand was strapped to his chest, protected and elevated. His smile had returned, though he was still a bit shaken, and he met his neighbors and Drew with relief.

"I'm so glad my mother wasn't here," Donny said. "She would have been sick with worry, seeing all that blood. Thank you for coming, Mr. Como." Turning to Christina and Drew, Donny said, "Thank you both for helping me. They said you guys did an amazing job."

"We're just glad you're OK," Christina said.

Mr. Como agreed. "You've been through quite a lot, young man, and I'm sorry to say it's my fault asking you to trim those bushes."

"No, I just somehow lost my grip," said Donny.

"Let me take you for an ice cream on the way home. It's the least I can do," said Mr. Como, "but first let me call your mother to let her know you're walking and well enough for ice cream."

Mrs. Meddleton kept Mr. Como on the phone for ten minutes, asking all kinds of questions about her son's accident, ending with, "I can't thank you enough for taking such good care of my son."

"No, Edith, you've got it wrong. I came home after it happened to find Christina and her boyfriend rushing Donny off to the ER. She had done first aid. She had us call ahead to the ER. I just followed her orders."

"Your daughter took care of my Donny?" Mrs. Meddleton gasped. "Is she a medical student?"

"No, she writes computer software. For hospitals. But Christina was an EMT, so she knew what to do, I guess." Mr. Como stumbled through his explanation as if he couldn't quite grasp what his daughter had done.

"Well, that girl has certainly missed her calling. I'm going to write a letter to the editor of the *Post* about my young neighbor who saved my son's life! Nice of you to take them all for ice cream after such an ordeal. Get your daughter two scoops."

CHAPTER 15

UNTIL HER TRAINING class started in June, Christina helped Gary with his account, Santa Clara Medical Center, a regional hospital in a San Francisco suburb. She loaded Santa Clara's defining characteristics into their profile. Their various ancillary departments of lab, radiology, PT, OT, speech and respiratory therapy, as well as all the nurse stations and hospital buildings, were enumerated in a spec book from which she populated the database. She entered their tax ID number, addresses, fiscal calendar, insurance plans, and associated details to be stored in memory for reference by the system's programs. Christina loaded text for dozens of demographic questions that would populate screens used in registering patients. She plugged in tables of regional zip codes and their corresponding cities and towns and marked choices reflecting decisions the hospital made for countless settings the system required. She built catalogs of tests that doctors might order and entered Santa Clara's supply items, one by one, into the database. She began to virtually see the hospital laid out in front of her in the data.

The process of building a new account was as interesting as the account itself. The project for new clients started with a copy of the model, which was then modified to site-specific specifications. The specs were written by a field director from a local office, someone who spent months on-site, tailoring the parameters to fit a client's needs. The model held many populated datasets, which might need only slight changes for a given site or require complete clearing out to be built from scratch.

Christina liked the idea that they started with a template for the functioning clinical system and then customized it for each hospital site as needed. What a smart approach—not having to start from scratch for every single client. Someone clearly gave a lot of thought to how the company could roll out this customized software without the unnecessary labor of starting with a blank slate.

"Christina," Gary told her, "there are two great ways to learn the system. One—build their database from a site's specs, and you'll get to know that hospital inside and out because all their information will be loaded into the hundreds of files."

"I'm doing that now, right?" Christina nodded. "What's the second way?"

"Number two is testing the software after it's been built. Try every function. Pretend you are a nurse, registration clerk, lab technician, or other hospital employee and mistype, backspace, enter junk text, and hit keys erratically to try and break the system or force an error. Look over every printed report and document. Run Dayend processing. Put in fake data as if you are a monkey who doesn't know how to answer the questions."

"What's a monkey got to do with it?" Christina laughed.

"If we can make our system so tight even a monkey can use it, we've hit the jackpot. The problem is most programmers expect the users to think like they do. That's a mistake. We need to build a system for anyone who might use it, including someone who thinks illogically."

"How do we do that?"

"We try to foresee any errant response and program accordingly. We plan for that condition. For example, if we ask for age, we don't want a user to type in 'old.' So, we check to ensure their response is a number up to three digits, presenting an error message if they don't. They can't get past that question until they've put in a valid response. They can't put in '3 years'; the system is looking for a number, so an error message must pop up and tell them 'Enter age as a 1-to-3-digit number,' for example."

"I see. That makes perfect sense." Christina nodded.

"To you and me it does. But believe it or not, we see companies peddling systems without any error messages or hard stops that could prevent junk data, and then they wonder why there's garbage in their database." Gary shook his head in disgust. "We don't want to be in the data scrubbing business, so we build a tight set of checks that prevent junk from being entered. We make sure input has the right length, matches an expected pattern, chooses from a valid set of entries. We make it foolproof."

"What do you mean by pattern match?" asked Christina.

"Say you have a phone number. We require them to enter it as a string of seven digits, with no spaces or dashes. The error message shows the format if they enter it incorrectly."

"What about area code?"

"We collect that as a separate field. It's got to be one in a table of valid area codes we have built."

"I like the spoon-fed approach."

"Garbage in, garbage out," Gary warned.

After weeks of entering all the Santa Clara data, Christina and Gary set about testing screen flows and menus, printed output and reports, screen layouts and system messages themselves before letting their colleagues take a shot. The Aura product suite was so new, there were less than a hundred people working on it at the time, while the other side of the house, the IBM side, had a thousand programmers. Gary and Robert talked about them like they lived on another planet or on the wrong side of the tracks.

Come time to test a system before deploying it to a hospital, the Aura side of the house banded together and held a quality assurance event, which they called the QA Party, after hours, where everyone was invited to bang away at the system with fake data to test it every which way. The account's programmers rewarded testers with free pizza and Coke on the company's tab. They all benefitted from a successful Install at a client site, and their side of the business was booming.

Christina had fun entering fake patients named Donald Duck, Michelangelo, and Winston Churchill into the system. She made up their addresses and devised elaborate but quasi-credible demographics and health scenarios for each fake patient, loading in "123 Main St, Anytown, USA" and "Rome, Italy" and "10 Downing St, London, UK." She assigned webbed feet, paint in left eye, and typhoid as their admitting diagnoses. She ordered EKGs, barium studies, blood counts, and electrolytes for her patients.

She intentionally tried to max out the number of characters in an entry, testing the software's ability to detect data that was too big to fit in its defined storage allotment. She tried to break the system, noting whether or not an error message alerted the user to an invalid entry. Christina recalled a college professor's sage advice—the computer only does what you tell it to do. She wondered if Gary's database defined a name to contain up to thirty-two letters, else it would exceed storage limits. She learned to pad long entries with trailing last letters and a final *Z*, like "ChurchillllllllllllllllllZ" to see if the system accepted the too-long answer entered by an unsuspecting user. If it did get through, she tested how it printed on documents. Did the lengthy entry show every letter until the last *Z*? Did it run into the next field on a printed form, making it completely illegible?

Christina considered QA a game, and she interrogated the systems like a computer-loving Dick Tracy. David and Gary both commented on her attention to detail, and she became a sought-after tester for any QA party. She loved finding system bugs or causing the system to crash. Better to find out the problems here at the QA party than after installing it in Santa Clara.

After the first QA, Gary walked to the parking lot with Christina. "You know, Christina, I'm glad they didn't offer a slice of pizza for each bug found, or you would explode."

"Very funny, Gary," she said, allowing the compliment to settle.

He showed her how to dial in to a hospital system. Each account had its own three-character identifier on the switchboard, enabling access to the site's separate region of code and database. Programmers went to the telecom room and patched into their account by plugging in the wires for their code.

"I feel like a switchboard operator facilitating a long-distance phone call," she told Gary. Christina came to know the switch's distinctive sound cadence—scratchy static, pause, scratchy static, eeyore, eeyore—and finally a resolving hum that indicated a connection had been made. This daily routine opened the site for programmers to do their work.

Christina became accustomed to the fast pace of innovations and improvements to the process of modifying model code and appreciated how the product evolved ever so elegantly. Just a few months later, the procedure in the telecom room was replaced by the use of a virtual switch which enabled direct access through a desktop computer terminal.

In June, orientation class began, with all the new hires from college recruiting events. Initially intimidated, thinking these folks were computer science majors, Christina took a seat in the back. Norm Peters, the instructor, whom she had known now for months, embarrassed her on the first day by calling out, "Hey, Christina, you're a three-month veteran around here, especially since half of these folks just started an hour ago. Why don't you help me out and share your experience as a newbie?"

Thanks, Norm! Christina nodded and briefly shared what she had been doing in her three months at HSA. Norm had been a high school math teacher before coming to HSA, and it showed. He insisted everyone introduce themselves before starting. Christina was happy to learn they were not all computer science majors. The recruits hailed from twelve states, mostly on the East Coast, and two dozen colleges. A few came from other jobs in the area. Christina was shocked to see Elena, a woman who had been her physics lab instructor at State, now working for HSA.

Orientation lasted three weeks, with Norm and guest speakers from within the company indoctrinating the recruits on company history, the various products sold, and new programming languages. Christina avidly watched product demonstrations, astonished at the striking visual differences between the IBM- and minicomputer-based products. IBM screens looked more like a reproduction of a punched card, with eighty lime-green dots that acted like placeholders on a blank black screen, awaiting input. The older products presented system messages only after an entire screen's worth of input data had been collected, requiring the user to know what format was required. By comparison, the Aura products, running in real time, prompted users with questions in English sentences. These products are easy to use, Christina concluded. Surely, they're more popular with hospital staff than those that look like punched cards. Clinicians communicate in full sentences! Their systems should too, she thought.

Half of each day of orientation was dedicated to teaching recruits to code in MUMPS, a text-based processing language specifically designed to handle strings of text well, by a team from Massachusetts General Hospital. It didn't require thousands of lines of code. It was its own compiler, database, and coding language in one. It allowed multiple users simultaneous access. Christina favored it over the laborious COBOL she had used at Global Life. It was quicker to write than Pascal and Fortran, and easier than the machine and assembler languages she used in college. She appreciated its powerful immediacy and had become adept at MUMPS even before orientation, considering it elegant and concise. Christina helped Gary write customized code because she already knew how to construct elaborate algorithms, query a database, and define variables from her experience programming in several other languages. She felt competent and capable, putting her knowledge to good use.

By early July, Christina was ready for her own account—Central Washington Medical Center, in Yakima, Washington. Or, as HSA folks referred to it, C-Wash. Gary continued as her mentor. She became officially a member of HSA's West Coast team, servicing clients in California and other western states, supporting the sales teams working out of Seattle and Los Angeles. There would be travel involved, one- or two-week trips on-site to install the software, train the hospital staff, and stand up the systems, or go LIVE, as it was known at HSA. With the typical three-month development timeframe, Christina estimated that might put her in Seattle sometime that fall! She was determined to build the best system she could for her client.

One morning just after she started on her own account, David called her into his office. "We have a team supporting a go-LIVE next week that needs a fourth person to round out their support schedule. Rhonda is taking Southern Nevada Memorial LIVE, with Marshall as the main programmer and Abby for operating system support. We've seen how far you've come since March and think you would be a great addition to their team. It'll give you a chance to see what a LIVE event is all about before your account goes up."

"I'm so new. Will I be able to contribute, or will I just observe?" she asked.

"Oh no, of course, you'll contribute. They'll put you to work! But don't worry. Rhonda will get you prepped, and you'll be paired with either Marshall or Abby on a shift. You'll correct issues identified during the LIVE event. Oh, just so you know, the hospital is right at the end of the Vegas strip. I'll be scrutinizing expense reports for any gambling debts you may rack up and try to expense."

"You're kidding, David!" Christina knew he joked around, but could this be true? Could the first work trip be a two-week learning gig on the Vegas strip? Christina could never have predicted this. And to think I could still be back at Global Life, padding around behind Doug, watching him enter a missing period on a line of code.

CHAPTER 16

"IT'S A SWELTERING 118 degrees in the shade here in Nevada's desert," the pilot announced as they approached McCarran International Airport. Las Vegas shone brilliantly through the haze as the Pan Am jet plunked down on a sizzling runway laid like ribbon on a barren expanse of sand dotted with an occasional prickly shrub. Christina blinked in the glare of a silver wing against the blue sky, gazing at Nevada's red-rock mountain landscape in the distance. She wondered what she had done to earn this opportunity and still couldn't believe her change in circumstances in just one year. *I literally went from watching green dots on a computer screen to building a hospital.*

She peeked up at the overhead compartment, hoping the disk pack she had stowed there had survived the turbulence over the Rockies. *I can't be the one who destroyed the data!* She had nestled the disk pack carefully within her coat and wedged it tightly against the side, next to her embarrassingly large suitcase. Since she had never packed for a business trip before, she brought everything she might need, which meant bringing the larger bag.

A passenger in the seat across the aisle had plopped a tattered canvas sack, very obviously stuffed with rolls of coins, into the bin, along with his moth-eaten wool overcoat, before slamming the door shut. His eyes never once moved from the bin during the entire five-hour flight. Christina guessed his anxious glances were because winning big with those coins was his last desperate attempt to hold on to any shred of dignity he had left.

Here she, too, was attempting to build her future in, of all places, Las Vegas. A hospital on the strip, whose six-story tower loomed large and conspicuously plain among its low but glitzy casino neighbors, was to be her training ground. Looking out at the tarmac, Christina watched men boarding planes as their loved ones waved from the airport gates.

She, too, felt the pang of goodbye. Hers was a goodbye to the tethers of her prior life, the intricate web of fear, doubt, oppression, and a dream that never came to fruition. She, too, would be a gambler of sorts. If she couldn't make good on her bet that she could do something to make the world a better place and live independently, then Dr. Solokoff would have been right when he told her she wasn't good enough. If she failed, her brother's cruel judgments would become mere foreshadowing, and it would further justify her father's opinion that she didn't need an education. The naysayers would have won. But a gambler relies on odds, she told herself. *I'm relying on my skills, not odds, and what's more, David and Gary are relying on my skills. They believe in me.*

Opening the luggage compartment, Christina was relieved to find the disk pack still nestled safely inside her coat, appearing unscathed from the long flight. She grappled with its unwieldy bulk down the aisle as she exited the plane, avoiding the questioning stares of fellow passengers. Her colleagues, Abby and Marshall, were waiting at the gate. It took two hands to carry the disk pack, and finally Marshall offered to relieve Christina of her burden.

"I apologize for not carrying it for you. I didn't realize it was half your size." Marshall took the device from her.

"It's OK, Marshall, I was fine lugging it for a while, but I appreciate the break." Christina rubbed her sore arm and gritted her teeth. She hated to admit it was heavy and vowed to work harder at the gym so a male coworker won't have to relieve her in the future. It had never occurred to her that she could pull a muscle working a cushy software job.

Walking to baggage claim, Christina laughed to herself as she passed one-armed bandits, as her mother called them. There seemed to be more of the bell-chiming, strobe-light-flashing, glittering silver slot machines in the airport terminal at McCarran International than people. Here in Vegas, there was no need to enter a casino to try your luck. Every airport corridor was lined with penny slots, and for the high rollers, dollar slot machines promised a bankroll. Signs for jackpots, exclusive baccarat tables, incomparable odds, and frequent payouts bombarded weary travelers as they made their way through the airport. The bandits were everywhere—at rental car kiosks, outside the restrooms, near the skycap desks where departing passengers could drop in their last few coins.

Christina felt in her trench coat pocket the heaviness of the roll of quarters her mother had insisted she take with her to play four at a time. "Wait until you are feeling lucky, Christina, to play my quarters," her mom requested.

Christina had been inside a casino once, in Atlantic City at age eighteen. Back then it reminded her of a smoky arcade for grown-ups who hadn't yet grown up and for sedentary seniors happy to perch on a stool at the slots after gorging themselves on the free buffet and before the bus ride home. Christina had felt overstimulated by the onslaught of flashing lights and sounds and smothering clouds of cigarette smoke in the windowless spaces. She wondered now if Vegas casinos were any different.

Outside the terminal, Abby, Christina, and Marshall shed layers of clothing, unprepared for the desert heat. The chrome door handles of their rental car burned their fingers, and they rode with the windows down to allow a breeze to mix with the suffocating dry air inside.

When they approached the glitzy Welcome to Las Vegas sign, Abby screeched the car to a halt and jumped out to take a snapshot.

"Do you guys want to get in the picture?" she called back to Marshall and Christina.

"Sure, why not," Christina said, taking her Polaroid out of her luggage. "I'll take one too."

They passed Caesars Palace, Circus Circus, and the Flamingo casinos before arriving at the three-tower Las Vegas Hilton, just a block from the famous strip. Check-in was a breeze, thanks to their friends in Travel, as Abby referred to them.

"I really can't believe the company put us up so close to the strip!" Christina said to Marshall.

"All the hotels are cheap here. Food is cheap too. They want bettors to spend their money in the casinos."

"They didn't put us up on the strip, though, not even in Circus Circus." Abby said, frowning.

"I'm happy with the Hilton. I like the exterior glass elevator, at least from the ground. I may change my mind after riding it, depending how high up our rooms are." Christina looked up, counting the number of floors. This is just cool. Wait until I tell Mom and Dad about this. Christina clutched her locket.

She boarded the rising fishbowl with trepidation and took a deep breath, then stepped out onto the twenty-eighth floor, a bit wobbly. The expansive view from her room didn't disappoint, with the desert stretching west for miles toward the mountains. The tail end of the strip glowed in the fading light. She could see the huge red cross painted on the side of Southern Nevada Memorial hospital and was fooled into thinking it was close by, unaware that the flat desert and watercolor skies distorted distances. The city appeared to be plopped down willy-nilly, its bloated streets and creeping sprawl of urbanization dwarfed by the endless surrounding desert and red bluffs backlit on the horizon by a reluctantly setting sun.

The team leader, Rhonda, was already at the hospital, briefing their leaders on what to expect for their LIVE event. Abby and Rhonda would take evening and night shifts, with Marshall and Christina covering day shift the next five days. Rhonda would stay into the morning the first day to get Christina and Marshall started. Marshall had been out for the client's Install trip and knew the site. He'd done two LIVE trips before this one and was experienced enough to guide Christina on their shift, but he was painfully quiet and never volunteered information unless asked. Christina had tried to draw him out by chatting with him at the gate before takeoff. She peppered him with questions he couldn't not answer. By the time they boarded, he had eased up a bit. Her persistence had penetrated his reserve, eliciting an occasional half smile. The threesome ate dinner together at the ample hotel buffet, leaving a surplus in their per diem allowance. Weary from the long flight and change in time zones, they retired early to get ready for the week ahead.

The next day, Marshall and Christina entered the hospital through a buzzing main lobby. It was the lifeblood of the institution, with greeters at the front desk smiling and jumping to attention when a patient asked for directions to radiology or the surgical waiting room. Brightly colored tile paths on the always just-buffed terrazzo floors helped patients and visitors navigate the spiderweb to their destinations—the pharmacy, the cashier's office, or admissions desk. A confusing maze of hallways, doorways and locked double doors, marked conspicuously 'STAFF ONLY,' presented a daunting experience for mothers ushering their children forward to Pediatrics and for seniors hobbling along to the lab, one hand gripping a handrail along the way. To those unfamiliar it was unwelcoming, but staff memorized the routes and shortcuts, using back stairways to rush to another floor or to make their way to the cafeteria. A sense of urgency among white-coated clinicians was palpable, in contrast with the slow, uneasy pace of visitors and patients. Badge-wearing housekeepers, X-ray technicians, and orderlies, clothed in scrubs of all colors of the rainbow, hurried silently in rubber-soled shoes in the giant institutional beehive. It reminded Christina of her days in the ER, though on a much grander scale, and she instantly felt at home in what was to become her new world.

The programmers descended to the lower level. Below ground lay a tangle of tunnels and corridors, with white concrete walls and dingy gray flooring that showed evidence of the incessant traversing of shoe leather and wheels, noticeably devoid of colored tile paths. Here the underbelly of the organization hummed and puffed. Much like the internal organs of its patients, the inner workings of the hospital lay beyond what is seen. Christina took it all in.

As the two wove through the hallways, they dodged carts clattering to the laundry. Steam billowed from the double doors of the hothouse that sanitized all manner of bedding, pillows, drapes, and bandages, and the pungent smell of bleach was enough to make their eyes water. Laundering linens for all those beds required an entire operation that employed dozens of staff. Several were now darting about behind the overstuffed carts, pushing them toward the steam.

This level also housed a massive warehouse, labeled Central Supply. Through its open doors, Christina and Marshall got a glimpse of its treasures, from bedpans to blood pressure cuffs, and plastic tubing to Steinman pins. Shelves held sutures of all strengths, materials, and thicknesses as well as disposable and single-use products. A pair of teenage candy stripers clad in pink-striped smocks and white pants moved swiftly from Central Supply, likely at the behest of a harried floor nurse in need of a crucial item, and almost knocked Marshall off his feet as they rounded a corner.

Passing the warehouse, Christina pointed out the sign for Facilities, a boiler room like one might envision on the lowest deck of an ocean liner, with shiny pipes winding up and around in a dizzying array. She and Marshall peeked in at the castle of metal as two uniformed and hardhat-wearing men carrying tools emerged from the sterile factory. Here generators and boilers, compressors and tanks, wires and nozzles and cranks and valves were laid out neatly in a grid. Each component was connected by a bright yellow stripe on the floor, guiding workers safely through the labyrinth, lest a hot pipe burn through a uniform sleeve or singe the hair from an unsuspecting arm whizzing by.

Like a bus marking neighborhoods along its route, they now passed by the pharmacy. Its mind-boggling cache of ointments, pills, IV bags, and anesthetics was secured within a wire cage. Technicians picked and pulled products from the sub-desert acre of shelves three times daily, filling as many small bins as there were patients, with that shift's necessary medications. It took hours to fill the cart with everything each patient needed for one shift in the four-hundred-bed hospital, and Christina noticed a person behind the cage selecting a package and loading it into one of hundreds of tiny drawers. A small annex to this space housed a tiny laboratory where pharmacists mixed and measured products under a gigantic hood, crafting specialized compounds and IV fluids for uncommon treatments.

Unfortunate patients ended their hospital stay at the morgue, which was usually on the lower level of the hospital, ominously close to the loading dock and waste disposal area. Christina was sure Southern Nevada's was no different. She had been in a morgue while working as a high school volunteer in her local hospital. A nurse had asked her to help push a stretcher with a deceased patient, covered by a sheet. They loaded the stretcher onto a shabby utility elevator and rode to the depths of the hospital and the morgue. She remembered the unmistakable smell of formaldehyde that had filled her lungs as she entered, wheeling the stretcher to an open space alongside a line of populated stretchers awaiting their placement in one of the refrigerated drawers stacked three high on the walls of the sterile tomb. She didn't mention any of this to Marshall as they passed by, carefully dodging broken beds and seatless wheelchairs in the equipment graveyard lining the hallways.

Just beyond the morgue and across from the tunnel to the parking garage was a nondescript door marked Computer Room. Maybe the refrigeration needed for dead bodies and computers was centralized by design, Christina wondered. For this and many rooms throughout the hospital, visitors and vendors gained entrance through locked doors only by being buzzed in by someone already inside the space. This computer room would become the programming team's home base for the next week.

Inside was a stuffy vestibule with a cramped work area. A collection of dumb terminals sat atop a counter strewn with cords and power lines, and wheeled chairs spun to face every which way. A door at the far end with a tempered-glass window revealed the cooled computer room, a miniscule and not-so-glamorous version of the HSA data center. Though it had the requisite raised panel flooring for the spaghetti bowl of wiring underneath and high-velocity air blown from below, this room's low ceiling and dim lighting was no match for the company's impressive data space. Here, a tape drive, disk drive, PDP minicomputer, console, and line printer comprised the lean offensive line for the hospital's automation team. All the equipment was shiny, just-out-of-the-box new, not a scratch or dent in sight. The modern technology looked out of place in a room that appeared to have been retrofitted from an old storage closet to house the new computer and its peripheral machines. When they buzzed to be let in, an operator scrutinized the HSA badges they wore around their necks. He said nothing after releasing the lock and went back to his work. They walked ahead and peered through the window to find a gloved and sweater-wrapped Rhonda sitting in front of the console. She waved them in. Christina buttoned her suit jacket and made a mental note to bring along gloves tomorrow.

"Welcome to Vegas!" Rhonda said, as they stepped around the line printer. "I half- expected a slot machine to be in here with our hardware."

Marshall, having gallantly carried the disk pack through the meandering halls, set it down on top of the disk drive and smiled. "Now that we made it here, to the basement computer room of the hospital, we may as well be on Mars."

"I forgot to tell you to come in through the parking garage entrance," Rhonda said, "It takes you directly to this hallway."

"I didn't mind the trek here. Now I have my bearings." Christina said.

"You weren't the one carrying the disk pack," Marshall reminded her as he pointed to the plattered parcel. "Three and a half million patient records delivered, as requested."

"I sure hope it wasn't damaged on the flight," Christina said.

CHAPTER 17

RHONDA LED THEM to the disk drive where she began to load the disk pack. She unscrewed its black plastic cover and nonchalantly lifted the machine's door, as if she was getting ready to throw a load of laundry into a washer. She lowered the pack into the machine, aligning its spindle to the receiving end inside the drive. Each platter surface containing the magnetically stored data would be read in tracks by heads that moved closer and farther from the spindle once it started spinning. Rhonda now handled the exposed pack like a pane of glass. A speck of dust, a fingerprint, or a droplet from an unshielded cough could wipe out someone's birthdate, a surgical note, a lab result, or address data stored on its tracks. She started up the drive by typing a command on the console, and the pack began spinning inside the drive. Christina double-checked by looking through the drive's transparent cover.

"That'll run well into the night to load the patient file. We'll have to check the console for any error messages periodically, but for the most part we can let it run. Meanwhile, let's go out to the office area and go over our plan for the week." Rhonda spoke quickly as she walked.

"While the file loads, we'll bring up Aura for our testing only. No users allowed on yet. We won't officially go LIVE and let everyone on until the patient index has fully loaded, likely not until tomorrow morning. Marshall, sign in with username

PRODTEST1, and Christina, use PRODTEST2. You guys test each function but don't submit anything into the system, other than to admit three test patients—an Inpatient, Outpatient, and Emergency, with last name TESTPATIENT. I'll clear them out before we let users on. When you get to the end of a page for other functions, hit Cancel so we don't store your test data. We just want to ensure every screen comes up as expected and looks OK."

"What do we do if something looks wrong or doesn't load?" Christina asked.

"Just record all details. Create a document, and we'll keep a running list to review at the interval meetings, usually every four hours, or more frequently if needed. Meanwhile fix whatever you can and check it off the list."

"Are we working here or in that refrigerator?" asked Marshall, glancing at the computer room.

"You can work here at the workstations but go in and check the console once in a while for any messages about our load or other system errors. I'll call in later this morning to see how things are going. Abby will come in around four for turnover with you."

"We'll see you again tomorrow morning, right?" Christina asked.

"Of course! We'll all be here to go LIVE, then we'll start our shift coverage."

Day one of the trip flew by. Marshall and Christina tested to ensure the system came up as planned, dividing up the work. They ensured all the data from hospital specifications had loaded properly. They checked random user profiles to ensure appropriate functions were allocated. Supervisors were granted more access than their staff. Clerks could view reports appropriate for their department but not those of other departments. Nurses had their own set of functions. IT staff had access to run console operations in addition to all user functions, which they'd need once the HSA team left. Christina was surprised at the diversity of jobs and roles at the hospital, which this file of user profiles so clearly depicted.

Christina reviewed the doctor database, noting there were more than thirty physicians with the last name of Smith. Ah, that's why the system required a registrar to ask about medical specialty, phone number, practice address, or other identifying information when asking a patient for her family doctor. If a patient responded only with "Dr. Smith," the registrar must probe for further information or risk assigning the wrong physician to the patient. Selecting the wrong Smith would mean the patient's doctor wouldn't be notified that their patient was in the hospital and wouldn't receive their test results.

Christina discovered that while the system might be working as designed, its success would depend to a large extent on how people used it. A failed or flawed business or clinical process could detract from a system's ability to serve the client. Though her peers were more interested in the computer than the people who used it, the human/computer interaction piqued Christina's interest. A hint of self-doubt crept up again. *Am I that different?*

She and Marshall printed every system artifact for the test patients they'd entered. That afternoon they perused all printed chart documents—face sheets, consent forms, insurance forms—checking for readability and accuracy. They verified that nothing printed where it wasn't supposed to be. They ran all the system reports and saw that the census correctly showed only their one test patient admitted to an overflow bed.

"What about the outpatient visit summary report?" asked Christina.

"Good point," Marshall said. "We need that and the ER visit summary too."

By four o'clock when Abby came in, they'd run through every viable function.

"I sure had a long walk into this place," said Abby as they buzzed her in.

"There's a door directly from the parking garage just down the hall. We forgot to tell you," Christina apologized. "But good news is, we ran through the system with just a few minor issues and no console errors. It should soon be ready for you to start looking at real patient data. The patient index load is more than halfway through."

"OK, let's see what you've found, and then I'll take it from there."

Abby took the issues list, nodded as she read through their list of items, and smiled.

"Not bad! You guys seem to have resolved most of these. I'll continue with what's left. I'll see you tomorrow at seven. Rhonda will run through the Dayend process overnight and confirm the load has been completed. We'll all come in tomorrow morning, and if Dayend ran clean, then we'll plan to bring the first users up at eight."

When the two young programmers emerged into the desert sun, Christina said, "Marshall, do you want to walk instead of hailing the taxi? I'd like to defrost in the heat after being in the computer room."

"I'm game, but I don't know how far it is."

"We can always hail a cab if we get tired," said Christina, and they headed east on Charleston Boulevard to Main.

"Or a limo. There are more limos here than anywhere I've ever seen."

Once they turned onto Las Vegas Boulevard, the strip's sights and spectacles assaulted their senses, startling them out of the bleary-eyed haze of the hospital basement they'd worked in for the last eight hours. Walking to the Hilton, they passed half a dozen wedding chapels. The cheesy places were adorned with white bows and fake flowers, faux greenery and heart motifs crammed into a makeshift church for two lovers and their tiny congregation of coerced witnesses. Marshall and Christina laughed at the gaudy altars.

They stopped to gawk at casinos, each more tacky or more glamorous than the next, advertising burlesque stages, theaters, and gimmicks to appeal to any vice. Under towering palm trees lining sprinklered lawns, Christina and Marshall rested and sipped drinks from the MacDonald's squeezed on a lot between Mac's Liquor and Gifts and a small RV park. There were restaurants for any taste or cuisine, hotels and motels for any budget, most with casinos, and smoke shops galore.

"Take a look at that, Marshall!" Christina pointed to a silo with FlyAWAY painted on its side, and "An indoor parachuting experience" written vertically so she had to cock her head to read it. "I've gotta try that."

"You kidding?" he asked.

"No, I'm perfectly serious. I had trained for skydiving once with my college buddies and never got a chance to jump because I chickened out. So, here's my chance at redemption. I'm feeling more confident these days and maybe I can actually jump this time. You have to come with me."

"I'm not really the adventurous type."

"Oh, come on. After a couple days at the hospital, we'll be itching for something to do. You said yourself that you can't spend more than twenty dollars at the casino, so this is a good alternative."

"I'll think about it."

By the time the two got back to their hotel, they decided to eat dinner again at the buffet, letting their per diem accumulate for a splurge later in the week. Maybe they would save enough for FlyAWAY.

The day of the LIVE event started with a small group meeting in the close quarters of a vestibule next to the computer room. The HSA team, the hospital's VP of operations, Mr. Opdenaker, and the director of information services, Nelson Garcia, and his two staffers crowded around the workstation counter. After Rhonda's introductions, Nelson leaned his head to the side and commented not so quietly to Mr. Opdenaker, "The consultants look newer than the PDP-11/70 we just bought to run the new system. That one there could have been my kid's babysitter." He glanced at Christina.

She watched him curiously. Does he think we can't hear him?

Aloud, Nelson addressed Christina. "If I met you on the street, I'd think you were one of our showgirls. Maybe you should trade in your computer for an ostrich-feather headpiece." He looked her up and down.

"I prefer working on a computer and not on stage, thank you. I look better in a suit than in feathers." Christina shot back. What an idiot! Christina wondered if she'd have to put up with these kinds of remarks from other clients too.

Rhonda pretended not to hear the awkward exchange and went on to review the phasing approach for letting users onto the system.

"First, we'll have nursing verify the manual census report. Then our team will retrieve those patient records from the patient index and work with admitting to load current patients' information into the system and assign them their beds. We'll run a system census and validate all is well."

"I'll help with that," Nelson said. "I know our nurses. Wouldn't want them to scare you away. Those women are like hyenas when something from IT goes wrong."

Christina stifled a gasp. Could he be more disrespectful?

Rhonda continued. "Um, we'll let the emergency room registrars on, followed by ancillaries, one by one, until all user departments are up and running. At that point, Marshall and Christina will field all issues until evening when Abby takes over. I'll be in for the night shift and to support the Dayend process."

"What do we do if there's a problem?" asked Mr. Opdenaker.

"Marshall and Christina have a beeper. Here's the number to call. If necessary, they'll contact me or Abby for assistance."

Nelson and Mr. Opdenaker exchanged glances. Christina stiffened. Was it their age or the fact that three women and a young man held the fate of the hospital's investment in their hands that made the two men skeptical? A fleeting image of Dr. Solokoff flashed through her mind.

Two hours later, the system was up and running, with most of the hospital's users clicking away at their terminals. Christina offered to make rounds to all the user areas to answer questions and inquire what problems they'd encountered, while Marshall was happy to man the computer console and work from the vestibule workstations. Nelson Garcia offered to walk her through the hospital.

"Thank you, but it's not necessary. I know my way around hospitals." Christina departed before he could respond.

There's no way I'll let him show me anything. I know his type, feigning chivalry only to rip you to shreds later because you needed help. The kind that smile and talk sweetly to your face, then badmouth you when you leave the room. She recalled the time her organic chemistry teaching assistant so gallantly offered to help her prepare for an organic chemistry exam. He patiently explained spectroscopy to her over several sessions of office hours, encouraging Christina with, "There, you're getting it," and "See, you know how to do it," only to embarrass her in front of the class when she dared to raise her hand to answer a question, and was only partly correct. "Christina, all that extra help I gave you and you're still getting it wrong?"

Yes, let Garcia help someone wearing ostrich feathers!

She set out for the first-floor admissions area, then made her way to every nursing unit and ancillary department, completing her rounds at medical records and the cashier's office. One nurse manager told her of a room on her unit that was no longer in service because of repairs being made, so Christina decommissioned the room in the beds database. There were a few other rooms in several units which had been made into private rooms since the system had been originally specified, so their characteristics had to be reset in the database and the total number of beds adjusted in order for the census to balance. Otherwise, Rhonda would find a serious error when the census job ran at Dayend. Christina took care of it before leaving the unit. The ancillaries had no issues other than new users whose profiles had not been built into the system back at Corporate because they were hired after the specs were written.

By lunchtime, Christina and Marshall had noted a few artifacts and forms with printing errors, a visits report that sorted by account number instead of by patient last name and one registrar whose access was set up erroneously with laboratory functions on their menu. None were issues she and Marshall couldn't correct that same day. She felt a wave of satisfaction as she compiled the issues list, made notes about what was done to correct or resolve the issue, then marked each issue resolved.

After turning things over at the end of the day to Abby, Christina and Marshall opted to catch a cab back to the hotel instead of walking. A rotating sign in front of a bank across the street showed the temperature as 120 degrees.

"I'll need my energy for FlyAWAY tonight," said Christina.

Marshall slid into the cab's back seat beside her. "Are you really planning to go?"

"Of course! I've been thinking about it since I first saw it. I called last night and found out all about it. I reserved a spot for us tonight, hoping you'd agree to go with me." Christina smiled at Marshall. "So?"

"What's involved exactly?" Marshall demanded a full debriefing.

"We go at seven. Sign some waivers, and they have a training class for forty-five minutes where we practice steering in the air and how to roll if we fall."

"Wait—there's a chance we could fall?" Marshall looked skeptical.

"It's just in case. There's a person in the silo who is your guide, and they monitor your flight and ensure you don't fall. If you get close, they guide you gently toward the blower."

"The blower?"

"There's a jet engine mounted vertically at the bottom of the silo, blowing air upward. It's covered by a metal grid so no one can fall into it. The guide stands on the grid and watches you."

"Where would we be?"

"We jump in from the top of the silo, spread out our limbs, and fly."

"How's it that we fly yet the guide remains standing?" Marshall asked.

"We are wearing a parachute suit! It fills with air once we jump into the wind of the blower, and we float. The guide is in street clothes, standing seventy-five feet below us, off to the side of the air stream."

Having convinced, or rather, cajoled Marshall, Christina decided to eat only a light bite at the buffet. Marshall was confident the engine's powerful fan could keep both him and the prime rib he ate aloft.

"It's the same $4.95 buffet price whether you eat steamed spinach or lobster, Christina."

They set out shortly before seven. At FlyAWAY, the lengthy waiver form's graphic depiction of the potential hazards and injuries their "guests" may experience gave Christina pause. How high did they say it was? she thought, as she fingered her locket. *Mom, I hope I live to tell you about this adventure.* Then she hurriedly scribbled her name before she could change her mind and got in line for the parachute suit, helmet, earplugs, and goggles.

"I guess we're doing this," Marshall said.

Less than an hour later, Christina burst from the doorway seventy-five feet in the air, waving wildly at the moving dot of the guide below. The guide flashed a quick thumbs up as she soared left, dipped right, tumbled head over heels, and spun around, her wide white grin all he could see beneath the helmet. Marshall looked green awaiting his turn but soon followed Christina. He didn't take his eyes off the guide and ignored Christina's motions to follow her spinning and zigzagging antics. As the blower velocity slowed to a light breeze, they floated lower and lower, until first Christina and then Marshall came within reach of the guide. The guide grabbed her arm and pulled her beyond the air stream so she could land on her feet.

"Thanks! What a thrill!" Christina said to the guide, removing her helmet.

"You're quite welcome! I hated for your flight to end because you were having such a good time up there. I like your spunk!" he said.

"I didn't realize I'd take a few years off my life on this trip," Marshall quipped. "Thanks, Christina. I would never have gone there if not for you."

Christina couldn't stop smiling as she boldly soared toward the sky in the Hilton's glass elevator.

PART II

1983–1984

CHAPTER 18

SITTING ON HER BED, Terry thumbed through a *Bride's* magazine and stopped at a page featuring Lady Diana in her wedding dress. "I like the puffy sleeves on her dress and her crown veil. What do you think, Christina?" she asked.

"It's quite ornate, Terry, with all the ruffles and that long train. And regal. I do think it's wise to get an idea of the style you like before you go out shopping for a wedding gown." Christina tried to be supportive though her mind was elsewhere. Images of her future apartment raced through her mind. Throughout the girls' friendship, their conversations were more like two airplanes traveling at different altitudes in opposite directions. When Terry talked about how many children she hoped to have someday, Christina commented about yesterday's biology lecture. When Christina talked about going to college, Terry talked about the outfits she wanted to wear to Homecoming. They could converse easily about dancing and choir, two of their shared interests, and what was happening in the neighborhood, but most of the time they enjoyed each other's company despite traveling in different circles and with interests worlds apart.

Flipping to the makeup section, Terry looked up from the pages. "Christina, I really can't believe you were in Vegas for work. And did that parachuting thing too. The farthest I got last month was going to the library for a book about wedding planning."

Christina smiled. "That's exciting! I can't believe you're getting married. And soon! I'll have to start calling you Mrs. Ross." Her expression became serious. "Terry, you sure you're ready for this big step?"

"Of course! Ryan and I love each other, and we both want this. You know I don't want to live at home any longer, and we don't see why we should wait. Besides, we want to start a family," Terry said.

Christina gulped, speechless. She managed to ask, "What do your parents think about it?"

"They love Ryan! And they're happy he has a good job in accounting, though the idea of me moving to Allentown is not so popular," Terry said.

"Will you be working?"

"I'll take time to settle into the apartment, then look for a job. Unless we get pregnant right away." Terry's eyes were glued to the step-by-step depiction of applying smudge-proof eyeliner.

Christina could think of nothing to say, so she fumbled in her pocket for the Polaroid photograph of herself in the parachute suit at FlyAWAY. She held it out for Terry to see.

"I wanted to show you this. You can see the entrance to the silo at the top. It was seventy-five feet above the engine. I had to jump out and let the air fill my suit for a second or two before beginning to fly. It was thrilling but scary until I relaxed and enjoyed the flight. You know how afraid I am of heights."

"I always knew you'd go places, Christina. I didn't think it would be flying in a silo, though."

"I was terrified at first but so glad I was able to muster the courage to do it and overcome my fear. It was a fitting way to celebrate my new job."

"Soaring to new heights?" Terry's sarcasm was palpable.

"Next month I'm moving out to be closer to work and on my own again. I have to decide among two apartments and convince my new roommate."

"What are your options, and who is the roommate?" asked Terry, now studying a page about bridesmaid dresses.

"Option A is to live in a garden apartment in West Chester. It's a little cheaper but not near anything exciting and closer to home. It looks like where my grandparents live."

Terry glanced up from the magazine. "You're not really selling it."

"The other is in a high-rise building in King of Prussia, right across from the huge mall and Bloomingdale's. It's in a growing area. I could run at the nearby Valley Forge park. But of course, this one is more expensive. Both apartments are the same distance from work, but this is over an hour from home."

"What about the roommate?"

"Diana Rubin is a friend of a friend at work. She's an artist, a photographer."

"Where does Diana want to live?"

"I think she'd rather King of Prussia because she works on the Main Line. I told her I'd look at a few places and let her know what I liked."

"If you really want to live on your own, as you did before in New Jersey, then distance from home shouldn't matter. And you know, in Jersey you didn't like living in a neighborhood without young people."

"You're right. The garden apartment isn't really my style either. Hopefully my savings in gas money can offset the extra rent. Thanks for helping me figure it out."

"We didn't really figure out my dress, though. I'm going to a few places Wednesday night to look at gowns. Will you come and help me?" asked Terry.

"Of course I'll come!" Christina hugged her friend and pretended to walk her down the aisle.

Diana agreed on the King of Prussia location, and the girls moved in on a hot Saturday. Christina had convinced a few coworkers to help with the move at the King of Prussia end, with the promise of pizza and beer. Her brother Dominic and the twins helped load her bed and dresser, as well as boxes of kitchen items, stereo equipment, and clothes into the trailer. When Dominic arrived at Christina's new place with the U-Haul truck, Diana had already unloaded and was chatting with Drew, who had arrived before Christina. In a matter of hours, the apartment was made habitable by the small group, despite frequent beer breaks and lots of kidding.

Drew was all business, directing the careful emptying of the U-Haul and calculating corner angles and heights to navigate the narrow hallways of the building with Christina's furniture and boxes. He greeted everyone upon Christina's introductions in the parking lot of her new home at Prussian Valley Apartments but remained otherwise quiet. He sipped his beer, listening to the people in Christina's new world bantering about the Phillies, the clubs to try out in the area, and the latest gossip from work. Drew occasionally commented on the sports talk, mostly about the Phillies season and how their roster was age heavy, with Steve Carlton and Tug McGraw skewing the otherwise young 1983 team. Dominic, also meeting Christina's work friends for the first time, paired up with Drew to move the larger pieces, and the two passed the time with side conversations about their favorite bands.

Once everyone but Drew had left after the long day of moving and Diana had decided to try out the shower, Christina plopped down next to Drew on the brocade couch Diana's grandmother had donated to the girls. She put her feet up on a box labeled Albums.

"So, Drew, what do you think?"

"The place has potential."

"It does, and with artwork on the walls and a few plants it will be really nice. Did you like my new friends?"

"Sure, they seem nice. Gary was friendly. Diana is a riot," he said, then opened a pizza box, grabbed a cold slice, and quickly took a bite..

Sensing he was withholding something, Christina asked, "What is it, Drew?"

"What do you mean?"

"You seem distant, not like yourself. You've been especially quiet all day. I really appreciate you doing all that heavy lifting."

Drew looked at Christina, then lowered his eyes. "I'll be honest…I can't help thinking how cool it would be if you were moving in with me today, instead of here, with Diana. You're starting a new life. Without me." Christina had never seen him look so serious.

"Drew, how can you say that? You're a big part of my life! I'll be only an hour's drive from you now, and we can spend more time together!"

"I'm not so sure you'll have the time. We've seen each other only a handful of times since you started this job, and now you're doing more traveling."

"Yes, I'll be traveling more for work now that I've been through training. That's an exciting part of this job. They're putting their trust in me. I'm starting to contribute. The work is important, and I like it. I've made friends here. And you can be part of whatever we do—if you want to. I thought you'd be happy for me, proud of me, Drew."

"I'm very proud of you. Never doubted you would go far. Just not that far."

"An hour?" Christina cocked her head to the side.

"It's not *the* drive that concerns me. It's *your* drive."

"What? That's absurd. I'm the same person I've been since you met me. I just now have an opportunity to use my talents, unlike the past couple of years, since that dreadful day with Dr. Solokoff."

"I know that incident still haunts you," Drew said.

"I don't know if *haunts* is the word, but I want to start building my future, and I can see myself doing this for a while. Just like you're doing at Keystone Cellular. You were fortunate to get a job right out of college that you loved. Did you envision designing cellular phone infrastructure when you started college?" Christina asked him.

"No, I didn't even know what a cellular phone was back then. Who did?"

"Exactly! So now I have a chance to explore new frontiers in healthcare, despite not going into medical school as originally planned. I had no idea this work even existed back then." Christina sought Drew's understanding, and admittedly, his approval.

"You're ambitious, and I see your world expanding. I just hope there's space for me, Christina."

Diana and Christina soon became friends as well as roommates. Diana was funny and always up for an outing, and the two learned their way around town together. Often they stayed up and chatted over late-night snacks, pondering lofty ideas and trying to solve the world's problems. They got to know each other's friends and swapped clothes. Nights out included dancing at Flanigan's and Houlihan's, plus Touché, the club at the end of their street, which was close enough that they could safely stumble home after a night out.

Diana's photography equipment and makeshift studio took up half their living room, but Christina didn't mind. There was plenty of room for the couch, TV, and plants. A six-foot rubber tree and tropical palm filled a corner where furniture could have been.

One rainy Sunday night when they were both home with nothing special to do, Diana explained to Christina how to set up a shot, how to see things like a photographer, and the purpose of the various lenses and filters she used, but Christina was happy to just enjoy the end products—the photos themselves.

"Diana, you've really got talent," Christina told her friend, perusing Diana's catalogue of prints. "I sure hope they appreciate you at the art school. I can see you fitting in better at *National Geographic* or *Time* magazine."

"Ha-ha, Christina. You're funny. And ambitious. Just like you—swing for the fences. People like me don't think that way," Diana said. She wiped the camera lens with a soft cloth and shook her head.

"What way?" Christina again wondered why she was considered different.

"Thinking the sky's the limit. That dreams come true. That there are no limits to what a person can do." Diana's face clouded as she moved toward the window and stared down at the highway stretching through the wet valley below.

"What? I'm twenty-two years old. I have hopes and dreams, and believe me, I've had plenty of them burst like soap bubbles on a July day. But that won't keep me from trying to do something more. The world sets enough limits for us to overcome. Why shouldn't we shoot for the stars? Even falling short would leave us with a spectacular view of the universe. How does that not make sense?" Christina reasoned, her voice rising an octave.

"It does make sense for you. Just not for me, for most people. I'm not from a wealthy family. I feel lucky to have a job. I'm lucky I've found a hobby I like, even if I'm not using it fully in my job. It's enough." Diana shrugged her shoulders and carefully packed a lens into its velvet case.

"Are you fifty years old? Have you given up on your dreams already? For the record, my family is not wealthy. I'm a granddaughter of immigrants with less than a high school education. My parents worked hard for what they have and taught me to work hard too. What's the harm in dreaming?" As she spoke, Christina crossed the room, reached for Diana's hands, and held them tightly, imploring her friend.

"Only good can come from it. If we stop dreaming, we die. And maybe those dreams will lead you to new dreams or places you never dreamed of, if you work hard enough. I hope you will dream, Diana, and work toward those dreams, because you are so talented. And worthy."

"Thank you, Christina. No one ever has encouraged me like that." Diana squeezed her friend's hands. "Who encouraged you?"

"Well, my mother was always saying how I could do anything I put my mind to. I never really believed her," Christina scoffed. She noticed a few yellowed leaves on the towering rubber tree in the corner and went over to snap them off. "Back then, I thought all mothers praise their children, regardless of their talents or lack thereof. And especially because I didn't get that from my father. He loved us but was indifferent, hardly noticing my older sister and me. My father encouraged me to work hard by example. He encouraged my brothers to follow their dreams. Not me or my sister. It was never clear what he envisioned for us other than being hard workers. I'm sure he thought we'd have our families someday and never gave anything further a second thought. What's ironic is my brothers have no ambition, and Sebastian is lucky he's not in jail. My father really couldn't understand why I even wanted to go to college. But our mother did."

"Was it because he never went?" Diana went back to fiddling with the camera.

"Maybe. Or maybe just the traditional Italian ways, you know, where women raise their families, take care of their husband, end of story." Christina understood her father's world but didn't see herself living in it.

"Huh. That's pretty grim. I mean, I'm OK with raising children someday, but that can't be all there is, can it? I can say from watching my mother, it's a pretty thankless job. She was always tired, an unsung hero," Diana said, as if noticing it for the first time in her lens, then looked up from behind the camera.

Christina nodded. "Mine too. She married young and had kids right away. But my mother quietly pushed back against oppression, getting an education after we entered school, working part time. She shoehorned her emerging self into the restrictions of her life."

"Thank God we at least have some choices now," Diana said.

"*Amen!* I want to make a difference somehow. And to make a difference, I know I must first take care of myself and not rely on someone else. My mother never told me that, but it's something I feel strongly about. Living in a patriarchal family and watching only my brothers somehow on the receiving end of that encouragement, I had to figure things out for myself.

"I'm trying hard to believe in myself, even if no one else but my mom ever did. I've had to justify why I wanted a college education. I am trying to refute a condescending advisor's belief that I won't make it, and now I see clients talking over me to the only other male in the room, whether or not he's competent or in a position of authority. I know I'm capable. That's what I'm focusing on now, trying to overcome a pervasive feeling of oppression, this external pressure to fail, or worse—fading away into oblivion." Christina had filled a water jug and focused her attention on watering the rubber tree in the corner.

"Oh, Christina, I didn't know you ever had doubts. You seem so confident and self-assured," said Diana.

"I fool people. On the outside I project what I want to feel inside. But I am slowly starting to believe in myself again. I know there are things I can do that others can't. There are people, male bosses even, at HSA, who believe in me. I'm learning I can make a difference. I hope someday, I can do something, even the smallest thing, to help the world. Even Drew doesn't seem to understand." Christina stared at the photos in her locket.

"Hospitals save lives, and from the sound of it, hospitals need people like you to keep things running. But how can a photographer make a difference?"

Christina set down the jug and turned to Diana. "Are you kidding? Your work finds beauty in the world, shares insights into social problems. People need to see that. Your photos are uplifting. Art is educational. It's important. People need beauty to counter all the ugliness that exists out there. They need to be shown things outside of their own little world, other ways of seeing things. I hope you will find the best way to share your art, Diana."

Diana looked at Christina over the tripod. "I never thought of it that way. Thanks for your faith in me! I don't think I have half the ambition, or hutzpah, as they say, that you do, but you've got me thinking. For now, though, Christina, I'm working at the school and hoping to make enough money to pay rent and my car payment and still eat. Sharing my art will have to wait a bit."

CHAPTER 19

HEADS TURNED AS the couple entered the cathedral. Drew, handsomely clad in a gray tuxedo, guided Christina as they led the wedding party toward the altar. Christina looked stunning in the pale gray stiletto sandals and the fuchsia silk gown Terry had selected for her bridesmaids. Christina's shoes pitter-pattered against the marble floor as she appeared to glide down the aisle. She winked at her family and grinned at Donny and Mrs. Meddleton, careful not to turn her head lest her updo sprout a stray hairpin. Drew and Christina took their places when they reached the altar.

Mr. Merullo escorted Terry down the aisle to deposit her alongside a noticeably trembling Ryan. She looked regal in the Diana-like gown with a ten-foot train trailing behind. Mr. Merullo's eyes were glassy as he lifted Terry's veil, kissed her cheek, and retreated to his seat beside Mrs. Merullo in the first pew. Terry was radiant, beaming at Ryan, who relaxed his tense shoulders when she took his hand. They rotated in unison to face the priest. While Drew never took his eyes off Christina, Christina watched the wedding couple's faces from her vantage point on the marble steps. Terry smiled nonstop for seventy minutes. Ryan's earnest expression broke only when uttering his vows. The couple nearly sprinted down the aisle when the organ blasted Mendelssohn's wedding march.

Terry asked Christina to assist with securing the long train around her hips before entering the reception in the adjacent church hall. As the two fumbled with yards of fabric in the ladies' lounge, Terry held out her hand to show Christina her ring.

"It's official, Christina. I'm married!"

"Congratulations, Mrs. Ross!" Christina hugged her friend, who was wrapped in layers of tulle and satin. "I'm really going to miss stopping over at your house when I go home to Delaware. It won't be the same."

"Christina, we can see each other in Allentown when you come to Drew's! Our place is close to his." Terry paused to admire herself in the full-length mirror, train pinned up in an enormous bustle.

In Allentown. Christina suddenly couldn't breathe.

Back at the head table, Drew was chatting with the groomsmen. "There's my girl now," he said as Christina approached and wrapped an arm around her waist. "Have I told you how amazing you look today?"

"Yes, Drew, thank you! And you polish up pretty well yourself. I definitely like the tuxedo. But I bet your shoes aren't poking through your heels and numbing your toes like mine are," Christina said, taking a seat. "The price of beauty…" she lamented.

She stashed the fashionable torture devices under the table for the remainder of the night. Drew twirled and twisted Christina around the dance floor in stocking feet, and she was relieved to be so comfortable with Drew. *He is gracious and thoughtful,* she thought. She knew Drew wouldn't care what shoes she wore or whether she wore an evening gown or sweatpants. She knew he accepted her at her best and her worst, and she loved him for that gift. *I'm lucky to have Drew. But why doesn't he get that I want to do something for myself?* She shrugged it off, wanting to enjoy Terry's special day. Christina and Drew danced to everything the band played, from the bump to the moonwalk. As they stopped for a breather, Donny Meddleton came by to get Christina back out on the dance floor.

"Donny, that hand looks good as new," Christina observed as he took her by the arm and strutted toward the band.

"It is completely healed, thanks to you and Dr. Aboud. I can't use it as an excuse for more time on exams, though," he said.

"How's school going? I can't imagine being at MIT. What'd you pick as your major?" Christina shouted over the band.

"Computer engineering. Maybe add a marketing minor later."

"I'm glad you're taking an easy course of study," she kidded. "Are you playing any ball?"

"Just club baseball. I need time to study."

"I know you'll do well. Let me know if you want a summer job. Our company is growing rapidly, always looking for fresh talent."

Drew had stopped to talk with their college friends, and when the song ended, he handed Christina her drink and embraced Donny with a wink. "Great to see you, buddy. I'm glad you're not bleeding."

When it was time to throw the bouquet, Terry motioned for Christina to take a spot in the front of the crowd of young women. Christina pretended not to notice and crept away. She hastily took a place at the far side of the throng of estrogen and behind young cousins whose mission was to catch the darn flowers and thereby be the next to marry. "What a stupid tradition," she muttered. Christina imagined how lovely the freesia and gardenia nosegay would look as a centerpiece on her otherwise bare dining table, then dismissed the thought. Sorry, not worth the humiliation.

On the drive back to the Comos, where they were staying for the weekend, Drew remarked on how happy Ryan and Terry looked.

"Yes, they looked happy…and young," added Christina, popping Supertramp's *Breakfast in America* cassette into the Saab's tape deck.

She turned up the volume. Terry's wedding program vibrated atop Drew's upgraded sound system's speakers and fluttered to the car floor. Christina hummed along, feeling the last gin and tonic affecting her memory for lyrics, then sporadically broke in with an exaggerated, "Be sensible, dah-ta-dah…Responsible…" and nearly shouted with sudden recollection "who I am!'"

Drew smiled and said, "That takes me back a couple years. Darling, do you know how often I listened outside your door as you screamed it from inside your tiny dorm room?"

"You what? Why wouldn't you just knock and come in?" She stopped singing for a few seconds.

"As I approached your door from across the quad, I could hear you blasting music. I liked to stand there and imagine you tossing a book aside and singing in full voice to no one in particular. I'd linger for a few seconds outside before knocking. You were always a force and knew what you liked."

Christina waved her hand and scoffed, "You're crazy, Drew," and resumed singing.

⌁⌁⌁

Just days after Terry and Ryan returned from their wedding trip to New York City, Terry called Christina one evening and insisted she come up to see their place and help her settle in.

"I'll tell you all about our time in New York when I see you," Terry gushed, "and maybe you and Drew can go out with us to the Roundtable Steakhouse."

"Sounds great, Terry," Christina said, "but I'm not sure how soon I can come for the weekend. I have a few trips coming up—they're sending me to Baton Rouge and to Chicago soon. If I fly out on Sunday, then a weekend trip won't work for me. And of course, I'd have to check with Drew."

"Why? Drew's door is always open for you, Christina! What's this about Chicago and Baton whatever?"

"Now that I did that LIVE trip in Vegas, word got around that I'm available to join other support teams. My boss thinks it's great for me to get that experience. When it's time to support our region, I'll be more than ready."

"How long will you be away?"

"Chicago's trip is for two sites, so I'll be gone a week. The other trip to Baton Rouge, Louisiana, will be a shorter trip," Christina wondered if Terry was listening. She heard dishes clattering in the background.

"Well, find out and let me know when you can come. How does Drew feel about all this jet-setting you're doing?" Terry's dishes had quieted down.

"Drew? I've no idea. He knows I'll be traveling, and I'm sure he's fine with it." Christina hung up after promising Terry she would come as soon as she could get away, though Terry's question about Drew had her wondering. What does Drew think of it? Why would he care where I have to go?

Christina had never considered that her traveling would interfere with her relationship with Drew. They had lived pretty far apart when she was in Jersey and were lucky to see each other once a month. Now that she lived in King of Prussia, he could stop over for dinner midweek if he wanted. The concern for Drew in Terry's voice kept returning to Christina. Her own apprehension mounting, Christina decided to call him that night. She sat on her bedroom floor, propped up against her bed, nervously combing the carpet with her fingers as she dialed.

"Just got a call from Terry. They're back, and she wants me to come up and help her settle into their place." The carpet fibers were now arranged in a rainbow shape.

"Great, darling, when?"

"That's just it, Drew. I don't know because I'm going to Chicago and Baton Rouge soon for work." She carved clouds in the carpet.

"I thought your region was Seattle?" Christina heard him open his kitchen window.

"It is. But David says the other teams need help, and it will help me when our accounts go LIVE. Now I'll get an up close and personal view of the country's healthcare facilities."

"David?"

"Yes, David. My boss. The one who hired me in the snowstorm!" Christina wondered how Drew forgot that, from all she'd told him.

"Oh, right. What did you tell Terry?" Drew asked. Christina heard rustling noises as Drew unpacked a bag of groceries.

"Same thing. I'll have to let her know." Christina was relieved Drew said nothing concerning her travel schedule and let the carpet be. "What's new at work?"

"We're starting to test fiberoptic components so we can eventually replace the coax cable with something better to cross the Atlantic. This cable will be exponentially faster because of the repeaters we're using. We'll place them every forty kilometers throughout its length. The fibers are super cool. Made of glass." Christina could feel Drew's excitement through the phone.

"Sounds like something out of *Star Trek*," she said.

"Not really. Fiber's been around a while, just not in the transatlantic. We're testing which diameter fibers transmit better over that great distance and which connectors hold up, considering they'll be underwater, with sharks, boats, and natural phenomena to contend with." Drew hastened his pace, explaining it with pride.

"Sharks? Never thought a shark would be interested in my phone conversations," Christina chuckled.

"It's not your words they're after. Apparently, the electromagnetic field attracts them and makes them go batty. We have to figure out how to reduce or eliminate the field. I call it job security." Drew minimized his contribution to the company, but Christina knew his brilliant mind would likely be rewarded with a few patents before this was all finished. She admired his modesty, how he never bragged about his achievements. It was one of the things she loved about him. Yet, with all his focus on his work, he still didn't seem to get hers.

"It's shocking how technology is exploding nowadays, isn't it, Drew? I'm just thrilled to have a small part in it. Someday maybe I won't have to carry disk packs across the country. I could just say, 'Beam them up, Scotty' like Captain Kirk, and the data will flow through the atmosphere to the hospital," she laughed, sprawled out on the floor.

He was quiet for a second, then said, "You're really into this job, aren't you, Christina?"

"Sure. I love it. I learn something every day and get to use what I know. I even have new ideas for how to make the system better. For the first time ever, someone wants to hear what I've got to say," Christina said, realizing Drew might take that the wrong way as soon as the words came out.

"I've always listened to you, darling. Haven't you noticed?" he whispered, intimately brushing Christina's vulnerability, yet he didn't acknowledge the fact she was enjoying her work and the chance to contribute. She found herself apologizing, again.

"Drew, of course I notice that. I meant in a job or in a serious way." She reached for her locket, moving it up and down along its chain.

Drew paused, then changed the subject. "I forgot to mention I joined a local soccer team. I'll be playing a couple nights a week."

"Soccer? Drew, I didn't even know you could play. Isn't it a bit more footwork than tennis?" Christina worried Drew could break a leg or worse.

"Yes, but I played in middle school. It's just a recreational team. Mostly guys from work. In a few weeks, you can come watch a match. If you're available, that is."

"I'd love to see it. I've never seen grown men play soccer before. I hope you don't get hurt with all that testosterone running around. Why wouldn't I be available?"

"I don't know, you might have a flight to catch or be in Moulin Rouge or Seattle or wherever. I'm afraid you're getting too busy for me," he added.

So, he does mind. She halted the locket at a point near her collarbone and exhaled.

Christina took a deep breath and then spoke deliberately. "Drew, I'm not too busy for you. I want to be with you. I also want to succeed in my work. I need to do this. For myself. And it's Baton Rouge."

"By yourself, you mean," Drew suggested. Christina heard him gulp. Was it the soda or a sigh?

"No, not by myself. For myself. I have goals. It's important to me to contribute to the world. In a hospital, good decisions can save a life. I also want to explore new places and see what lies beyond the three-state circumference I've lived in. I want to be financially independent and support myself, not rely on my parents like my brothers do. Or on a husband, for that matter. It's something I've worked for and why I went to college. Just like you've worked hard to get where you are. I hope you can understand that, Drew." She drew rain coming from the carpet clouds.

"I understand it means I won't see much of you." His words sounded muffled. He either turned his head away from the phone or was whispering.

"You have my heart, Drew. Whether I'm with you every day or

not." She felt her heart thrashing back and forth within her chest.

"I hope the soccer boys will keep my mind off you, while you're out doing your thing," he said, "but don't stay wherever they send you, OK?"

"I promise. I'll be back. They're just trips. Maybe twice a month. And promise me, you won't let those head butts destroy your memory of me!"

"That's not possible."

Despite Drew's sweet response, Christina felt, for the first time in their four-year relationship, a heaviness she couldn't ignore.

David's briefing for the Chicago sites was short and to the point. Swedish American was having trouble getting all the registration staff trained, so the HSA team of Abby and the account-owner, Rex, spent more time on training than fixing issues. Abby requested Christina specifically when asking for additional resources. The other site, Rockford Memorial, had a team of three out there but got delayed due to problems in field engineering. And their uninterruptable power supply was faulty, with another one on order. Once their hardware was up, they'd need a fourth programmer to get them back on schedule. Christina would spend three days at Swedish and two at Rockford, which was just across town.

Alice in Travel suggested Christina fly out Sunday evening to avoid O'Hare chaos on Monday mornings.

"We'll book you a rental car, and you'll stay at the same hotel as the other teams. You'll fly out Sunday."

"When are the others flying out? I'd rather fly with them," Christina said.

"They're already there. And oh, it's about an hour-fifteen-minute drive from the airport to the hotel in Rockford," Alice noted.

Chrstina pasted a fake smile on her face. *I'll be driving alone in the rental car. Somewhere I've never been. At night. Suck it up, Christina, you wanted adventure and independence, and so it begins.*

Christina left the apartment in King of Prussia at 3:40 p.m. and drove twenty-five minutes to Sugarman Subaru on Essington Avenue, where, thanks to a tip from David Stokes, she would leave her Honda for the week. A Sugarman attendant would drive her in her own car to the departure terminal, then drive the car back to the Subaru lot, wash it, keep it for the week, and deliver it to her, spotlessly clean, upon her arrival in Philadelphia. *Cool! I could get used to this first-class service.*

At 4:15, right on schedule, the attendant dropped her off at the United terminal. Christina checked her luggage at the curb with the skycap, smiled and handed him a dollar, then hustled to the gate. She gripped the punched card boarding pass, silently thanking God for Travel, who attended to every detail for those flying all over the country from Corporate. This time, with no disk pack to carry through the airport, Christina felt light carrying only her briefcase.

She had just stopped to get a hot pretzel when she heard static and then a pleasant voice descending from the overhead speaker. "Last call for boarding United Flight Number 177 for Chicago." She darted to her gate with fifteen minutes to spare before takeoff at 4:40. *It took longer for her to drive home to Delaware than it took to leave her apartment in King of Prussia, get to the airport, and take-off.*

As Christina was loading her trench coat and briefcase into the overhead compartment, someone called her name.

"Hey, Christina, over here." A grinning Gary Wentworth was squeezed into a seat a few rows behind her in the Smoking section, waving his long arms above the seatbacks.

Stunned to encounter a familiar face, Christina walked toward his seat. "Gary, why are you on this flight? Are you going to Rockford too?"

"No, I'm heading to Seattle by way of Chicago. I could have gone through Denver, but Alice told me you were on this flight, so here I am. Voila!"

"What luck!" she said. "Do you smoke?"

"No, I don't smoke, why?"

"Alice couldn't get you a seat next to mine?"

"Alice is good, but not that good to get a choice of seats at the last minute. I'll wait until they close the door, then if that seat's open, I'll grab it. If not, I'll listen to the Seahawks game once they pass out headsets. They're looking pretty good this season, might make the playoffs."

"OK. Don't let me interrupt the game. I brought *In Search of Excellence* to read. And I have my Walkman."

After Gary sweet-talked the stewardess into letting him move into the empty seat next to her, Christina said, "Who would've thought I'd know someone on my flight?" then sneezed. The smoke from a few rows back wafted through the entire cabin, in complete disregard of its insidious infiltration into the No Smoking section.

"You'd be surprised how often it happens. HSA keeps the airlines in business. I've run into people from work in Denver, Chicago, and Atlanta, all the major hubs. We crisscross the country. Neither rain, nor sleet, nor fog, nor snow; if there's a hospital in need, we go. Or something like that." Gary would be good company for the ninety-minute flight. He never mentioned the Seahawks as the two chatted away. Anyone eavesdropping on their conversation couldn't have known they'd just spent forty hours of the previous week together in their one-hundred-twenty-square-foot office.

"I guess a lot of us travel Sunday nights too. Gary, do you want half of this pretzel? I wasn't sure if I'd eat before driving to the hotel."

"No thanks. I'll get dinner at O'Hare during the layover. Want to join me?" Gary asked.

"Why not? Alice guaranteed my late arrival at the Best Western."

"Best Western? Traveling in style, I see. When you come to Seattle, we go first class." Gary teased.

"I'm too new to make demands. So how do you get the choice accommodations, Mr. Frequent Flyer?"

"First, we take the red-eye flight to Seattle. It's half the price of daytime flights, so we can spend more on the hotel. We book the SeaTac Marriott, which has an amazing indoor pool and hot tub."

"I'm glad you've got it all figured out. Can't wait to go!"

Christina thought only a few minutes had passed, but they were already landing in Chicago. Gary had her laughing the entire trip. She motioned to the stewardess for a can of Tab to soothe her throat, parched from laughter and the lingering cigarette smoke. Once they deboarded, Gary waited for a table at Pizzeria Uno, while Christina retrieved her bag and returned to the terminal to dine with Gary.

"You'll love this pizza, Christina. It's deep-dish, Chicago style. Stuffed crust. Whenever I come through O'Hare, I eat here. And given a choice between coming through Denver or O'Hare, it's O'Hare hands down because of Uno. Though, once in Denver I did pass John Elway in the airport."

"Who?" Christina looked sideways.

"You're funny. Wait, you really don't know him? He's only the best quarterback the Broncos have ever had, the best in the NFL!" Gary sighed. "He could sweep the floor with Jaworski. Want a beer, Christina?"

"OK, good to know. Since I'm driving alone in a state I've never visited before, in who knows what kind of rental car, to a local hotel in the dark, I'll pass on the beer," she said. Gary might have thought she was dutifully cautious, but Christina was duly apprehensive about all the firsts. *I hope I don't get lost. I hope I have no trouble driving the rental. I hope my work goes well… fingers crossed.*

"Don't worry about the rental cars. They're made to be abused. Be sure to accelerate over speed bumps, toss your empty soda cans in the back seat, and forget about washing the windshield. And leave the tank empty when you return it," a sufficiently stern Gary advised.

"OK, note to self." Christina wrote in the air with an invisible pen.

Gary shook his head. "I keep forgetting, you're a newbie!"

"Give me a few months, Gary, and you won't recognize me."

"I don't doubt that for one instant, Christina Como. My star mentee." Gary raised his beer mug in her honor.

Gary was right. Christina did love the gooey, deep-dish Chicago-style pizza, though she felt a few pounds heavier after consuming a couple of slices. After dinner, he went on toward his gate, and she went to the Hertz counter gold line, where the advertised "seamless key pickup" worked as promised. She got keys to a grandpa-blue sedan and was soon heading west on the I-90 tollway.

CHAPTER 20

A YOUNG WOMAN AT the Hertz counter had torn a paper map from a one-inch-thick tablet and carefully highlighted the route Christina should take to Rockford's Finest Best Western, before wishing her a good trip. Midwestern hospitality? Christina half expected to be called Ma'am instead of Miss Como.

There was no worry about speeding. The Chevy Malibu, when floored, maxed out at fifty-five. Christina had to roll down its windows to flush out the cloud of cigarette smoke left behind by the last driver. I'll have to ask Alice to reserve a no-smoking car for me next time. Little more than standard suburbia silhouettes were visible from the toll road, though she recognized Schaumberg and Naperville as she passed signs for their exits. As she checked in at the hotel, the desk clerk handed Christina a message that had been left for her. Waiting for her room key, she read the handwritten note from Abby on a folded page with "Rockford's Finest" hotel logo emblazoned at the top.

> *Meet us at the hotel lobby bar at 8:30 p.m.*
> *—Abby*

Checking the Swatch wristwatch Drew had given her, Christina picked up her pace. She'd have just enough time to freshen up before meeting Abby and Rex.

"Impressive bar we've got here, don't you think, Christina?" Abby motioned for Christina to take the single remaining seat at the bar of only six stools. "Not exactly worth rushing to."

"I'm not picky. I literally just arrived. Oh, I forgot about the time change—we're an hour behind now." Christina pointed to the Molson Canadian tap and smiled at the bartender who sauntered over with a frosty mug.

"You know Rex," Abby said, looking his way. "It's his account."

"Hi, Rex. We met once briefly outside David Stokes's office." Christina extended her hand, noticing his shirt cuff was missing a button.

Rex shook her hand harder than necessary. "How could I forget Snowstorm Hire?" He passed his tongue quickly across his lower lip.

"Beg your pardon?" Christina raised one eyebrow, rubbing circulation back to her hand underneath the bar.

"Word has it you stayed to interview while all the rest of us went home in the snowstorm. Blizzard, in fact. And later that day, Elliot apparently called everyone's office, and whoever was not at their desk got a black mark against them."

"I only stayed because I was already there and took a day off from my job to interview. Not to make anyone else look bad." Why am I justifying myself to this guy?

"No matter. Nowadays, you're referred to as the Blizzard Bug Fixer." Rex's dagger eyes pointed straight at her. He did that weird lip thing again.

"Is that better?" Christina stared right back at him. Was it he who made up the belittling moniker?

"It certainly is," Abby answered, "and that's exactly why I asked to have you come out with us. We've been stuck here since last week because the hospital named only a few core trainers, leaving no one to train the ER and night shift, so we've been tag teaming training night and day. And not getting any fixes done."

"Thank you for requesting me?" Christina half smiled, unconvinced she should be grateful.

"You can do the fixes, even train the reg clerks if you like," Rex said.

"Whatever you need me to do. I haven't done training, but I'm willing to try. Especially since I once worked in the ER. Maybe that will help."

"You worked in the ER too?" Rex leaned back in exaggerated shock. "I suppose you also juggle knives?" Rex rolled his eyes and smirked at the bored bartender, who suddenly perked up and moved closer to them, arranging limes.

"Not in my skill set. Yet, that is," Christina responded. "Right now, I'll have to muster all my skills to get to my room and get a good night's sleep before tomorrow. When are we starting?"

"I'm leaving at 7:30 for Swedish. I'll grab breakfast there, then meet the IT folks at eight," said Rex.

Christina downed the last sip of her Molson, leaving two dollars on the bar to cover her tab and a tip. "OK. I'll meet you in the lobby. No knives, I promise."

Rex showed his uneven teeth in a wry smile and raised his glass toward Christina. He reminded her of her brother Sebastian. *I'll need to be careful around him.*

"I'll see both of you at the end of your day and will take evening shift. G'night!" Abby hurried down the hall, leaving Rex and Christina eyeing each other.

Back in her room, Christina sprawled on the bed. She hadn't told anyone she made it there. Both Drew and Mom would worry. *Do they think I can't do anything for myself?* She dialed a credit card call to Drew and asked him to let her mother know she arrived safely. Too tired to stay up and answer her mother's inevitable million questions about her first solo travel, Christina found it funny her mother had not worried about the Vegas trip. Then she knew why—this time she had gone *alone.*

Relieved that Drew graciously agreed to relay the message, Christina fell asleep with his voice echoing softly, "Goodnight, darling. I love you. I'm happy to call your mom."

Christina laughed as she met Rex in the parking lot Monday morning. "There must have been a fire sale on Chevy Malibu."

"Not a fan, but we usually get these or a Pontiac. In Indiana, they gave me a '78 Pacer to drive. Rode around like a damn fish in a fishbowl!"

"I didn't know those still existed."

"I gave Travel an earful when I got back. Next trip Alice made sure they comped me a Jetta."

I bet he did, thought Christina, hoping his scathing manner would improve as they worked together. Rex's tie was tied loosely around his neck, his shirt was unbuttoned at the throat, and his worn pants with a frayed hem met the ground as he walked. Is he cheap or just careless?

At Swedish American Hospital, the familiar scent of disinfectant greeted Christina and Rex as they entered the lobby. It was soon replaced with the smell of bacon frying on the griddle as they neared the staff cafeteria. For $1.45, Christina got a classic bacon and eggs breakfast, complete with jam, toast, and tea to start the day. Another way to save part of the per diem allotment—eat breakfast and lunch at the hospital. Gary had told Christina that if her daily meal expenses were less than the allotted thirty-five dollars, she could just claim the full amount without providing receipts.

Rex introduced Christina to the hospital IT team, who seemed relieved to have another person on-site even before hearing the plan.

"She's supposed to help us with fixes." Rex's dubious statement hardly masked his disdain.

Christina ignored him and went straight to reviewing their issues list. She noted at least a dozen items where documents printed incorrectly. Easy fixes, no doubt, but indicating Rex had not adequately QA'd his work. There were access problems—a user's profile gave them the wrong or incomplete set of functions or none at all. Several standard model reports had not been customized as per the site's specifications. Still more were missing data fields or sorted incorrectly. There were registration screens where prompts were inexplicably omitted. Screens showed blank or nonsensical error messages, making it difficult for a user to know how to correct unacceptable input. Christina rubbed her temples.

There were two fatal errors from Dayend jobs, halting the nightly process. The census job, a critical step in resolving counts for admissions, discharges, and transfers of patients throughout the day, would be top priority. The other failure was the master file audit, an important tool for system security because it told management who changed what in the system. Christina found it incredible that Rex had not corrected the many glaring and avoidable errors before coming on-site, but he hardly spent any effort dressing himself either. His carelessness explained why he was still considered an associate programmer despite his three-year tenure. After perusing the issues document, Christina found nothing she wasn't prepared to fix. A wave of satisfaction washed over her, and she was eager to get to work.

Rex had scheduled a registration class for 9 a.m. and suggested Christina observe and assist with questions the core trainers might have. Christina watched Rex demonstrate how to preregister a patient, make changes, then cancel a visit. The class learned to select a patient from the database if they'd been to the hospital before and carry forward the patient's prior information. Rex showed how to apply charges to their account after treatment. He entered a test patient with first name Darth, last name Vader, and advised the class to always use obviously fictitious patients and made-up data when testing the system or during training. Rex chose a cast of villainous characters for the demonstration.

When Rex finished, Christina acknowledged his work, hoping to gain his trust. "Great job! I think they liked the *Star Wars* data, and it kept their interest. I particularly like how you gave Vader the diagnoses of sore throat and laryngitis."

"Once you do this a few times, you've got to find ways to liven things up and entertain not only the students but yourself. Darth Vader's my idol."

"That so? Rex, if you want a break from it, I'd be happy to hold some classes in between fixes."

"Great! I hate dealing with these old bats. We have three more today, so you can do the afternoon classes. In the meantime, knock out issues."

"Besides the census job, what are the top priorities?"

"The print issues are next. Your boss, David Stokes, told me on my first Install that although we consider printing issues a minor thing because they're easy to fix, customers always consider them a big deal. Everyone sees them. They scream 'error' to a user, even if all the processing in the system works like a charm. The visual component matters."

"That's good advice! David really cares about our clients. I've seen him jump on a call to iron things out with an irate client, saving a team member from being raked over the coals, only to have the client laughing and thanking him in minutes."

"Yeah. I'd kill to have David as my manager. How'd you get so lucky?"

"Say, Rex, why don't we record issues on a spreadsheet and add a priority column so we can sort it? If the client designates a priority, we can note it there, or we can determine priority based on the print rule you just mentioned or other criteria. What do you think?"

"I think I wish I thought of that!"

Christina converted the text document to a spreadsheet and added a few more columns for additional information. Rex said to give top priority to any system job that aborted, any Dayend job that failed or prevented processing of a subsequent job, and print issues because of their client visibility. Lesser priority was assigned to menu or master file changes, adding new users, reports, and screen changes. They were satisfied with their plan and set to work on the fixes. Christina took the census and print issues, and Rex started on the rest.

Though she appeared outwardly confident and welcoming to the users in her first core-trainers' class, Christina's stomach was flip-flopping. These students had been selected by their management for their years of experience at the hospital and respect from their colleagues. Most were old enough to be her parents, or grandparents. She greeted each by name as they entered the IT classroom, thanks to the picture badge each wore around their neck. Introducing herself, she shared a little about her work in the ER. Christina told them of her past experience registering patients with an ancient typewriter and having to rely heavily on the handy bottle of White-Out liquid.

The class responded to her warm and candid introduction. Instead of using Rex's villain theme, she choose names for test patients from movies she thought this demographic might know—Martin Brody, occupation: beach town police chief, and diagnosis: shark bite; mob boss Don Corleone, in for a gunshot wound to the head; and Flashdancer, presenting with a broken ankle. Her students used pop culture examples to have fun learning the system. At the end of the day, Rex and Christina met with Abby to brief her on their progress.

"We fixed the census resolution job and made a dent in the backlog of printing issues." Rex claimed a joint effort though he was conducting class while Christina did the work. "Christina led the afternoon training classes while I started in on reports and functions. I decided we needed a better tracking system for our issues and created an issues spreadsheet, with columns for details like priority, responsible party, status, and notes," hissed Rex. He licked his lip, like a snake before striking its prey.

Christina had been nodding along, ignoring his allusion to a team effort, until his egregious claim about improving the issues tracking. She winced at the scalding lie and caught her breath, then stared at Rex with a set jaw, waiting for him to correct his false claim, but he didn't.

He basked in Abby's admiration. "Rex, that's fantastic! Why haven't we been doing that all along? It sure beats the handwritten annotations we have on our printed list. It'll be convenient to sort and filter issues as we update the client or Corporate. You've earned your free dinner today, for sure."

Rex wagged a finger close to Abby's face. "You be sure to tell my boss, Abby."

Christina's eyes shifted to study the tile grout on the floor of the stuffy conference room. Those accolades should have been mine, and Rex knows it. He gloated with false pride. She said nothing while her stomach churned.

She was cast back a few years, in the backyard with Sebastian. Her parents had left within minutes of hearing news of the accidental death of their mother's only brother, leaving Sebastian in charge. Christina seethed, stopping with the garden hose poised midair, while he proudly told her parents that he gathered the siblings around and convinced the children to chip in and clean the entire house while their parents were away. It was Christina, however, who had rallied the family to surprise their parents with a clean and orderly house to return to, while her brother camped out in the basement with his buddies for the night, watching a game, munching on snacks, and drinking beer. The next morning she reminded Sebastian, as he staggered up the stairs, to dispose of the empty bottles and trash his gang had left downstairs, because she and the others had done enough work. Only then did Sebastian look around, noticing all they'd done without his help. "I guess I trained you well." He sneered with the sarcasm of a lazy foreman.

She remembered her mother, visibly shaken and grieving, walking through the immaculate house, which had been left in a state of disarray two days ago, and into the manicured yard. Her mother looked side to side in wonder. "Wh-who did all this? Who cleaned the house and spruced up the yard?"

"Aw, it was nothing, Ma." Sebastian feigned a modest grin. "I thought it was the least we could do with all you had going on."

Their mother was speechless, but their father was not. He seemed taken aback by Sebastian's uncharacteristically gentle concern.

"That's quite a responsible thing to do, son. Your mother has been through a lot these couple days, and the last thing she needed was to come home to a wreck."

Christina couldn't believe they fell for Sebastian's lie. She dropped the running hose right where she was to go to her mother and hug her, then she rode down the street to Terry's. Sebastian watched her retreat. She felt the smug glare of his deception burning through her as it always did when his greedy ego snatched the limelight from its rightful owner. She spat in disgust. She'd told Terry, "I wish I had spoken up then and told my parents what really happened, but the thought of Sebastian pouncing on me in retaliation as soon as he had a chance made me swallow my words."

"Earth to Christina… You with us?" Abby said, jolting Christina into the present.

Christina nodded slightly, and Rex's chair screeched across the tile floor as he got up and said, "You take it from here, Abby. I'm ready for dinner."

The radio saved Christina from having to speak on the ride back to Rockford's Finest. She rolled down the window and gazed out at the wooded landscape passing by. How do trees stand so tall and strong despite the constant barrage of winds?

"I've made other plans tonight, Rex. You go on to dinner without me."

I'd die before eating alone with Rex.

On Wednesday, her last day at Swedish, Christina took over the remaining core-training classes, leaving Rex to work on issues without her. She welcomed the chance to teach the classes and hear directly from the users how they felt about the system. Later that day, she met with the Rockford team leader, Melanie McCormack, to get acquainted before showing up to work the next day. The hardware was finally installed, and Melanie's team had begun the database load. On Thursday they'd proceed with testing the system.

Christina met Melanie's team Thursday morning, and they divided testing roles among the four programmers. A few hours later they brought up the system and gave the first users access. The team staggered their breaks to provide continuous coverage. When Christina returned from a late lunch, her head was throbbing, her body was damp with sweat, and her throat felt like it was clogged with cotton balls. As the afternoon wore on, her fingers stumbled on the keyboard.

Melanie looked over and said, "Christina, are you OK? You're as white as the walls!"

"No, I think I'm running a fever. I haven't felt well since lunch."

"Why don't you go back to the hotel and rest up. We'll finish out today without you."

"I hate to leave the team in a lurch."

"Don't worry. We can't have all of us getting ill now, can we."

She spent the next twenty-four hours sick in the hotel room. Quarantined, Christina wanted nothing more than to be home in her bed instead of being stashed away in the damp room at Rockford's Finest. She resisted the urge to call her mother who she knew would offer a sympathetic ear and whose soothing voice could comfort her like a steaming bowl of vegetable pastina.

What self-respecting adult calls their mother from a business trip to complain of a sore throat? No, I can't. When I called her from Bloomfield that time I was sick, Mom insisted I drive home. She hung up in a huff after telling me, "You've made a choice to move out. I can't help you much from two hours away."

This time, Christina dialed the hotel desk instead, asking them to send up an extra blanket and a box of tissues. I'll call Drew later, but right now I need to sleep.

CHAPTER 21

"CHRISTINA, THERE'S A LETTER here for you," her mother said, and Christina knew she would be holding it up as if Christina could see it through the phone line.

"Who's it from?" Christina cradled the phone between her neck and shoulder as she unpacked her suitcase, which had sat for days while she battled strep.

"I didn't open it, honey, but it has a First State Emergency Services logo on the envelope."

"What? It's probably junk mail. Go ahead and open it, please." Her mother began reading.

September 15, 1983

Dear Christina,

I've been thinking about that day you came in with the patient, your neighbor, I think, who had the hedge clipper injury. The young man who was a baseball player. Your quick thinking saved that boy from bleeding out. I'm writing for two reasons. One—how is he doing, and is he back to playing baseball? Please extend my best wishes to him when you see him.

My second, somewhat selfish reason for writing, is

to ask about you. How's your new job going? I'm sure you are almost running the place by now and they're lucky to have you. If you learn as quickly there as you did here, you'll be their star employee. I'm eager to hear about the medical software product itself and wondering if it might help us out here in our little ER. When you are in town again, it would be great for us to catch up over lunch, my treat. I'm off most Saturdays unless there's a community disaster.

I certainly understand if you're busy, but if you do get a chance, please drop me a line.

Your friend,

Ali Aboud

"Dr. Aboud?" Christina stopped unpacking, stared at the phone's handset, and asked her mother to confirm.

"Your friend, Ali Aboud," her mother confirmed.

"Mom, he was my *boss*! Yes, he was friendly, and he taught me a lot, but he was *Doctor* Aboud to me. I can't believe he wrote to me."

"Nice of him to ask about Donny. Apparently, he thinks you saved Donny's life!" Her mother sounded proud.

"Mom, he's being kind. Anyway, read me the return address so I can write it down. I'll meet him when I come home next. Why not?"

"Exactly!" Her mother read the address and pronounced an exaggerated "*Doctor* Ali Aboud."

"Oh, Mom, I forgot to tell you I got sick in Chicago last week."

"What? What happened, sweetheart?" The chicken-soup voice made an appearance, and Christina couldn't help but smile.

"Strep throat. I started feeling bad late Thursday and couldn't speak or stand straight. I stayed in the hotel until I could fly out the next day. It was pretty awful."

"Oh, Christina, poor thing."

"My coworkers brought me food and even the front desk helped by bringing me extra tea for the kettle and blankets. They opened the cable TV channels for me, on the house, so I could watch MTV. They gave me two free movies on LodgeNet. I watched *Flashdance* and *Risky Business*! You have to go see it, Mom. Tom Cruise! I do like that midwestern hospitality."

"But to be sick in a hotel. How terrible." Mom's mothering instinct kicked in once again. "Christina, you don't have to do this, you know."

"Do what, Mom?" Christina slammed her now empty suitcase shut.

"All that traveling. Trying to make it on your own."

"Who am I, Mary Tyler Moore? Mom, you watch way too much TV. I love what I'm doing. I could get sick at home just as easily. Besides, I'm over it. I shouldn't have mentioned it."

"Maybe you can ask your friend, Dr. Aboud, what he thinks."

Yukon Jack's eatery and bar held a long-standing presence in the college town. Though it had been there when Christina was in college, she had never seen the inside. Christina couldn't afford to eat out as a student. She knew some rich kids in her dorm who raved about the place. It seemed more upscale than the run-down townie bars and diners and the Shipwreck on Main Street. Its patio dining and colorful umbrellas on the terrace invited patrons to dine alfresco. She had walked by it every day to get to work at the ER.

Today, she would be one of those patio diners. Dr. Aboud suggested they meet there, as it was close to the ER, and he could stop over if needed. She could see him already seated outside at a table under an umbrella as she walked down the street from the municipal lot. His street clothes—fitted jeans and light-blue wool sweater—threw her for a second. He looked more relaxed and less serious than she had ever seen him wearing his clinic scrubs and white coat. He somehow appeared younger, sitting back in a leisurely way and watching the flow of students stroll by. He could have passed for a graduate student himself or a young professor.

"Christina Como, how great to see you again." Dr. Aboud got up as she scooted around tables to where he sat by the railing.

"Dr. Aboud, what a pleasure!" Christina said, extending her hand. Rather than shake it as she expected, Dr. Aboud clasped both of his hands around hers and smiled.

"Please, call me Ali. I'm off duty now. And I still look around for my father sometimes when someone calls 'Dr. Aboud.'"

"OK, then. Ali." Christina unconsciously touched the locket around her neck and regained her composure. "It's hard to believe I've been away from the ER life for a couple of years. Tell me, how have you been? How's everyone doing there?"

The nose-pierced waitress appeared and took their order. Before answering Christina, Ali ordered the Blue Hen burger. She asked for a crab-cake sandwich.

"There are two new doctors on staff now, enabling me to cut down on the number of shifts I work and my on-call schedule. There's been a string of students who passed through for a reality check to see if their pre-med studies will bring the job satisfaction they envision. Few of them stay more than a semester, and few of them compare to you, Christina."

"That's kind of you to say, and I'm glad you are getting a bit more time off. I thought you lived there because you were there no matter what shift I worked."

Christina couldn't believe she was sitting there as a guest of Dr. Aboud. For four years she had walked by this place and disregarded it as out of reach. Now, as a guest of an esteemed patron, she took in details that for years she had ignored. The smell of burger drippings falling into the coals of a hot grill mixed with the exhaust from a passing diesel truck hung in the air. Then a whiff of pot as a group of students ambled by just inches from their seat along the patio railing.

"As a new physician I wanted to put the time in. Learn all I could. But now I appreciate the help and relief from my colleagues."

"Are any of the staff and nurses still there that I knew?"

"Many of them are. Pam still talks about you seamlessly moving between front desk registrar to suture-substitute."

"Pam? The clerk supervisor who was pregnant when I worked there? She always laughed at my poor typing! I was so embarrassed and almost regretted my choice of woodshop instead of typing in ninth grade."

"The very same. She never mentioned your typing. She still talks about your willingness to chip in no matter what was needed. The students we get in here now don't volunteer to do anything and just wait to be told what to do. They want to start in doing open-heart surgery, gripe about prepping the rooms, and barely glance at the office staff." Ali pursed his lips. He took a bite of his burger and focused on Christina.

"Please thank Pam for her kind words. I tried to make at least the registration process and vital signs painless." She watched students walking by the restaurant as if from miles away.

"Yes, you did. Treatment involves more than a procedure."

Ali's heartfelt regard for patients, together with his technical prowess, was evident to Christina the first day she worked with him. She remembered him patting the arms of elderly widows, making puppets for children from surgical gloves, and reassuring worried parents.

"The entire experience, from the time someone walks in the door, to when they leave with their discharge instructions, is trying and stressful," Christina said, "for the patient *and* their family. I know more can be done to improve the process, especially now that I'm seeing the inner workings of the hospital." She swallowed a bite of her crab-cake sandwich and sipped the iced tea.

"So, tell me about your work." Ali leaned closer.

"I'm what they call an Installations programmer for a new product called Aura."

"What does Aura do?" He smiled at the server who refilled their drinks.

"Basically, it provides a means for registering, discharging, and transferring patients. It maintains a patient database for easily calling up patients' demographics and brief prior history. It has a module for communicating orders to other departments within the hospital and printing requisitions to notify them when tests are needed."

"I can see how that would be extremely helpful for the hospital," Ali said, nodding. "But how does it help clinicians like me?"

"More accurate historical patient information is readily available on the system to whoever needs to access it. Less dependency on the paper charts. It eliminates care bottlenecks, reduces waiting time for an X-ray, lab work, or other testing because those departments get the request instantly. No need for couriers or pneumatic tubes to send requests to other departments."

"I could see if you came in before for a similar illness?"

"Yes, you'd see a brief summary of earlier episodes of care. For example, you could see if the patient had been in the ER just two days ago, who treated them, and their discharge diagnosis. Having that information available to you immediately or knowing that they haven't been in the hospital since they had an emergency appendectomy five years ago could provide insights into their current problem."

"That would be useful. Most of the time when our patients present, we have no idea of their history, their prior health, their home situation—nothing. It's as if they come in cold. We can only treat what's immediately known."

"There are many future modules planned. Pharmacy, lab, and radiology are being considered. Another benefit to the hospital is that by capturing orders, the system eliminates the need for a person to manually enter charge data. Our system captures charges and sends them over to the billing system at night. There were people who simply typed in charge data all day long to catch up on what was ordered and done yesterday. We've eliminated that."

"I can see where a hospital would love that, but not so much the employee who loses their job."

Christina wasn't surprised that Ali's empathy reached beyond patients to employees. "We offer retraining for new roles," she said. "There's a new need for system operators, for example. Interested employees can be upskilled and not lose their job."

"Good. So, what is it you do as an Installations programmer?" In less than fifteen minutes, Ali had asked more questions than anyone had ever asked Christina about her work.

She told him about the model customization and testing. "Much of the modification is done through utilities that have been designed by people I consider geniuses at HSA. Dozens of programmers use those utilities to customize it for the client."

"It takes dozens of people to do it? That sounds expensive!" Ali commented.

"It can be built for one hospital in just a few months by one or two programmers. Much cheaper than hiring programmers to develop an in-house system." Christina was already realizing the business case for the product and believed in its potential to change healthcare. "We also write new code when there's a feature they want that is not in the model. The part I really enjoy is designing a new feature altogether."

"Do you do this work at each hospital?"

"Much of it is done at our corporate office in Lenapy. We have a huge data center that makes NASA's control room for the moon landing pale in comparison. We build the custom system there and then travel to the hospitals to install it. We deliver their own database of patients, do final testing, and train a few staff. We go back a few weeks later to bring it LIVE in production mode once they're ready."

"You have done this in a few hospitals already?"

"Yes, I've been to several sites so far. But my assigned region is the West Coast. Mostly Seattle and LA, and I'm told we are now covering Alaska."

Ali's eyes widened. "Christina, that's exciting. I haven't even been in that many hospitals during my years of internship, residency, and practice!"

"I find it fascinating. You know, Ali, I was so disappointed not to go on to medical school. I thought my dreams of working in healthcare were gone forever. But this opportunity has given me another chance, one I didn't even know was possible. This is a totally new field where we use computers to improve healthcare. And it's really just in its infancy."

"I'm eager to see where this will go. Is there a product for the free-standing ERs to use?" Ali's intent expression led Christina to believe his mind was three steps ahead.

"I'm not aware of that yet. We have a product pipeline a mile long right now. Lots of wish-list items from our clients. You see, the company started ten years ago to process hospital billing. It now has over eight hundred hospitals using the shared billing system, and every one of them is a potential client for the clinical systems. The sales team is insane, selling what we call vaporware—products a salesman dreamed up but we have yet to develop. Maybe someday we'll develop products for ERs and clinics but for now we have plenty of work."

"I hope you will keep me posted on that. I can already think of what I would need automated or streamlined at the ER."

"Your input would be invaluable, Dr. Aboud!"

"It's Ali! Remember, we're *friends*, Christina. And thank you."

"OK, Ali." Her face felt hot. "I know the company has physicians who consult on product development. You can get involved with that if you're interested."

Christina would never have thought she might have anything of interest to say to this kind, educated, accomplished man. No one, not Drew and especially not her family, had ever regarded her in this way. Ali not only listened—he mined her insights. He asked meaningful questions, commented with interest, and offered feedback. She dared to think he might consider her a peer.

"Possibly, when they start looking at clinics and ERs. You'll have to let me know."

Christina's delight in his interest sparked a flurry of ideas in her head. Before lunch was over, they agreed to keep in touch.

"The idea of a collaboration between two industries—medicine and software—is novel, but this could revolutionize healthcare, Christina! I can't wait to see where it goes."

"Thank you for lunch, Ali, and for listening to me go on and on about the job. I sometimes get carried away."

"The pleasure is mine, Christina. Oh, I almost forgot! How's your neighbor doing—the one with the hand injury?"

"Donny? His hand is good as new. He missed only a couple weeks of pitching after you treated him. Now he's a freshman at MIT, studying computer engineering."

CHAPTER 22

CHRISTINA RETURNED TO the office Monday morning with a newfound fervor. The conversation with Dr. Aboud left her with countless ideas about what computers could do for his ER. She told Gary about his interest in an ER product.

"I'm sure we'll get to it eventually, Christina. Right now, though, the company recently bought a lab product to incorporate into the model and is looking for other systems for radiology."

"Gary, we are really at the tip of the iceberg here, aren't we?"

"You could say that. All I know is that the Seattle team is out there selling stuff we don't have. I've been on the phone with Margaret Green every other day talking about what exactly we can and can't do. Your site is one asking for the moon, and David and I keep having to say, 'No, no, no.'" He held up both palms in surrender.

"Could I sit in on those calls, Gary? I'd like to hear what it is they're asking for."

"Sure, I'll tell David, for next time. Programmers don't often want to listen to these demands because they're outrageous and it causes more work."

"Maybe those clients are just ahead of their time."

There were more accounts Christina supported before going to Seattle for her own Install. Baton Rouge was an interesting site because they had a billing system that had not come from

HSA, which posed unique problems when sending Aura's data to it. Each system defined the data in its own way, making it difficult to interpret by the other system. Much of Christina's work there involved reformatting Aura data before populating interface messages to meet their billing system's data requirements.

Baton Rouge itself felt like a foreign country to Christina. Everyone spoke with a drawl. At first Christina could hardly make out what they were saying. The pace of the IT and hospital staff, too, was decidedly relaxed, as was their demeanor when something went wrong with the system.

"Christina, honey," one manager called to her, raising a steaming mug of chicory coffee to her lips, "do you think maybe this report could be fixed to show the parish alongside the street address?"

"We capture religious affiliation as part of registration, but not the parish," Christina replied.

"Honey, not parish, like with priests and all. I mean parish, like counties or regions. That's what we call neighborhoods down South here."

"Oh, I'm so sorry. I'm not familiar with the term in an address."

The manager brushed it off while Christina racked her brain for a solution, trying to compensate for her ignorance by quickly accommodating the request.

"I can add a column for it to the report, no problem, and a place to collect it on the registration screens. Should it be a list to choose from or free text? If you want a list, I'll need you to tell me all possible entries—give me a list of all parish names—and I'll build a file to hold those choices."

"Oh dear, I don't know all that."

"Well, for now I'll add a new text field on the screen and won't make it a mandatory field, so it can be skipped. I'll add the field to your reports wherever Address appears."

On the drive back to her hotel that evening, Christina thought how kind the manager had been about the whole parish misunderstanding. Nothing like the tongue lashing from Sebastian she always got when she simply asked the meaning of a word. Six years ahead of her in school, her brother gloated over knowing something she hadn't learned yet, as if not knowing were a moral failing. He continued to demean and ridicule her until it became clear that she was a quick learner and he was not. The gap in their knowledge closed by the time she entered high school, and he flunked out of college.

Her oldest brother had never left their home state except on family vacations, yet here she was, finding her way through the streets of a Louisiana city. Spanish moss swung from overhanging branches of the massive oaks that lined both sides of the street. The town was deserted, with only the screeches of barred owls penetrating Christina's thoughts. The friendly southerners disappeared once the sun began to set, replaced with hidden but desperately screaming cicadas and insistent frogs.

Though Delaware was no metropolis, she felt like a city girl in the backcountry here in Baton Rouge. With the Maurepas Swamp to the east and the Mississippi River to the west, and breathing in the humid air, Christina sensed a constant soak of water smothering her tanned skin beneath her silk blouse. She tried hard not to think about the palmetto bugs that the well-meaning hotel clerk had warned her of. "Best to avoid those buggers," he said, handing her the room key. "The devious hiding creatures inhabit all of Baton Rouge. Else you feel a scurrying on your leg or worse, like somethin' crawlin' on your pretty dark hair." She gulped at the thought of it.

It was clear Christina was a visitor, or as they say, "not from these parts," but the hospital *Aaaah-Tee (IT)* folks went out of their way to make the HSAers feel welcome. The CEO, Simon

Deveaux, took a special interest in the interface and spent hours with Christina discussing the billing system and how important the feed from Aura would be for their revenue cycle. She learned that more than fifty percent of the hospital's patient mix were Medicare patients. When the government's strict reimbursement requirements were not met, payment would be denied. Simon told her private insurance would follow suit, though state insurance regulations could mitigate some denials.

Christina learned how a hospital stays in business from Simon. He painted a clear picture of how it all worked together, scattering a few French words and southern idioms throughout his personal mission to school Christina, all with an endearing Creole accent. She loved listening to his unique way of speaking and appreciated his guidance. He took a liking to Christina and tried to persuade her to make another trip back to their site.

The site was one of the most welcoming she visited. One shy operations supervisor even brought her homemade "prawl-eens."

"Oh, I don't take credit," the man said. "These here are sent in by the wife, a good woman."

She paused before popping the "prawl-een" in her mouth. Though his intentions were complementary, she thought, I'm sure his wife has a name. Women are not interchangeable like forks in a drawer. It seemed disrespectful to refer to his wife in that way.

A systems operator furnished the HSA team with fresh beignets every morning. Christina found it challenging to eat the pastries without dusting her keyboard and navy-blue suit with all that confectioner's sugar.

Just weeks later, in the Harlem section of New York City, Christina and Gary found themselves locked inside a metal-fenced cage in the attic of a historic hospital. With no spare workspace for the visiting programmers, the hospital rigged up a couple of workstations inside a locked area that housed medical record archives. She and Gary had to call a security guard to let them out whenever they needed to leave for meetings, use the restroom, or go to lunch. Cords and wiring wrapped around the workstations and wove between water-stained rafters above to an unknown power source. Once, glancing up from her screen, Christina caught a glimpse of something along the solid wood wall outside the barricade and gasped. She pointed to a stretcher with a large lumpy shape in a black rubber enclosure.

"Can that be what I think it is?"

"Holy sh—! Is the morgue up here too?" Gary walked to the fence to examine the shape more closely. "I gotta tell David about this. I'm OK with being flexible about working conditions, but this is too much! And here I thought you just found another bug. A real bug."

"I'm glad I'm not up here alone. Somehow the cicadas and palmetto bugs of Louisiana seem harmless now."

That trip precipitated a set of contract conditions HSA management drew up to ensure their teams had a safe work environment at client sites.

"Did you know we were changemakers, Christina?" Gary was all smiles as he waltzed into their office one morning with the policy memo in hand.

"I'd have preferred a damp, windowless conference room and no changemaker role, thank you. I'm pretty sure the morgue wasn't up there, but who knows what was in that bag."

Their apparent goodwill, despite working in deplorable conditions, left the site requesting more of them. The historic hospital was just one of a set of facilities in the city, and the health system's administrators wanted to bring all their sites onto Aura. Only a short train ride away from Philadelphia, those site visits were often squeezed into the schedule on a moment's notice. On subsequent visits, Christina wore knee-high boots and carried mace in her briefcase, but after that first impression, the IT director varied their workspace between a basement computer room and an unused therapy lobby. Twice he put them in a richly paneled executive boardroom.

Christina traveled on support trips until the month before her account was ready to install. She was eager to see her account, C-Wash, come into the Aura world.

When she held a QA at Corporate, she was overwhelmed by the participation from her colleagues as Aura's teams came together to help out. They tested thoroughly so that newbies presented the most solid software to their first site. A few, like Rex, however, got kicks out of discovering errors. Rex was known to squawk and make a loud fuss to ensure everyone heard him find an oversight. But Christina had done her homework, staying late into the evenings for weeks to bang away at her system and hunt down any glaring errors her peers might otherwise find. She was hell-bent on delivering a quality product. She wanted to make David and Gary proud.

Christina created dozens of test patients, including Snow White and all seven dwarfs, every member of *The Brady Bunch*, *The Partridge Family*, and *Happy Days* TV shows, bandmembers from The Who, Styx, and The Go-Go's, and even Jack Torrance from Stephen King's novel, *The Shining*. To lighten her mood and elicit a chuckle, she entered his diagnosis as "suffering from writer's block." Christina ordered tests for her patients, changed their addresses, added next of kin contacts. She pored over reports of admissions, transfers, discharges. She tallied census. She created fake employees in every department, from housekeeping to respiratory therapy, and tested their access to the system.

Adding her own name and credentials to the doctor database, Dr. Christina Como checked out medical records and dictated abstracts. She scrutinized screen layouts and evoked error messages, giving the system a full workout like no other. Gary tried coaxing her to leave as he shut down his beehive terminal and called it a day a half-hour after quitting time, but Christina declined, murmuring, "I'll be done soon, Gary, you go on ahead," her eyes glued to the black screen eerily illuminated by its green letters.

Twenty-three pizzas were delivered like clockwork on the day of QA. David Stokes stopped in Christina's office to wish her well and grabbed a slice for the road as he slipped out, saying, "I can't wait for tomorrow to hear how it all went." Abby and Rhonda, Rex, and Melanie came by for their test assignments. Gary, acting as Christina's assistant, doled out tasks to them and the others who came to contribute their expertise. Jack Walters, rarely seen outside his corner office, took a walk through the halls of Aura Installations and wished Christina well with her first account. She had no idea he took the trouble to know who was working on which assignments and was even more astounded he knew her name.

"Thank you, Mr. Walters. I hope to make the company proud."

She cringed inwardly once she got the words out. I sound like a schoolgirl brownnosing a teacher. It was common practice to go by first names at HSA. The most senior leaders were often referred to by employees with their first and last names. Only clients were shown the respect of honorifics. Their founder was simply "Elliot" to all.

Christina wasn't expecting the programmers from nightshift customer service or the group that deployed updates to the model system who showed up to help. A recent hire in David's group said he hoped to learn on her heels tonight and asked for easy functions to test since this was his first QA. Robert helped by monitoring system capacity, tracking any load or response time delays, and auditing a stress test when multiple users exercised the software at once.

A LIVE hospital might have hundreds of simultaneous users. If performance at her QA with forty people brought a system to its knees, Christina could correct any jobs that were hogging system resources and slowing everyone down before going on-site. Usually if there was a slowdown, it meant a job was still running in the background instead of closing down overnight or a job was looping incessantly. Better to find out here in Lenapy than in Washington. Christina held her breath when the buzz around the pizza died down and folks went back to their own offices and started testing.

Rhonda, Bryce, and Marshall offered to run reports and desk-check them for problems. Elena, Christina's old TA from college, pulled her aside and whispered, "Don't worry about tonight. You'll do great! I know how careful you are in your work! If you were giving out slices only when a bug is found, we'd all starve tonight."

Until Elena mentioned it, Christina didn't realize how tense she had become. *What if the system is riddled with problems? What if I missed something big? Will David Stokes regret hiring me? Will my move to King of Prussia have been for nothing? What if Dr. Solokoff was right—and I really am not good enough?*

Her spiraling thoughts were interrupted by Gary handing her a paper plate with two slices and a can of Diet Coke. "We can't have the guest of honor passing out tonight from low blood sugar. Once we get going, you may not have time to eat."

"Gary, thank you. I'm so nervous, I'm not sure I can stomach anything right now."

"Nah. Piece of cake. You forget, you've had the best mentor there is."

Robert glanced up from his screen where ever taller bars on a green graph showed increasing user activity. "And the best office-mate/question answerer too."

Christina's shoulders relaxed, as she realized how grateful she was for these men and women who'd shown her nothing but support since she'd started at HSA. These people are not critical like Sebastian or Dr. Sokoloff. I'm so grateful to not be dismissed or treated with indifference, as I am by my own father. David, Gary, Robert, Norm, even Jack Walters treat me with respect. They want me to succeed. They believe I can.

An hour later, there had been just two programmers who had come into her office, both with minor issues. One had found a View Patient screen that was wonky and another had found a typo in an error message.

"Gary, it seems woefully quiet. Why aren't we hearing anything?"

"No news is good news, Christina. If there's a problem, believe me, you'll be the first to know."

"Maybe they all left after pizza."

"Nope, they're here. I can see 'em hacking away," Robert confirmed.

Gary agreed. "Yes, I'm running census right now. We're running eighty-seven percent occupancy, and the ER is filled to capacity, with twenty-one patients waiting for a bed. From the looks of it, our teams have been busy admitting and registering like there's no tomorrow."

Robert added, "This is more than we usually see."

"More what?" she asked.

"More activity!" Gary looked at Christina and laughed. "They are desperate to find stuff, believe me, so they're going ballistic entering data. If they had to stop for bugs, there would be far fewer patients in your system right now. I'd say it's going well."

"I'm going to send out a broadcast message to let everyone know to inform me of any issues they've found so far. I can't bear the thought that I'll be inundated at eight o'clock with no forewarning." Christina sent the message out and drummed her fingers on her desk.

Marshall was the first to report.

"Christina, I printed order requisitions for five tests each across sixteen ancillaries. All I found was speech therapy had no assigned printer so their requisitions couldn't print, and the ordering doctor and family doctor printing in each other's field on the neurology consult req—the field labels were simply reversed. I'm afraid I haven't earned the half a pizza I had tonight."

"Marshall, thank you! That's a lot of printing you've done, but I'm not sorry you couldn't find more bugs. Here, have more pizza. Say, have you done any flying lately?" Christina smiled, knowing she could easily resolve those issues.

The programmers came by her office, one by one, over the next hour. Most came up short, with nothing to report. She scanned their log sheets to ensure they'd tested what they were assigned, and to her amazement, most had finished their task with few problems. With a dozen minor issues reported by the thirty-nine who had QA'd that night, Christina handed Gary the audit after everyone else had gone.

"Twelve issues?"

"Yes." Christina lowered her eyes.

"As in 1-2?"

"Yes. One dozen. Two more than ten. The product of three times four." Christina thought he was mocking her.

Gary hesitated for what seemed an eternity. "Well, all I can say is you must have had one hell of a mentor, young lady." His sudden laugh startled her, and her worried expression morphed into a giggle.

"I'd say we call it a night. A successful night. Good job, Christina. Tomorrow when we come in, we'll force Dayend to run and wrap this baby up in a bow. I can't wait to show you Seattle."

CHAPTER 23

"KOH-NEE-CHEE-WAH," pronounced pleasantly over the airport loudspeakers, greeted Christina as she exited the plane. For a moment, she thought her long flight had taken her to Japan instead of Seattle.

"Welcome to SeaTac Airport," the speaker continued. Gary and Abby were a few steps in front of Christina, hustling toward the Hertz counter before another customer landed the upgrade they hoped for.

"We'll need a decent engine to get us up Mount Rainier and over the mountains to Yakima," Gary had said before running ahead.

The Seattle airport was squeaky clean. Its immediate surroundings sparkled under a rare bright sunny sky, light bouncing off a landscape freshly washed by rain showers. To Christina, everything looked brand-new. Buildings and roads still bore the bright white of fresh concrete, contrasting with the surrounding evergreens that stretched upward as if climbing the lone towering mountain in the distance.

"Christina, you brought good luck!" Gary put his hand to his forehead to shade his eyes. "It's a rare day, indeed, when you can see the glacial top of Rainier from the airport."

"We're going there?"

"Yup! The wonderful thing about Install trips is that there's no pressure to hang around the hospital on weekends. So, between this week and next, we'll take the weekend to check out Mount Rainier. Abby and I have been talking about it for months. We've both been out here a few times but never had a chance to do it until now. We'll start the patient index load on Friday after we've finished our Install, and it'll take a day or two to run. By the time we return from our mountain trek, it might be finished. Or not."

"I'm still pinching myself that we can take the weekend off out here and the company pays."

"Don't go thinking they're looking out for us, Christina. It's far cheaper for them to put us up for a night or two than to fly us home and back to C-Wash again for the second week. But I do appreciate it, regardless of the reason!"

"I will definitely take advantage of it too. Especially since they continue with the per diem for meals."

"We can't exactly cook like we do at home from a hotel room. It's the least they can do."

"Gary, you cook? I didn't take you for the domestic kind."

"Not really. But don't tell Corporate. Even my regular Thursday night cheesesteak from Jim's is cheaper than eating anything out here. So again, it's the least they can do, having us live on the road and all."

"Tough life." Christina feigned pity, and Abby played an air violin.

As the three drove southeast from the airport, Christina gaped at sweeping views of Puget Sound disappearing between massive concrete piers supporting intertwined elevated roadways. Ramps were stacked three or more high in places. She marveled at the modern highway system and wondered why there were none like that back East. Noticing the absence of streetlights, Christina soon spotted the reflective grapefruit-size half domes that delineated lanes of traffic.

"I'm not sure I'd ever want to change lanes if it meant driving over one of those braille dots. I'm glad you're driving, Gary."

"Just wait until we climb the mountain. I'll have you take a shift along the switchbacks. We can drive up to about eight thousand feet where the road ends."

"I hope you're kidding. I rode in a car on Mount Washington once. It scarred me for life."

Gary looked in the rearview mirror at the sun shining over Puget Sound. "Let's hope this peak leaves a better impression."

They continued eastward, spared a harrowing journey over the mountains by a dramatic but level pass lined with increasingly brown brush and exposed rock sheers on either side. The landscape got drier the farther east they drove. Evergreens had vanished from the horizon, replaced by scrub bushes and tufts of faded weeds. In the three hours it took to reach the Yakima Valley Holiday Inn, they'd driven through several climates, from lush wet coastal to moderate highlands to semi-arid and desert.

Pulling her luggage from the trunk, Abby said, "I hear they're starting to develop a wine country up in the higher elevations. I think we'll have to check it out."

"Maybe we can ask Margaret where to go," said Christina. "I feel like I know her so well after talking to her for months about the account. I can't wait to meet her in person."

"She's one of the best field directors there is," said Abby.

"Yeah," said Gary. "And the hospital team I met at the spec review is nice too. There's Adam Olson, the IT director, a laid back, likable guy. Nothing ruffles his feathers. He has a small team and is a hands-on leader. I watched him lie down on the computer room floor to extract a bit of broken tape caught in the drive spindle. His operator said he couldn't kneel down because of an old knee injury, and Adam sprang into motion."

"That's refreshing." Abby said.

"Yeah, and he did it with a smile. Got up and dusted off his pants and resumed our meeting as if nothing out of the ordinary had happened."

Gary was absolutely right about Adam. When she was introduced to him, Christina immediately put her defenses at ease.

"I hear I'm lucky enough to get the star recruit, Christina, and I'm mighty pleased to meet you." Adam shook her hand vigorously and welcomed her to his office.

"I'm not sure who told you that, Mr. Olson, but I'm delighted to be here. I feel like I know you through all your data that I've pored over for the past few months."

"Got it straight from David Stokes himself. Now there's a straight shooter if I ever knew one. And please, it's Adam. No self-respecting cowboy goes by 'Mr. Anything' in these parts."

"I'm the lucky one, Adam. I've had Gary here as my mentor, and Abby took me under her wing at a few different sites already."

A black-haired middle-aged woman wearing a cobalt-blue shift and matching jacket entered Adam's office. "I see the party has already started without me."

"Margaret Green, always a pleasure," drawled Gary. "I'd like you to meet Christina Como."

Margaret flashed a dental-white smile and dropped an armful of three-ring binders containing the system specs onto Adam's desk, just missing a framed photo of Adam wearing a cowboy hat and standing in a herd of cows.

"Finally, we meet! Welcome, Christina, to Central Washington," Margaret said, clapping her hands together.

Fifteen years her senior, Margaret was closer to Christina's mother's age than her own, but she acted more like an older sister. *I can't believe my good fortune—working with these people on my first account. Did midwestern hospitality extend this far west?*

The week was spent loading and testing the software, getting familiar with the three-hundred-fifty bed hospital itself, meeting department heads and core trainers, and reviewing the specs that Margaret had painstakingly written nearly a year before. The hospital database disk packs had been hand-carried by Kip Carmichael, one of the Seattle sales team, weeks ago when he was traveling back from Corporate, sparing Christina the burden of carrying them aboard her flight. Her diligent work left more than enough time for them to be sent out early, unlike Marshall's or Rex's last-minute scrambles. Abby worked most of the week in the computer room, chatting with the field engineers and assessing the hardware installation. She found a drive to be missing, which wouldn't affect the Install but would be critical to stand up the system LIVE. Abby and an engineer tracked it down and installed it.

Gary and Christina loaded the software and finished testing earlier than anticipated, so they used the extra time to show Adam around the system. Christina demonstrated and Gary narrated the show. Adam occasionally slapped his knee or let out a "whoop-tee-do."

"You folks don't know how long I've waited for this. And it's pretty slick, from what I see in that demo. I've been here ten years, and I was the only one who'd even heard of a computer then. I kept planting that bug in our CEO's ear until he went batty. Then your sales guy, Kip Carmichael showed up every month for a year, toutin' Aura this and Aura that, until our CEO couldn't say no much longer. I'm like a kid on Christmas morning."

"You'll definitely be cutting down on all that paper going back and forth between departments," Gary said. "And save nursing time reconciling the census. Not to mention eliminating charge entry for the ancillaries—because it all happens behind the scenes."

"We have three nurse managers who reconcile census each shift. It takes them the better part of forty minutes. That's time better spent on patient care. And my CFO will be thrilled to know charges are sent across to the finance system daily, ready to bill soon after a patient gets discharged. Now our data entry folks are backed up four or five days, and that's after they receive the charge slips from everyone. The departments seem to take their good ol' time collecting those pink charge slips and sending them to us."

"You will also see less wear and tear on the pneumatic-tube system. No more having nurses and unit clerks sending notes to X-ray and lab via the tube. Though I do like the *whoooop* sound it makes as the tube is sucked into oblivion behind the hospital's walls and ceilings," Christina said.

"You can't imagine the problems we have with that tube system. One day it went down, and nobody could figure out what happened. Suction completely lost. Finally, rumor got 'round that night shift OR sent along a taco to a friend in radiology who was complaining the cafeteria wasn't open. A taco! Can you imagine? What a mess—and smell—for days. Darn jam was up in the ceiling above the surgical waiting room." Adam raised his arm and pointed at the ceiling tiles. "I'll be the first one to show up when they bury that tube."

"A taco! What a wild prank." Christina covered her mouth with her hand, giggling.

"And don't get me started on spelling errors and typos we see on doctors' names," Adam said "We got fifty variations of Dr. Brzezinski. There's only one in the state. He's a busy OB who pulls out every baby this side of Chinook Pass, noted on ninety percent of the seven thousand newborn charts we file each year. Fella's busier than a cattle vet in the valley. I'll be happy when there's only one of him in the list for folks to choose. No more clerks making up anagrams we have to decipher and fix in order to get those deliveries paid by Blue Cross. Aura will rein them all in."

Christina liked his colorful descriptions, particularly the cattle lingo. She wondered why a guy like him was working with hospital computers.

As they walked the hospital corridors, Gary and Christina saw Adam's hand in promoting the new system. There were posters telling staff to "Get Ready for Something Big," showing a horse and rider carrying a computer terminal headed for Mount Rainier, and "Climb Aboard the Train to the Future," showing staff in scrubs mounting a steam engine before it plowed upward toward the sky. The conspicuous propaganda always included a plug for the new system typeset in an oversized, forward-slanting font. It was big news around town. In this small town where everyone knew each other, the easterners stood out. People stopped them on the streets to ask if they were there to deliver the future to their hospital.

"You'd think we were celebrities, with this warm greeting in Yakima," Christina told Gary.

"We are. We're bringing modernization right here to Yakima Valley!"

Gary pretended to pontificate, stepping onto an imaginary soapbox, swinging his arms. "I told you before, Christina, we're the changemakers."

CHAPTER 24

THE WEEKEND BROUGHT the promised trip to Mount Rainier, which jutted up from the horizon like a single candlestick remaining on a dining table after a celebration.

"How high is it, exactly?" Christina asked.

Abby consulted the AAA guidebook she had in her lap. "Says here, Mount Rainier is over fourteen thousand feet high. It's actually a volcano, and towers over most of the other Cascades, except for Mount Shasta and Mount Adams. Around here, they call it The Mountain."

"I mistook the glacier on top for clouds in the sky." Christina couldn't take her eyes off the behemoth. "I saw it when we flew over. I was sleeping when the pilot made an announcement and woke up to see a gigantic land mass just outside my window."

Cattle were the only living things awake and moving when the three left Yakima to follow the Naches River up through White Pass and along the Tieton River. Gary's curiosity got the best of him when he spotted a sign for the Tieton Nature Trail Suspension Bridge.

"We're stopping here to stretch our legs," he said, jumping from the driver's seat.

A sign loomed large at the trailhead, hard to miss with its red DANGER warnings.

Watch out for rattlesnakes.

Do not approach.

**Bridge is not suitable for
small children.**

No pets on bridge.

**No swimming. River currents change
unexpectedly.**

"How small a child?" Christina's breathing became shallow.

They walked the mostly level quarter-mile trail until suddenly the bridge came into view. With netting for sides and child-size gaps between boards, this was more like a swinging obstacle course than the bridges Christina knew. The words *suspension bridge* had called to mind the stately Delaware Memorial Bridge, a multi-lane span that welcomed motorists from New Jersey to Delaware. But only forty feet separated this bridge from the white water beneath it, even fewer where the boards sagged in the middle, and it swayed erratically in the wind. Christina steeled herself to cross it. FlyAWAY was higher than this, and I can swim. She stroked the locket around her neck, saying a quick prayer.

Gary raced ahead. Christina gingerly navigated across the metal plates, hands outstretched, grasping the netting and occasional poles along each side. Abby inched forward behind Christina. The bridge resonated with their footsteps. Christina shuddered as she first remembered then quickly tried to forget the fate of the undulating Tacoma Narrows suspension bridge, whose collapse she had once seen on film in physics class before a discussion of landmark engineering failures. Picking up her pace and singing, she made it to the other side. Looking back at their trek, the three remarked how lucky they were that it had not rained because that metal path would have become slick as a luge track. Just ahead, the trail was flanked by towering basalt columns, black and sleek as if honed by masons for city skyscrapers.

"This was a good stop," Abby said, "but I'm anxious to get to the mountain. No more stops until we get there, OK?"

The trail was not a loop, so they turned around and crossed the bridge again. Neither Abby nor Gary noticed the sweat pouring down Christina's face as she got in the car, drew in a deep breath and laid her head against the headrest. The suspension bridge and the churning waters below reminded Christina that one careless step could be catastrophic. Though everything had been going well at C-Wash, Christina was still apprehensive about her first account, and with another few weeks before they'd go LIVE, a lot could still go wrong. One slip and she could be back on her parents' doorstep, her brother Sebastian spitting, "See, Christina, you really aren't good enough." Her heart raced, but Gary interrupted her spiraling thoughts when he said, "Hey, look ahead! There's the park entrance."

Approaching Mount Rainier National Park, the group stopped at the visitor center, picked up maps, and filled their water jugs.

"Let's do one or two stops at overlooks, then drive up to Sunrise Visitor Center where we can park and hike around," Gary suggested.

"Sure. The ranger said it's at 6,400 feet, and it's the highest point you can drive. There's another eight thousand feet above it. I don't mind driving a bit if you want a break, Gary."

"OK, thanks, Christina. Then I'll resume after the overlook."

Christina maneuvered the grandpa-mobile up moderate grades. She glanced at the turn-off lanes for runaway cars coming down the mountain from the opposite direction, deciding to pull the gear shift on the steering column into low gear. No telling if there was any gravel or slippery spots ahead. Then she delicately wove around switchbacks as they ascended, avoiding a look at the guardrail and landscape that plunged downward just feet from the road. After an hour's drive and only four miles from the visitor center, Abby asked her to stop at the next overlook.

"It's gorgeous scenery, Christina, and you have to see it before we move up into higher elevations and things change. I know you haven't taken your eyes off the road!"

They parked after waiting for a spot to open. Crowds were already forming. Visitors clamored to see the park before the first heavy snowfall announced the arrival of winter season on the mountain and park roads closed until spring. Abby, her Minolta in hand, rushed over to see a vertically mounted cross section of the largest Douglas fir found on the mountain. At thirteen feet in diameter, the disc had been cut from a 257-foot-tall specimen felled by a wildfire. Christina tried counting the rings to determine its age and lost count after 140. A stranger offered to take their picture, and the three lined up, dwarfed by the fir spectacle. Most of the trees lining the slopes were Douglas firs, interspersed with a few smaller cedars and hemlocks. Hundreds of them pointed, stretched, and fingered cloudless blue skies, their rough red-brown bark contrasting with the deepest of green foliage. The endless, dense timber stands prevailed up to an elevation of thirty-six hundred feet. Christina had never seen such prolific natural forests on slopes that leaned just left of vertical.

Gary resumed the drive. Afraid to blink for fear of missing a sight, Christina wished her head was mounted on a lazy Susan to take in the panoramic views. The road became increasingly steep and winding, and the car chugged along, using every bit of its six cylinders. They stopped at Sunrise Point where they could see Mount Baker, Mount Adams, and Glacier Peak through thinning crystal-clear air. Now dormant volcanoes of the Cascade Range surrounded them, rising in splendor. Tall grasses swayed and rolled like tides. The color mix of trees, snow, meadows, sky, and lakes fanned before them in a dizzying kaleidoscope.

Gary shook his head, "I was born in the Adirondacks, but I can tell you we got nothing like this!"

"I can't imagine a more beautiful place on earth," Christina marveled.

"It's getting near noon, so we'd best get on up to Sunrise and hike before too long. We'll need to start our way down by four o-clock to make it out before sundown," Abby said.

They parked at Sunrise Visitor Center and grabbed a hearty hiker's sandwich at the outpost before setting out to hike above the tree line. Determined to touch the snow on Winthrop Glacier, one of twenty-eight glaciers on the mountain, the three headed out on Wonderland Trail. Stopping at Glacier Overlook, they could see Emmons Glacier several thousand feet below them, its pristine bluish frozen field flowing downward to lower elevations. Its smooth ice was studded with truck-sized boulders and debris carried from earlier rock falls. Glacier lilies peeked out from patches of snow. Meadows of colorful paintbrush, pink mountain heather, subalpine daisies, and lupine spread before them like an artist's palette.

Christina caught a faint whiff of pine as she gazed down at the stands of Douglas fir at lower elevations, dazzled by the sage green lakes colored by glacier sediment sparkling in the reflected sun. Abby tried to capture the expansive view by positioning Christina and Gary in the foreground for scale. While the overlook was a feast for their senses, they continued up the increasingly steep trail, lined with huckleberry meadows. As they began to feel the air thinning, vegetation gradually disappeared and gave way to rocky gravel. Walls of gray andesite chiseled by long-ago lava flows flanked the uphill side of the trail.

Bounding ahead of the others, Christina froze at the sound of a raspy slide, followed by a feeble "Whoa" and thump. Abby, having stopped to snap photos of a fuzzy marmot poking out from behind a boulder, lost her footing and careened down the slope and off the trail. Gary rushed down the trail to her point of exit and called to Abby, lying motionless twenty feet below.

Christina picked her way back to Gary. "Did she answer?"

He shook his head, eyes fixed on Abby.

"Abby, can you hear us? Move your hand if you can," Christina yelled down.

Nothing.

"Gary, we need to get down to her. If you anchor us from the trail, I'll connect your belt and our jackets to create a line. I can use that to scale down close to her."

The makeshift rope got Christina within six feet of Abby, and with a few calculated steps, she was at her side. Abby's eyes were closed, but her chest was moving.

"Good, she's breathing." Christina examined Abby's exposed skin. A thin line of blood trailed between her sock and her pants. She knelt beside Abby and said, "Abby, it's Christina. You had a fall. Are you OK?"

Abby's eyes fluttered open. "Where's my camera?"

"Your camera! I think you may be lying on top of it. Before you try to roll over, let's see what you can do. I'll instruct you so we don't cause any harm, OK? Easy, easy does it."

"I think I'm fine."

"First, look at me. Do I look blurry or fuzzy?"

"No, just a bit dusty."

"I see you didn't break your sense of humor. Can you move your hands? Feet? OK. Arms? Bend your knees? Good. Can you turn your head a bit? Oh, that looks like it hurt."

"I must have banged my shoulder, but I can move it. Head's OK."

"All right. How about I help you sit up, nice and slow. Then we'll see how that is."

Perched precariously on the grade, Christina braced herself just below Abby and helped her into a sitting position. She was relieved to see color return to Abby's face. "Good. We'll sit here a minute, then see if you can wiggle your toes, rotate your ankle."

"Aaaahhhhhh, shoot. My left ankle is telling me it's here."

"You took a nasty cut on the outside of that ankle. Must've hit a rock on your tumble down. Your other leg OK?"

"Yeah, seems fine."

"I'm going to wrap your ankle to support it until we can get you checked out." Christina wriggled her silk base layer top out from under her sweater and used it like an ace bandage to bind the ankle. "Lucky for you, the cut stopped bleeding. We can deal with that later."

Christina looked at Abby's face, noting that her pupils seemed equal size. "Do you think you can make it up to the trail with my help?"

"I should be able to, though my ankle is screaming right now." Abby scrunched up her face, and Christina noticed Abby's eyes were moist.

On the trail above, Gary waited patiently and watched the women.

"How's she doing?" he called down.

"Good. We're going to try to stand up, and we'll use the line to pull ourselves back up to the trail. I'll stay behind Abby. We'll need you to hold the line and pull her up as she gets closer. Her left ankle might be sprained."

Abby inspected her camera. The lens had cracked, but otherwise it was intact. "My weight was too much for it. I knew I should have lost those ten pounds."

With Christina behind her, gently guiding her footing for three long strides, Abby grabbed a sleeve of the jacket line. Gary held the line's other end firmly.

"There you go, Abby. I got you from up here. Pull yourself along with your hands if you need to."

From behind, Christina kept a wide stance a couple of feet below Abby, prepared to catch her if she were to tumble backward. Hand over hand, Abby progressed up the incline to the trail, nearly collapsing onto Gary. Christina sighed as she stepped onto the trail.

"Wow, that was close. Let's take a minute here to catch our breath. I think we should head back to Yakima, though, and let Abby rest up."

"Agreed," said Gary, despite Abby's protest.

"I hate to be a drag, guys."

"It's getting late, and we don't want to push that ankle of yours."

"Gary, do you think you can break that branch in half?" Christina pointed to a fallen branch jutting into the trail just ahead.

"'Course. Maybe not with my bare hands, but I can step on it!" Gary trotted up to the branch and jumped on it with all his weight. "This good?" he said, holding up two lengths.

"Perfect. I'll create a splint for Abby's ankle. Can I have your bandana? I'm running out of spare clothes, and we'll need your scout knife to clip off any sharp edges on the branches."

Christina fashioned a primitive splint by placing the branch lengths on either side of Abby's ankle and securing them in place with Gary's and her own bandana. Then Gary lifted Abby to her feet.

"Can you bear weight on it now, with the wood supporting it, Abby?" asked Christina.

"I can bear my weight. It hurts, but my pride is hurt more. Let's go."

Heading back down the trail with Gary in front and Christina behind her, Abby cried out only once when she slid briefly on the gravel path. Once they got her back into the car, Gary and Christina went into the Visitor Center for water to wash the cut and keep Abby hydrated.

"How bad is it, Christina?"

"I don't know. Since she blacked out, there could be a concussion. Her leg is cut but that should be fine. It's the ankle I'm most concerned about. Looks like a sprain, hopefully nothing worse."

"Ugh, I can't believe it. Good thinking with that rope line you concocted. How'd you come up with that?"

"My EMT training. I had to improvise here, having no supplies, but Girl Scouts taught me how to do first aid in the woods. I'm glad I had a clothing layer to spare and we could shed our jackets. Thanks for the belt."

"Glad to oblige. Let's get her back."

"Gary, we'll need to watch her for concussion. I think we ought to get her checked at C-Wash's ER." Searching her pockets, Christina frowned. "I want to call ahead and let them know we're coming, but I don't have any dimes."

She found a pay phone outside the gift shop and dialed the operator. "Credit card call please." She read the sixteen-digit card number to the operator and asked to be connected to the ER at Central Washington Hospital.

Abby rested while Gary drove down the mountain. Christina tried to keep her awake in case she'd had a concussion, chatting about the park and asking Abby about the photos she took.

"I'm getting carsick," Abby moaned as Gary zigzagged down the mountain.

"Can't help the road," he said, trying to make light of it. Christina had told him nausea or vomiting would be a red flag. "But I'll take it easy."

"No driving awards for you, I'm afraid." Abby still found humor in the situation.

Ninety minutes later they pulled up to the porte cochere at Central Washington's emergency room.

"Hey, I'm not sure I feel like working tonight, guys."

"You're not working. You're a patient." Christina was already out of the car and opening Abby's door.

Staff emerged with a wheelchair and rolled Abby into the vestibule. A nurse thanked them for the heads-up on Abby's situation. Meanwhile, the ER clerk had called Adam Olson to let him know one of his HSA team was coming in as a patient. Adam rushed through the entrance as they were giving information to the registration clerk. Abby had already been whisked back to triage.

"What on God's earth happened?"

Gary told Adam about Abby's fall on the side of the mountain.

"It's a wonder you could get her back to the car at Sunrise." Adam shook his head so hard the cowboy hat nearly toppled off. He caught it and held it to his chest.

"It was so nice of you to meet us here, Adam. I'm sorry we interrupted your Saturday evening," said Christina.

"No worries, there. My ranch is just a few paces down the road. My wife insisted I come when we found out something happened. I want to make sure they patch up our girl good as new!" He disappeared behind Staff Only doors. Gary and Christina took a seat in the waiting room.

"What a day! I didn't realize how tired I was." Christina slumped in a stiff chair.

"And I'm starved. But I'm sure glad we got to see a glacier at that lookout!"

Just then Adam emerged from the treatment area and motioned for them to come over. "Doc wants to know how you found a park medic up on the mountain."

Gary glanced at Christina and said, "Uh, no medic. Christina wrapped her ankle, cleaned the cut, and assessed her other limbs. Made the splint. Even noted her eyes, err, I mean, pupils, looked good but wanted to watch for concussion."

"She felt nauseous on the ride back," Christina added.

Adam Olson regarded Christina. "You don't say! How's it you knew what to do?"

Looking down at the floor, Christina mumbled, "I once was an EMT and a Girl Scout."

Adam spun around and dashed back through the doors, returning moments later with a smiling resident beside him.

"You the Girl Scout?" the doctor asked, eyeing Christina.

"Uh, yes, that would be me." Christina looked at Adam's cowboy hat and wanted to crawl into it. *Funny he chose to ignore the EMT reference and instead made fun of my Girl Scout experience.*

"Well, young lady, I must say I never had a patient come in with a fir branch splint, but it did the job just fine. I think the ankle is sprained, not broken. Abby's in X-ray now to be sure. Here's the silk underwear—I mean ace bandage—that you used to wrap it." He winked dramatically.

Christina grabbed the silk top from his hand and shoved it into her pocket. She said nothing in response but wondered if he had inherited two copies of the condescension gene.

"No stitches needed for the laceration, it was neat and clean. It'll heal up good as new with a few butterfly closures. The brief blackout is a concern so we're doing a head scan to be safe. Likely a mild concussion. Your friend is lucky you were there. I know there's not much in terms of medical care on the mountain, because they often end up here. We're the closest facility east of the park. Let me know if you ever need a job."

Adam put up his hand. "Now, wait a minute, Doc. We need her to put in our new system."

"Thank you, Doctor. Will she be OK to fly home?" Christina asked.

"Assuming the X-ray and CAT scan are clear, she should rest for a couple days. We'll give her crutches. She'll be clear to resume normal activities as long as she can remain off that foot."

"Oh good. We'll put her to work as soon as she can." Gary smiled. "Adam, do you have any workstations we can hook up in Abby's room?"

CHAPTER 25

MOVING AURA INTO production happened a few weeks later. C-Wash, with Margaret's help, efficiently scheduled a hundred core trainers who went on to teach the remaining employees. They were ready, thanks to Adam's careful planning. When Christina had talked to him to confirm the plans for LIVE a few days before flying out to Seattle for their second trip, he minimized his efforts.

"Christina, I'm a cattleman outside the hospital. I'm used to rounding up eighty head of steer day in and day out. Just got to show 'em the way from A to B. That's all I did here. Our nurses and techs and admit clerks are lambs compared to my herd and a lot smarter too."

He gave them credit for learning the system. Christina admired Adam's faith in his staff, in stark contrast to Opdenaker's and Garcia's disparaging remarks about Southern Nevada's employees. How'd they put it? Oh yes. "How will any of them get this right?"

"Yes, Adam, I noticed that myself during the Install training. They caught on quickly and seemed eager to learn all they could. They'll be more than ready to go LIVE next week."

The way people talk says a lot about them, Christina was learning, and she vowed to craft her words as positively, if not so colorfully, as Adam Olson. She also took a page from his book about believing in the good in people and voicing it.

The Friday before they flew out, Christina had gone to the first-floor computer room at Corporate to begin the final database load. She deftly mounted the reel onto the empty spool and threaded it along its path. Closing the drive door and pressing Load, Christina felt a surge of adrenaline. In a matter of days, she would cross this final hurdle as her hospital came up and started using the system she built. When she, Gary, and two other programmers boarded their flight, she finally let out a sigh, knowing their data was transmitting over the wires as they flew. It would be Monday morning before the file finished processing, so the group had planned a few outings in Seattle before heading east toward Yakima. Abby, unfortunately, was still on crutches and couldn't join them.

During an underground tour of Seattle, Christina learned the city had resided some twelve to thirty feet below its current street level during the 1800s. After a fire that destroyed much of Pioneer Square, the city was rebuilt at a higher elevation, addressing the frequent flooding and problematic sewage backup. What remained was a ghostly city under the city, a popular spot for tourists like the HSA group. Much of it had further deteriorated after it had been condemned eighty years before. Christina admired the resourcefulness of the original business owners, who simply moved their operations to the new ground floors, leaving their old establishments—windows, doors, and all—as dim basements of the now street level buildings.

Fascinated but anxious to return to daylight, Christina soon filled her lungs with the salty air blowing off Elliott Bay as they made their way down Madison Street. They browsed market stalls and watched fresh fish being tossed around by fishmongers at Pike Place, and they deposited coins in Rachel, a giant bronze piggy bank, as shadows from the Seahawks' Kingdome pointed east. After enjoying a meal of fresh pink salmon from Alki Beach, they headed to the Space Needle to watch the sunset.

Nestled shoulder to shoulder with her coworkers and two dozen strangers in an ascending room, Christina held her breath for the three-quarters of a minute the elevator took to reach the top of what could have been a location for the Jetsons. Giggling and remarking that the Space Needle was born the same year she was, Christina ventured out onto the observation deck six hundred feet above ground. Dazzled by the 360-degree view of Puget Sound, the Olympic Mountains, and Lake Washington, Christina glanced down at an unexpected glass floor and felt her internal organs implode. Gary hurried over to guide her to a nearby bench.

"Whoa, somehow I was not prepared for that."

"I should warn you the floor rotates, too, so if the clear floor doesn't mess with your head, the ever-changing vista might."

She willed herself to recover from the shock and emerged onto the outdoor deck once again, this time, snapping photos with her Kodak Instamatic so quickly she came to the end of her film cartridge and raced back inside to buy more film at the gift shop.

"I promised my brother Dominic I'd take a lot of pictures," she told Gary, who waited while she browsed.

As they stepped out onto the observation deck once again, a stiff breeze kicked up and fanned Christina's dress out and up, pinning it against her chest. Instantly turning around toward the inside wall, she adjusted her clothing back in place and then covered her face with her hands.

"I'm going to have to start calling you Marilyn, now," was all Gary said.

"Marilyn?"

"Yeah, Marilyn Monroe. That was quite an iconic moment. I wish I'd had your camera."

"You wouldn't!" Christina's eyebrows met her hairline.

"No, of course not. But you got to admit, it was pretty funny."

Gary stepped out to view the sunset and let it go at that. He could have made off-color remarks to humiliate her, like Sebastian would have.

"Thank you, Gary. You're very sweet." Christina felt lucky to have Gary for a mentor and a friend. His sense of humor was razor sharp, but his kindness cut through with the precision of a surgeon's scalpel. She was relieved it was only he who caught her at the inopportune moment. The others were busy looking out at the Sound.

Christina arrived early the day of LIVE to check that everything was in order before starting the process of converting Aura into production. The patient index database had successfully loaded after running forty hours, while she and the team flew to Seattle, toured the city, and drove through the mountains to Yakima. After an initial meeting with Adam and his operations team, Christina and Gary set to work.

They broadcast a message to all active terminals indicating the system would be shutting down momentarily and telling users to log off. With users on doing their last-minute training, a warning told them to finish up. Once everyone was off, Christina went into the computer room and performed an orderly shutdown from the console. She was impressed that Jack Walters himself had devised the process of ending jobs systematically, closing open files and finishing any background processes that may be consolidating data or removing data fragments. The shutdown jobs closed gaps in storage and shut down all peripherals, like printers and drives, until finally no activity was present in the computer's central processing unit. She likened its tidy resolution to the process of carefully wrapping a gift and tying it up with a bow.

"OK, we're down," said Gary, looking over Christina's shoulder as the last system message displayed on the console. "Next step is to copy code from the training region to the PROD region."

"Yes, I remember that from Southern Nevada. I also have the step-by-step instructions from the Go-LIVE manual, which I will follow to the T. No sense in relying on memory and possibly missing something."

She typed in a few commands on the console. The system spat back a lengthy series of messages, indicating successful completion as hundreds of modules were copied into PROD. Once all programs had migrated over, the next step was to manually declare which databases to copy.

"I want to be sure not to bring all our test patients into PROD. Someone might get excited if they see a film star up on 4North," she joked, and she specifically left out populated beds from the list of files to copy.

"Everyone but him, I'd say. Once the files come over, we'll run a census to ensure no patients came over from training. It should amount to zero percent occupancy."

"Yes, and we'll want to check the user profiles to ensure the latest new hires are in there. Adam gave me a few new names and their function lists this morning, and I added them just before you came in."

Within the hour, the software had been converted to production, and the reports showed everything was in order. Christina and Gary ran a few functions to validate basic access. They tried a few registrations and canceled out before committing any false data into the database. They made a few innocuous master file changes and loaded one test patient, "PROD, Test" into an overflow bed to flex the software. They immediately canceled the test patient's admission so as not to skew census tallies, which hospital administrators so carefully monitored. All good.

"OK, I'll let Adam know he can let admitting on in fifteen minutes, to start loading the current inpatients and assigning their beds," said Gary. "I'll hang out here in IT and watch for console messages if you want to go up to admitting and support them as they load."

"I'm so looking forward to this part. Seeing the system come to life—it's almost like giving birth!"

"Christina, I never thought of it like that. Hopefully, it will be much less painful!" Gary grimaced. "It's really refreshing to see your excitement about this. After a couple of years, I'd forgotten how much I enjoyed my first LIVE."

She spent the next few hours in admitting as they registered hundreds of inpatients. No problems were found. Later that morning, nursing managers came in to validate the system census against their manual tallies.

A gray-haired nurse wearing white clogs, pen stashed in her uniform pocket alongside bandage shears and a stethoscope, shook her head. "You can't imagine how long I've looked forward to the day when we don't have to go around manually counting heads, Christina. Do you know how much nursing time it takes to do that in a three-hundred-fifty bed hospital? By the time you've done it, some patients have been transferred or discharged, so it's never accurate. And now the system can do it in a matter of seconds."

Christina smiled, knowing the system would free up nurses to do more of what they went into nursing for—to deliver patient care. Gary had stopped in to see how it was going before turning things over to Christina and the other programmer who would support day shift and work into the evening. Gary would return later with Christina to run Dayend processing. The first Dayend run in PROD sometimes presented issues, and he wanted to ensure things went smoothly for Christina. Bryce, on loan from the operating systems team, would round out the twenty-four-hour support coverage.

They phased in user access to allow inpatient activities to run in PROD all day Monday, monitoring the system load and ensuring response time was maintained. On Tuesday they allowed outpatient and ancillary departments onto the system, with Christina present as they loaded their patients in, and on Wednesday they brought up the emergency room and medical records. By Wednesday evening, all user areas were on the system, banging away, as Gary put it. Christina couldn't believe the sense of pride she felt in seeing this come to be. She couldn't wait to call home and tell them. I'll tell Drew when I see him.

"Mom, They're up!" Christina exclaimed, forgetting the time difference when her mother picked up the phone.

"Christina? Is everything OK?" Her mother's voice sounded groggy. "I'm sorry, honey, I was sound asleep. What's going on?"

"Oh, Mom, I forgot it's after eleven there. I just left the hospital here, and we're three hours behind you. I called to let you know everything has gone really well in Yakima. My account came up, and it couldn't have gone any better!"

"Fantastic, honey, I'm happy for you. You're just getting back now? It seems late to be working."

"I've put in lots of hours this week—wanted to make sure it went well. And I wanted to see for myself how the system is being used. Most people at the hospital like it, though some are timid about using the 'machine.' I try to coach them through it, saying they can't break it, and if they do, it's my fault, not theirs."

"I'm sure they'll learn."

"Yes, in just three days, we already have a few experts. Of course, they've been well prepared and well trained. Adam made sure of it."

"Who's Adam?" Her mother yawned.

"Oh, Adam Olson is the hospital's IT director and a local cattle rancher. He's been terrific to work with and promised me a ride on a steer when this is all over."

"A steer?"

"Never mind. I won't keep you up and run up the long-distance charges. I'll call you when I'm back in Philly."

Conquering the LIVE was a boost to her confidence that Christina didn't realize she needed. Suddenly, things became clear. She found nothing more exciting than being on-site at a hospital, working in the microcosm of the well-oiled medical machine. The pressure to perform was purely internal. She wanted to solve their system problems and help her clients get back to their patients instead of fretting about a screen malfunction or printer jam. A few trainers commented on her dedication, thanking her personally.

Adam Olson was the biggest fan. He could have been a one-man sales team for Aura, enthusiastically promoting the system and the HSAers who came on-site to his colleagues throughout the state of Washington. His influence didn't go unheeded. Soon, three more sites out of the Seattle office signed with HSA, and both Gary and Christina were requested by name.

David Stokes was pleased as punch and started bringing Christina out with him for spec reviews. They'd travel to client sites after a deal closed to discuss any customization requirements and learn about their needs. Soon Gary led these trips, with Christina there to assess the feasibility of changes or new features a site wanted. They enjoyed staying at the SeaTac Marriott, especially in the winter months, and took advantage of the Olympic-sized indoor pool.

Though the spec review trips were short, usually two days long, they tried to schedule them so they could tack a weekend day onto the trip and explore the area. Christina came to know Ivar's on the banks of Puget Sound as the place for fresh salmon. The fish was a foodie's dream, but Christina's favorite part of dining there was the water view. Margaret had taken David and Christina to the restaurant after a site visit, and Christina made it a point to return for a salmon dinner with the captivating view whenever she traveled to Seattle.

Spec reviews were a different kind of trip than those for installing Aura or going LIVE. Before traveling to the site, they'd have poured over Margaret's detailed description of the hospital client and three or four notebooks of specifications, which laid out file contents and idiosyncrasies of that particular hospital. They would have reviewed and challenged some of Margaret's proposed screen layouts or reports, often devising more succinct or novel solutions altogether. Christina thrived on finding more efficient ways to meet the needs, and as David watched her scribble a design or outline a process that could work within the existing confines of Aura functionality, he saw her potential as a skilled developer.

It was in a meeting with the client that David first recognized Christina's unique talent for listening to the business or clinical case for the request and her understanding of problems from a user's perspective. Clients often told the field office they wanted Christina to come back to brainstorm ideas for new features. Sales started calling Christina directly to find out if they could sell features that Gary called vaporware, knowing if she could think of a way to do it, they could sell the customization to fund its development. David Stokes gave her authority to make the call as to whether it was feasible or not.

But not all trips were smooth sailing.

CHAPTER 26

ST. LUKE'S IN TACOMA was an account assigned to Mitch Donaldson, a new programmer on David's team. Mitch was one of the stars from the most recent round of Aura recruits. He was also incredibly modest despite his obvious talent. Christina went out for his Go-LIVE as the lead, having been warned in advance by Gary that the hospital IT director, Joni Savage, did not let anything go unchallenged. Christina thought nothing of it. At the first meeting to review the LIVE schedule, Joni started in by announcing the board was not behind the project.

"Most of them didn't support the idea of installing Aura and voted instead to replace their HSA financial system." Joni flattened her lips, glaring at Christina and Mitch.

Christina didn't take Joni's bait. "What was it that changed their mind, Joni?"

"Our CEO coerced, I mean, convinced them an investment in Aura and clinical systems would serve the hospital better in the long run." Joni's eyes flashed at them. "So, nothing must go wrong with this Go-LIVE. All eyes will be watching and waiting for an opportunity to prove their initial reservations." She pounded her fist on the desk to punctuate her conclusion.

Mitch became ashen, looking at Christina, who kept her composure.

"Of course, Joni. We will do everything to make this a success. Mitch has done a fine job testing the system back at Corporate and again when he installed it. Your own people have flexed the software for weeks. We anticipate an uneventful conversion." Christina's calm assurance lay before them in stark contrast to Joni's abrasive threats. Inside, Christina's blood pressure rose in response to Joni's attempt to undermine their work. She also thought it unbecoming of Joni to disparage her own hospital's CEO and the employees who tested the software.

"You'll be the first to know if it isn't." Joni glared at Christina and Mitch.

"We will actively monitor and address any issues. You can page us anytime. Our team will cover 24/7." While familiar pangs of self-doubt raised her heart rate and began to constrict her breathing, Christina squelched them with deep breaths and dissociated herself from Joni's verbal attacks. She outwardly maintained her cool, steeling herself against Joni's deluge of rage.

Christina viewed Joni as someone afraid of the little bit of authority she'd been given and wielding it in the face of others. Joni reminded her of Sebastian, who as the oldest, was the one their parents often put in charge of the siblings. Christina told herself that in voicing threats and making demands of others, Joni was trying to wield control, like Sebastian did. He'd shout orders and insist they follow rules he made up and which their parents had never declared. But he revealed his own inabilities when she or Dominic questioned him. When challenged, Sebastian resorted to using his physical size to push Christina and intimidate Dominic into complying.

But Christina knew Joni's verbal attacks would not escalate to blows like Sebastian's did. Though Joni may have intended to intimidate them, just as her brother tried to intimidate her, Christina wouldn't succumb to Joni's threats, suspecting she'd back down if challenged or if met with neutrality. Sebastian could only beat Christina down with physical attacks. She had learned to dissociate herself from her body, and he never beat her mind. Christina had developed a knack for responding to aggression with apparent confidence, and now she tried to muster all she could. Her resolve left Joni fuming.

But Joni's warning rocked Mitch. He wore a pained expression as they left the meeting and walked to the computer room. "She's really angry, Christina." He worked with shaking hands on the keyboard as they performed console operations and prepared for the LIVE. "You know this is my first account. I worked hard to get things right, but who knows what they might find?"

"Look, Mitch, you're not in this alone. We had a department full of people testing back at Corporate, and the hospital has been interrogating the software for weeks. We should have no surprises. But if we do, we'll take care of it. I'm here, and Rhonda and Marshall will cover the other shifts. We can call David and get any other help we need."

He acquiesced and they worked silently side by side. As they were clearing out test data before bringing Aura LIVE, Mitch gasped and drew back, burying his face in both hands.

"Oh no! I just wiped out the index!"

"You what?" Christina wasn't sure she heard him correctly.

"I accidentally deleted the entire patient index file from PROD. It's got some three million records and took over a day to load."

"Oh, boy. Let me check. Maybe it's not gone after all."

She walked to the console and typed in a few commands, scanned the system messages, and returned minutes later to Mitch, who by now, had sweated through his oxford shirt and wiped his forehead with a stiffly starched white handkerchief.

"Mitch, you're right. It's gone." She paused to think a minute. As the lead on this LIVE, Christina racked her brain for a solution. "But we can get it back," Christina said matter-of-factly.

"We can?"

"Yes. You know we run a system backup every night. We ran a backup of both Training and Prod environments last night in preparation for LIVE. We can restore the file from last night's backup."

"But that could take days!" Mitch paced the room, mopping his brow.

"No, it won't. With everyone off the system, and since it's here on the drives and not running over the lines like our initial load from Corporate, it will run faster. And there will be no need to worry the hospital."

"Won't we have to tell them?"

"I'll tell them we are testing the restore process, a necessary step to ensure we can recover if anything is lost during Go-LIVE. It is true—it's just that we don't always perform a restore on day one of LIVE. But Joni doesn't know that. We'll have to make up time by letting more users on at once when we do go up."

"Christina, do you think it will work?" Mitch stopped pacing.

"I know it will. Besides, I want to see a restore work in a LIVE environment myself."

Days later, St. Luke's was LIVE, and the site had no idea of the grave mishap that had occurred. Since Joni catastrophized even the slightest errors, no occurrence was more dire than the next. She would storm into the computer room waving a requisition with a typo or screen print of a function with an insufficient error message. Christina welcomed her and thanked her for finding those errors each time, knowing full well Mitch would fix them before Joni finished complaining about poor quality. By the end of the week, the restore had completed, and only a few minor issues remained. Joni, lower lip pursed, simmered quietly when her CEO congratulated the HSA team at the recap meeting.

Christina had informed the other programmers of the restore situation. They worked their shifts as planned, but Christina and Mitch put in long hours to make up the lost time from the restore. It was only after it was well underway that she breathed a sigh of relief, though she knew she had made the right decision to recover the lost data. She set up a conference call with David and Gary to share the events that had transpired.

"We've had a setback here at St. Luke's, but we've recovered at this point."

Christina told them what happened and how she initiated the restore to recover the deleted database.

Gary shouted into the phone, "Way to go, Christina! Way to turn a tough situation into a creative test of the system, all the while assuring the client that all is well. Testing the restore. . . now *that's* a good one." She heard Gary clap a few times in the background.

"It was a sound decision, Christina, but you should have let us know before proceeding. We could have worked out a solution."

Christina had never heard David sound this serious. "What other solution would there be?"

"That's not the point. Your decision was the correct one, but if it hadn't been, things would get out of hand quickly. You have all our resources back here to help you, and we could have managed the client for you. Your first lead and you didn't call for help."

Christina's stomach acid boiled up into her throat. "I'm sorry, David. I didn't think I needed help. I didn't want to bother you when I knew how to fix it." Her self-reliance was being called into question, and she didn't know how to react. It had been a protective self-defense from years of Sebastian's preying upon her inabilities and had helped her become independent. She'd become determined never to give anyone reason to doubt her abilities. But now that self-reliance interfered with her ability to trust those who offered help.

"No need to apologize. You took charge and knew what to do. I don't think we'd have any other solution here. It's just that you need to keep us informed as you go. Use the resources you have in our team."

"Of course, David. Now I know. I'll do a better job communicating next time and ask for help. And I want you to know Mitch worked like a dog to catch up."

"Sounds like you did too," Gary said.

"We expedited our schedule to get back on track. Mitch and I pulled double shifts and brought ER, outpatient and ancillaries all up on day two. Lots of coffee and those sweet apple fritters in the hospital cafeteria kept us going."

"How did Joni handle it?" asked David.

"Joni, to my surprise, handled it well. She doesn't discriminate with her distaste for anything. I told her we were taking extra precautions and testing the restore process before going LIVE, to ensure her board would not regret their decision to move forward with Aura. She thanked me, then went away muttering as always."

"I don't think she'll ever admit the system is good, but we know it is."

"True, but her CEO is enthusiastic, and he signs the checks."

"And Christina—don't beat yourself up over this. We expect to have to guide our new leaders a bit when they're on-site and handling any rough spots with the client. I was just taken aback at the thought of you having resolved the problem before we even got wind of it. In the future, just keep us in the loop. Tell us what you're thinking before you do it. Thank you for what you did and for handling Joni."

"I didn't want to let you down. And I didn't want Mitch to take the fall for this. He is one of the best programmers we have, David, and everyone makes mistakes. I tried to reassure him. I know how external pressure feels, and I'm sure Joni's threats interfered with his work."

Christina hung up and sighed, thinking about her failure to communicate in real time and not asking for their help. She was relieved they didn't make her feel less than. Days later, when she arrived back at Corporate, David called her into his office.

CHAPTER 27

"YOU'RE GETTING A raise, Christina."

"I am? I thought you called me in to fire me for not informing you of the restore incident."

"And how do you feel about snow?" David asked.

"Snow? Am I being transferred?" A look of horror crossed her face.

"I put in for a raise for you after the restore incident."

"I don't understand."

"You thought of a good solution and executed it well, all while managing a formidable St. Luke's administrator. Informing us is something I know you won't forget in the future. But few of our programmers would have gotten us out of that jam so easily, and I want to formally recognize that. I must get approval first, since you've been here less than a year. And no transfer, but you're going to Alaska."

"Alaska?" Chrstina tried to make sense of what David was saying. "It's nine months. I've been here nine months, David."

"Yeah, OK. Seems like the Seattle office has covered lots of ground. They're up in Anchorage now, and they want you to accompany them to Providence Hospital, help them seal the deal."

"But David, I don't know a thing about selling!"

"You won't need to. They want your opinions on the goofy stuff

Providence is asking for. Whether we can do it or not. It may make or break the deal."

"Alaska! When?"

"Next week, and I should know soon about your raise."

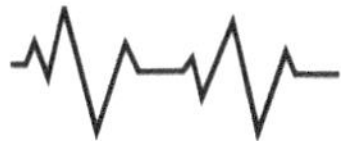

It took two flights to get to Alaska. United Airlines took her to Chicago, and then Christina boarded an Alaska Airlines flight to Anchorage. Arriving in Anchorage midafternoon their time, Christina thought the sky looked strange. Oh, I forgot, it must be dusk! She had read that the sun sets around four in the afternoon in December. The pilot announced it was a balmy thirteen degrees, clear skies, with about twenty-six inches of snow on the ground.

Margaret, who had gone to Providence Hospital with the sales team several times, had given Christina basic but crucial information in preparation for the trip. Margaret would be writing the specs for the account if they signed.

"It's a bit more casual there. You won't need to wear heels. I wear a suit with boots."

"Oh—hadn't thought of that, Margaret."

"The computer room is housed in what looks like a portable classroom in the parking lot. You'll be crossing back and forth to the hospital at least a couple times each day."

"No kidding. In the snow?"

"Yes, they plow it, but there's always a covering of snow. And invest in silk undergarments. You'll need a layer underneath your suit blouse even with a jacket on, and the silk is weightless and not bulky. Light wool sweaters are good too. You might need one under your jacket."

"Oh, right." Christina wondered how she could look professional if she was bundled up, wearing all that clothing.

"Also, ask at the Hertz counter when you get your car, and they'll show you what you need to do to plug in your engine, so it starts up when you go out."

"They're electric cars?" It sounded like something from a sci-fi novel.

"No, silly. They use engine-block heaters to keep the cars from freezing up. The hotel's garage has plugs for you to use."

"I never knew there was such a thing! I grew up around Philadelphia, and other than a few ski trips, I'm not really a winter outdoorsy girl."

"It's a way of life there. In any case, the roads in Anchorage will be plowed, but there's always a few inches of snow on the flat, straight roads. I can drive them OK, and I'm from Seattle. We don't get snow here."

"What's the hotel like?"

"We stay at the Hilton Anchorage. It's a nice high-rise with a pool and decent restaurant. Do be careful there by yourself, though. A young woman like yourself traveling alone is a real novelty there."

"Why's that?"

"Mostly men live in Anchorage, except for the native Alaskan women. Men went up there in droves the past few years to work the oil. The Hilton will have business travelers and oil men. You go anywhere else in town, and you'll likely be the only professional woman."

"Thanks for the warning. I'll be careful. I'll stick to the hotel, and I'll be meeting your field team there."

Christina was glad she had cornered Margaret for travel tips. Because of the extra clothing and unfamiliar weather, she packed a carry-on suitcase along with her checked luggage. At the last minute, Christina decided to stay through the weekend so she could ski at a local ski resort. When would she make it up to Alaska ever again? Though uneasy about skiing alone in Alaska, she fought back her anxiety, determined to take advantage of the opportunity, and packed her ski coat, ski gloves, and goggles. And she opted for her wool pants from the navy surplus store because her stylish ski pants wouldn't be warm enough. She'd rent skis at the mountain.

Christina was lucky her warmest clothing and ski gear were in the carry-on bag. Alaska Airlines lost her checked luggage during the connection in Chicago. Oh great! My work clothes are all in that bag. She spent the few days at the hospital alternating between her wool ski pants and the jeans she'd traveled in. The sales team made light of her unusual attire.

"No worries about your clothing here. We're happy to see you, even if you look more ready for snowmobiling than brainstorming a software enhancement." Kip Carmichael led the Seattle office and was known for both his sense of humor and his keen sales strategies. "Besides, there are so few women around, none of the men would know the latest fashions anyway."

If that was supposed to make Christina feel better about her lost luggage, it didn't. But after meeting the hospital leaders, including several nuns wearing business clothing and identifiable by only a short headpiece, she relaxed a bit.

The nuns shared unusual requests for handling the collection and storage of names, due to indigenous people coming into the hospital and staff being unfamiliar with their naming practices. The hospital's patients included a mix of English and Inuit and many other native Alaskan names. Patients often used different names on subsequent visits to the hospital, which compromised care, the nuns explained, because prior visit history couldn't be called up by the system if a matching name was not readily found in the database. Aura's name algorithms didn't account for reversals of first and last names, various formats of the same name, and other idiosyncrasies. To further complicate matters, often native Alaskan babies weren't named until they were thirty days old or more.

Intrigued, Christina took copious notes, asked for examples, and flooded them with questions about these unique circumstances. She learned that many locals had never before received institutionalized care. Others were wary of the hospital. It was also the first time she learned of health disparities—the health gap between native Alaskans and newcomers to the state was more pronounced than in other states. There were clusters of diagnoses reflecting common industrial accidents among those working the pipeline. Native populations showed high incidence of common diseases. The sisters passionately and diligently described their unique circumstances to Christina in meetings that lasted hours. They needed solutions that the model Aura system didn't yet provide.

In one of Christina's frequent trips between the computer room in the parking lot and the main hospital building, she spotted a four-legged, antlered animal ambling between rows of vehicles. She stopped, frozen mid-step, to watch the beast stealthily cross within fifteen yards of her position, utterly unfazed by her presence. Once inside, she rushed to tell her colleagues. They assured her the moose were harmless and would not charge unless it was mating season, which fortunately had passed. Before seeing one in person, Christina thought moose were about the size of a large horse. She was amazed to hear the Alaska moose might weigh up to sixteen hundred pounds with a shoulder height of seven feet. *If only I had my camera! Drew and Dominic will not believe this.*

Thanks to a friendly hotel bellman, Christina got the hang of plugging in her car. Driving was manageable though a bit tricky in the evening because the sun had already set hours before she left the hospital. What had melted during the brief period of sunlight froze up again to become surface ice. Roads were plowed just enough for a car to squeeze through the single lane flanked by five-foot-high snowbanks on either side. She found it hard to adjust to leaving for work in the morning in utter darkness and returning again in darkness after a normal eight-hour day. Her jaunts across the parking lot to and from the computer room were the only times she saw the light of day. By late morning the sun rose, only to disappear just a few hours later.

Working in her travel and ski clothes for days, Christina returned to the hotel Friday evening to find her lost luggage had finally been delivered, though by then she had replaced necessary items with amenities from the hotel and drugstore.

One of the computer operators told Christina about the best place for local skiing, and she couldn't wait to try it. Saturday morning, after a hearty buffet breakfast at the hotel with the sales team, Christina set out for Mount Alyeska while the others left for their flight out.

Driving south along the Seward Highway, dimly illuminated by the still starlit sky, the waters of Turnagain Arm on the south side and the untouched snow meadows of Chugach State Park to the north were barely visible. Less than an hour later, she arrived at Mount Alyeska, pushing her trepidation deep down as she found her way to the ticket office and ski rental. The helpful staff outfitted Christina with skis fifteen centimeters shorter than her own skis, advising her the shorter length was better in heavy powder conditions. A lanky teen behind the counter remarked when she told him about her 175s and asked her what it's like to ski Vermont's icy runs on Killington.

"That's the only skiing I know. We always have icy conditions back East, unless you ski during a storm when you can get a few inches of surface powder. You learn to cut deep on turns by the sound of scraping ice and release quickly before you lose control. I'm a bit leery, to be honest, about skiing here in powder."

"Just remember to lean back on your skis and exaggerate your turns. If you lean forward, you'll end up digging deep into the snow and get stuck."

"Thanks for the tips. I'm hoping to get in a few easy runs, just the green runs for now, until I feel comfortable in the powder."

She stepped onto the lift platform as dawn emerged, reached briefly into her jacket for the reassurance of her locket, and was immediately swept up by a speedy quad chairlift. *Now I know why there are no lengthy queues here like those back East!* Watching the sun's rays peek through a cloud mass, Christina took in the magnificent views of Turnagain Arm cradled by bluish glaciers and snowcapped forests pointing upward from steep slopes. Having skied in New York's Lake Placid, Killington, and even Quebec, Christina decided the difference here in Alaska was its vastness. All Christina could see, for as far as she could see, were white mountains. Intermittent patches of blue sky pierced the increasingly gray cloud cover. Yet, there were conspicuously few people. *Oh gosh, did I even tell Mom or Drew where I was going skiing today? There's no need to worry. Kip knew I was coming here. I'll call Drew after skiing.*

At the top of the lift, which was only halfway up the mountain, Christina stepped aside and pulled her point-and-shoot camera from her jacket pocket, clicked a few photos, then quickly pulled on her mittens. She checked the trail map to confirm she was on an easy slope, and slowly traversed the top of the run in a wide turn, feeling the weight of the powder on the front of her skis.

"I almost forgot to lean back. He said to exaggerate the movements, and I understand why. I'll plow right into a drift of my own making if I don't heed his advice!" Christina said aloud, after all there was no one anywhere around her to hear. "Where is everyone who was renting equipment? The chair lift is empty."

Taking her time going down Aleut Invitation, Christina stopped on the side of the run several times to rest. The powder skiing tired her more than skiing on granular snow. By the end of the run, she had adjusted to the new style and was comfortable with the technique. Before getting on the lift again, she waved down a ski patroller.

"Is there a better beginner hill I could try? I'm wondering why no one is on this one."

"Given the sky, we're in for a storm. Pretty soon you won't be able to see on this run. Clouds will open up, and we'll get ten inches within the hour. You're better off taking the Alyeska lift to the top and skiing the bowl. No clouds that high. Everyone's heading there."

After a frigid nineteen-minute ride up, with snow and wind pelting the tiny bit of exposed skin on her face, Christina wondered if she'd made a big mistake coming here alone. I can't let my nerves, or the fact that I'm a young woman in a strange place, prevent me from trying new things! As the only occupant of a three-seat chair, Christina felt her chair listing to one side. For a moment, she panicked. I could fall off this chair and no one, not anyone in the world, would know to look for me here, buried in a snowbank. Or ski patrol might find me if I'm lucky. Then airlift me back to Providence where they could wheel me before a terminal to work while I wait in the ER. I thought they said there would be no clouds up here. It's hard to tell it's daytime in this whiteout.

Just then, the chair broke through the clouds and entered another world. The sun appeared in a sky bluer than the Caribbean Sea. Evergreens swayed, their limbs dancing upon a powdery stage. Red, blue, and yellow specs crisscrossed the mountains. Here are all the skiers! The bowl was like nothing Christina had ever seen.

I can hardly believe this is the same mountain I was on just a few minutes ago. Here was a warming sun, fresh powder, and air that was crystal clear and snowflake-free. She peered at the upper bowl from high above, as if gazing into a snow globe after all the white flecks had settled. Scenes like this exist only on TV when I watch the Olympics. I can't believe I'm here.

Exiting the lift, Christina again checked her trail map. Runs were impossible to distinguish because of the open bowl, though she could make out regular, rhythmic mounds of a mogul hill off to one side. Better avoid that, she thought. "I need a beginner or intermediate run," she said aloud, not realizing there was a group of people nearby.

One woman removed her goggles and said, "You could try Main Street to the Imhofs and pick up Blueberry Hill toward the bottom. It starts out blue, intermediate, and ends easy green. We're doing that run now, if you want to join us."

"Thanks! I'm here alone and nervous about skiing the bowl. I'd enjoy having company."

"Most of the bowl is black diamond, or double black diamond, so you should stick with us. Oh, I'm Samantha, Sam for short, from Portland. Just follow me."

"Great, Sam. I'm Christina, from Philadelphia."

They whisked downward. At one point, Christina fell gracefully after relaxing into the slope and forgetting to keep her tips up. Powder had accumulated on her tips, and she couldn't extract her skis. Sam called to a friend from downslope, "Hey, Landon, can you go over and help Christina?" pointing with her pole to a snow-covered mound waving a pole.

A spray of powder swooshed nearby, and Christina looked up to find Landon perched just below her on the slope, smiling. His splash of snow just missed her.

"Are you Christina? Sam asked me to check on you."

"That's me. I forgot to lean back."

"Better take off your skis to get out of that mess. I'm Landon. Extend your pole to me and hold on so I can steady you. We can't have you roll down the mountain. Are you OK?"

"Thanks. Just embarrassed. I was so busy enjoying the ride and the view, I forgot the conditions."

"Why, conditions are great!" Landon narrowed his eyes.

"Oh, yes. They are," Christina said, stepping into the binding, shaking snow off her skis, and once again standing upright. "I'm just so used to icy, granular snow. I really have to think about what I'm doing here. It's almost a different sport entirely. And I love it!"

Taking the tram up to the upper bowl, Sam and Landon chatted with Christina like old friends all the way up the mountain, asking Christina about her work and skiing out East. They introduced their friends, explaining the trip was a reunion of college friends from UC Boulder. Christina and her new friends took a break from skiing to eat lunch at Seven Glaciers restaurant. Atop the summit, they sat at outdoor picnic tables, popping tops off bottles of beer and gulping down steaming bowls of chili.

"Sitting out here, I now understand why western skiers always look suntanned," Christina told Sam.

"Yes, but we have tan lines around our eyes." Sam laughed and removed her ski goggles to reveal white racoon circles.

Promising to look them up if ever she got to Portland, Christina left the group midafternoon to return to Anchorage before nightfall. We'll have to find a client in Oregon. Who knows, maybe I will go to Portland someday. I would never have dreamed I'd be here, in Anchorage. Or Seattle, or Chicago, Harlem, or Baton Rouge, either.

Her world had enlarged tenfold in less than a year. There were more opportunities than she could count, and they were coming at her as fast as she could catch them. Despite all that needless worrying about skiing alone, Christina ended up having a great day at Alyeska and making new friends from Oregon. Her traveling adventures far outdid the thrills of clubbing with Erik in the city. Those days seemed eons ago.

252 • SILICON VALLEY EAST

worrying about skiing alone, Christina ended up having a great day at Alyeska and making new friends from Oregon. Her traveling adventures far outdid the thrills of clubbing with Erik in the city. Those days seemed eons ago.

CHAPTER 28

BEFORE YEAR-END, Christina made three more trips. The Los Angeles office had a record sales year, and David's team absorbed some of those accounts. Christina worked a LIVE trip for St. John's in Oxnard, California, and held spec reviews at Bay General and Scripps in San Diego. Each time, she spent the weekends exploring the area, sometimes with her coworkers, other times alone as she became more comfortable with solo travel.

In San Diego, her team stayed at a new inn on the hotel circle. A cold spell blew in, and Christina adjusted the heater in her room after shivering had kept her from falling asleep. Suddenly, flames burst from the wall-mounted unit, igniting lacy curtains hanging above. She jumped out of bed and dialed the front desk, yelling, "FIRE! My heater's on fire!"

"What idiot pulled the fire alarm?" A shirtless Gary was standing outside in the hotel parking lot in his sweatpants at one o'clock in the morning.

"It's not a false alarm." Christina stood shivering, pulling her bathrobe tightly around her, as they watched fire trucks pull up. Firefighters sprinted through the hotel entrance.

"How do you know?"

"I know."

"Christina! What happened? *You* pulled the fire alarm?" Gary's mouth stayed open.

"Of course not, Gary! There was a fire in my room, so I called the front desk. They must have pulled the alarm."

"So, all these people, woken up in the middle of the night, out here in their robes, hair rollers, pj's, and worse, have *you* to thank for this?" Gary was laughing hard now.

"It's not my fault! The heater caught fire!"

"Who uses a heater in San Diego?" Gary broke out in a wild roar. "That's one for the books, Christina. Only you…"

After the trip to St. John's in Oxnard where Christina was training a new team member, Marie, the two drove up the coast and toured San Simeon's Hearst Castle. On the drive back, they stopped at a rest area and saw men with shaved heads wearing orange robes standing in the shade of overhanging oaks. They were selling baked goods at a stand, fundraising for their church. Christina sampled a free bite and bought a few bags of cookies for the ride back to LA.

"Why don't you open up those treats you bought, Christina?" Marie shouted over the wind blowing in from the open windows as she drove down Pacific Coast Highway. "I'm starving. We'll get back too late for the buffet at the hotel."

Christina tore open the bag and handed Marie one of the cookies. She bit into one, pausing to read the bakers' story on the back of the bag.

"Those bakers are followers of Hare Krishna. This tells the story of their religion and invites us to join them. They're complete vegetarians," Christina told Maria. "The cookies are vegetarian too. Does that mean no eggs?"

"Who knows? They're delicious. Cinnamon." Marie smacked her lips.

"Welcome to California."

Christina leaned back in the wind, laughing to herself, looking west toward the Pacific. Imagine that. Today, I met my first vegetarian in California.

David Stokes offered help to the Midwest office again, this time sending Christina on an Install trip to London, Ontario. She was curious to see how the universal healthcare model impacted hospital workflow. Midway between Detroit and Buffalo, on the northern shores of Lake Erie, Queen's Hospital and its universal healthcare presented a decidedly foreign experience to the HSAers. It wasn't the Canadian location that intrigued them. The sheer volume of patients adorning waiting rooms, lounges, lobbies, and corridors shocked the Americans. Apparently, hospitals offering free care were in high demand. Patients could wait months for appointments and sometimes resorted to waiting on-site for a chance of landing an appointment due to a no-show.

Because free care meant Aura's charging feature was not utilized, which shortened their installation process, the HSA team had extra time to discuss wish-list features with the hospital leaders. What Queen's Ontario wanted was a scheduling module that would facilitate efficient use of hospital resources, relieving overburdened clerks and harried clinicians from managing appointment demands. HSA, however, hadn't yet included scheduling in its development plan.

After C-Wash went LIVE, David had started Christina on a high-profile charge-interface project. She wrote code to translate Aura's charges into a formatted record that could be transmitted and read by a McDonnell-Douglas financials system. It was a custom solution that, if successful, would open opportunities for Aura to be sold to clients that didn't use HSA billing, thereby extending the Aura market considerably. Christina found it astounding that one piece of data could look so different depending on how each system defined it. A name in one system might be stored all together as "Last, First, Middle Initial," and as three separate data elements in another. She figured out how to map each data element to its counterpart on another system and reconfigure each element to match the required format. Programming interfaces, she thought, was a lot like learning Spanish and French. There weren't always foreign words that matched what she would say in English, so she'd figure out a combination of words in the other language to convey her meaning.

She recalled fondly her first exposure to interfaces in Baton Rouge with Simon Deveaux speaking in his eloquent accent. She called Simon to tell him about her project and thank him for his early lessons. Foreign system interfaces, as they were known, became a lucrative market for HSA. David Stokes built a team dedicated to these projects as demand increased, with Christina at the helm.

After all the traveling she'd been doing, Christina looked forward to taking a breather over Christmas to catch up with her family and friends.

I can't wait to go Christmas shopping! I'll have a bit more spending money from David's generous raise and a lot to celebrate on New Year's this year.

CHAPTER 29

"CHRISTINA, I'M PREGNANT!" Terry gushed into the phone. "Four months! Ryan and I are so excited. We're due in May."

Christina nearly dropped the phone. "Terry, really? I wondered why you didn't take champagne when you I saw you at Christmas! How are you feeling?"

"To be honest, I feel like crap. I've been sick as a dog, and I've slept more than I've ever slept in my life. I haven't even finished with the apartment, but that can wait."

"Oh, I'm sorry. Maybe you'll turn a corner in the second trimester."

Terry's pregnancy became laden with difficulty. Her morning sickness didn't end with the first trimester, and she started getting headaches and severe abdominal cramping. At twenty weeks she had an ultrasound that didn't reveal any serious conditions for her baby, though the baby was tracking smaller than typical. Weeks later, Terry's headaches became acute, and Ryan insisted they see her obstetrician. Terry's blood pressure was high and remained high for weeks. She was finally diagnosed with preeclampsia, a complication dangerous for both mother and baby. At twenty-nine weeks, Terry was hospitalized. Ryan called Christina to let her know. She drove to Allentown to see her friend the next day.

Entering Lehigh Valley Hospital where Terry had been admitted, Christina felt a strange sense of déjà vu. Christina had entered similar doors in dozens of hospitals in the past year, but under business circumstances. This time, her friend was lying in danger in a maternity unit where she could hear both the joyful cries of new mothers and wails of those experiencing an impending birth. Christina hastened her pace and, alone in the elevator, said prayers. When the elevator stopped at the eighth floor of Lehigh Valley, its doors opened to a pastel-colored unit. In dim lighting, nurses gathered and spoke in hushed voices.

Terry was lying in bed with her eyes closed when Christina arrived carrying flowers. Trying not to wake Terry, Christina glanced around the room, noting a monitor humming next to the bed with an eerie green line spiking erratically as it traveled across the small screen. The curtain was drawn, and Christina hoped there was not another patient beyond it in the next bed. She set the fragrant gardenias on Terry's bedside table. Terry's eyes blinked open.

"Is that you, Christina? At first, I thought I was dreaming of a sweet garden. It's hard to know what's real and what day it is in here."

"Yes, it's me. I came as soon as I could. Oh, Terry." Christina took her friend's hand, not knowing what to say.

"I'm so happy to see you! I'm incredibly bored here. I've been in bed for what seems like months. But at least the headaches aren't as bad now. Those flowers are beautiful, and they smell great." Terry pushed a button and lifted the head of her bed.

"Is it OK for you to sit up?"

"Yeah, I sit up to read, or watch TV, or just for a change of position. I'm fine as long as I don't get up out of bed. I get dizzy, and they don't want me to fall or bring on labor."

"So, you feel OK otherwise?" Christina looked at her ill friend, so vibrant just a few months ago.

"Yes, I'm more worried than anything at this point. It's good I'm here in the hospital because Ryan is away all day at work and at least here I have people helping me. They want me to rest as much as possible so that we can delay delivery until at least thirty-two weeks. That's seventeen days away."

"But then you'll deliver?" Christina wondered if Terry could hold out that long.

"Yes, the baby is doing well now and just needs to grow a little more so his lungs develop. They're more worried about me because of the high blood pressure."

"His lungs? It's a boy?"

"Oh, we didn't want to know at the ultrasound. But I think it's a boy. Look at this belly! There's a basketball in there." Terry stroked the ball under the thin white hospital gown.

"I just can't believe in a few weeks you'll be a mom! Do you have everything you need?"

"Right now, I can use something to read. I've read every magazine they have in the lounge here and went through all the motherhood books. I could use a beach read to get my mind off babies."

"That I can provide! I just read *In Search of Excellence*, but you don't want a business book. How about a Danielle Steele or Sydney Sheldon novel?"

Driving back to King of Prussia, Christina blinked back tears and felt her lip quivering. The thought of losing Terry was almost too much. The thought she might lose her baby was worse. After all, weren't she and Terry just children themselves not long ago? Though she tried to keep the visit upbeat and make Terry laugh with her stories about the hotel fire and monks selling cookies, the sobering thoughts of Terry's plight rattled Christina. While I was out having the time of my life, seeing the country, working hard but with little responsibility outside of work, my dear friend was fighting for her life and that of her baby. How could our lives have taken such divergent paths?

Two weeks later, Ryan called Christina.

"They've scheduled Terry's delivery for tomorrow. The baby is doing well, considering, but Terry's blood pressure remains too high for them to wait any longer."

"I'm glad you let me know, Ryan. I'll call her as soon as we hang up."

Terry sounded relieved when Christina phoned. "I'm glad we aren't waiting any longer. I was so worried about whether I'd make it to the birth, and I'm ready to focus on the baby. I know the baby is not as big as full term, but they tell me this is the best for both baby and me."

"I can't imagine what it's been like for you and Ryan, Terry. I wish there was more I could do. I'm sending you a hug through the line."

"I feel it! Thanks for the book you sent. I'm almost finished. I'll try and wrap it up today because I don't know what's in store after tomorrow."

"Terry, you know I'm praying for you. And I can't wait to meet your baby!"

There was nothing more to say. The next day, Christina kept watching the clock and checking her messages between the spec review meeting and calls with the McDonnell product manager about their data dictionary. She had trouble concentrating on her work and decided to spend the rest of the day testing. It required less brain power than writing new code.

Ryan called moments after Christina arrived home for the day. Diana had answered the phone and handed it to Christina with an anxious look, knowing she was waiting to hear about Terry.

"We have a baby girl, Christina!" Ryan sounded elated. "Terry is stable. The C-section went well."

"Oh, thank God! A baby girl! What's her name?"

"Danielle Theresa. She's a tiny girl, just four pounds, two ounces. They'll keep her here in the neonatal intensive care unit for a while, and Terry will stay for another week or so."

"I can't wait to meet Danielle! Please tell Terry I'm so happy for you all. Ryan how are you holding up?"

"I'm good, now that I know Terry is OK and the baby is here. These past few weeks have been a nightmare worrying about both of them."

"You get some rest now. I'll come see Terry on Saturday, and hopefully they'll let me meet the baby!"

The NICU was one area of the hospital Christina had spent little time in. She knew they held strict protocols for visitors, keeping the sick and premature babies safe and secured in the glassed-in nursery behind locked doors. She had been on a NICU unit just once, for a printing issue at Southern Nevada. Their chart documents didn't show the tiny babies' weight accurately. Weight in ounces was not shown on adult orders, but that level of precision was needed for infants. Christina's admittance to the unit had been like entering Fort Knox, she recalled, not only for security but for the babies' health. She also remembered seeing the tiniest of babies cradled in the palm of a neonatologist's hand, small heads swathed in the tiniest of pink or blue hand-knitted caps and handwritten name cards in each incubator, marked with the names of baby and mother. The NICU was a hub of activity, with nurses huddled around an infant adjusting breathing tubes or IV lines or drawing blood from a foot so tiny it could fit in an espresso cup. Christina immediately understood the need to show weight in pounds and ounces for these littlest of patients and logged on to a computer workstation on the unit to fix the printed documents right then and there.

Visiting Terry on that chilly first Saturday in March, Christina found her friend to be upbeat and beaming with pride, though moving slowly because of her stitched belly.

"I'll ask the nurse to bring Danielle over to the window so you can see her. I'm sorry you won't be allowed into the nursery. They won't bring her out until she's over five pounds."

Peering through the glass before the nurse went in, Christina tried to figure out which one was Danielle among the little faces in pink hats she could see. There was one baby with dark hair peeking out from under the cap. Without reading the name card, Christina pointed, "That one must be Danielle!"

Terry brightened. "How did you know?"

"The hair was a giveaway. She's got your mane, Terry! She's adorable."

"Poor Ryan. Danielle has dark hair, dark eyes, and my dark skin, though it's hard to tell because of the jaundice. But I really see nothing of him in her." Terry didn't take her eyes off the baby.

"Maybe she'll have Ryan's mannerisms or math abilities?"

"Right now, she sleeps all the time. They even have trouble feeding her—she falls asleep. If she doesn't start gaining, they will need to use a feeding tube. I hope she can gain weight on her own. And she needs oxygen because her lungs aren't fully developed yet, since she was taken so early."

Just then, Christina saw the IV bag for Danielle's fluids squeezed together, emptied of its contents. No nurses were in sight. Christina raced out to the nurses' station and flagged down a nurse hurrying by.

"Please, excuse me. The IV for Danielle Ross has finished. Can we get another one started right away? I know she needs her fluids. I was looking through the window with her mother, Terry."

"Thanks, we'll get another one going. You a nurse?"

"Just visiting. Friend of the family." Christina walked back to Terry, who was pressed against the glass, her eyes glued to Danielle.

"Terry, it must be so hard for you." Christina put her arm around Terry and squeezed her tight.

"I'm glad I'm here in the hospital with her. But when I'm discharged, I'll be able to come in and stay with her as long as I want. I'll have to gown-up to go in, but at least I can hold her hand, sing to her, and soon try to feed her. Ryan, too, can go in."

"It's amazing what they can do for the tiniest patients."

"These nurses and doctors are saints. They are so patient and kind. They treat Danielle like she's their own. I know she is in good hands."

Christina left after a short visit, not wanting to tire Terry. She reminded Terry to call her any evening, whenever she needed a break or wanted to talk. She'd be home a few weeks between trips and would be eager to hear how Danielle was doing and how Ryan and Terry were adjusting to parenthood. Terry had smiled weakly and grabbed her hand as Christina was leaving, saying, "You know I've always wanted a daughter."

CHAPTER 30

CHRISTINA FELT A heaviness in her chest as she drove to Drew's from the hospital. The thought of seeing Drew after they hadn't seen each other much in the fall and spent only a few days together at Christmas burdened Christina with guilt. He'd tried repeatedly to get her to come to Allentown, but her travel schedule at work kept her away more than she'd anticipated. He missed her, and she missed him, but she was so busy she hadn't called him from the road as often as she should have. She didn't want to have to apologize for enjoying her work. She hoped they could just pick up where they'd left off but knew deep down things were different now. She was different now.

And the new concerns for Terry and her baby left Christina sick with worry. Not only must Terry now recover from her own surgery, but she also bore the weight of not knowing when her baby would be coming home and if the early birth resulted in other, more serious, medical conditions. Though Terry voiced none of those concerns, Christina felt them, having lived most of her childhood with Terry by her side. Words weren't necessary.

Picturing the NICU's clinical staff in her mind, Christina thought how little was done to meet their specific needs and those of their patients. This unit dealt with both joyous and heart-wrenching events on any given day, serving their tiny patients, distressed parents, and all too frequently, bereaved families. Needs for small supplies, urgent requests, and specialized equipment and pharmaceuticals placed demands unlike those experienced on any other hospital unit. The computer system was certainly not tailored to their operation. She wondered what staff would want in a system for a specific NICU module.

A security feature that ensured only the babies' mothers and fathers had access to the unit or alarms if the baby left the unit would be useful, considering the military measures currently in place to monitor babies and visitors. Age-specific and weight-specific ordering practices could be considered in screening orders for medications, supplies, and other items inappropriate for preemies. If the system collected more delivery details and maternal health factors, clinicians could use that information for better treatment decisions. Christina's mind raced with possibilities centered around NICU-specific care and treatment. She cared little about the charges their care racked up and more about facilitating that care.

Drew was loading his gear into the trunk of his car when Christina pulled up to his apartment building. She'd come to watch his soccer game, and they planned to spend the evening together before she'd leave on Sunday.

"Hey. There's my girl. It's been way too long." Drew opened her car door and leaned in to caress her cheek and kiss her. Christina let his hand cradle her head for a moment before stepping out.

"Oh, Drew. I've just come from visiting Terry. I met Danielle! She's so sweet and so tiny. I can't imagine how Ryan and Terry are holding up with all that's happened."

Drew wrapped his arms around Christina, and she felt his strength lifting her spirits.

"I know Ryan's doing OK, especially now that Terry is OK. He says the baby is healthy, just small from being delivered so early. They'll be fine, Christina."

"It's just that we almost lost Terry! And now she's in the clear but the baby isn't."

"Ryan says as long as the baby gains weight she'll be fine. The lungs will develop as she matures. They'll bring her home soon."

"I hope so. Terry has wanted to be a mother for as long as I've known her. She's having to leave all the mothering up to nurses now. My heart breaks for her. I just hope Danielle gets bigger and stronger so they can take her home soon."

"It'll happen before you know it."

They let go of each other to unload her bag from the car. "Are you ready to watch the game?"

"You bet. The fresh air will clear my head."

Christina sat in the bleachers in a row to herself. A few players' wives sat on the bleachers around her, but they seemed to be paying little attention to the game. Kids busied themselves in the dirt, blowing bubbles, or kicking a small ball around the sidelines. Their mothers, eyes hidden behind sunglasses, seemed interested in neither the game nor the children, instead enjoying perhaps a moment's peace.

Christina waved at Drew as he moved into position before the game started. Drew nodded, then focused on the goal line. From that point on, he didn't look her way. She sat forward on the bench as his team scored a goal after he had dribbled the ball down more than half the field and passed it to a teammate. She jumped to her feet and cheered. No one in the stands reacted with more than a single clap, and she felt foolish. She watched the rest of the half with waning interest, using golf-tournament clapping when Drew's team scored.

What a good day to run, she thought. I'm here, sitting, watching Drew play. He hardly knows I'm here. I'm like a mother who arrives to watch her teenager's game when the teenager wants nothing to do with her and only to cavort with his friends. She felt out of place among these families of players. At the half, Christina tried to catch Drew's attention but couldn't as the team huddled. Retrieving her running shoes from Drew's car, she took off casually around the field and broke into a sprint just out of sight of the pitch.

I've never been a good watcher. As long as I'm back before the end, Drew won't care. What has Drew been doing all these months, besides work and soccer? I've been to eight states, moved into an apartment, and passed my go-LIVE hurdle. And now I'm supporting a friend in life-changing circumstances. Is he waiting for me?

As Christina rounded the woods, turning toward the pitch, a wind whipped at her face as did the sobering thought that things were out of sorts. She was just gaining her momentum. He was already at steady speed. She was not ready to take the foot off the pedal or relinquish the driver's seat. He was settling into gear. For her, there was still much road ahead. She sprinted the remaining mile.

I must tell Drew. We're at different places on our journeys, our separate journeys. I can't let him continue thinking it's just a matter of time. I just don't know how it could work and certainly not in the way Drew envisions. I love him, and he loves me, but is that enough?

Christina slowed to a walk as she neared the stands, huffing deep breaths with her hands on her hips. The run had cleared her mind of the cobwebs that had accumulated over the past few months. Her life, while seemingly at a crossroads, seemed easy. Her friend's challenges were only beginning.

"What did you think of the game, Christina?" Drew wiped his forehead with a towel.

"You made some good passes," Christina said, finally catching her breath. "Why don't you just take it in to score?"

"My job is to get it down to the guys who score. Tee it up, so to speak."

"I obviously don't know much about soccer. Looked like you could have scored."

"Sure, I might have."

Drew never was one to steal a show from anyone, though he easily could. "Did you leave after a while?"

"Yes, I tried to catch you, but you were busy. I went for a short run, came back and caught the end."

"Bored?"

"Just needed some air."

Drew introduced Christina to a few of the guys on the team. The goalie, who worked with Drew on the fiberoptics repeater, extended a sweaty taped hand to her.

"Ah, Christina. Drew's told me about you," he said as he wiped his hand dry with his glove. "I hear you're the coding medic."

Christina swatted Drew's arm. "That's one thing I've never been called."

"Don't mind him, Christina, he only half listens when I talk. I told him how you saved Donny's hand and that you write software."

"Drew's very proud of you." The goalie winked at her and said, "Definitely a good catch!" His hands encircled an imaginary ball, pretending to save a goal.

On the way back to Drew's, Christina again brought up Terry and the baby, and the NICU.

"Drew, they have no software specific to that unit. Those babies have special needs, needs like no other patients in the hospital. They are fighting for their lives before they've even started. The staff are amazing, patiently working on a miniscule stage, on fragile bodies smaller than a bag of flour. They work through tiny armholes in incubators smaller than most backyard coolers, to soothe and care for these little people. And the computer does little more than collect orders for bloodwork and supplies. It could do so much more."

"I'm sure that will come with time, Christina. Technology is exploding every day now."

"True, but these babies don't have time. They need to get stronger and bigger and go home to their parents, not live their nascent lives in a hospital incubator. Companies like HSA will come along and someday develop systems for specialties, but right now the focus is on billing."

"I thought you wrote clinical systems?"

"Our system, Aura, collects patient information and orders, basically to streamline operations and ultimately feed accurate demographics and charge data into the billing system. We aren't focused on improving care. At least not now." Christina stroked her locket and looked at the photos. My mother would understand.

"Maybe another company is looking at doing that?"

"I don't know."

"Say, why don't we go out and have fun tonight. There's a movie, a comedy, which I've been wanting to see."

"What is it?"

"*National Lampoon's Vacation*," he smiled. "I want to see that smile of yours return to that beautiful face."

Drew was right. The historic Allen Theatre had been running the best releases since the beginning of movies, and that night was no exception. The movie had Christina laughing despite her serious mood after her visit with Terry and the heaviness in her heart from her necessary decision about Drew. They settled back in their seats, passed an enormous bucket of popcorn back and forth, and enjoyed themselves like teenagers on a date. Drew kept his arm around Christina, and for two hours they let Chevy Chase and his screen family entertain them with their arduous trip to Walley World.

What had started as a trying day ended in laughter and bittersweet love. There was no denying the happiness she felt with Drew. Christina could have stayed there, longer than the weekend—forever, really—and never wanted for anything in Drew's arms, enveloped in Drew's secure love. But she couldn't. She never took the easy road.

She stared out the window at a moon obscured by clouds. *There's a huge part of me that doesn't fit well with Drew's plans for us. I have to be honest with him. It has to happen before I leave.* She lay silent instead of chatting herself and Drew to sleep that night.

After downing a cup of coffee and picking at a toasted Eggo waffle early the next morning, Christina stared at the table. This morning, instead of lingering in bed, she had risen quietly. She stole into the kitchen and brewed coffee. Drew rose to the enticing aroma, made his way into the kitchen, and popped a waffle into the toaster.

"You're up early. Couldn't sleep?"

Christina couldn't bear his concern. She took a sluggish breath and heaved a burden up through her chest and into the waffled, coffeed air between them.

"I need a break," Christina announced to the napkin in her lap.

"What? Is the work too much, darling?" He sat down to eat and turned toward her.

"The work is fine. The work is great. It's us, Drew."

Drew's fork, a bite of waffle teetering in its tines, stopped somewhere between his plate and his chin, wavering ever so slightly. He froze in that pose, waiting for her to explain.

She mustered the courage to speak so he could take a bite.

"I love you, Drew, more than anything, but I don't see how this can work. I'm not that powerful woman in the perfume commercial. I can't bring home the bacon *and* fry it up in a pan. Turns out I'm pretty good at bringing home the bacon, though. And I'm just getting started. With no desire to fry anything."

She gripped her locket so tightly her knuckles were white when she opened it to face her father's photo. Maybe he was right after all. Maybe I have no business trying to do something. Maybe I'm nothing more than a dreamer. But her mother's face beamed.

"I'm not asking you to cook for me, darling."

"I know that, Drew. I just need to figure things out for myself. I have no role models. As much as I love you, and I know you love me, something will have to give. My work is just taking off, and I'm finally coming into my own. Either I cut back, or you do. And I never want you to cut back for me." She paused and added, "I'm not worth it." Christina held the napkin to her face. Drew saw the edges wet with tears.

"No, Christina. You are worth it to me. We can compromise and work it out." Drew shoved his plate to the side and took her hand. "Look at me, darling."

"I can't."

"You can't look at me?" His voice was hardly more than a whisper.

"I can't compromise, Drew." Christina looked at Drew, searching.

"Christina, you're one of the most giving people I've ever known! You truly listen, you bend, and you give, and you give."

"I want to give myself an opportunity now. To grow, to learn, to accomplish something. In ways I want to, not in ways everyone else wants me to. I must do this alone."

"What are you saying about us?"

"I'm saying now is not the right time for us. And I don't know how long I need, so I don't want you to wait for me. Live your life. Know that I've loved you."

Astounded at the finality of Christina's words, Drew slouched back in his chair. He fell silent as Christina turned and gathered her things from the apartment. She walked back into the kitchen and stood before him, close enough to hear him swallow hard as she examined the graining on the wood floor beneath them. Drew gently lifted her chin and kissed her first with gossamer wings, then fiercely as she answered by wrapping her arms and legs around this sweet man as if to never let go. Christina tried to look away as he kissed away tears, looking at her with the most tender expression, one that insisted this would not be their last embrace.

By the time she got on the turnpike, her shirt collar was soaked. Mascara trailed down her neck. The locket had opened, the tiny photos of Christina's mom and dad gazing straight ahead, oblivious to their daughter's anguish. Have I made the most terrible mistake? Was there a way to compromise that I missed? Could I make this work with Drew and still move forward independently?

Her tears were shaken dry by an ambulance whizzing by. Its red and blue spinning lights and blaring sirens announced that someone was gravely ill or injured. Her thoughts went back to the NICU, to Ryan, Terry, and Danielle, sobering Christina out of her own misery and into their heartache.

Their next few weeks were touch and go. Danielle had nibbled at the nipple but was not taking in enough nutrition. Doctors guided a feeding tube through the baby's purplish pursed lips into her stomach. It would remain there at least until Danielle was discharged from the NICU. Terry spoke through tears when she told Christina over the phone, though she had suspected it would be necessary. Christina tried to reassure Terry but had so little knowledge of newborns. Infants who were brought to the ER where Christina worked had been redirected to the Children's Hospital ER. Other than babysitting an infant occasionally and watching her new niece, Christina could count on one hand the number of times she had held a baby. Danielle was smaller than a child's babydoll and had lost more than ten ounces since birth. Christina had learned the impact of low birth weight on infant health in a child development class and knew Danielle would face challenges ahead. Terry said it might be months before they could send her baby home. Christina hoped Terry could muster enough courage to accept it.

She wouldn't burden Terry with her own loss, though she longed for Terry's matter-of-fact assessment, her "Christina, what were you thinking?" and her supportive hugs despite not under-standing her friend's choices. Terry loved Drew, for it was through him she met Ryan. Ryan would find out about the breakup from Drew, and eventually Terry might know before Christina could tell her. Christina was willing to take that chance rather than distract Terry from her baby.

Neither girl had ever understood each other's choices. Each simply accepted them like the inexplicable odd pieces in the challenging puzzle of the friend they treasured, putting the odd pieces aside until the puzzle's full image emerged.

PART III

1984–1986

CHAPTER 31

"HAVE YOU HEARD the big news?" Gary rose from his desk as Christina entered the office.

"Whoa, Gary, can it wait until I get my coffee?"

"I'll walk with you because it can't wait." He followed her down the hall and to the coffee station. "Reagan is coming." Gary flashed his teeth in a smile wide enough to knock his glasses off kilter.

"Are you Paul Revere? What do you mean, 'Reagan is coming'?"

Gary shoved a memo into Christina's hand. She saw it had been written by none other than Elliot himself to inform employees that the president was coming to Springton Grove on Wednesday to give a speech. HSA would be closing at ten, and all employees were to vacate the buildings so that the Secret Service could prepare for the visit.

"So, we get the afternoon off that day? I like the sound of that."

"We may be forced from the building, but there's no way anyone will be driving anywhere if the president is in town. I'm sure we won't even be permitted to go to our cars until he's cleared out. Besides, the memo from Elliot says we are *encouraged* to stay and support him."

"Are you kidding? We have to stay and listen to him?" Christina had no interest in politics, other than the one time on the NYU campus when she marched along with the nuclear arms protestors. "I voted for Carter."

"That's too bad, Christina. It'll be quite an event to see no matter who you voted for. We can bring our lunch outside and make a day of it."

"If a picnic is involved, I'll go."

By Tuesday morning their building was inundated with officials in black who examined every corner, conference room, and office. Programmers got little done at their desks and canceled client calls because phone lines were being used by the government. People whispered in the hallways about the Secret Service, speculating about why Reagan was coming to Lenapy to face the nation. Christina admitted to Gary that all the novelty was getting exciting.

Arriving at work on Wednesday, Christina gasped when she spotted a sniper on the roof of the data center, aiming a rifle toward the parking lot. SWAT teams had stationed themselves on every corner and atop her building. Gary pointed out a helipad in the open field beyond the data center where they would deposit the president. An area around the helipad was already cordoned off by officials and barriers. A podium and stage appeared in the large green between HSA and the adjacent Burroughs campus. Christina wondered how this equipment and all those people materialized overnight.

Grabbing a boxed lunch and snacks from the HSA café to carry them through the afternoon, Gary, Robert, Christina, and David set up their camp near the edge of the spectator's field. Soon Mitch and Abby joined their group, and by eleven-thirty the field had become a sea of faces, not a blade of grass visible. A local high school band marched by, its tubas and trumpets swinging and cymbals clanging to the beat of "Hail to the Chief." Flags popped up and waved overhead. Enterprising teens pulled wagons selling buttons, stickers, balloons, and all kinds of patriotic paraphernalia.

"You were right, Gary. It's quite a spectacle. I've never seen anything like it, except for a Fourth of July parade in Washington, DC."

Christina was glad she had worn her Reeboks and sunglasses, though her navy suit reminded her of the circumstances of this picnic. Clever David had thought of bringing folding lawn chairs, but Christina couldn't see over the crowd while sitting. She leaped to her feet when a voice came over the loudspeaker. "TESTING, TESTING," it screeched.

She pulled Gary's sleeve. "This is what I imagine an outdoor Who concert is like, without the business suits, of course."

"Hardly, Christina. Man, you've led a sheltered life. We need to take you to one of those concerts! They're a lot more fun, and there's people smoking weed and no snipers."

The announcer came back on, and soon the formalities began. Pennsylvania Governor Dick Thornburgh spoke briefly and welcomed Reagan to his state. News cameras zoomed in on the stage. She overheard a reporter on camera stating, "They were expecting three-to-five thousand in the crowd today here in Lenapy. Our sources tell us it's upward of twelve thousand right now as we wait for the president to come onstage…"

Appearing on stage in a flash of pageantry and welcomed by thunderous applause, President Reagan loomed larger than Christina had expected. She felt a smidgen of interest. There was still no explanation for why he had chosen to come here. Philadelphia was the local hub of talent, with the University of Pennsylvania and Drexel and dozens of higher education institutions, while Lenapy and the western suburbs were sleepy towns beyond the reach of train and transit. The corporate park itself was shiny new construction amid rolling hills, farmland, and dairy cows. Maybe that's why he came, to address urban sprawl?

She soon got her answer when Reagan wasted no time expressing his delight at being in the "workplace of the future," the hub of innovation and technology along the Route 202 high-tech corridor. Looking around as if for the first time, Christina acknowledged the neighboring businesses—Burroughs, Vanguard, Safeguard Scientifics, and a few pharma incubators. Is investing innovative? Banks don't seem to use advanced technology—I still have to enter the bank to cash a check.

The president went on to tout this corporate park and others like it across the country as a home for big ideas, where we will grow American innovation and lead the country into the twenty-first century.

Christina eyed Gary and laughed. "Did you know we are doing that?"

"We're the leading edge, remember?"

Reagan also mentioned statistics that shocked them both. Their little high-tech corridor held over two hundred firms employing ten thousand people.

"No wonder there was a waiting list for my apartment!"

Her ears perked up when the president mentioned simplifying taxes for the average employee. Having filed taxes herself for only two years, Christina already dreaded the paperwork ahead of her next tax season. She wasn't familiar with tax brackets, beyond the fact that her father complained about his. Christina did understand the push toward innovation and funding for new technology. It caught her ear and her curiosity. Maybe this presidential visit was a good thing.

Reagan spoke of his proposed tax plan as one that would liberate Americans from "tax bondage," closing loopholes and foreign tax havens that benefit only the wealthy, possibly eliminating the 1040.

"I'm all for that," Gary said.

The president promised to lower capital gains taxes, capping them at 17.5 percent, thereby spurring innovation and fueling technological advances. He wanted to make it fairer for small businesses and new businesses, researchers and innovators currently squeezed out by capital gains. He predicted that lowering the capital gains tax would blast the economy to new heights and bolster the venture capital market.

"I'm going to have to read up on this venture capital idea. All I know about capital gains is that I have gains from buying our stock at the company discount! My dad says I need to hold on to that stock for a while to reduce short term gains taxes."

"Not a student of macro- or microeconomics?" Gary asked.

"That is a No, with a capital N. I took micro and dropped it after falling asleep on the first day of class. Maybe I'll listen to a book on tape. Can't be any worse than Professor Dullsville's class."

"Somebody as smart as you? I'd think you'd be all over those graphs and figures."

"I never got that far. Walked out the door and sold my book on the spot to a smiling freshman who had just added the class, poor soul."

Echoing his acting days, the president made every effort to connect with the audience. He praised the Route 202 corridor and its companies that developed large integrated systems, comparing what they did to his experience with *disintegrating* systems in Washington. He alluded to hacking as something he knew from his work with Congress. "They hacked my defense budget to nothing," the president quipped. Christina and her friends groaned at his dad jokes. But his vision of a tax system that worked in the technology age of silicon chips, engineering, and robotics made some sense to Christina.

There was one promise that stuck in Christina's mind. Reagan said the country needed to fund high-risk industries like those right there in the Silicon Valley of the East. He wanted to boost incentives for entrepreneurs and areas where innovation was exploding, places like the Silicon Bayou, Silicon Mountain, and there in the Philly 'burbs. The crowd had clapped and cheered until the last few minutes of the president's speech, when a cold drizzle sent many listeners on their way. Her group packed up chairs and headed to the parking lot. As Christina was exiting the field, the news reporter she had seen earlier waved her down from under a giant 6ABC NEWS umbrella.

"Excuse me, miss. May I talk with you?" The serious look on the woman's face made Christina wonder if she had gotten hurt or was in some sort of trouble. Christina looked over her shoulder to see if there might be someone else the reporter was talking to, but the reporter pointed a finger at her and nodded.

"Sure, how can I help?"

"I've been here for hours, and my crew and I couldn't help but notice the majority of this twelve- or fifteen-thousand-person crowd consists of men. Can I ask you a few questions?"

"OK." Christina motioned to the others to go on ahead without her.

"What is your name, and do you work here in Springton Grove?"

"I'm Christina Como. I'm a programmer for HSA. I work in that building over there." Christina pointed to her office on the third floor.

"A programmer! What do you do exactly and how long have you worked there?"

"I write software for hospitals and customize our model product to meet clients' specific needs, then travel to the site and install it, with a team of engineers and other programmers."

"So, you are one of the innovators President Reagan was talking about."

"I wouldn't say—"

The reporter interrupted. "Christina, what do you think of the president's tax plan?"

"I like the idea of simplifying the tax system, and I'm very supportive of incentivizing technology innovation and funding businesses that advance technology."

"What innovation would you like to see?" the reporter asked.

"Me?" Christina paused to collect her thoughts. "Well, I'd like to see more software systems that support clinicians in the hospital and their patients. We've been focused on billing and insurance and collecting patient demographics, but the true improvements to the health of patients will occur when our systems prevent medical errors, retrieve their patients' history, and use it to inform care and treatment decisions. We really need to streamline our emergency rooms and facilitate care in the NICU where patients have urgent needs."

"Are you a programmer or a nurse?"

"A programmer, with experience as an EMT. I've seen first-hand how sorely automation and accurate data is needed in urgent care and in all of clinical care."

"Christina, I have to say, it's refreshing to hear a young woman like yourself with big ideas. You are exactly the kind of person the president was talking about." The woman turned abruptly and stared directly into the camera, "Marissa Porter, 6ABC NEWS. Back to you, Larry."

"Before you leave, I need to get information from you." Marissa handed Christina a clipboard with a form to fill out, including her signature, permitting them to air the clip. "Thank you for the interview! Do you mind if I contact you if we need more for the story?"

"You're welcome. I don't mind." Christina then added, "Marissa, will this be on the news?"

"Sure will. The six o'clock and eleven o'clock! Channel 6, maybe on World News too. Tell your friends."

Christina rushed home to call her mother. "Mom, you need to set the VCR."

"Christina? What are you talking about?" Mrs. Como had never touched the machine.

Christina launched into a full explanation of the day's events, talking so fast her mother had to stop her a few times and ask her to slow down and repeat a few things. Diana, her roommate, was watching and listening, eyebrows rising higher and higher, holding her hand over her open mouth as Christina relayed what happened.

"Wait, Christina, let me tell Dominic to set up the tape. We've never had a TV celebrity in the family, and I don't want to mess it up. I'll put your brother on. You tell him what and when to record, OK?"

After repeating the story for Dominic, Christina told him to put Mom back on the phone.

"Mom, can you please call Ali Aboud and let him know? I know he'll be interested."

Christina searched her kitchen cabinets and refrigerator for food to make a quick dinner, until Diana came up with the great idea of ordering cheesesteaks. "We're too busy to make dinner tonight, Christina. We have to call everyone we know before the news comes on at six." They would spend the rest of the evening on the couch, calling their friends to tell them to watch the news, then discussing it with those who called afterward, while waiting to watch it again at eleven.

The presidential visit made headline news for all Philadelphia TV stations that night. ABC followed coverage of the speech with a special Dollars for Tech segment that featured Christina's interview and Marissa Porter's commentary on how the crowd skewed male, highlighting a need to get more women into these high-paying jobs.

"Were they wearing blinders?" Christina asked Diana, who hadn't been there. "There were women spectators there—well, at least some. Two of my female friends from HSA were in our group alone, but they left early. Marissa Porter must have been looking for an angle."

Diana spoke like a photographer. "Well, looking at the camera footage as they panned the field, you can't see many women at all. Maybe they left to pick up their children from school instead of listening to a political speech."

"Or more likely, took a much-needed afternoon to themselves. I did find it odd that many of my coworkers weren't around. I don't know how they could have gotten away, with all the security and road closures. Anyway, I'm proud to have represented the increasing female contingent in the computer industry."

"Were you nervous talking on the camera? You certainly didn't appear to be."

"I was stunned when Marissa stopped me, so I didn't really think about it. I was still thinking about the problems yet to be solved and how incentivizing development might expedite that."

"To me, you sounded like someone who knew what they were talking about and not just someone going gaga over a celebrity's—I mean president's—ideas."

At work the next day, Christina was shocked by how quickly the campus had been restored to its pre-Reagan state, with not a patriotic ribbon or black-suited official in sight. An HSA letterhead envelope waited on her desk when she arrived.

CHAPTER 32

TEARING OPEN THE envelope, Christina read the message, handwritten by a heavy hand with an extravagant forward-leaning slant.

> *Christina,*
>
> *I saw the ABC News interview. I'm proud to have you on our HSA team. Your comments were intelligently articulated and insightful. I'd like you to meet me for lunch at noon in the executive dining room to discuss your suggestions for future products.*
>
> *Elliot McMaster*

She'd been told about the executive dining room by the Seattle sales team. They had the honor of joining Elliot and his senior staff for a celebratory dinner there upon breaking the sales record among field offices last year. They couldn't stop talking about the carved mahogany panels, the immense granite tabletop, and of course, the lavish gourmet meal served to them by gloved waiters with the fine wines chosen and poured by a New York City sommelier. Kip gushed about the melt-in-your-mouth filet mignon, cooked to perfection, and lobsters the size of footballs.

Christina wondered if she would regret having eaten breakfast but knew her nerves would have overcome her on an empty stomach. At least she had dressed in her easy go-to professional outfit—navy interview suit paired with a silky white blouse—Christina had been too tired to think about her outfit after being up late watching the news. Her clothing was now the least of her worries. How does one have a casual conversation with the founder of the company and offer suggestions for his products without coming off as a cocky brash up-and-comer?

David Stokes came into her office just as she finished reading the letter. "I hear you got an invitation from Elliot." He grinned.

"You knew about this?"

"Only to confirm your office location with Elliot's assistant and that you are on my team. I took all the credit for hiring you."

"What did that get you?" Christina shook her head.

"I was hoping it would get me an invitation to the lunch, but it didn't. You're on your own." David handed her a blank piece of paper.

"What's this?"

"I'd like a Christina Como autograph, please. I don't have a photo of you to sign, so this will have to do."

"You're funny, David. I'm terrified! What business do I have telling Elliot what to develop, what the products should do, discussing the billing system *he created*?"

"Elliot is approachable, despite his larger-than-life size and gruff exterior. And Jack Walters will be there too. He knows you. I've told him all about you already."

"David, why me? I'm just a girl from Delaware who not too long ago was told she wasn't good enough to pursue her dreams. I can't bear the thought of getting reamed out by Elliot. He'll tell me I'm getting too big for my britches. I shouldn't have talked to that reporter." She stared at the envelope until the tears in her eyes dissipated.

"No, Christina, whoever told you that was dead wrong. Elliot has no intention of berating you. You have ideas worth hearing. Why *not* you? You've proven yourself over the last year, and we have high hopes for you. Most of our people punch out at five and never give another thought to hospital problems or better solutions. They go home to their TVs and barbecues and shut their brains off until eight the next morning."

"I don't own a barbecue grill," she said, wiping her wet cheek with her hand.

"No, you go in there and hold your head up high. You tell them what you saw in the ER, what you see and hear when you're on-site, what our clients want and what their patients need. You listen and observe better than anyone around, no sense in keeping that to yourself."

"Hey, I resent that, David." Gary had been nodding in agreement until David's "better than anyone around" comment. "Just kidding! Though, as her mentor, I should also be invited to the lunch."

"The only one getting a fancy lunch is Christina. But if you could put in a good word for your boss and your mentor, we'd really appreciate it." David winked. "I felt like a proud papa seeing you on the news last night."

Christina wondered if her own father would share that sentiment or see it as yet another instance of his daughter being uppity, living in a dream world.

The morning hours passed like rising floodwaters. Combing data dictionaries for discrepancies provided enough distraction until it was time for Christina to go before the wolves. Why do they want to hear from me? Does Elliot want to publicly shame me? Who am I to tell them what their company should do? Until I came to HSA, no one had ever, ever in my life asked for my opinion on anything important. And I learned early not to voice it, else suffer the consequences. If I tell them what I think, I'm likely to get laughed out of the room or maybe even fired for the audacity of my suggestions.

Christina fully expected to be put in her place. She'd rehearsed an apology to these men who had spent the last ten or twelve years building a software company that led its client-base into the world of computers. Her stomach lurched and her legs wobbled, but she took deep breaths and focused on the importance of helping NICU babies and the ER patients. That focus fueled her confidence, helping her summon the strength to advocate for them.

Jack Walters was in the dining room when she knocked and was let in. "Christina, I'm Jack Walters. We met when you had your QA."

"Mr. Walters, I mean Jack, of course I know who you are. Thank you for stopping over to wish us well that night. I'm sure you had more important matters to attend to."

"Nothing more important than the quality of our product, Christina. We rely on people like you to put our best foot forward. From what I hear from Adam Olson, you did a bang-up job out there in Yakima. And patched up Abby, one of our best people, to boot."

Adam Olson had reported back to Jack Walters! Christina suddenly felt her face radiating heat. One good thing about my olive skin is that a blush of embarrassment is not always visible. Just then, a lumbering Elliot and two other men burst into the room. The men waited to take their seats after Elliot had settled into the oversized padded leather chair at the head of the table. He motioned for everyone to be seated. Jack Walters facilitated introductions.

"We all watched the news clip, Miss Como. Can I call you Christina? I wonder if you had spoken to our PR team before agreeing to the interview."

Here was the admonishment Christina expected.

"I wasn't aware of a PR team, Mr. McMaster. And I hadn't prepared for an interview. I was stopped by a reporter as we were dashing from the field when it began raining."

"Call me Elliot," he said, reaching for his dinner napkin and opening it with a flourish. "For someone not prepped to talk with the media, you did well. You had that reporter hanging on your every word."

"I just answered her questions as straightforwardly as I could. I'd never been to a political event before and honestly know little about tax reform."

"But you know about software. And hospitals."

"I'm learning, sir," Christina said respectfully.

Elliot looked over his shoulder for an imaginary general. "We're not in the military here. It's Elliot, remember? David Stokes says you're the best he's got. Olson out in Yakima wants you back there, and you knocked the habits off the nuns in Alaska and the crawfish from the Creoles down in the bayou. Even Opdenaker in Vegas was impressed, and that's one tough nut to crack."

"Thank you." Christina nearly choked on her ice water at the mention of Opdenaker, recalling his comments about her youth.

"So, we're going to have a nice lunch here, and we'd like you to tell us what you are seeing out there in the hospitals, where you think we could look at development."

They're not here to torment me. They want to hear what I have to say! Christina took a deep breath and started in. Her passion for the patients, for the nurses, physicians, and technicians, and for making healthcare work better for those who needed it came through loud and clear.

While she loved computers, she told them, she considered software merely a tool for solving big problems. She admitted she was not enamored of technology for technology's sake but because of its potential to change lives. Trying to keep her remarks brief and pointed, she focused on the opportunity to simplify the process, to facilitate better and more expedient care, to make the job easier for dedicated clinicians who labor long hours and in challenging circumstances. "I know we can do more," she concluded.

She had hardly touched her poached salmon, hollandaise asparagus, or Crab Louis and spring vegetable medley as the men scarfed up their meal along with her words. When they started talking to each other about the eighteen-month development plan, she stole a few bites of the meal she wished she hadn't been too nervous to enjoy.

Jack Walters looked her way and said, "Christina, I know you were hired into Installations, but I think we'd really like to have you work in Development. The pipeline for clinical systems is just starting up, and you could thrive there. What do you think?"

"That's tempting. I'm in the midst of the interface project for David Stokes, and I would hate to leave him in the lurch. David gave me the opportunity to work here. I owe him a lot. And I find the Installations site travel fascinating because I see how the operation runs. I'm not sure I'm cut out for heads-down coding in Development, frankly."

"I'm not talking heads-down coding. I'm talking product management and systems analysis, where you set the direction and own the design. You'd be going out to sites to collect requirements, gather insight, research the market. Then come back and translate that into a product framework. You could write specifications or even write code if you'd like. You could finish your project for David before starting."

Jack Walters had presented an offer she couldn't refuse.

Two days after the president's visit, Christina got a call from Ali Aboud.

"How nice to hear from you, Dr. Aboud."

"It's Ali, remember? I wanted to congratulate you on your TV debut, Christina. You were a star! All of us here in the ER watched and cheered for you. We could feel your empathy for patients and desire to improve healthcare through the airwaves, in your voice. We are all so proud."

"I was caught off guard, Ali. I'm not even sure what I told her, so I'll have to listen to the playback. I had my brother tape the segment."

"And thank you for having your mother tell me about it. Is it true the company is still focusing on the billing software?"

"It seems so, because it is the revenue cash cow, and hospitals need to bill to stay afloat. I know we are developing Aura, but it is a long development cycle, and we haven't tapped ancillaries yet."

"And the ER?"

"Not on the radar, I'm afraid. Rumor has it we bought a lab system from a small business a while back, but it hasn't been made part of the product yet. Same for radiology."

"I see. Sounds like it could be years before we get anything for our stand-alone ER."

"That's the problem. Not only ER, but the OR, NICU, oncology—there are specific needs the computer could address, if we had the resources. I'm starting to think about what it would take to start up a business. Reagan's talk got me curious. Do you know anything about venture capital, Ali?"

"You're asking the wrong guy. I know emergency medicine. That's pretty much all I do. But I have friends in all kinds of specialties. And I know a hospital administrator who knows about finance. Whitt Bates. I could put you in touch with him. He'd at least be able to tell you where to start."

"I'd hate to waste his time."

"Don't be silly. He owes me a favor, anyway, from back in med school. Call him. And keep me posted. Maybe I can be on your clinical advisory team?"

"Talk about putting the horse before the cart! I'm going to research this a bit while getting started with HSA Development. I'll learn how products come into being. It'll allow me to make new contacts too. This time next year I'll be in a better position to seriously consider doing something on the side."

"I'm on board. But let's do it sooner than next year!" Christina could hear Ali's excitement and was flattered he thought she could someday start a business.

Her phone rang off the hook for the next two weeks. Diana had to pop another tape into the answering machine because messages for Christina had exhausted the recording space on an entire tape. Each night after work, Christina listened to messages from reporters and journalists wanting to hear more about her story. *What story? I'm not all that.*

There were messages from recruiters looking to fill software jobs, one offering her twice her current salary on the spot. A representative from the University of Pennsylvania Wharton School of Business invited her to apply for their MBA program, mentioning scholarship money was available. Mixed in were well wishes from friends and acquaintances, her old college roommate, and Drew. "I saw you on the Philadelphia News, Christina. Just wanted to tell you how great you were, and I miss you." That one stopped her cold. Diana brought over a box of tissues and put her arm around Christina's shoulder.

"The price of fame." Diana shook her head. "With six million viewers, you're bound to reach someone you don't want to hear from."

"Maybe I did want to hear from Drew, but not in that way." Christina's shaky hands brushed her damp cheeks.

A few random callers left messages asking weird questions. One strange message from Rex left her seething. "I will now be calling you 'Suck-Up Celebrity,'" he hissed.

Diana made a face. "Who is *that*? What a nutjob."

"Some guy at work who seems to have something against me. Gary says he's just jealous."

Diana listened attentively as Christina skipped through messages on the tape, deleting the junk, pausing to replay a few. "This beats watching *Wheel of Fortune* or a sitcom." Diana began tinkering with backdrops and lighting equipment in her photography corner of the living room.

"I'm glad you find it entertaining," scoffed Christina, "but what are you doing with the camera?"

"I'm setting up to get a portrait of you. When you become famous, I want to be the photographer who captured you while you were innocent."

Christina pursed her lips. "I'm not sitting for any portrait tonight." She stopped to replay a message. It was from Adam Olson, asking Christina to call him back in the evening, after work. She didn't recognize the phone number as one from Central Washington Hospital.

"It must be his number at the ranch." She scribbled down the number he left.

"Ranch? Who's Adam Olson? Sounds like a big guy."

"He's a client in Washington State. And a cattle rancher. Maybe he wants me to come round up the cows." She pretended to ride a horse and swing a lasso.

"What a combination of talents he has," Diana said, smiling. "I can't wait to hear more about this one. Call him back!"

"I will, I will, maybe tomorrow. Let me get through these."

The next message was from Terry. "Hey, Christina, Ryan switched on the eleven o'clock news when we came home from the hospital last night. I thought I was hallucinating from exhaustion when your face flashed up with the headline, 'Dollars for Tech.' Are they giving you money? Rather than drop into bed, I stayed up to watch. Ryan and I are proud to claim we've known you well before you became famous. Call me."

The last message was from her brother Dominic. "We got it. You looked good, kid."

CHAPTER 33

WHEN CHRISTINA RETURNED Adam Olson's call about the news interview, he greeted her like an old friend.

"Christina! Boy, was I bowled over when my wife and I tuned into the nightly news the other day and sure enough, there you were! Talking about innovations we sorely need on national TV! You were the talk of the hospital next day, with everybody saying, 'There's our programmer, on TV with the president.'"

"Adam, I wasn't anywhere near the president, but it's awfully kind of you to call. The reporter somehow caught me in the crowd."

"You know, I got to thinking about what you said about the ER and NICU. I know we just installed Aura, but now that it's going so well, our board is chomping at the bit to get ancillaries and the whole hospital automated. Problem is, HSA isn't moving fast enough for us."

"Well, Adam, since we talked, I'll soon be leading Development for the pharmacy product. That'll be the next release. They're also working on an app for labs and soon radiology. Probably within the next three years."

"Yeah, Kip made sure I knew all that, and we'll likely sign before too long, but folks are getting antsy. At that rate, could be years before we see anything for our specialty units like ER and NICU. I don't suppose you could persuade Jack Walters to step it up on those?"

"I can certainly try, but the company has a three-year development plan already in place. I'm frustrated with the pace as well. I'd love to develop ER and NICU, plus OR, oncology, and scheduling. I have a list a mile long in my mind, Adam."

"Christina, you said you were interested in the president's proposal to fund innovation. What say you consider going after that funding yourself and creating these apps to work on top of Aura?"

"Adam, how in the world could I get funding? I'm just starting in Development and with MBA classes. I don't know the first thing about running a business."

"Christina, you know software, and more importantly, you know the market need. You know the potential to improve clinical outcomes with computer software that is currently unavailable. I think I can help you—that is, if you're interested."

"Help me do what?" Christina couldn't believe where this conversation was going.

"Listen," Adam continued, "you're a go-getter. A doer who listens. One who cares. You have the insight and drive in you to make things better. We can get people around you to do all that other stuff, get you a board, get you the support you need to bring this baby home. I know a guy here in Washington, in Bellevue, who started a personal computer software business. He's got big plans for that, and I know he can offer advice. I can get him out to my ranch and have you pick his brain. His name is Ford Burch."

"Let me think about it, Adam. I have a friend who is an ER doctor who also offered help and advice. Seems there's a lot of interest. And a sense of urgency."

"Our patients need it. Our docs need it. Why *not* you? A small business could be agile enough to deliver quickly, without all that red tape that drags down a big company like HSA. Give it some thought, and I'll check in with you in a couple of weeks. We can't waste any time."

Ali and his friend, Whitt Bates, made the drive to King of Prussia to meet with Christina over lunch one Saturday at Bookbinders Annex, at Ali's suggestion. The three sat in a booth near the back where they were unlikely to be overheard. No telling if an HSAer might be dining nearby.

Whitt got right to the point after the server brought their meals, the menu's special for Whitt, grilled oysters for Ali, and Maryland crab soup for Christina. "Ali tells me you're thinking of starting up a software business."

"At this point, I'm trying to understand what starting a business is all about. I have ideas for a product, and I'm certain I could build it, with additional resources, of course."

"I know she can build it." Ali turned to Whitt and nodded. He squeezed the half lemon wrapped in cheesecloth over the oysters, which were carefully arranged on a circular platter with indentations to hold each in place, as if they might otherwise swim away.

"First question is, Why wouldn't you try pitching it to the company you work for, instead of going solo?" Whitt asked, dumping flakes of red pepper onto the plate piled high with opened mussels and clams that seemed to be smiling up at him from their comfortable bed of linguine.

"I could do that. Jack Walters is approachable. However, the company operates on a three-year development plan, broken into two major releases. I've seen it, and their plan does not include the products I want to develop. The market can't wait."

"I can tell you the basics of what you'd need to start up. Number one—a good business plan that maps out the company vision, products and services, market analysis and strategy, and budget and financials."

"I'm good with all that except budget and financials. For budget, I can identify the technical resources needed in terms of programmers, hardware, and staffing, but I'm at a complete loss as to how to determine the associated dollars."

"I can get you figures if you identify the needs," Whitt said. "I know lots of people who live for budgets and figures."

"Yeah, that's a real deficiency of mine. Even in the MBA program, I'm dreading the accounting." Christina grimaced.

"That's a role you can hire out. Most of the skills can be hired, except for the tech skills, which are far more in demand than there are people who have them. It's the leadership and vision that makes a company. The CEO doesn't need to be all things. That's why finance guys like me always have work." Whitt smiled. Christina would have thought his medical degree offered enough job security.

"How do you hire if you're just starting up with no money?"

"You dig deep in your own pockets to start up, you get loans, and a skeleton crew who is willing to do some initial work with the promise of equity. A lot of businesses start as a side gig to real jobs until they get funded."

"I can definitely do work on the side and maybe convince a few others to join me."

"Meanwhile, as you develop the product, or a 'proof of concept' of the product, you have a team looking for funding, backers, and investors."

"Seems like a lot is resting on good faith," Christina observed.

"Your business plan has to be bulletproof. It's what will get you attention from those willing to take a chance on a return for their investment. If you draft one, I can review it and start to fill in the blanks."

"You'd do that for me? Thank you, Whitt."

Whitt dug into the last of his Frutti di Mare, twirling the pasta with his fork. "For you and for Ali. With you and Ali as partners,

I'm excited. Ali is my best friend. If he says someone or something is worth taking a chance on, I'm all in."

"Good of you, Whitt. But how can I help?" Ali asked, forcing his last oyster from its bone-china-white shell with a miniature seafood fork.

"I'll need a team of advisors for product input. Any docs you know who might be interested, from ER, NICU, OR could help with that. If you could spread the word and put them in touch with me, I'll take it from there," Christina said.

"We'll need board members. Some of those folks could be on the board or simply be an advisor," Whitt added. He and Ali had already become her partners.

Christina's head was spinning as she drove home to her apartment. She immediately got to work on the business plan. Mapping out the products and their rollout was easy. She was already doing that at HSA. An unexpected excitement grew inside her, stirring up those embers she thought had long since been extinguished. To think these men are interested enough to gather their friends and support my wild ideas!

CHAPTER 34

AFTER MOVING TO DEVELOPMENT, Christina skyrocketed at full throttle into the ever-burgeoning demands for computerization. Her fear of being stuck at a desk writing programs with little exposure to the pulse of the industry vanished by her second day. Jack Walters saw to it that Christina attended all the market research meetings with leaders across the country, including some of her prior clients. The push was on to deliver a pharmacy solution.

Christina crisscrossed the country shadowing hospital pharmacists and observing drug ordering, dispensing, and administration procedures to understand the entire process. She watched operators fill carts for medication distribution. She sympathized with nurses trying to decipher a handwritten log of which patient received which drug. They often resorted to guessing between 10 milligrams or 1.0 milligrams, the ink and handwriting obscuring a possible decimal point on the page. Occasionally, pills dropped when technicians loaded the tiny cart drawers.

Christina watched pharmacists leafing through pages and pages of a patient's chart to review details in the patient's medication profile before confirming or suggesting a prescribed medication. It was their job to identify any drugs a doctor ordered that could potentially conflict with another the patient was taking. The sheer volume of information pharmacists digested and considered before approving a drug order was mind-boggling.

Her mind was filled with ideas of where the computer could make an impact. Storing and organizing all the details on a patient's drug profile were tasks well-suited for automation, enabling the user to peruse history easily. The ready retrieval of pertinent information could expedite clinical decisions. She also knew it could do more. Wouldn't it be great to have the system tell the pharmacist if the drug a doctor ordered was wrong for that patient? Maybe it was one that would interact with another medication, or maybe the dose was too little or too much based on the patient's weight, age, or condition. Maybe the drug was similar to another the patient was given, thereby causing a therapeutic duplicate and perhaps a cumulative overdose.

Christina's hand couldn't write fast enough to record everything she observed. She started carrying a small tape recorder to dictate her thoughts and record conversations she held with clinicians. Poring over transcripts when she returned back to Lenapy, Christina distilled the notes and conversations into a set of requirements for the design of HSA's next application or release. Building on what they already had in their orders product, they'd add features that facilitated medication selection, produced warnings of potential harmful effects, and serviced the manufacture of IV admixtures.

Pharmacy was not the only area she tackled. Nurses, becoming fans of the computer after using automated order entry, wanted devices at the bedside. They weren't happy about having to jot down notes on paper at the bedside and then return to the unit's central station to enter orders into the system. Using the Aura system, nurses reported walking hundreds more steps each day than before the system was implemented, which Christina confirmed through time studies and by wearing a pedometer as she shadowed nurses on their shifts.

Terminals, however, were expensive and bulky. Placing a clunky terminal next to each bed was physically impossible in many hospitals where monitors and medical equipment laid first claim to scarce real estate at the bedside. And clinicians needed easy access to the patient without having to squeeze around any extraneous equipment in the room.

Christina and her colleagues considered using wheeled devices, to save nurses a few trips back and forth. They looked at designing a handheld device, one that nurses could carry around to patients' bedsides, entering and retrieving information from the portable device. But circuit boards themselves were too big to fit in a palm, and lead components made them heavy. The HSA team tested a few portable devices for feasibility. The best one was the size of a clothes iron, but nurses caring for twelve or more patients on a shift might end up lifting the six-pound brick hundreds of times a shift. Device wiring and cords for stationary devices made the weight issue seem trivial. HSA decided to defer bedside terminals, hoping that advances in device technology might someday improve portability. In the interim, the company sought other ways to reduce manual nonclinical work that nurses did throughout their workday.

Dozens of repetitive and labor-intensive nonclinical processes involved in healthcare were evident at every hospital Christina visited. From Scripps and Bay General in San Diego to Mayo Clinic, Cleveland Clinic, New York Presbyterian, and Mass General, the burden on clinicians included as much information shuffling and sifting as it did caring for patients. Clinicians confided in Christina after days of her empathic inquiries, telling her these tasks were not what they'd envisioned themselves doing when they chose a healthcare profession. Non-care processes became even more burdensome as legislation and insurance layered on demands, purportedly to improve care and reimbursement. Christina wondered if it wasn't at the *expense* of patient care.

In a briefing with Jack Walters, Christina explained the pharmacy's manual review of medication records and the tedium of finding all relevant details before approving a drug order. On the other end, once that drug was in the cart drawer, ready to be given to a patient in a bed, nursing often struggled to decipher illegible administration notes in order to give the correct medication in the proper dosage to the correct patient in the correct way at the appropriate time. Sometimes, the patients were transferred or discharged by the time the written report was compiled and distributed, making it even more difficult for nurses to ensure they were administering the medication to the right person. Spills, missing pills, extra doses, staff changes, canceled orders, and waste contributed to the confusion. Any deviations from the instructions were to be noted. Opportunities for human error and omissions were rampant.

It was a tedious and manual process that the entirety of nursing collectively hated about their work. Christina felt their pain. It was chaotic at best and potentially fatal at worst. Following a nurse manager and unit nurses around for days, Christina saw the medication administration role for what it was—a huge time sucker, ridden with potential for errors—life threatening errors. Jack Walters' eyes widened, and his jaw dropped at her description of the process. Christina was emboldened by his interest and proposed an idea to Jack.

"I think we can win nursing, Jack, despite not delivering a bedside solution. We can automate the medication administration process, freeing them up to administer the meds without the unwieldy work of making sense of an immediately outdated manual report. We can develop 'the MAR,' or Medication Administration

Report, as part of our pharmacy product development. It will be an enormous gain for nursing, the pharmacy, and especially the patients."

Jack whistled and nodded approval. "This is what we needed here in Development. Someone whose ear is to the ground and whose heart is with those patients and those clinicians."

Her ideas for the product became more refined as enthusiastic sites contributed their ideas and identified process inefficiencies. Christina used her listening and observation superpowers, asking questions, probing for whys. She canvassed the country's institutions and started to see consensus forming when dissimilar sites cited the same pain points, the same operational nightmares. They all experienced medication issues with undecipherable handwriting, misplaced decimals, unreadable units of measure, and spelling problems arising from similarities between drug names. Compounding name confusion was the fact that pharmacy staff utilized the drugs' generic names while physicians and nursing staff used brand names. From North Shore Hospital on Long Island to Methodist Houston and all the way up to Queen's in Ontario, Christina questioned, documented, and interviewed experts, gathering as many friends as requirements in her travels.

On her second trip to Providence Hospital in Anchorage, this time with David Stokes and a new development programmer, the nuns welcomed Christina back with a gift of a locally made whale-bone rosary. Sister Mary Xavier, the hospital CEO, put her hand to her heart when Christina immediately put it around her neck. Christina then wore it whenever she went to Providence. She'd tuck her locket in a velvet jewel box in her dresser drawer before flying out to Anchorage, donning the rosary in its place. Providence was now signing for the future pharmacy product, and Sister Mary continued to influence design as Christina honed the product.

With her colleagues, Christina ventured out of the city into Alaska's wilderness, this time in mild weather. They visited Portage Glacier and Denali National Park. The turquoise-bluish ice of the glacier set against a powder blue of the sky and a midnight blue of the waters in Portage Lake left Christina with an unforgettable image of natural beauty. The majestic Denali soared from the earth, viewable from over a hundred miles away, as they made the three-and-a-half-hour drive from Anchorage. Its sheer vastness in a pure and untouched wilderness was unforgettable. In this spectacular sample of Mother Nature's best work, Christina found an understanding of the limitless capability of the human spirit.

Miles on her frequent flyer account increased substantially, as did her savings account while she lived on per diems on the road. The higher salary, thanks to the promotion David Stokes lobbied for and another increase with her new role in Development let Christina breathe the fresh air of financial security. She knew her Honda was not meant to last much longer, and soon she'd soon be using her savings for a new car.

Christina spent the few weekends she was home in King of Prussia working on the business plan and researching what it takes to start a software development company. On the road, she took weekends to explore local sites. In Ontario, Christina bought a Trivial Pursuit game and expensive perfume for her mother. Her dollar went a lot further there than in the States. From a Houston research trip, she drove to Galveston, Texas, for a Mardi Gras parade, returning with two pounds of brightly colored beads tossed from floats bedazzled with flowers, lights, and all manner of bling. In Long Island, pressing the pedal to the floor on a rental, Christina sped along highways once traveled by F. Scott Fitzgerald's characters. She imagined the stately and manicured estates in full dress, welcoming men clad in tailored tuxedos and bejeweled women in gowns of imported silks to their gilded extravaganzas.

Those weekend side trips not only gave Christina a chance to clear her head but also distanced her enough to solidify her thoughts and weave minute details into design for HSA's pharmacy software. She also spent hours on the road formulating ideas for the software applications she envisioned for ER and NICU, but she knew she had to get the pharmacy development experience first.

Christina realized multiple releases of the pharmacy software would be required to deliver all the features she identified. But she was convinced they could provide a base product in six to eight months. She thought of her friends on the Seattle office sales team and chuckled. Kip could start selling pharmacy now and by the time the product was ready, have a dozen clients signed on and waiting.

Jack Walters stopped in her office one day. "Can you give me an example of the name issue? I don't see why they use different names for the same drug." She appreciated his desire to understand. He was not one of those leaders who sat back in an ivory tower.

"I've learned pharmacy uses generic names for a couple of reasons. The hospital buys drugs in bulk, they look for deals among manufacturers, and they stock those they have negotiated as part of what they call the hospital formulary. The formulary of all drug products a hospital stocks is one of the biggest expenses in running a hospital. Hospitals continually shop for the best pricing, sometimes forming groups with other sites to negotiate volume discounts. Brand names in a formulary may differ over the course of a year because of the various deals made with suppliers. For continuity's sake, pharmacy uses the generic drug names. The pharmacists know the scientific nomenclature of products, which is sometimes reflected in the generic name. There is often no therapeutic reason to prefer one brand over another." Christina stopped to take a sip of her coffee.

Jack nodded, stepping in from the doorway. "Can you give me an example?"

"Ibuprofen. That's a generic name. Clinicians might know it as Motrin or Advil. When drug makers' salesmen call on physicians to educate them on the medications' usage, they promote their brand-named products. Nurses, like the doctors, come to know drugs by those brand names. Also, generic names are often not as easy to say, remember, or spell as the catchy brand names."

"Makes sense. It seems an impossible feat to learn the many names for the millions of drug products out there."

"With more being discovered every day! Pharmacy is in the business of learning their therapeutic qualities and, of course, the names. The computer can facilitate it by serving up the typical uses, dosage, and interactions for a trained pharmacist or pharmacologist to consider."

"How so?" Jack took a seat on the corner of Christina's desk.

"The FDA requires all commercially available drug products to have a National Drug Code or NDC number, a national drug product identifier. A dataset contains all drug product information, based on the NDC code. We can develop software that creates a subset of that data for each hospital formulary. Then it could interrogate each medication order against that data to determine drug interactions, therapeutic duplicates, specific dosage guidelines, and the like.

"We'll have the system do much of the screening that pharmacists do manually now and allow pharmacists to override any system warnings based on their knowledge of the patient and the drug. We can flag typos in orders with misplaced decimals, thereby avoiding excessive or inadequate dosage. We can flash a warning of a patient's drug allergies if one of those drugs is ordered. We can flag drug interactions or inappropriate orders for a given condition. We can notify pharmacy before an order is about to expire and request a renewal, thereby ensuring continuous care with no interruption to the medication schedule. We can reduce medication errors. We will save lives."

Jack stood up. "I want you to tell Development. Your passion for this, Christina, will inspire them to do their best to make this product sing."

Before her move to Development, David Stokes had encouraged Christina to take advantage of any of the professional training the company offered. Heeding his advice, she squeezed in as many classes as she could between travel. She took a Presentation Skills course with Gary, where she learned to emphasize important points without waving her hands around. Suppressing her animated gesturing took lots of practice. Christina became increasingly more comfortable making persuasive speeches, her usual butterflies lying dormant.

Christina knew Development would require more design work than she'd been doing in Installations. The Structured Systems Analysis course stepped her through the product life cycle and the formal processes involved in systems design. She was grateful to have this under her belt before her job changed. Technical training was ongoing at HSA, as technology changed weekly. Recalling her four years in college, Christina wondered if she hadn't learned more in the two years since graduating. The company kept feeding training to motivated employees, and Chrisina took full advantage of any opportunity to learn.

Weeks after the Reagan news story and her interview, she had called the person at Penn's Wharton School who had left her a message about a scholarship. Nothing could convince Christina to quit work then and go back to school. There was too much at stake to leave. The university representative suggested she consider taking night classes to get a few credits underway before deciding to enroll. An understanding of business, and how software could become its own big business, was now of interest to Christina. Weeks later, she was among those hustling from their day jobs to night classes. Wharton even waived her tuition for the first nine credits. If she were to enroll in one of their programs, the waiver would continue. They're taking a chance on me because of a news story!

With busy days and nights, between work, travel, thinking about a future business, and now classes, Christina's cup was overflowing. She found other students who also traveled for work. They exchanged notes when one missed a class. After class one evening, Christina settled into an empty seat on her SEPTA train. One of her classmates, the only other female in the program, then boarded the same car. Christina rushed over to introduce herself.

"Hi, I'm Christina Como. I'm in the class you just left."

"Natalie Valentine. I go by Nat."

"Seems we are the only two women."

"I'm used to it. Not many in the sales world," Nat said, reaching up for a handgrip as the train started moving.

"What do you sell?" Christina grabbed a pole to steady herself, resting her power briefcase on the floor between her knees as the train sputtered forward.

"Imaging equipment. X-rays, ultrasounds, CAT scanners, you know, the big box equipment."

"Sounds expensive."

Nat nodded in agreement.

"I write hospital software," Christina said. "We may have some of the same clients."

"We could use somebody to write software for our machines. It's still like chipping hieroglyphics onto stone tablets." Nat mimed hammering a chisel. "Hey, how 'bout we vow to ditch our heels in class next week?"

"I have my Reeboks in my briefcase. I was dying to put them on all night."

"Deal!" Nat grabbed Christina's hand, and they shook on it. Christina liked Nat's directness and knew at once they'd be friends.

CHAPTER 35

THE PHARMACY PROJECT was well underway. They'd be QAing the first release soon, and Christina set about looking for a beta site. Because of reduced licensing fees and the opportunity to contribute to product design, hospitals clamored to be selected. The site must have sophisticated Aura users who would provide feedback and view the product from a global perspective, not simply looking after their own interests but cognizant of differences between their own operations and those of other hospitals. They must also tolerate inevitable errors as the product became refined before market. HSA preferred a location close to headquarters to facilitate daily on-site support and decided on a two-hundred-bed community hospital in West Chester, just twenty minutes from Corporate.

One weekend Christina left the beta site to drive to her parents' home. It was only another thirty minutes' drive. Her mother always welcomed Christina home, and her father asked the same question each time. "How are you doing up there in King of Prussia by yourself?"

Each time, Christina answered the same way. "I'm fine. I'm not by myself. You've met Diana, my roommate. And I'm not there much, anyway."

Why can't my family grasp the idea of me living independently? Why do they think I need someone paying my bills or taking care of me? I know they all wonder what happened with Drew. He had become part of the family, and they assumed I'd marry Drew after college. Questions about that sometimes spoiled an otherwise enjoyable time at home.

"You're always working or traveling for work, Teen. Why don't you want to have any fun?" Dominic turned to her as they sat on the porch swing.

"I like what I'm doing, Dom. I've made new friends in my classes, and I meet so many people on the road. I'm not always working." She tried unsuccessfully to help him understand why a twenty-something girl wanted to be on her own. She was now able to comfortably pay her bills and save money.

"I mean real fun, Christina." Dominic pressed her, planting his foot on the ground so the swing jolted back at a steep angle.

Christina held on, unfazed. "I've had dates. I've gone to concerts. I still run. And you see where I've been from the postcards I send. I'm seeing the world, I mean, the country."

"Been to a party lately?"

"Our company anniversary party was a blast. They hired a band. The food was over the top. Champagne flowed like rivers in spring thaw. We danced and took breaks outside on the patio overlooking the expansive golf course under the stars. I took two days to recover."

"A party with the bosses looking on? That doesn't count."

"Oh, Dominic. I have plenty of fun. You'll have to come out with us sometime in KOP. You know Diana and Gary, and you'll meet more of my friends."

She knew Dominic didn't understand and also knew he had only her best interests at heart. But like her mother, he seemed to think he knew what's best for her. They don't get my passion for this work. They don't get that I've made true friends here. They think I need a boyfriend or to get married to live happily ever after.

Christina hardly saw Sebastian when she was home. She avoided him as much as possible. She had felt his hatred of her intensify since the day he realized that her potential and ambition far exceeded his. Since he dropped out of college, he was unable to hold a steady job. Now at nearly thirty, Sebastian still behaved like a preteen. He cared only about beer, ball games, and boisterous boyhood pranks. Although he'd ceased being a boy long ago, his playground bully face had neither aged nor softened. Christina suspected his detachment stemmed from the fact he couldn't get away with pushing her around anymore. He had lost his target. His old target had become a force he was no longer prepared to confront.

When they were alone, Christina fielded her mother's more probing questions about her life. "Has there been a love interest after Drew, honey?" "When will you think about settling down?" "Aren't you worried about jetting all over the country, staying in hotels alone, driving on unfamiliar roads in a rental car? It must be exhausting."

'No, not now, and no, no, no, and no, Mom," she protested. "Mom, when I wanted to go to medical school you were all for it. Now that I have a different path, in a job that I love, you have doubts." Christina fumbled with her shirt collar and realized that her locket was not there. I must have forgotten to put it on after returning from Alaska. Do I really need to wear the locket anymore? She stood up straighter.

"I just wish you could come home to stay."

"Mom, things are different now. I'm living on my own. And making it. More than making it. People believe in me. They put their trust in me. They listen when I talk. I'm not just someone's sister or someone's daughter or someone's anything. I'm me. I'm happy."

Christina drove back by way of Allentown to see Terry and Ryan. Terry cradled the baby, wrapped in a pink polka dot blanket, as if she'd been doing it all her life. "Can you believe it, Christina? We're finally home after nearly three months."

Danielle weighed five pounds, ten ounces. Still small and with the feeding tube through a port on her tiny belly, she was getting stronger and now kept her eyes open longer, gazing up at Terry or Ryan as they held her. "They say they'll take the feeding tube out when she reaches six pounds, so maybe in a month or so. The doctors have been really great. A nurse comes here twice a week to check on her. At this point, they say Danielle may be more susceptible to respiratory illnesses but otherwise she'll be fine. Maybe smaller than if she was delivered full term. And I'm almost back to normal. The blood pressure came down, and they say it may have just been this one pregnancy and may not happen next time." Terry's eyes were bright.

"Next time?"

"Yes, Ryan and I will start trying for our second within a month or so. Danielle needs a sibling or a few siblings. I'll be home taking care of Danielle anyway. She has to be fed constantly and monitored, so I can take care of another."

"That seems ambitious, with all you've been through," Christina tried to hide her disbelief, seeing Terry had her mind made up. She held Danielle and felt the baby's tiny hand wrap around her pinky finger, wondering what the future held for this baby who was not yet out of the woods, despite her mother's optimism. The weight of that uncertainty bore down on Christina yet didn't seem to burden Terry.

"Tell me about what's going on with you, other than talking to news reporters. I'd like to hear what it's like in the outside world."

Christina noted the time. Her world spun in another galaxy. She decided not to try to explain it to Terry. "I'm going to Penn now, for business classes at Wharton. That takes up most of my free time outside of work."

She kept the visit brief, knowing both Terry and the baby needed rest. Driving away from Allentown and back to her apartment, Christina watched the sun setting in her rearview mirror. Gone were the days of her and Terry giggling and swapping albums. No more bike rides around the neighborhood or games of *H-O-R-S-E* on the driveway. The two friends' divergent paths were now growing further apart, toward opposite poles. Where Terry followed a straight path toward her childhood dreams, Christina's path twisted, and she had stumbled. The sharp turn she'd been forced to make had sent her in a direction she had never considered. Her resulting journey provided not only an unexpected opportunity for meaningful work but also an autonomy and independence she had so fervently sought but, until now, didn't know how to achieve. Christina hardly recognized her own life. How different from the one her family wanted for her. How different from her own vision just a few years ago.

Christina now had more in common with Diana, her photographer roommate of months, than with her lifelong friend. Diana's talent outpaced her drive, due to her lack of confidence and her fear of the audacity of dreaming big. The daughter of a deadbeat father and a single mother who typed in a steno pool to pay the bills, she had little support from home. She was lucky to have picked up an old Nikon camera from a neighbor who was moving. Diana learned to use it by photographing kids in the neighborhood and capturing Philadelphia street scenes for fun. An art teacher in middle school discovered her interest and let her borrow lenses.

In high school, Diana became proficient in the darkroom,

winning awards for her creative street scenes and landing a scholarship to the Pennsylvania Academy of the Fine Arts. Diana took the first job she was offered out of school because she needed money. The scholarship dollars ended at graduation, and her waitress side hustle wasn't enough to put gas in her car and eat. She couldn't wait for "the right job" to come her way. Three years later, she was barely making ends meet yet grateful to survive in the periphery of the art world.

Recognizing Diana's talent, Christina helped Diana develop a clientele of her own outside her school job. Whenever anyone at work mentioned wanting a family portrait or a photo of their dog or house, Christina raved about Diana's work and sent them her way. One corner of the living room in their apartment was permanently draped with white sheets, a standing tripod, and a gigantic umbrella, waiting for Diana's next take. It was just a matter of time, and the right client's photo getting into the right hands, before Diana would make it big, Christina thought. In the meantime, she did all she could to encourage her friend to expand her side business and, with it, her dreams.

"Not bad for a Polaroid or an Instamatic," Diana would say, after viewing snapshots from Christina's travels. "Maybe next time you could try to zoom in a little on the subject and show less background," or "Consider where the sun is before angling your shot."

"Diana, I never thought of that. When the camera is called 'point and shoot,' well, that's all I do. Who knew there was more to it! I bet your students love you."

Sure enough, Christina's Instamatic photos improved. Fewer and fewer had streaks of sun glare creeping in from the edges. Her shots became more focused on the subject she wanted to capture. Photos with darkened backlit faces became a thing of the past, thanks to Diana's advice. When she went to pick up her photos one day, the cashier at the Fotomat in King of Prussia Mall's parking lot commented, "Who's using your camera now? There are some really good ones in these last few rolls."

"No one but me, thank you!" Christina drove away, proud of her improved pictures.

Diana began compiling a portfolio from her side work, at Christina's insistence. "Once you collect a diverse sampling, you can apply for jobs that pay you to *do* photography instead of teaching it."

Marissa Porter, the news reporter who had interviewed Christina, had told her to keep in touch, so Christina phoned to ask a favor.

"Marissa, I have a friend who's a talented photographer, and she's developing a portfolio. Would it be possible for her to accompany you for a day and get a feel for what it's like to shoot a story? Maybe take her own shots? I'd really appreciate it if you could help her out."

Diana went along with Marissa as she covered the opening of Philadelphia's Market East Station. Christina was excited for her friend, knowing that these shots of scenes around Philadelphia would be easy for Diana. Having grown up riding SEPTA, her roommate was familiar with the crowded stations and trains. Christina remembered Diana telling her that while other riders dozed in boredom, she would scout potential angles to photograph the inside of train cars and the jostling of passengers when doors opened. Her photos showed the chaos she'd observed on platforms as trains approached and retreated. Diana had the eye of a skilled artist.

At first Diana followed a few steps behind Marissa's cameraman, Luciano, but then she ventured off to find her own take. Marissa and Luciano went about their work, and Diana picked her way through the crowd. Diana had become so engrossed in the scene they went searching for her when the station shoot was over. Next, they visited the city's Public Works Department for a story about contaminated public drinking water. Diana focused on the stern faces of officials explaining the failure. She zoomed in on the contrasting faces in the crowd. Their expressions demanded answers and solutions so their families could safely drink Philadelphia's tap water. She wandered through the crowd unobtrusively, with only the continuous clicking of the camera's shutter revealing her presence.

Two days later, Diana returned to the apartment after spending all evening in the darkroom at school. "I think I have a good one for the portfolio!" She handed a few prints to Christina.

"This close-up showing both the official and that woman in the crowd is incredible, Diana," Christina said, inspecting the prints. "You can simultaneously see her angry frustration and his defensive righteousness. Priceless!"

"I thought it odd Marisa's cameraman just panned over the crowd quickly and then spent all his time on the public official. Officials always wear the same expression, especially when they're trying to justify a failure in their department. How boring. The crowd was much more interesting to me."

Her photos revealed Diana's insight. The train station shots were equally compelling.

"I like this one where you captured the tedium of commuting, exhaustion on the faces of riders, the everyday occurrence of suited tote-carrying workers scurrying to catch their train. It reminds me of rats running in a maze. Diana, you've outdone yourself. What did Marissa say about them?"

"Oh, I didn't send them to her. She was just doing you a favor. I'm sure she's already forgotten I was there."

"Diana! Marissa has to see these. She won't forget you were

there when she sees them. I saw the news footage of the same event. It pales in comparison. Maybe he's been at it a long time, but Luciano's shots seemed uninspired to me. Maybe they could use a fresh eye at 6ABC?"

CHAPTER 36

MARISSA SHRIEKED WHEN she laid eyes on Diana's prints. "My gosh, girl, were you at the same place I was with Luciano?"

Diana caught her breath. "You don't like them."

"You kidding? Your prints put my guy to shame. Look at that woman pleading with the councilman! I can feel her frustration right through the film! And that train station. Was it really that claustrophobic? There's hardly room to cross your fingers on the platform. Since it's all behind me when we're taping, I can't see the whole picture. You really brought it to life, Diana. Luciano will be envious."

"I'm glad you like them, Marissa."

"You'll have to come with us again. I'll talk to my producer," Marissa promised.

Diana accompanied Marissa every couple of weeks and got a variety of shots to add to her portfolio, including one especially poignant portrait of a mother, sitting at a bus stop and cradling a baby in her arms, as gunfire erupted around them. Marissa asked if she could buy it, then framed it and hung it in her office at 6ABC. Her producer studied it and asked when Luciano took it.

"Oh, that's not Luciano's work. It's by a photographer named Diana Rubin."

"She really captured both the fear and love on that mother's face," the producer said. "See if she wants a job."

Diana couldn't believe one photo prompted a job offer. In talking with the producer, she found they were looking for a photographer for their human-interest segments. She showed him the few prints from her growing portfolio and from her college capstone project. The job she was offered at the end of the interview paid four thousand dollars more than her current salary at the art school, and its benefits were better. She started two weeks later. For Diana, the role offered her a chance to work in her field and more than pay her bills. It also offered the added benefit of growth potential.

To celebrate Diana's new job, Diana, Christina, and Marissa met for dinner at an upscale restaurant on Philadelphia's Main Line with outdoor dining on the terrace. The women enjoyed French food and wines and mostly each other's company. The conversation bounced from the latest fashions to the best clubs to the problems in the city until finally the server told them the restaurant would soon be closing. Marissa became a frequent visitor at Diana's and Christina's apartment, often bringing along a French Burgundy or a Tuscan Montepulciano for them to try.

Meanwhile, Christina juggled work, travel, and classes with development of her business plan. Christina decided to approach her classmate, Nat Valentine, to weigh her interest in joining the business project. Nat answered her friend's call with her usual energy.

"Hey, Christina. You having trouble with that econ assignment too?"

"Ahh, no, that's not why I'm calling, Nat. I have a proposition for you."

After launching into a pitch that she had honed in the shower, practiced with Diana numerous times, and recited in her head while running the five-mile loop in Valley Forge, Christina waited for Nat's response.

"Wow! That was quite a pitch. You sure you've never done sales? Of course I'm in. I can use it for my marketing case study assignment to boot! I can already think of where to launch and which conferences to plug into. And I can tap my existing clients. Who knows? I can jump from big box sales to vaporware."

"Does this mean we're partners?" Christina laughed into the phone, adding another name to her growing list of supporters.

It was a rare occasion when both Christina and Diana were in the apartment on weekend nights. One Friday evening, Diana was arranging new backgrounds in the corner of their living room for the next day's portrait session. Christina sat at their kitchen table working out design details for the ER product, as she did every waking moment and even during fits of insomnia. She had finalized the business plan except for the numbers that Whitt would soon provide. Adam Olson had agreed to give her more time to get details in order before pressing her further. She had then moved right into product design based on preliminary requirements she had collected. Christina wanted a solid specification document to show prospective developers, hoping to entice them to join the company by showing a feasible and elegant design that they could start programming immediately. If they could begin with a few screens and reports, there would be enough to demo for potential investors and clinical advisors.

As the girls took a break and waited for their food delivery, Diana asked Christina if she had told Marissa about her project.

"No, I haven't said anything because there's nothing to tell quite yet. Once my plan is ready, I'll tell her. I can't let word get back to HSA before I have a conversation with Jack about it. I'll probably go in early one day next week to discuss it with him."

"Aren't you just ready to explode with excitement?"

"Diana, to tell you the truth, I'm terrified. What if I fail? All these people thinking I can do something special, and what if I can't?"

"Hey, where's my old friend Christina? The one with ambitions and confidence for days? You're the one who told me to shoot for the stars. Now it's your turn." Diana patted her friend's arm.

"I don't know. The plan is good, but I don't want people to risk losing their jobs or having false hopes for something I can't deliver. If it was only me involved, that's one thing. But we're up to a dozen people now. It's a grave responsibility. I hope I'm good enough for it."

"You've got a dozen people involved already? My gosh, who all's on board?" Diana set out paper plates and grabbed a couple of sodas from the fridge.

"Ali and Whitt are my partners. So far, we have two of Ali's colleagues from Doctors for Emergency Service as advisors. Whitt is handling everything financial as a second job. My friend Nat Valentine is doing marketing strategy and wants to lead the sales team. I contacted a smart kid I know from MIT, Donny Meddleton, who is studying computer engineering. He wants to be a developer and will use anything we do before it officially becomes a company for credit in his independent study. He's learning MUMPS now. And he's got two classmates to join him."

"You got three MIT engineers? My gosh, Christina. Who else is on this dream team?" Diana called back from the kitchen. She had forgotten hot pepper.

"My colleagues, Abby and Bryce at HSA, have been sworn to secrecy and don't know the full plan yet, but they agreed to do preliminary operating system and backend development work. Abby has an old PDP machine she got from the company when they migrated to VAX. They were giving them away. Imagine, having one around for show." Christina raised her palms in wonder.

"She happens to have a commercial computer in her possession? Does she live in a data center?"

"I know, crazy lucky for me, huh? Anyway, it's enough to start with. Though I'll have to buy peripherals."

"OK, now you're talking nerd language." Diana waved a finger at Christina.

"Console, tape drive, terminals, printers, that kind of stuff. I can get them used and build a few components if I get back issues of *Popular Electronics* from the library."

"You're starting to scare me now. Anyway, who else—"

A knock at the door interrupted Diana, and she hurried to answer it. She paid the delivery man, then brought the paper-wrapped cheesesteaks to the table.

"Whitt is a member of the BMES, the Biomedical Engineering Society. That's what he did before going into hospital finance. He knows someone there, Cameron Nickle, who is currently working on programmable pacemakers. Cameron founded a company that will offer a pacemaker whose pace and other settings can be adjusted externally by a physician based on the patient's condition. He'll be a great resource. We may run into similar start-up issues. Whitt told him about our project, and Cameron agreed to be on our board, given his expertise in device programming. I can't wait to meet him. He's in Boston.'

"What about the cattleman?' Diana asked, taking a bite of the gooey sandwich.

"Adam Olson. He's in. It's just that I don't want to get him in officially yet, because of his relationship with Jack Walters. He'll do it, with bells on. I'm just sensitive to my current situation with HSA and don't want to burn any bridges."

"I suppose that's wise. Adam must know other people out west too. You want a national market, right?"

"He does. He already mentioned a guy he knows personally, who started a software company out near Seattle. Said he could put me in touch with him when I'm ready. Sounds like a great resource.'

"If he's developing software, wouldn't his company be a competitor?" Diana looked up, concerned, holding her cheesesteak midair, dripping sauce.

"I don't think so. Adam said he's doing something with *personal* computers, for regular people to have in their homes. Home computers. Can you imagine?"

"It sounds like something out of George Orwell's *1984*. Anyway, the more the merrier, I guess. All that brain power in one room makes my head hurt."

"I also have Sister Mary Xavier in mind to sit on the board."

"Sister who?"

"My client in Alaska. Sister Mary Xavier. She's their CEO. Smarter than any nun I've ever known, and I had eight years of nuns as teachers in grade school. She and I get along well, and she's an early adopter, er, she wants to be the first to get the latest technology. She's the one who gave me the whalebone rosary. I know she'll support us in some way. But I'll have to wait to bring her in, too, until after the Jack talk."

"Surely can't hurt to have someone praying for you, Christina." Diana put her hands together and knelt at the table.

"I'll need all the prayers I can get. I use that rosary she gave me every single night. I pray to God I'm doing the right thing."

"You are! And what about Marissa? She can get you publicity, spread the word, do a follow-up to her 'Dollars for Tech' feature segment."

"I'll see if she's interested. I'd love to have her involved in public relations. Or help Nat with marketing somehow."

"And you can let me know when you want a group photo."

"Diana, of course!" Christina nearly spit out the last mouthful of Tab. "I'd love for you to be our company photographer! We'll contract you for all our photo work."

Christina finally started eating her sandwich and stopped to look at Diana.

"Oh, Diana, I'm sorry, you're probably sick of hearing about all this, and you're getting ready for your new job, too."

"No, it's very cool. I'll take good pictures. You can pay me in cheesesteaks for now, Christina. Meanwhile, I'll take a few shots as you work. Then I'll be able to say, 'I knew her when…' Ha!"

CHAPTER 37

THOUGH NO LONGER sharing an office, Christina and Gary remained close friends and often caught a ball game or Happy Hour together with the group of regulars. One cold February night, Christina was at Touché celebrating her twenty-fourth birthday with her date, Colton Locke, and Diana, Marissa, Gary, and their group of work friends. Colton was a grad student from London, working at HSA on an internship. When he heard it was Christina's birthday, he convinced her to be his date that night. "No strings," he promised. Christina agreed, "Sure, why not? It's 1985, after all,'" and they decided to meet there after work.

Colton was a good-natured chap, which was the word he often used when referring to his friends. He entertained Christina with stories of pub crawling and said he once met Lady Diana, "before that bloke, Charles" was in the picture. Colton was a good dancer, and they enjoyed her birthday evening with the large group. Christina's roommate took on the role of introducing Marissa to the others before the two women left for another club.

Well into the evening, Christina stopped dead on the dance floor. There, across the crowd, was Drew, looking uncomfortably out of place and scanning the room as people jostled by with drinks. His eyes met hers, and he lifted his glass in her direction. Wondering what brought Drew here, Christina excused herself from Colton, who shrugged and flagged down a buddy to chat. She walked between dancers, careful to avoid those with full drinks in their hand, until she reached Drew.

"Drew, what on earth are you doing here?"

"I came to celebrate your birthday!"

"How would you know I was here?"

"I admit, I've been to a few of your favorite spots trying to find you. Then I thought to call your brother Dominic. After a bit of convincing, he told me you'd be here."

"He did, huh?" Christina couldn't believe Drew was here. Or that Dominic had let him know where to find her. Why does Dominic always think I need to be taken care of! When will he learn?

"Happy birthday, Christina." Drew leaned toward her. She dipped her cheek low at the last second and his lips met the air.

"Th-that seems like a long trip on the chance you'd find me, just to wish me happy birthday," she stammered, moving away from the thudding speakers.

"A chance worth taking. Anyway, I'm here. Want a drink?" Drew's casual retreat to their old ways of interacting puzzled her. Her thoughts were thankfully interrupted by Gary, who observed the scene from his post at the bar and ambled over to them.

"Hey, Drew, how's it going, man?" Gary shook Drew's hand and clapped his shoulder. Not waiting for Drew to respond, Gary turned to Christina and asked, "Christina, where did that date of yours get to? I can't see Colton sitting out 'Funkytown,' unless maybe he's waiting for you."

Christina mouthed a quick Thank-you to Gary.

"Oh—I'm sorry, Christina, I didn't realize you were here on a date. I was hoping we could talk privately." Drew looked away, squeezed the lime in his Tanqueray and tonic and gulped down the drink.

"Drew, this isn't really a good time. I'm here with my friends, and Colton, for my birthday."

"I can wait until you go home." Drew persisted. "If you're going home, that is."

"Dude, how about you and I go watch the game at the bar. Or I could challenge you to a game of Pac-Man. Let Christina enjoy her night." Gary nudged Drew's elbow toward the bar.

"I'm leaving at midnight tonight. I have to work early tomorrow," Christina called after him, checking the time. It was 11:20.

Christina left Drew with Gary. She found Colton talking with Mitch and Abby, who had come to join the celebration.

"Seems like that guy was on a mission from the likes of that serious expression he wore." Colton spoke with his polite British air.

"Just an old friend who wanted to wish me a happy birthday."

"Old friend, my arse." Colton cocked his head, then grabbed her hands and pulled her to the dance floor. Christina laughed, knowing Colton was a good sport, never taking himself too seriously.

Before the midnight hour, Christina worked her way around the room and said goodnight to her friends. Colton walked her back to her building up the street. They had meant to simply go out and have fun together, and they surely did. Colton knew he'd be going back to London, and Christina was relieved there were no expectations on either one's part. They parted after Colton insisted on giving Christina the Colton special embrace in honor of her birthday, which meant a bear hug followed by a low dip and kiss.

Gary had seen the two leaving and distracted Drew with a discussion of the recent Super Bowl. After a while, Drew looked at his watch. He scanned the room again but didn't see Christina. He waved down the bartender and picked up the tab for both himself and Gary before leaving. "I'm going to try and catch Christina at her place."

Christina sighed as she entered the apartment, immediately kicking off her heels and collapsing onto the sofa. Minutes later, Diana came in with Marissa, laughing and stomping the ground as they tried to catch their breath.

"What's so funny?" Christina called from the couch.

"Oh, I didn't see you there, birthday girl! Just that some weirdo was hitting on Marissa, and we couldn't get past those clodhopper shoes he was wearing," said Diana. "Is Colton here?"

"No, we went separately. I have an early morning tomorrow. But I think Drew is coming over."

"Wait, what? You were with Drew tonight?" Diana looked wide-eyed from Christina to Marissa.

"No. Drew showed up and insisted we talk. Gary was nice enough to come over and save me. He took Drew to the bar, mentioning something about my date. Drew got the message and said he'd wait until I left."

Just then, they heard a single knock on the door.

"I'm just leaving, anyway. I'll get the details from Diana tomorrow." Marissa opened the door and let Drew in, smiling as she left.

Diana greeted him. "Hi, Drew, how've you been?"

"Good, Diana, I'm good. How's school treating you?"

"I have a new job now, at Channel 6. I'm sorry, but I'm going to be a party pooper and take a quick shower before bed. Goodnight, all." Diana left Christina facing Drew in the living room.

"You didn't have to wait for me, Drew. It's late."

"I wanted to see you on your birthday, Christina, like I've done every year since we met."

"It's no longer my birthday. It's after midnight."

Drew sat down next to her and took her hands in his. Her mind flooded with memories at the touch of his hand.

She finally managed to say, "You could have let me know you were coming."

"I knew you'd say don't come. Or I was afraid you'd say that." He looked at her stack of papers piled high on the floor and his eye caught sight of the business law textbook. "You're reading business law for fun?"

"I had a date, Drew. Colton. It's not serious, but still."

"I'm sorry. Of course you'd have a date. I wasn't thinking."

"I'm not reading law for fun. A lot has happened since we last talked." Christina didn't take her hands away from his.

"I know. It's been months. Feels like years to me. Last time I heard your voice was on the news. Way too long ago." He reached for his coat, and Christina thought he was leaving. "That's why I'm here." Drew fumbled with his coat and pulled something from his pocket.

"Christina," he said, looking intently at her and turning her head as she tried to avoid his gaze, "These months have made me realize I want to spend every birthday with you. Every occasion. Every one of life's big and little moments. I want to share them with you. Christina, will you marry me?" Drew opened the small box he'd taken from his coat pocket to reveal a stunning diamond ring, an emerald cut on a delicate white gold band.

"Drew, please." Christina hugged her sides and hunched over, burying her head in her lap. Drew could see her shoulders trembling as she sobbed, gently at first then lurching in fits. She instinctively reached for her locket, quickly inhaling when she remembered she had never found it.

"Will you try it on?" Drew asked quietly.

Christina gulped for air through her sobs.

"I want you to have it. You can take your time to answer me. I love you. I can wait for you to be ready, darling. I think you still love me. I hope you still love me." He set the opened box down in front of her.

Christina looked up as she pushed matted hair from her forehead, away from her clouded eyes. "Drew, I've started a company. A software company called Helios. I'm the founder."

Drew blinked. He started to speak and paused. Then he gathered himself and said, "For a minute there, I thought you were going to say you started to love someone else. But you didn't." Drew paused before continuing, and Christina wondered if she had unintentionally given Drew false hope.

"We're meant for each other, Christina. I think of you every moment of the day. Of your hair falling in gentle cascades onto the graph paper in our physics study group. Your nervous laugh just before our Wild Mouse cart plunged down the tracks on Seaside Pier, your puzzled face as I held a death grip on your ankles when you teetered on the Shipwreck bar."

Chrstina fixed her gaze on Diana's tripod in the corner, wishing it could hold her up.

Drew continued. "I love your animated retelling of the piping plovers skittering over the sand to pluck a chip right from your hand, your confident and nurturing command while tending to Donny's bloodied hand. I see your slim shoulders rocking back and forth, guiding Chigger through a sloping meadow of wildflowers. I feel your heart breaking with empathy for Terry and Ryan when you describe their experience in the NICU. I see your passion for those NICU babies and the ER patients. These images of you are permanently imprinted on my retina. You're part of me, Christina. The best part of me, within me."

"Drew, don't." Christina pressed the heels of her hands into her eye sockets.

"Maybe now isn't the right time, darling. I'm impatient. But if we love each other, I can wait. You do your thing."

She said nothing, her eyes still covered.

Drew went on, "I have something I want to do. I've been accepted to graduate school, and I'll be moving to Boston. Keep the ring and promise me you'll think about it. I want to hear everything about your company, and in time, you'll tell me. I'll go now and wait to hear from you." He left a business card face down next to the ring on the coffee table, picked up his coat, and walked out of the apartment.

Diana found Christina stretched out on the sofa, sound asleep the next morning. When she started to tiptoe to the kitchen, a small white piece of paper fluttered on the coffee table. Her eyes landed on the diamond ring, and she clapped her hands over her mouth, stifling a gasp. Picking up the card from the table, Diana looked puzzled as she read what was printed—"Massachusetts Institute of Technology, Graduate School of Electrical Engineering and Computer Science."

CHAPTER 38

Jack Walters was known to arrive at HSA in predawn hours, and his Datsun 280Z was the lone car in the otherwise empty parking lot when Christina pulled in. She wanted to get this done early, with plenty of time to leave before anyone else arrived should he fire her on the spot. Regretting the second cup of coffee, she wished her nerves and the caffeine hadn't left her shaking like leaves in Aspen on an autumn morning. Steadying herself with deep breathing, Christina walked the empty corridors to Jack's office, power briefcase in hand.

His door was ajar, and Christina peeked through the crack and saw his head bent over the work on his desk. She knocked, three solid taps.

"It's open, come in." Jack looked up. "Ah, Christina, what can I do for you?"

"Good morning, Jack. I'm sorry to interrupt your work. I have something I want to discuss with you and thought it best to catch you before the day gets too busy."

"Sure. What is it?"

"Jack"—Christina set down her briefcase—"you and I both know how well received the pharmacy product is and that customers are lining up to install it. All our clients tell me how much they need clinical solutions. Beyond pharmacy and lab."

"Yes, and we're working on radiology soon too."

"I'm aware of the thirty-six-month plan, and I'll get right to the point. I've been asked to see if you would consider expediting development for an ER product."

"ER, huh?" Jack sat back in his chair, rubbing his hands along the leather armrests, his eyes fixed on the Stanford campus paperweight barely holding down a foot-high stack of papers beside his terminal. She wondered if he missed his days teaching undergraduates about modern computing.

"Also, NICU and OR. The demand is outpacing our development plan."

"Christina, you know a lot of thought went into that three-year plan. You were involved. You know we have to get lab and radiology out there because of their large volume and the revenue those areas generate for the hospitals."

"Of course, I realize their importance. Same could be said for ER and OR, in terms of revenue generation." Christina paused to gather her composure. "I was hoping we could also work in these other crucial apps simultaneously, during that time frame."

"With our resources, lab and radiology are all we can deliver in that timeframe with the quality we have come to expect. HSA is also developing more revenue cycle products, and we compete with them for company funding."

Christina nodded then spoke quickly. "You know my heart is with the clinicians and patients. I want to do more clinical development and deliver it fast. I've been working on a plan, which I have shared with interested parties. I've assembled a board of advisors and am ready to launch a company to develop the software. That is, after hearing from you that HSA is not embarking on that development in the near future. That's why I'm here."

Jack's mouth opened and no words came out. He studied Christina for a moment, then cleared his throat. "I knew you were sharp. That's why I got you on our team."

"Believe me, I appreciate everything you've done for me. I have done my best for HSA and our clients. I'd stay here if we could proceed along those lines."

"You know, I see a lot of myself in you, Christina. That fire in the belly, that passion. Your determination. I admire that in you. I won't hold you back, even if that means you'll become a competitor."

"Jack, I'm hoping to become a sort of partner. My software can be integrated with Aura, as an add-on, if you will. I was hoping you'd agree to be an advisor."

"A sort of friendly fire arrangement?" Jack smiled. 'I'd be a fool to impede you. I'll support you, though I'll need to clear that with our legal department before I can accept any official role. Can I ask what got you started on this?"

"It was the Reagan visit, really. When that reporter asked me what innovation I'd like to see, the question lit a spark in me. I couldn't get those ideas out of my mind. Why not do it myself, go after funding, start up with a new product, develop what's so urgently needed and perfectly feasible? You know I was an EMT. I've a close relationship with an ER physician who has convinced me of the urgency of ER's needs. Together, we've assembled a team."

Jack's thoughts came at her fast. "If it becomes, I mean *when,* it becomes an MVP, we should talk. You know HSA buys up niche systems."

"MVP? I'm sorry, I'm only two classes into my MBA."

"Minimum viable product."

"Oh, of course, when it goes to market. We are just weeks away from an MVP demo to prospective backers. An HSA purchase could be a terrific opportunity down the road. Though we are thinking beyond ER to other products, as well, so maybe we'd wait until the full suite is developed."

"I'm sure you won't stop at ER. Just keep that thought in the back of your mind."

"Will do. Oh, and Jack, a few of your employees have been working at night with me."

"Not only will we lose you, but you're also taking my staff? That'll be tough to take sitting down."

"Aside from those who are already engaged—there are only a handful—I'll sign an agreement to not hire your employees for a period of six months."

"I see you've done your homework. Who am I to hold a good man, er, I mean, woman down?" Jack shrugged his shoulders and frowned. "I need you to do a couple things, though. Will you stay on board a few months to consult on pharmacy as we roll it out? And can you refrain from telling our people until after you've gone?"

"Yes and yes. With two exceptions—Gary Wentworth and David Stokes. I owe a great deal to them. I owe them an honest explanation. Without them, I wouldn't even be here."

"So, I take that to mean neither of them is working for you now? You got to leave me a couple of my A-team players."

"You have my word."

CHAPTER 39

CHRISTINA COULD HARDLY wait to call Adam, but because of the time difference and her need for privacy, she resigned herself to taking the next few hours to review the latest pharmacy contracts and put Helios temporarily out of her mind. At lunchtime, she raced back to her apartment to call him.

"Mornin' to you, young lady. How's it going with plans for Helios? I've been out of the saddle waiting to hear."

"I have a lot of news for you. I wanted to discuss things with Jack Walters first before updating you, to be sure I'm heading in the right direction and not burning bridges."

"Fair enough. Don't let the horse out of the gate too soon."

"Yes. Jack confirmed HSA is not developing ER, NICU, and OR anytime in the next three years. I wanted to be sure that was true before going any further."

"And?"

"I've assembled a team for Helios development. Recruited talent for a board of advisors and engaged a lawyer for the business set up. I've written a business plan, with help from Whitt Bates, my finance guy, which I'll send you for review. I've written specs for ER-GO, the ER product, and have started myself, three interns from MIT, and a couple of HSA developers on writing code. It'll function on its own and optionally integrate with HSA's Aura. We'll have a high-level MVP to demo within a few weeks."

Adam whistled into the phone. "You've been running on high test, Christina! I knew you'd come through and felt certain HSA was not going to keep up. I'll review your plan right away. What else do you need at this point?"

"We are in urgent need of development space. We are working in silos now with everyone writing code on paper at home and meeting at Abby's to load it onto the system, but we'll need to assemble soon as a team in one office, with equipment and a small data center. We also need to recruit investors and secure loans. Adam, I'd like to ask you to chair our board."

"You won't believe your own luck. After we last talked, I started scouting around Pennsylvania for farmland to raise dairy cows out East. I found two hundred acres out in Glenmoore, Chester County. It has a big farmhouse and a few outbuildings, a pole barn and machinery garage."

"Adam, that's exciting. You want to raise cows here?"

"Always looking for greener pastures, Christina. Why not there? Especially if I'm going to need to stay involved in my software investment!"

"Does that mean you'll be joining us?" Christina was jumping up and down in her living room.

"Done deal. Also, I won't need all the buildings' space on the property. Maybe you could use the farmhouse for Helios's offices and an outbuilding for the data center. I mean, if you think that could work for you. Would be good for me to have the place occupied, aside from the herd manager and feeders, folks who'll work the place."

"My gosh, Adam, what a generous offer! How can we do it?"

"I'm coming out to look at the place. You should come along with your decision makers, of course, and check it out, see if it'll do. If we both like it, I'll expedite the transaction. It's vacant now so we can move quickly."

"This is beyond amazing. It sure is my lucky day."

"Oh, and Christina, I think you'll want to meet with my friend, Ford Burch, the fella I told you about who's working on personal computer software. He was where you are now a couple years ago, and he can share lessons learned. Nice guy, too, and he rides. I know I promised you a ride, so come on out, and I'll get him over to the ranch. Maybe invite my Washington Hospital Association colleagues as well, round out the group. They'll be interested in hearing what you've got planned. There may be investors in that group."

"Adam, I can't thank you enough! And by riding, I hope you're talking horses and not that steer you mentioned before. I'd love to meet Mr. Burch and the WHA, give them my pitch."

"All right, a horse. But maybe you'll try a steer? No pressure. And Christina, you're definitely doing the right thing. I knew you could."

Christina's next call was to Sister Mary Xavier, who told her the Anchorage thaw was starting and she and the sisters were looking forward to some evening hikes as the days lengthened. "We had an incident with a bear pawing at the hospital entrance a few weeks ago. I thought of you, Christina, and how shocked you were that time you encountered a moose. How are things in Pennsylvania?"

"Sister, I'm calling with some news and a request." Christina launched full speed into her pitch, pumped by Adam's offer. "And Sister Mary, I'd like to invite you to join our board."

"Bless you, Christina," cried Sister Mary. "When did you find time to do all that, dear?"

"I've been working on Helios every waking hour since the president came to Lenapy last year. After work at HSA, of course.

We just released pharmacy, so the heat is off a bit. And with Jack Walters aware of my plans now, it will make things a bit less stressful. I'll be staying on as a consultant to HSA on pharmacy through the rollout, on an as-needed basis."

"Oh, to be young and have all that energy, dear! I'm excited for you, and for the industry. We need people like you who understand our mission and develop technology to execute it. Yes, I'm honored to be on the board of Helios. Send me the plan."

"Sister, I'm thrilled you're joining us. Soon we will meet in Yakima to share details with potential investors and clients. Adam Olson will be hosting it. It would be great if you could attend."

"Things are moving fast, Christina. You be sure to take good care of yourself. I always pray for you, dear, and now I'll keep you in my prayers twice a day. We'll talk soon!"

Similar enthusiasm came from Baton Rouge's CEO, Simon Deveaux, and Marissa Porter and both agreed to board membership. Marissa was already thinking of follow-up stories from the Reagan visit to pitch to her producer, and Christina's steps toward innovation aligned well with her ideas.

Christina held meetings for the local team and whoever else could make it in a field at Valley Forge park. In bad weather, they crowded into her living room or at a back table in Bookbinders Annex. The interns and programmers couldn't believe they might soon have real office space. Jokes had already started about the development team sharing their campus with livestock. They began defining requirements for the computer room and workspace in preparation for Christina's assessment of the space on Adam's farm. Whitt would go with her and Adam to evaluate the site.

Christina's legal advisor, Julia Keene, drew up agreements and bylaws for the board members and proposed agreements for her, Whitt, and Ali. She drafted compensation options for the developers and initial staff. Things were coming together at warp speed.

CHAPTER 40

CHRISTINA DROVE THE familiar back roads through Chester County, thinking about how best to share with her family all that had transpired. Her mother knew she was working on a side project of her own and going to school at night. She lamented in their phone conversations how infrequently they'd seen Christina these past few months.

Christina decided that after her parents learned about the company, she would ask them to help her with seed money. Between what she, Ali, Whitt, and the others had put in, their funds would suffice for a short while, but they'd need more. However much her parents might offer would be helpful. Holding the steering wheel with one hand, she instinctively reached for the locket and remembered again that it was no longer there. In its place was nothing but Christina's own neck and shoulders, supporting a head full of aspirations. Would her parents support her now or not?

Christina thought the best way to bring them up to speed was to have them read her plan while she spent a few hours unwinding at Carousel. Being around the horses would provide a well-deserved respite, and a ride through the fields would bring the peace she needed. Alone on the trails, Christina would tell Chigger exactly what she would say to her parents, and he'd simply nicker or whinny his approval.

Slinging the saddle onto the horse's back, Christina felt weights dropping from her own shoulders. She inhaled the aroma of sweet hay mixed with barn smells and let the rhythmic clopping of Chigger's hooves lull her into a meditative calm. The idea of working on Adam's farm with horses nearby that she could regularly consult with brought joy to her soul.

The Comos sat around the kitchen table, the pages of her document spread out between half-empty cups of coffee and plates holding crumbs of biscotti when she returned from her ride. Her father held the page detailing the bios of board members and staff bios, his mouth agape.

"You've got people from Alaska to Louisiana, cattle ranchers to college kids rallying behind you! How in the world did you pull this off, Christina, and when?" Her father seemed astounded at the presentation. "How long have you been at this?" He looked at her as if she were a stranger appearing unexpectedly at his door.

After removing her boots at the front door, she stepped into the kitchen in stocking feet, pulling off her riding gloves one finger at a time, and glanced at them sideways. "I've been busy." She poured herself an espresso.

"It's no wonder we haven't seen you much, honey! Working your job, going to Penn, and starting up a company in a matter of months. We had no idea." Her mother brought her hands to her face, her fingers resting along her jawline.

"Well, Mom, I told you I had a project, and you knew about school." Christina dunked her biscotti into the dark liquid and continued. "I wanted to wait until I talked with HSA to officially launch the company. I didn't want to burn bridges, and I had to know that HSA was not heading in that direction before I committed."

"A project? This is more than a project, Christina," Her father said.

"It seemed more like a pipe dream at first. But then I heard the president speak about America leading in the technology space and how the government was fostering innovation. Because of what I knew from talking with Ali and my customers, the idea would not leave my head. It consumed me to the point I had to act."

"Christina, the business world is not kind. There are people who will chew you right up and spit you out. It can be ruthless, vile, and unforgiving. Especially for a woman." Her father's lips drew tight.

Brushing aside his comment along with a few biscotti crumbs that dropped to the table, Christina said, "I've been in that world now for a few years. It doesn't take long to see that some people stagnate like a dammed-up reservoir and others propel themselves into the future like waves onto a beach. I'm one of the waves, I guess. I've traveled to more states than you and Mom have seen in your lifetime, and I've been in dozens of hospitals across the country. I listened. I saw a need. I know what can be done. I've worked hard to formulate a plan. I know what *must* be done. So, I'm doing it."

"Why not stay at HSA and do it there, sweetheart?" her mother suggested. "Let them take the risk?"

"They're taking a different direction. They're a big company, not so agile to flex with the market easily. It'll be years before they can get where I'll be. I'm ready now. I have people who believe in me, who are helping me, who believe we can do it. What do I have to lose, really?"

"But it takes money, not just smarts, Christina."

Her father's skepticism tasted more bitter than the espresso in her cup. "I have savings. Whitt and Ali are putting up seed money. Adam is giving us a six-month waiver for rental space when he buys the farm. We are giving staff equity and options, and we'll be pitching investors for funding this month. I'm not asking for your approval or permission. I'm asking you for a loan, to be repaid, with interest."

"How much do you need," her mother stated rather than asked.

"Ideally, twenty-five thousand. That can help with salaries and equipment we'll need the first few months. You read the budget. You could loan me the money to be paid back, or you could be an angel investor who gets paid with a stake in the company, if you'd rather."

Her father remained silent.

Christina pressed on. "I figure my college scholarship saved us close to five thousand dollars on my education, so hopefully you have that available to lend me, and you haven't needed to support me the past few years like you've done for Dominic and Sebastian. But I would appreciate any amount you could loan me at this time. I'll pay it back."

"We'll give you the five thousand, Christina." Her mother looked directly at her, then turned to her husband and asked, "And maybe we can loan her the rest?"

Still Mr. Como was silent.

"You can think about it and let me know. I'll be here all weekend. Right now, I need a shower." Christina cleared her cup and plate from the table and started to walk upstairs. She refused to plead with her father. She'd get another loan if she had to, before begging him for a cent. Why would I think he'd support me now, when he tried to convince me I didn't need a college degree? When he hardly acknowledged my scholarship? When he always thought the boys would amount to something and never considered I might?

Her brothers burst through the front door and stopped suddenly upon seeing the serious expressions on their parents and sister.

"Christina, honey," Mrs. Como got up and wrapped her arms around Christina. "I'm so proud of you!"

"What'd *she* do?" asked Sebastian, rolling his eyes.

"More than you'll ever do in your lifetime." Christina ascended the stairs.

"What was that all about?" Dominic was in the driveway, buffing his Mustang to a glossy shine when Christina stepped outside. "Dad looked like he did that time his company was sold and he wasn't sure if he still had a job." He stopped rubbing for a second and looked her way.

"Nothing like that, Dominic. I told them I'm starting a company, and he about lost it."

"You're what?" Dominic set the polishing aside, taking a seat next to her on the porch swing.

Christina started from the beginning, telling her story for a second time that day. "I never get tired of talking about this. I'll never get tired of working on it either." The work not only kept her interest, it energized her, replenished her reserves, and made her feel more competent and alive than anything ever had before. Dominic could feel the electricity, and a grin spread across his face.

"Teen, I didn't know you had it in you. I mean, I knew you were going somewhere. It just never occurred to me you'd be the one to solve a problem like that and lead a bunch of big wigs into the cause. I'm with Mom. I'm proud of you too. My sister, a company president."

"Thanks, Dom. But it's not quite there yet. I didn't expect to do this. I didn't set out to do this. I'm the same Christina, the one who watches, listens, figures things out, and works her butt off. And turns out, I got this figured out. With help, of course. It's nothing

I could do alone." Christina had finally learned to lean on others for help. To trust those who believed in her.

"Christina, what ever happened with Drew?"

"Drew moved to Boston, Dom. End of story."

Her brother peered at a loose screw on a swing board that was missing its companion bolt.

"I like Drew, Teen, more than our own brother," Dominic said, biting his lower lip and picking up the missing bolt that had fallen. "When you get to the point of building that data center, maybe you can give me a job doing the telecom work. I'm not married to the phone company, you know, and I'll work hard."

"Maybe. I don't want to involve you in something that may not work out. I'd hate to drag you down with me." Christina's eyes watered.

Dominic offered her his handkerchief. She knew he recognized that recurring shadow of self-doubt, the one he had seen many times, and was sorry she let it show. This time, though, Dominic spoke up to thwart it for good. "The way I see it, Teen, you're pulling people up with you. Why don't you forget all that self-doubt once and for all and realize you're destined to succeed? Forget Sebastian's, Dad's, and everyone else's crap you've tolerated for way too long. There's no way you'll fail. You can do it."

She nudged her elbow into his ribs, then jumped from the swing and ran out into the yard. Her brother raced after her, laughing and circling her until they both fell to the ground, like they'd done when playing together as children. Christina caught a glimpse of her mother's wistful face as she watched them through the kitchen window.

"Dom, can you see Mom? She looks like she's witnessing one of us precariously perched atop the swing set."

CHAPTER 41

TERRY'S SECOND PREGNANCY was nothing like the first. At thirty-four weeks, she was the picture of health, not a hint of pre-term labor or high blood pressure. Terry and Ryan were still enjoying walks through their neighborhood, pushing little Danielle, cooing and batting at toys, in the stroller. At home, Terry chased after the crawling baby with glee, despite carrying her daughter's sizeable sibling in her burgeoning belly. Danielle was still small for her age but growing on her own. She constantly battled respiratory illnesses, which, fortunately, set her back only temporarily. Ryan and Terry took it all in stride and having gone through a difficult first birth, anticipated no issues with the second.

The couple moved baby paraphernalia to one side of their living room and did little else to prepare for Christina's visit. Terry pulled a baked ziti and tray of meatballs from the freezer, and Ryan played with Danielle as the three fell into the easy exchange of old friends catching up after a long time apart. Terry told Christina that she was becoming good friends with one of the NICU nurses who lived in their building and had cared for Danielle for months. The nurse told Terry about a new program at the hospital in which parents of preemies shared their stories and offered support for new NICU parents.

"I'm going to join this program once the new baby is born. I'd do anything to help those parents avoid the anxiety we went through when Danielle was in the NICU. I'm sure there are tips I can share," Terry said as Christina set the table for dinner.

"You'll be so busy, Terry. A new baby, a soon-to-be toddler, and NICU supporter. Be sure to take care of yourself. Your babies will need you at your best!"

"And me too," Ryan added, as he carried a flailing Danielle into the kitchen. "Danielle didn't want me to pick her up because she was headed toward the stereo. It'll be a miracle if the machine survives those little hands pushing all the buttons and turning the volume knob all the way up. Sometimes we forget Danielle has been near it, and when we turn it on, we both jump out of our skin."

"Gotta love those Bose speakers you have, Ryan. Soon they will be blasting nursery rhymes and Disney songs instead of The Police."

"Not instead, Christina, in addition to. Our kids will grow up with good music." Ryan put Danielle in the highchair.

"And they'll learn to sing," Terry called over her shoulder, removing the ziti from the oven.

"You guys are the quintessential parents! I still can't believe it."

"A lot has happened since the wedding, that's for sure."

"Yes." Christina paused, then said, "I have some news to share with you."

Repeating the story, in abbreviated form over dinner for Terry and Ryan, Christina spoke with a newfound confidence. They asked all kinds of questions, which Christina took as a good opportunity to practice responses she could use in future pitches to investors.

"Something lit up in you when you were talking to that reporter, Christina!" said Terry. "I could see your wheels spinning, and I thought to myself, she's up to something."

"I really wasn't then, but after that interview I couldn't stop thinking about it. Talking with Ali cemented it in my mind."

"Who's Ali?" Ryan asked.

"He's the ER doctor, Rye, who Christina worked for. I met him when we ran into him on Main Street that time going to the Shipwreck."

"He's now my business partner." It was the first time Christina said those words.

"Maybe if the farm works out, Christina, you'll let us take the kids over to see the animals sometime?" Terry asked, sprinkling parmesan over the ziti.

"Of course. I'll show them the computers and the data center, too."

"Recruiting already? Now that's the Christina I know." Ryan smiled, shoveling a spoonful of pureed ziti into Danielle's mouth. "Hear that, Danielle? Auntie Christina thinks you'd rather see a computer than a cow."

CHAPTER 42

As Whitt pulled up to the airline terminal, Christina scanned the sleepy crowd pouring out from baggage claim. Adam had taken the red-eye flight from Seattle, so he'd have a full day to check out the site and meet with the Realtor. Suddenly a ten-gallon hat bobbed above the throng of passengers.

"That's him!" Christina knew Adam spotted her when he tipped his hat her way.

"That's what I call service." Adam hugged Christina and smiled at Whitt.

"Hi, Adam. Whitt Bates." The men shook hands, and Whitt tossed Adam's bag in the trunk. "Good to finally meet in person. I feel like I've known you for years, from all that Christina's told me."

"Whitt, Christina's been singing your praises since day one. Said she couldn't have done the finances for our plan without you. And I studied those figures with a microscope. They're solid. Rock solid."

"Adam, Ali is meeting us for lunch after we visit the property. We have about an hour's drive to the farm. We figured you'd be more comfortable in Whitt's sedan than in my Honda."

After maneuvering around turns on the Schuylkill Expressway, they settled into a smooth ride on the Pennsylvania Turnpike. Whitt recapped their attorney's recommendations since their last call with Adam. Christina updated him on development efforts, noting how close they were to being able to show ER-GO's proof of concept, with a functioning demo not far behind. Though Adam had come to Corporate HSA a few times, he had forgotten about the traffic around Philadelphia. He asked about the town of Glenmoore, wondering if the farm was surrounded by highways.

"No real town there, Adam. It's a tiny village, with one crossroads. The only traffic around will be your cows." Christina remembered all the open space in Yakima and knew Adam would like the western side of Chester County.

Whitt turned onto a gravel road that ascended an incline and wove through an evergreen forest. Eventually the lane deposited them in a clearing beside a flat meadow enclosed by split-rail fencing and stone walls. A stately stone farmhouse rested at the far corner of the clearing, opposite a giant red barn with sloping roof. Beyond the barn, acres of green pastures rolled and sprawled as far as they could see.

"This could be a set for a civil war film!" Adam whirled around for a 360-degree view. "I'll bet we find solid shot here in these fields." He stepped over a sharp rock jutting from the soil. "Definitely fertile land here for dairy cows and horses."

The sound of tires on gravel caught their attention as Adam's Realtor parked.

"I see you found the place." The agent ushered the group into the farmhouse. Low door heights posed a challenge for Whitt's height, and Adam removed his hat. The stone walls were eighteen inches thick, adorned solely with cobwebs and dust.

"The place has been vacant a while. The farmhouse, that is. Farm's been worked up until last year. Cows all left when the owner thought he had it sold to a developer who was going to put up a slew of manor homes. Deal fell through when the county put up a fuss."

They walked through the main house, which dated from the late 1700s, then through two additions, a clapboard addition built a century later and one built within the last twenty years. The stairs to the original second floor were mighty steep. Only Christina could stand erect on that second floor, the headroom cramped by sloping ceilings. The additions were more habitable, although less charming, and the second addition had modern heating and plumbing and a decent kitchen. All told, the farmhouse totaled over five thousand square feet. It could easily work for a few dozen staff, thought Christina.

From there, the agent walked them to the barn. Its cavernous interior could accommodate a three-ring circus. Aside from a few birds' nests and an obvious leak near the sliding barn door, it was in good shape. They spent the next hour walking the grounds near the farmhouse and inspecting the empty feed silo and the greenhouse, now overrun with plantings that thrived despite abandonment. Farther out were a milking shed and a stable perched on a hill next to a riding ring. A stunning property in terms of potential and colonial charm, it left each one to their thoughts, imagining all that might take place in the future on grounds with a history that went back centuries.

Departing the site just as a cold spring rain descended from billowing gray clouds blown in from the west, the group silently took in the expanse of nature before them. They circled much of the property along narrow country roads to get a glimpse of its distant pastures, many of which were hidden from view by a border of pine forest. They spotted a small lake on the property and a creek that ran through the northwest corner. Christina wondered if Springton Grove might have looked similar to this farm before it had become home to HSA and other companies setting up shop on its suburban corporate campus.

The decision, ultimately, was Adam's, though Christina could think of no reason the farm couldn't be Helios' temporary home while the company was in its incubation period. "This here could be a sweet addition to the Olson family ranches," Adam said as they thanked the Realtor and drove off to meet Ali. "You see, my grandfather was originally a dairy farmer in western Pennsylvania, before packing it all in to move out West. My family still has ties to PA. I might even be able to convince one of my sons to run this place someday."

"Does that mean you are interested in making an offer?" Christina asked.

"I sure am. And I wonder if you think the farmhouse could work for Helios while you get started? I know it's a bit rustic, but we could look at replacing those old windows to reduce the drafts, and I'd have to upgrade the electric anyway to modern standards."

"Adam, we are all used to working in frigid computer rooms, so drafty workspaces aren't a problem for our team." Christina had never received such a gift. "We can absolutely make it work. We'll be responsible tenants."

"We can draw up lease terms, with the idea of adjustable rates as we grow, Adam," Whitt interjected. "We don't expect you to rent it to us for free. Ali, Christina, and I have pooled our funds for seed money, and we are going after loans and investors. We should know in a matter of months if we can expand Helios through development and into the market. The farmhouse itself has plenty of space for our R&D and operational team now and possibly for the next year."

"All right then. I'll call my Realtor after lunch. We'll meet Ali with the good news! I just hope you won't be too put off as we move in the cows and farm operations. I'd like to settle within the month and be up and running shortly after."

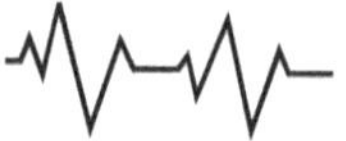

Christina accompanied Adam on his flight back to Seattle. Whitt and Ali would be joining her in two days for the meeting with WHA, the Washington Hospital Association. On the lengthy flight, Adam gave Christina a rundown on all the attendees, their hospital's pain points, administrative challenges, and interest in clinical systems. She listened, asked probing questions, and jotted notes to inform her presentation and to share with Ali and Whitt. She and Ali would be presenting the proof of concept and pitch. Whitt was at the ready for financial inquiries and to address any operational questions that arose.

The day before the WHA meeting, Adam had invited his friend, Ford Burch, out to the ranch to meet Christina. She wasn't expecting the lanky young man wearing a V-neck sweater and wire-framed glasses who pulled up in his sleek futuristic DeLorean and bounded to Adam's front step. She and Adam were sipping tea on the veranda. Christina had expected an older man, maybe Adam's age, since Adam had told her they were old friends.

"You're Chris Como?" Burch seemed just as surprised to see Christina as she was to meet him.

"It's Christina," she corrected him with a smile.

"Adam, you know I had in my mind you said it was Chris, so I'm thinking I'll meet some prep guy you know from back East. Anyway, what a pleasant surprise."

"Don't let her youth or beauty fool you, Ford. Her mind is as shrewd as they come."

Christina acknowledged Adam's comment with a dismissive roll of her eyes. "Just how is it you two became friends?" Adam poured tea for his friend, then handed him a rough ceramic mug.

"This guy started renting a cabin of mine a while back. Said he needed someplace quiet to think and read. No distractions. My cabin was pretty bare bones, out in the mountains between here and Seattle."

"Sounds like a nice retreat to me."

"Pretty soon he kept coming back. I'd bring a couple horses out, and he'd explore the cedars 'round the cabin. Then he came out to the ranch. Rest is history." Adam whacked Burch's shoulder. "Turns out, he was busy thinking up the next big software product while riding my horses, then went back to his lab and wrote the code."

"I can understand how horses bring out your creative side." Christina looked at Burch. "I spent a lot of time riding as a kid. I found it relaxing and got a lot of my own thinking done on horseback."

"I knew you two would get along. She's got a software company in the works, Ford, like I told you. I'm on her board. I thought on our ride we can fill him in on Helios, Christina, and over dinner maybe Ford can offer some pointers, seeing how he's doing so well with PerComp."

If the side trip to Washington yielded nothing for Helios, Christina would have been content with the daylong ride through the valley and then winding up into the hills through dense timber forests. This place is inspiring in itself, she thought, and best appreciated on horseback. The conversation and company were even better.

Christina enjoyed the quick wit of Adam's friend and appreciated his passion for technology. He envisioned getting a computer in every home in America, just as she envisioned software for every clinician in the hospital. They shared an interest in solving complex problems through technology and a penchant for hard work. They both felt lucky to call Adam, old enough to be their father, not only a friend but a supporter.

The meeting with Washington Hospital Association and Adam's business associates from the Ranchers' Alliance was intended to be a casual afternoon gathering of Adam's colleagues, held in the huge reception hall of central Washington's rodeo grounds. Folks started sauntering in by ten in the morning, taking time to stroll the grounds and observe the few animals on-site in the livestock pens. Some attendees who arrived early, having driven a few hours from the coast, walked around, peeking into stalls and pacing corrals to stretch their legs. Others sat back on wooden benches in the grandstands, taking in the country air and reconnecting with old friends and business buddies. Most came because of Adam's personal invitation. Adam Olson greeted everyone by name as they rolled in, stopping to pat some on the back and embracing others. He was well known throughout the state.

Having been on the bandwagon for hospital improvements for over a decade, Adam was known as both a motivator and an innovator. He would sometimes browbeat reluctant administrators, with his cowboy charm, into focusing on care outcomes as much as revenue. He had led the charge toward automation, convening a committee to explore computers in other industries with the hopes of bringing technology into healthcare. Others had dealings with Adam as a rancher and agreed there wasn't a more honest, hardworking rancher in the state. They all knew Adam in his various roles, and when the man had a request, like this one to listen in on the latest developments coming to healthcare, they came at once to honor it.

Adam got up in front of the group and introduced the guest speaker, C. Como, the CEO of Helios, a new company working on _linical solutions for emergency and neonatal care, surgical suites, and more. He drew in the ranchers with a quip about the staggering number of their cattlemen who end up at hospitals across the state. He cautioned them to open their ears and their bankrolls, to support the efforts of forward-thinking individuals who take the bull by the horns and get in the ring to make change happen. When he handed the microphone to Christina, the crowd was shocked to see a petite young woman take her place behind the podium.

"Hello, I'm Christina Como, the founder of Helios. And because I can hardly see over this, I'm going to step out in front of the podium and tell you about what we've been doing at Helios." Christina took a deep breath and launched into stories about industrial accidents, community disasters, and personal mishaps that sent scores of people to emergency rooms every day, many waiting hours for treatment, standing, bloodied, before reception desks or crouched over them, debilitated by pain. She moved on to premature infants in the NICU, struggling to survive even before their lives had a chance to get started and then described parents helplessly watching nurses and doctors fumbling with calculators and conversion charts to confirm medication dosages or retrofit adult supplies to fit the littlest of patients.

Christina painted a graphic image for her audience of a patient anxiously awaiting critical heart surgery, delayed in the prep and holding area while doctors frantically searched for their medical chart to review prior conditions that might put the patient at risk. Her empathic description of patients and their loved ones experiencing today's healthcare system left attendees pulling handkerchiefs from pockets to wipe their foreheads or eyes.

Then she introduced her partner, Dr. Ali Aboud, who proceeded to share his experiences as an emergency care physician. Ali expressed sheer frustration that patient longitudinal records are

unavailable during emergency care, forcing him and h⁃
to treat only what is immediately apparent because of a ⌐
accessible medical history. He described critical delays in treatment,
waiting for imaging or lab or other diagnostic procedures because
of communication bottlenecks, scheduling conflicts, and shared
resources within the hospital. He told a story of a patient who
needlessly expired on a stretcher in the hallway, somehow lost in
the shuffle when no ER beds were available, and staff were unable
to locate the patient in the corridor. Eyebrows raised and whispers
spread across the room as he motioned for Christina to resume
discussion of their solution.

"Ali and I have worked amid these frustrations and unnecessary
barriers to care. We've heard from clinicians and administrators
who agree we can do better. They are working with us, sharing
insights, suggestions, requirements, and guidance. We started with
the emergency room and have built our first product, ER-GO.
It'll be generally available within the next three months. On the
heels of ER, we have a NICU, OR, and scheduling solutions
planned for development. We will tackle every clinical area in the
hospital, one by one, until hospitals can get back into the business
of *delivering* care, letting computers handle the mundane, the
routine, the calculations, storage and streamlining. We will deliver
a solution that improves patient outcomes and enhances clinician
satisfaction and efficacy, and restores their passion for their work
as vital emissaries for health."

Christina was pacing the stage, looking directly at individuals
in the front rows and addressing those across the room, her tiny
but animated figure commanding their attention.

"We have a proof of concept now to show you, and the full
prototype is being alpha tested as we speak. This product uses
the latest software technology to solve ER's challenges around
patient history, patient tracking as they move through the ER

and diagnostic areas, and operational challenges. These issues result in lengthy stays and bottlenecks. Our product facilitates bed availability and throughput by triaging and carving out fast track paths for less acute patients, moving them through and out of the system quickly to enable focus on the sickest, most acute patients. The software suggests, records, tracks, and streamlines care so that clinicians can provide the care they're trained to deliver, without the roadblocks of manual systems, poor procedures, poor communication, errors in judgment, or the inevitable human error in written records. I'm going to show you ER-GO now. But first, let me ask if you have any questions."

There was one man in the far back who poked his hand up.

"I have two questions: How do we get ER-GO, and how can I invest in your company?"

Whitt fielded the question as Christina prepared to demonstrate the product. Christina spotted Ford Burch toward the back of the room just before the lights dimmed for her demo.

CHAPTER 43

Momentum from the Washington meeting catapulted Whitt, Christina, and Ali forward into business. The demo and pitch had resulted in investments and loans of over $250,000, enough to cover R&D expenses for months and fund necessary hardware and telecom purchases. Ford Burch himself wrote a check for $50,000, with the note, "No interest loan." Nat Valentine was already calling on her hospital big box customers and introducing them to Helios. After word spread from their colleagues in Washington, the prototype garnered interest from other state hospital associations.

Nat and Christina pitched and demonstrated ER-GO at the American College of Emergency Physicians conference in Las Vegas, after Ali's persuasive and compelling introduction. His personal experience as an ER physician generated not only their trust but enthusiastic responses from the crowd even before the demo began. Nat left the conference with sixteen follow-up appointments. Several attendees contacted their hospital administrators during the conference and obtained verbal agreements to purchase ER-GO. Nat had Julia draft a letter of intent, and a few prospective clients signed before the conference ended. She scheduled visits to those sites within days to further build relationships and personally obtain their signed contract agreements.

Christina contacted Marissa Porter as soon as she got back to Philadelphia. They arranged an interview as a follow-up to

Marissa's original Reagan visit story, highlighting the innovation angle of Christina's efforts to launch Helios and the initial interest and backing by industry professionals from healthcare and the growing computer industry. Diana snapped photos throughout the taping, capturing Christina's passion and tenacity. Marissa ended the interview with the question, "So, Christina, when will you be contacting the White House to get your hands on that funding President Reagan promised for developing technology for the twenty-first century?"

In ten days, Nat returned after a late flight. Seven signed contracts for ER-GO, two with prerelease pricing options for the forthcoming NICU product, were stuffed inside her briefcase. Christina was still up, hunched over her kitchen table, writing out the ER-GO beta site plan, when she heard pounding on the apartment door. Nat strutted into Christina's apartment, dramatically waving a stack of forms.

"Whoa, is that what I think it is?" Christina tried to reach the papers that Nat was using to wildly fan her from over her head.

"In the absence of palm fronds, this will have to do. But don't think I'm going to feed you grapes!" Nat set each contract on the table in a neat stack, deliberately placing the signature pages on top for effect, and then held up an open hand and two fingers.

"Seven contracts for ER-GO? Seven signed contracts for our first product?"

"And two for our NICU vaporware," Nat added.

Christina grabbed Nat's hands and the two jumped around in circles in the living room, kicking off their shoes and shouting, "We did it! We did it!" until Diana staggered out of her bedroom, wondering what all the commotion was about.

"We got seven clients, and $250,000 in investments and loans. Helios is officially in business, Diana!" Christina was reeling from the news. She couldn't quite grasp what this meant.

They believe in me. They believe in what we can do. *I* believe in what we can do. What I can do. I'm no longer letting small-minded people define me. I'm defining myself, and my future, with each passing day. Falling onto the sofa, Christina stared up at the ceiling, ecstatic, overwhelmed with satisfaction.

"Nat, we have to let Ali, Adam, and Whitt know right away. I'll call the team together for a celebration kickoff, maybe at that restaurant on the Main Line we like. Really do it up. After all, we're now officially in business."

Nat got out her Rolodex and started making calls, waking up Whitt and interrupting Ali between patients. Adam had just come in from the fields when Christina called him.

"We're in business, Adam," was all she had to say.

He hooped and hollered. She heard him stamping the floor with those cowboy boots.

"Christina Como, I knew you could do it!"

"Helios would be nothing without your help, Adam. Thank you!"

"Now you let me make some calls to the board. You go on and celebrate tonight, with Nat and Ali and whoever else is in town. I'll raise a toast from out here."

As Nat skipped from one proud member to the next, Christina retreated down the hallway, into her bedroom. There was one call she needed to make. Pressing 4-1-1 on her push-button handset, she waited for a telephone operator to come on.

"What city and state, please?"

"Boston, Massachusetts. Can you please give me the number for Drew Dawson?"

THE END

ACKNOWLEDGMENTS

Inspiration for this book came from my own passion for healthcare and computing, two marvels of the modern world which I experienced first-hand early in my career. Surrounded by hardworking and often brilliant colleagues, I enjoyed working in an industry that only a few years before didn't exist! It was an exciting time, full of firsts and rife with opportunity. I feel lucky to have begun working when women's and men's roles were changing, and when society started becoming more accepting of choices.

I am grateful to the clients who candidly shared with me their experiences of imposter syndrome, in unwelcoming workplaces, with hostile coworkers and bosses, and of adverse childhood events. Your insights helped me develop characters and scenes that bring realism to the novel. Unfortunately, many undesirable behaviors described in this book still exist today. In writing the story, my hope was to shine a light on the devastating impact negative beliefs and behaviors have on young people and their ability to believe in themselves. Those who succeed often undermine their own success or suffer from imposter syndrome. And, I wanted to spotlight the incredible buoyant effect a kind word, acceptance, and encouragement can have on an individual's world view and sense of agency.

I want to thank the many mentors I've been fortunate to know throughout my career. You have not only taught me, encouraged me, and challenged me, you embodied the Chinese proverb about teaching a (wo)man to fish. Your guidance served as a model when I wrote the characters who became Christina's supporters.

I am grateful to the dedicated healthcare workers and innovative computer programmers who worked together to develop the first software for the medical industry. Neither could do so alone and together contributed to the health of millions. Their efforts have undoubtedly saved lives.

I want to thank those women who joined the early days of medical computing and applied their talents, often as the only female in a conference room or before a terminal. Your courage and leadership have opened doors to health tech and traditionally male-dominated fields for countless young women over the past four decades.

I am indebted to readers of my early drafts for their honest feedback and heartfelt investment of time and energy, especially Lucille Payne, Bruce Rule, Bridget Carrick, and Lynn Bishop. Your thoughtful critiques pushed me toward better writing. Thanks to Lisa Ashley, Deanna Bledsoe, Diane DeSantis Hoffman, Julie Maloney, Karen Redfearn, Rachel Reichert, and Mary Lou Sinkey for reviewing the manuscript and especially for your interest and support.

This novel would never have come to be if not for the wisdom and camaraderie of the Rehoboth Beach Writers Guild Novel Group. Our gatherings were a consistent source of inspiration and reinforced my desire to become a fiction writer. You have become trusted partners in my writing journey, and I am grateful for your advice and friendship.

I'd like to extend special thanks to Tuck Crocker, who answered my call for tech and company descriptions with enormous detail and enthusiasm. We apparently shared many of the same colleagues and clients yet never met. Thank you to Harold Strawbridge, John Galvin, Susan Chindemi, Vince Giorgi, Daniel Emig, Alena Malatesta, Robin Ratliff, Karl Kiss, Karen Babala, Domenic Parisano, John Engle, Michael Bowers, Bob Haist, Tom Trestler, and Vincent Cauvin, for contributing information about eighties technology, hardware, company practices, and road warrior stories.

I thank my editor, Alison Imbriaco, whose attention to detail and fact-checking is astounding; my cover designer, Crystal Heidel, who really got Christina and captured her essence so brilliantly; and Christian Storm for the print book interior and ebook. These professionals truly elevated my work.

Thank you to my children, Christopher and Monica, for their support and for giving me a pass all those times I texted instead of calling because it was late when I finished writing for the day. My mother, Helen DeSantis, has heard every bit of progress, each bout of writers' block, and listened as I talked through scenes or characters while I was writing this book. Thank you for being my sounding board!

Mostly, I want to thank my husband, Kevin, for his tireless scrutiny of every iteration of the manuscript, every word choice, description, and metaphor, and his advice on sports and cars references and eighties pop culture. You have been a loving and supportive critic who tolerated many late dinners as I remained at my desk polishing paragraphs.

To all the many people I've met along this incredible journey into fiction, thank you!

GINA MARIE WILSON is a holistic executive coach, formerly a software developer and healthcare strategist. She is the author of nonfiction books, *Skills That Build* and the Delaware Press Association 2023 Award Winning *Fearless First Year*, which guide readers toward personal and professional development through evidence-based techniques used in her coaching. Gina's fiction writing uses inspirational stories to shine a light on challenges readers face in society, families, and workplaces. She is an active member of the Rehoboth Beach Writers Guild. Gina lives with her husband in coastal Delaware, where she loves spending time with her family, beachcombing, and paddleboarding on the bay.

Gina Marie Wilson is available for select readings and lectures. To inquire about a possible appearance, please contact the author through her website's contact page.

www.ginamwilson.com

ALSO BY

Gina Marie Wilson has also published nonfiction books as Gina M. Wilson, MS.

Skills That Build: The Hard Science of Soft Skills for Work and Life
ISBN 978-1-7370829-0-3, $21.00

Fearless First Year: A Student Guide for College Transition, Success, and Well-Being
ISBN 978-1-7370829-2-7, $19.99

Available at **ginamwilson.com** *and wherever books are sold.*

9 781737 082934